DAUGHTER

of the

BURNING CITY

AMANDA FOODY

DAUGHTER of the BURNING CITY

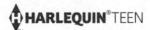
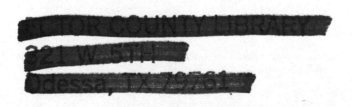
H HARLEQUIN TEEN

ISBN-13: 978-0-373-21243-9

Daughter of the Burning City

HARLEQUIN®TEEN
TM www.HarlequinTEEN.com

Printed in U.S.A.

For my Quidditch team:
Ryan &
McKenna &
Parker &
Alex &
Connor &
Erica.

CHAPTER ONE

I peek from behind the tattered velvet curtains at the chattering audience, their mouths full of candied pineapple and kettle corn. With their pale faces flushed from excitement and the heat, they look as gullible as dandelions, much like the patrons in the past five cities. The Gomorrah Festival hasn't been permitted to travel this far north in the Up-Mountains in over three years, and these people look like they're attending the opera or the theater rather than our traveling carnival of debauchery.

The women wear frilly dresses in burnt golds and oranges, buckled to the point of suffocation, some with rosy-cheeked children bouncing on their laps, others with cleavage as high as their chins. The men have shoulder pads to seem broader, stilted loafers to seem taller and painted silver pocket watches to seem richer.

If buckles, stilts and paint are enough to hoodwink them, then they won't notice that the eight "freaks" of my freak show are, in fact, only one.

Tonight's mark, Count Pomp-di-pomp—or is it Count

Pomp-von-Pompa?—smokes an expensive pipe in the second row, his mustache gleaming with leftover saffron honey from the pastry he had earlier. He's sitting too close to the front, which won't make it easy for Jiafu to steal the count's ring.

That's where I come in.

My job is to distract the audience so that Pomp-di-pomp doesn't notice Jiafu's shadow-work coaxing the sapphire ring off of his porky finger and dropping it onto the grass below.

A drum and fiddle play an entrancing Down-Mountain tune to quiet the audience's chatter, and I let the curtain fall, blocking my view. The Gomorrah Festival Freak Show will soon begin.

This is my favorite part of the performance: the anticipation. The drumbeats pound erratically, as if dizzy from drinking several mugs of the Festival's spiced wine. Everything sticks in this humid air: the aromas of carnival food, the gray smoke that shrouds Gomorrah like a cloak and the jittery intakes of breath from the audience, wondering whether the freak show will prove as gruesome as the sign outside promised:

The Gomorrah Festival Freak Show.
Walk the line between abnormal and monstrous.

From the opposite end of the stage, behind the curtain on stage right, Nicoleta nods at me. I reach for the rope and yank down. The pulley spins and whistles, and the curtain rises.

Nicoleta struts—a very practiced, rigid strut—into the spotlight, her heels clicking and the slit in her gown revealing a lacy violet garter at the curve of her thigh. When I first created her three years ago, she had knee-shaking stage fright, and I needed to control her during the show like a puppet. Now she's so accustomed to her role that I turn away, unneeded, and tie on my best mask. Rhinestones of varying sizes and shades of red cover it, from the curled edges near my temples to the tip of my nose. I need to dazzle, after all.

"Welcome to the Gomorrah Festival Freak Show," Nicoleta says.

The audience gawks at her. Like the particular Up-Mountainers in this city, and unlike any of the other members of my family, Nicoleta has fair skin. Freckles. Pale brown hair draped to her elbows. Skinny wrists and skinnier, child-like legs. Many members of Gomorrah have Up-Mountain heritage, whether obvious or diluted, but these northern city dwellers always expect the enticingly unfamiliar: sensual, audacious and wild.

The audience's expressions seem to say, *Poor, lost girl, what are you doing working at Gomorrah? Where are your parents? Your chaperone? You can't be more than twenty-two.*

"I am Nicoleta, the show's manager, and I hope you're enjoying your first Gomorrah Festival in...three years, I hear?"

The audience stiffens; they stop fanning themselves, stop chewing their candied pineapple. I curse under my breath. Nicoleta has a knack—a compulsion, really—for saying the wrong thing. This is the Festival's first night in Frice, a city-state known—like many others—for its strict religious leaders and disapproval of the Gomorrah lifestyle. Three years ago, a minor rebellion in the Vurundi kingdom ousted the Frician merchants from power there. Despite quickly reclaiming its tyrannous governorships, and despite Gomorrah's utter lack of involvement, Frice decided to restrict the Festival's traveling in this region. I can't have Nicoleta scaring away our few visitors by reminding them that their city officials disapprove of them being here, even at an attraction as innocent as a freak show.

"For those of you with weaker constitutions, I suggest you exit before our opening act," Nicoleta says. Her tone rises and falls at the proper moments. The theatrics of her performance in our show are the opposite of Nicoleta's role in our family, which Unu and Du have dubbed "stick in the bum." Every night, she manages to transform—or, better put, *improve*—her entire demeanor for the sake of the show, since her own abilities are too unreliable to deserve an act. Some days, she can pull our caravans better than our two horses combined. Others, she needs Tree to open our jars of lychee preserves.

9

"The sights you are about to witness are shocking, even *monstrous*," she continues. A young boy in the front row clings to his mother, pulling at her puffed, apricot sleeves. "Children, cover your eyes. Parents, beware. Because the show is about to begin."

While the audience leans forward in their seats, I prepare for the upcoming act by picturing the Strings, as I call them. I have almost two hundred Strings, glowing silver, dragging behind me as I walk, like the train of a fraying gown. Only I can see them and, even then, only when I focus. I mentally reach down and pluck out four particular Strings and circle them around my hands until they're taut. The others remain in a heap on the wooden floor.

"I'd like to introduce you to a man found within the faraway Forest of Ruins," Nicoleta lies. Backstage, Hawk stops playing the fiddle, and Unu and Du reduce the tempo on their drums. I yank on the Strings to command my puppet.

Thump. Thump.

The audience gasps as the Human Tree stomps onto the stage. His skin is made entirely of bark, and his midsection measures as wide as a hundred-year-old oak trunk. It's difficult to make out his facial features in the twisted lumps of wood, except for his sunken, beetle-black eyes and emptiness of expression. Leaves droop from the branches jutting out from his shoulders, adding several feet to his already daunting stature. His fingers curl into splintery twigs as he waves hello.

From backstage, my hand waves, as well. If I don't control Tree, he'll scream profanity that will make half these fancy ladies faint. If he works himself into a real tantrum, he'll tear off the bark on his stomach until blood trickles out like sap.

His act begins, which is mostly him stomping around and grunting, and me yanking this way and that on his Strings to make him do so. I crafted him when I was three years old, before I considered the performance potential of my illusions.

The six other illusions wait with me backstage.

Venera, the boneless acrobat more flexible than a dripping egg yolk, brushes rouge on her painted white cheeks at a vanity. She pouts in the mirror and then pushes aside a strand of dark hair from her face. She's beautiful, especially in her skintight, black-and-purple-striped suit. Every night, the audience practically drools over her...until they watch her body flatten into a puddle or her arms roll up like a croissant.

Beside her, Crown files the fingernails that grow from his body where hair should be. He keeps the nails on his arms and legs smooth, giving him a scaly look, but he doesn't touch the ones on his hands and head, which are curled, yellow daggers as long as butcher knives. Though Crown was my second illusion, made ten years ago, he appears to be seventy-five. He always smokes a cigar before his performance so his gentle voice will sound as prickly as his skin.

Hawk plays the fiddle in an almost spiritual concentration while what's left of a chipmunk—dinner—hangs out of her mouth. Her brown wings are tucked under her fuchsia cape, where they will remain until she unfolds them during her act, screeches and flies over the—usually shrieking—audience. Her talons pluck at the fiddle's strings at an incomparable speed. Her ultimate goal is to challenge the devil himself to a fiddle contest, and she figures by traveling with the world's most famous festival of depravity, she's bound to run into him one day.

Blister, the chubby one-year-old, plays with the beads dangling off of Unu and Du's drum. Rather than focusing on their rhythm, Unu and Du bicker about something, per usual. Du punches Unu with their shared left arm. Unu hisses an unpleasant word loudly, which Blister then tries out for himself, missing the double *s* sound and saying something resembling *a-owl*.

Gill snaps at them all to be quiet and then resumes reading his novel. Even wearing a rusted diver's helmet full of water, he manages to make out the words on the pages. Bubbles seep from the gills on his cheeks as he sighs. As the loner of our family, he generally prefers the quiet company of books to our boisterous, pre-show jitters. He only raises his voice during our games of lucky coins—he holds the family record for the most consecutive wins (twenty-one). I suspect he's been cheating by allowing Hawk, Unu and Du to forfeit games on purpose in exchange for lighter homework assignments.

"Keep an eye on Blister," I remind the boys. "Those drums are flammable."

"Tell Unu to stuff a drumstick up his—" Du glances hesitantly at Gill "—backside."

"That's your backside, too, dung-brain," Unu says.

"It's an expression," says Du. "I like its sentiment."

It would hardly be a classic Gomorrah Festival Freak Show if the audience couldn't hear my brothers tormenting each other backstage.

"I'll stick it up both your assholes if you don't shut it," I say. They pay me no attention; they know I never follow through with my threats.

"A-owl," Blister says again.

"Language, Sorina," Gill groans.

"Shit. Sorry," I reply, but I'm only mildly chagrined. Blister's been hearing all our foul mouths since the day he came to be.

One by one, they perform their acts: the Boneless Acrobat; the Fingernail Mace; the Half Girl, Half Hawk; the Fire-Breathing Baby; the Two-Headed Boy; and the Trout Man. The audience roars as Hawk screeches and soars over their seats, cheers at each splash of Gill flipping in and out of his tank like a trained dolphin. They are utterly unaware that the "freaks" are actually my illusions, projected for anyone to see.

The only real freak in Gomorrah is me.

"For the finale," Nicoleta says, as I hurriedly smooth down my shoulder-length black hair, "a mysterious performer who's been with Gomorrah since her childhood. She's the Girl Who

Sees Without Eyes, and if you remain in your seats, she'll reveal wonders you can see, hear, smell and even touch."

I greet the audience as Unu and Du wheel Gill's massive glass tank offstage. The hem of my black robes swish across the floor, and a hood drapes over all but my violet-painted lips. Count Pomp-di-pomp murmurs to the plump woman beside him, perhaps his wife. Another person Jiafu will need to sneak around during my act.

The room holds its breath as I remove the hood, only to reveal my mask.

"Take the mask off," a man shouts from the back.

"Those who see her true face turn to stone," says Nicoleta. Of course, that's horseshit. I just hate the screams, same as Tree with his bark skin, Unu and Du with their two heads and Hawk with her wings and claws. As good as we have it in Gomorrah, no one wants to be a freak.

The fiddle and drums fade to silence as I raise my arms.

The tent's ceiling and grass floor disappear, replaced with colorful galaxies so the crowd seems suspended within the cosmos. The woman beside Count Pomp-di-pomp shrieks and lifts her feet off the endless, black ground and then wipes the sweat from her forehead with her pearl-studded glove.

Nicoleta jabbers a spiel about the wonders of my sight, as if my lack of eyes allows me to see more than everyone else. Between my forehead and cheekbones is flat skin, but I can see just the same as the rest of the world. I'm an illusion-worker, the rarest form of jynx-worker, gifted in mirages real enough to touch, smell, hear and taste. My most intricate illusions are my family and the other members of the freak show: living figments of my imagination.

I've never met another illusion-worker—only read about them—but as far as I know, I am the only one born without eyes who relies on my jynx-work to see. No doctor or medicine man can explain how this works. Maybe I don't see like

13

everyone else does—it's not as if I could test that out—but I see, color and all, and I'm not one to question things I don't really need answers for.

I throw all of my energy into this performance, so much that my Strings are fully visible to me and tangle at my feet. I avoid moving around onstage, in case I trip. Normally, the Strings aren't solid, but when I'm commanding this much power? My ankle just might catch, and I'll topple into the front row.

Fabricated constellations whirl past, and the audience grips the edges of their seats. The planets orbit the room as if the tent marks the center of the universe and that universe is performing for us, its revolutions a celestial dance and me, the musician.

During my ten-minute act of shooting stars, crescent moons and burning suns, I'm too consumed by the exertion of my performance to notice if Jiafu stole Count Pomp-di-pomp's ring. The illusion dissipates, and I lower my hands. I stare around the tent with exhilaration, and my chest heaves up and down beneath my thick robes. I was marvelous.

The audience claps. Count Pomp-di-pomp's sapphire no longer glistens on his finger. Which means Jiafu managed to steal it undetected.

The seven other illusions join me for our final bows and farewell to the audience. Tired, I struggle to maintain control of the two more problematic illusions, Tree and Blister. One slip, and Tree could trample the audience under his clubbed feet. Or Blister could hiccup and set the tent on fire. Again.

Jiafu lurks in the back of the tent and picks his teeth with a steel comb. I avoid his gaze so the audience doesn't turn to where I'm looking. His body is cloaked in shadow, barely visible against the black and red stripes of the tent, except for the whites of his eyes and the light reflecting off his comb. With his scarred face and patched-up clothes, he looks like a beast who just crawled out of the kennel.

The illusions exit stage left, except for me and Gill, whom

I wheel in his tank to stage right. I rarely see him without his diver's helmet, which he wears whenever outside of his tank. His chin-length black hair is suspended in the water, and his skin prunes all over, even his silver-toned face, like a piece of rotten fruit. His smile for the audience disappears the moment we're out of sight.

"Why was Jiafu here?" he demands.

I smile and tilt my head to the side. "Who?"

Before he can answer, I slip around him backstage. I don't feel like listening to any of his lectures tonight. I know Gill means well, but we've argued about Jiafu before, and we're both more stubborn than mules and keep kicking up the same dirt. Neither of us will change our minds.

Venera is seated at her vanity, scanning her makeup collection and slathering a glittery lotion across her brown skin. As per her daily ritual, she'll wash off her stage powder and reapply a new look for the Downhill parties later tonight. Hawk bickers with Unu and Du about which game they'll play—chess or lucky coins. Blister reaches for his favorite top from his cauldron cradle while Crown leans forward in his chair to help him. Besides Gill, only Tree is absent—he prefers to stay outdoors when we're not performing.

I've barely reached my own vanity when Nicoleta corners me.

"Why do you keep working for Jiafu?" she asks. Between her and Gill scolding me and everyone else bickering with each other, my only moments of peace are on stage. "He isn't trust—"

"You all *know* why I work for him. Or am I the only one who cares about Kahina?" I tear off my mask and toss it on the vanity. The money I earn working for Jiafu goes to medicine for Kahina and her snaking sickness, a malady she's battled for an impressive five years. Although Villiam, the owner of the Gomorrah Festival, adopted me as a young child, it was Kahina the fortune-worker who raised me. It was Kahina who taught me to play lucky coins, to love nature, to embrace being a misfit.

And while Kahina didn't exactly raise my illusions, they love her as much as I do. She visits often with gifts of sweets and handmade knits.

Nicoleta sighs and fiddles with the ruby hairpin tucked behind her ear. "I know why, but there are safer ways to earn money, Sorina. I just don't want Jiafu to start expecting things from you, to keep you working for him even when Kahina…gets better."

I ignore the hesitation in her words. Kahina will improve. If the snaking sickness intended to claim her, it would have slithered its way into her heart years ago.

"Jiafu adores me," I say. "And he's terrified of me."

"The way every man should see you," Venera chimes in from beside me as she applies her signature black lipstick. I covertly hold up a hand, and she high-fives me behind my back. At least Venera is always on my side.

"Jiafu knows I'm not one of his cronies," I tell Nicoleta.

Nicoleta purses her lips. "What if Jiafu gets caught by Up-Mountain officials?" Nicoleta is an ardent supporter of what-ifs. "He could take you down with him."

"Could you stop? You're giving me anxiety," Venera and I say together.

Of all my illusions, Venera and I are the most alike. I made her to be the perfect best friend for me—fashion-savvy, fun and stop-and-stare gorgeous. The younger-looking illusions—Hawk, Unu and Du and Blister—are like my younger siblings. Crown: my grandfather. Gill: the voice of authority. Nicoleta: the bossy older sister. And Tree is…Tree.

I hunt through my various masks—all small, covering only the eye area—and select a simple one with matte sequins, a satin interior and a spider design on the top right corner. I never venture into public without a mask, where Up-Mountain children can gape while their parents call me *monstrous*, or *an abomination*, or any other colorful choice of word. I have no eyebrows, no eyes, not even indents where eyes should be. When I was younger, I tried to cast an illusion of these features, but something about the cold emptiness in my fake eyes looked even more unsettling than my normal appearance—nor could I maintain the image for more than a few minutes. Though I made peace with my face years ago, I don't have the thickest skin—it only takes a single whisper or sickened stare to reopen old wounds.

But I have nice lips, I remind myself. I line them in blood-red lipstick, which pairs devilishly with my dark mask. My skin is fair, my straight hair so black it's almost blue, like the people who live in the Eastern Kingdoms of the Down-Mountains. I don't remember my home before Gomorrah, but Villiam has told me stories about how he adopted me in one of those kingdoms, and Kahina has made a point to introduce me to foods from my homeland, like sugar-coated tanghulu that a vendor sells near Skull Gate. But none of us discuss my past often; otherwise we might dwell on what my fate could have been, had Villiam not found me, an eyeless slave girl. Sometimes I wish I remembered. But when I speak to others in Gomorrah with stories like mine, I feel relieved that I don't.

"Tonight is meant for fun," Venera says. "Save your bickering for another time."

She's right. Tonight we're all attending a show at the Menagerie, a rare, expensive treat we indulge in whenever we save enough for the tickets. The Menagerie is Gomorrah's gaudiest, most exciting and most overpriced attraction.

Blister darts out from behind me and holds up his hand. I give him a high five. Afterward, he moves on to Venera. He does this after every show.

"Are you ready to see some tigers and dragons?" Venera asks him.

He roars in affirmation, and Venera laughs and pinches his cheek.

Crown appears in the doorway with Unu, Du and Gill—

who looks rather sour—behind him. They are changed out of their costumes.

Unu and Du rub their hands together. "The cherries are on you, Sorina," Unu says.

I lost the last game of lucky coins. "Only one bag for you guys, though."

"But there are two of us," Du complains.

"You've only got one stomach."

"You'd hardly know that from the way they eat," Gill mutters. He jokingly flicks Unu on his ear. Flicking is his way of showing affection.

"We should leave now, or we'll be late," Nicoleta says. As if anything in Gomorrah starts on schedule, or our family is ever on time.

We march out of our tent into the dense smoke of Gomorrah and head north, toward the games neighborhood. It's a bit of a detour, but the food in that neighborhood is better than anywhere else—sticky buns that melt on your tongue, nuts dipped in honey like beetles preserved within amber, saltwater taffy you can buy by the yard. Plus, most of us can't resist wasting a few of our coins on a game or two. Unu and Du get a kick out of having people guess their weight with their two heads. Crown has a special gift for ring toss. Nicoleta, when she's feeling up to it, can make the bell chime when she smashes the airbag with the hammer.

My family does not go anywhere quietly. Tree's steps thunder as if we're walking with a crowd of one hundred rather than nine. Hawk squabbles with Unu and Du, who keep rubbing her feathers against the grain. Venera and I walk, arms linked and chatting about the yogurt face masks we might try tonight. The paths of Gomorrah are narrow and winding, sometimes only wide enough between tents for a single person to slip through. But we don't care about stopping traffic. The residents let me pass because I'm the proprietor's daughter, an association that brings me an uncomfortable amount of notoriety and weighty expectations. The visitors nearly lunge out of our way after one look at Unu and Du's heads, Crown's curling yellow scalp of nails or Tree.

We approach our favorite vendor of licorice-dipped cherries—Gomorrah's signature treat—and Unu and Du steer us aside.

"How many bags am I buying?" I ask.

Each of them shouts how many they want.

"I'm not buying fourteen bags." I hold up my flimsy coin purse. "You guys are milking me dry."

Crown fishes in his pocket for change before Du stops him. "You can't help her. She lost. Rules are rules."

Lucky coins is a sacred game in my family.

I curse under my breath and thrust my entire savings—one week's worth, since I can't save anything more than a few days—into the vendor's hands. His eyes light up as he hands us a full quarter of his stock.

Afterward, with our teeth sticky from black licorice and our lips stained red from cherry juice, we head toward the Menagerie singing one of Gomorrah's folk songs.

Wicked, wicked to the core. The city will burn forevermore.

Or mostly singing. Unu and Du shriek to drown out Hawk, who, as always, is trying to show off her vocal range and make everyone else sound bad.

The Menagerie's spires tower into the smoke that covers the Festival like an endless expanse of storm clouds. Its tent is so black it appears like a hole, seeping the color away from its surroundings. Pink, red and violet streamers—Gomorrah's colors—ripple in the breeze at its peak.

The line outside snakes around the tent, and we grab a place at the end. Because the Menagerie is such a popular attraction, stands for kettle corn, palm readers and charms salesmen clutter its perimeter.

"Care for some coins?" a man asks Hawk. He bites the coin,

and his teeth clack against the bronze. She turns her back to him, a pro at dealing with persistent vendors, but he continues, "Solid. Good quality. I have the Handmaiden, the Red Jester, the Harbinger—"

"We have enough coins," Nicoleta tells him. We all know the coins sold in this part of the Festival attract more tourists than actual players. The gambling neighborhood sells the characters of real and rare value.

Perhaps it is the stern edge in Nicoleta's voice, or perhaps the vendor knows a lost cause when he sees one, but he doesn't pester us again, even though we remain next to his stand for several more minutes. He moves on to the Up-Mountain patrons behind us, who marvel at the thin coins and ask the vendor how to play.

"It's your face," Hawk tells Nicoleta. "He can see the lack of fun and warmth in your eyes."

"I resent that," she says.

Unu and Du tug on the sleeve of my night cloak. "Will you buy us some spiced wine?" Du whispers eagerly, his hazel eyes sparkling in the white torchlight. Unu, on the other hand, stares at their feet.

"You're eleven," I say.

"That's an arbitrary number you made up."

"*Arbitrary* is a big word for you."

Du gives me one of his classic Du expressions. He leans his head back and scrunches his entire face together like he's eaten a whole mouthful of sour-cherry drops. He uses this to feign being insulted.

Normally, I might say yes, but the spiced wine in this area of Gomorrah is highly potent—meant to get guests drunk and happy to spend. "Sorry, kiddo." I pinch his cheek. "I'm too responsible a sister for that."

The Menagerie tent opens three minutes later, and the queue of guests shuffles inside at an excruciatingly slow pace past the ticket booth. The entrance is a hallway lit by iron lampposts on either side so that our shadows stripe across the grass floor. In between the lamps stand taxidermied animals from the Down-Mountains. We pass an Eberian snow tiger, its pelt winter-white and its stripes hooked and curled at the points. A chimera hunches to our left, its goat and lion heads frozen in midhowl.

"You're the goat for sure," Du whispers to Unu.

There's a leopard dragon, a few falcons and exotic birds, and one panda—all previous performers at the Menagerie. As a child, Villiam took me to the shows to watch the panda, who now watches *us* with vacant eyes.

The Up-Mountain guests point and gawk at the creatures we've seen a hundred times. They chatter incessantly and fan themselves, occasionally turning around to sneak peeks at us. I hear a woman say we must be in some kind of costumes. Hawk hugs her arms and her wings close to herself. Gill flicks her on the shoulder, and she manages a smile.

We have all learned—or tried to learn— to ignore the comments that follow us.

We enter the main part of the Menagerie, a huge open room with a circus ring, several trapezes and a collection of balls and hoops. My family slides into benches toward the back—we can never afford front row. The air smells of stale manure and kettle corn.

"Happy family night," Venera says, and we raise our bags of licorice cherries in a sort of cheers.

For the next few minutes, I am caught up in the excitement of the Menagerie. I live for the anticipation of a good show. My legs twitch. I constantly change my sitting position. I eat too many of my snacks before the show even begins, and my stomach cramps from all the sugar. The others chatter to themselves about the last time we visited the Menagerie, when an acrobat

21

broke his leg. Gill murmurs to Nicoleta—the only one who really listens to him—about the boring novel he's reading.

Then I notice the noise outside. Shouts. Running. It grows louder, loud enough that many in the audience turn around, as if to see the commotion through the red-, pink- and purple-striped tent walls.

"Does that sound rather panicked to you?" Gill asks to my right. "Like something's wrong?"

"I'm sure nothing's wrong," I say. Shouts and strange noises are business as usual in Gomorrah. Probably some drunkards passing through.

"But doesn't it *sound* like something is?"

I listen closer. There are shouts. Feet running. Maybe…maybe the sound of horses, as well. I can't be certain, but it does seem like more than a few drunkards. As the proprietor's daughter, destined to one day become proprietor myself, I should inspect the commotion. But it's family night. At the Menagerie. I don't want to give up my seat. I'm sure it's nothing important, and if it is, Villiam will take care of it anyway.

A man in a black tuxedo with a red undershirt strides into the center of the circus ring. He clears his throat, and the audience quiets. "I apologize, but the ten o'clock Menagerie show has been canceled. Tickets can be fully refunded at the booths at the north and south entrances. Please exit in an orderly fashion through the way you entered. We hope you enjoy the rest of your time at the Gomorrah Festival."

The noise of the crowd immediately grows into an uproar. Among the shouts and complaints, Unu and Du's and Hawk's are some of the loudest.

"That's rubbish," Du sulks. "*Our* show is never canceled."

"It's probably from whatever is happening outside," Gill says. "It mustn't be anything good."

"You're right," Nicoleta says. She stands. "We should leave now. Before the rush."

Most of the audience remains in their seats, as if sitting around long enough will bring the manager back and force him to start the show. But the manager nearly sprinted out of the circus ring, so I doubt anyone will return. Clearly whatever is happening is important.

I grab my bag of licorice cherries and try not to let the true extent of my disappointment show. This is the *Menagerie*. What sort of pandemonium does it take to shut down Gomorrah's biggest attraction?

"We better hurry if we don't want to stand in line for the rest of the night waiting for our money back," Nicoleta tells us.

We gather our few belongings and file out of the stands. The audience crowds in the hallway, and the eight of us link arms— Nicoleta carries Blister—to avoid losing each other. Once we approach the exit, the commotion grows louder.

Screams.

"What's going on?" Hawk asks. "Tree, can you see anything?"

Tree doesn't answer. He swats at a fly buzzing around his leaves.

"It's officials," the man in front of us says.

"Officials? Like Frician city officials?" I ask, confused. "What are they doing at the Festival?" They allowed us to come to Frice. Have they changed their minds? Will they force us to leave? It wouldn't be the first time a city-state has rescinded an invitation after gazing at Gomorrah's intimidating burning skyline up close. It looks like Hell itself has shown up on their doorsteps.

"Causing trouble," Gill says, always stating the obvious. Anything involving Up-Mountain officials means trouble.

We'll have to cut our plans short—the Menagerie, the fireworks show, all of it. Officials love to target jynx-workers, and even if I'm the only true one among us, our appearances will make us stand out. I could joke about how it has something to do with us being abominations to their god. But the joke is

23

less funny here, considering all the blood that has been spilled for thousands of years in the name of that same god in this city alone, not to mention in the rest of the world.

No, it isn't much of a joke at all.

"Straight home," Nicoleta says. "Does everyone hear?"

"Yes," we chorus. No one argues with Nicoleta when there's a crisis.

We step into the smoky night air, right in the middle of the clearing that was once filled with vendors, fortune-workers and laughing guests. Now, everyone is running. White-coated Frician officials on horseback charge dangerously close to the Gomorrah merchants packing up their stands. The officials brandish clubs and holler at passersby. Several brandish swords and crossbows.

Gomorrah is chaos.

CHAPTER TWO

The coin merchant's table crashes to the ground, and lucky coins cascade onto the grass in a rushing clatter. The official whose horse overturned the stand stops and dismounts. I hold my breath and squirm closer to Gill as the merchant drops to his knees and collects his fallen merchandise.

"We need to hurry," Nicoleta says. She points in the direction of a nearby path for us to flee.

The official picks up a coin and examines it. "The Harbinger? He looks like a demon." He throws the coin into the merchant's lap. "Are you a jynx-worker?"

"No," the merchant says, his voice strong. He stands to meet the official's eyes.

"Then what are these for, if not divining?"

"It's a game. Collector's items."

"A *game*," he mocks. "A *festival*. Pretty words for a city of rot and smoke. Nothing about this place is play."

Gill tugs on my arm. The others have broken apart and are running for Nicoleta's path. "It's time to *go*," he says.

I eye the ticket booth behind us, loath to lose all the money we spent. We saved for this night. I won't let a few Up-Mountain officials force us to throw our money away and terrorize us in our own home.

I disentangle myself from Gill's grip. "I'm getting our money back."

Gill's eyes widen in alarm. "There are more important things."

"No. Family night is a whole month of saving, and we didn't get to have it. I'm getting. Our money. Back." I say this sternly enough so that Gill won't argue with me. And he doesn't.

"Be careful," he says.

"Always am."

I whip around toward the ticket booth. A crowd surrounds it, shouting at the girl inside, who's shouting right back. There are twenty yards between them and me, plus a few officials in their white coats on whiter stallions beneath the Menagerie's banners, admiring the chaos around them and tormenting those in costume, searching for jynx-workers.

Villiam always told me the Up-Mountains hate us because they are afraid. He's told me stories that date back two thousand years, when Gomorrah was once a true city in the Great Mountains—a narrow strip of land dividing the two continents. When its sky-line was blue instead of burning. When jynx-workers wielding fire and shadow could dominate regions at any end of the world. Even though anyone can be born with jynx-work in their blood, it was the Up-Mountainers who turned away from it, and the Down-Mountainers who came to celebrate it. The Up-Mountains—from the wintry tundras in the north, to the humid bayous in the south, across cultures, across peoples—united under their common-held fear and warrior god. Now they are powerful, and even the most capable jynx-worker is no match for the massive Up-Mountain armies.

It will only take a few minutes to retrieve the money, I tell myself. Screams ring out behind me. Figures appear and disappear in the constant Gomorrah smoke. Hooves thunder past.

I'll be home in a few minutes. Like hell I'm leaving without our money. I am the proprietor's daughter, and I will never be afraid while within Gomorrah.

My illusion-work is not entirely for entertainment. A useful trick I've learned while living in the Festival is to convince someone they are looking at one thing, when really they are looking at something else. A sleight of hand, of sorts. It's significantly easier than persuading someone there's nothing to see at all.

I cast my usual trick: a moth.

To those around me, there is no girl passing them in a long cloak. There is no person. No shadow, even. There's a moth, fluttering from torch to torch in lazy curls, oblivious to the hysteria around it. A torn scrap of paper drifting in Gomorrah's smoke. If they concentrated or stood at a distance, they would glimpse the outline of my body, blurry like a reflection in a pond. But no one is going to stare that closely at a moth.

With my illusion protecting me, I pass the officials without notice and head to the booth. I shelter behind a tentpole, blocking myself from the view of those in the clearing. Once the illusion fades, I don't want an official to harass me because of my eyeless mask. Or worse, for someone from Gomorrah to recognize me as the proprietor's daughter and demand I stop the officials. As if they'd listen to a sixteen-year-old, small Down-Mountain girl. A jynx-worker. A freak.

I let go of my illusion and push my way to the front of the those crowded around the ticket booth. Inside, the frazzled girl shrieks, "You all *live* here! Just come back tomorrow!" Somewhere to our right, another vendor stand is knocked to the ground with a crash, followed by the thudding of wooden jugs of spiced wine.

She's right. Everyone in the group has mixed features and wears Gomorrah trousers and tunics. Those in Gomorrah are known for their stinginess, and waiting a whole day for our money back isn't going to cut it—not for me, not for anyone here. Those tickets cost a fortune.

A child screeches. I briefly look away from the booth, but it is an Up-Mountain child. He has nothing to fear. His father shushes him and pulls him away from the frenzied horses.

Be careful, Gill told me.

I'm definitely not being careful.

"Today you say money back, tomorrow you'll change your minds," one man says. He holds out his grubby hand beneath the glass opening of the booth.

"Where's the manager?" another asks.

"He's calming the swan dragon," the girl snaps. Her eyes fall on me, in the fringe of the crowd, and they widen. "You're Villiam's daughter." The others turn to me, and I curse under my breath. They all recognize me, but I know none of them. I shouldn't be here. "Take care of them. The Menagerie has to focus on its animals and the safety of the Gomorrah patrons and residents first. If you all return first thing tomorrow, we'll refund your tickets."

She scampers away from the booth, leaving me with the unruly group. She was smart. The Menagerie, being Gomorrah's most profitable attraction, receives Villiam's special attention. Right now, I should care more about their needs than those of a few residents. That is what a proprietor would do. A proprietor would have their priorities straight.

The group watches me expectantly. A proprietor would also know at least a few of their names, and I can barely remember the names and faces of the neighbors I've had for eight or more years. But they all know mine. My face is the most recognizable in the Festival. I do not search for anonymity, but I hate to glimpse the repulsion or pity in their eyes.

"It's for your safety," I stammer. "The swan dragon—"

"—is older than shit," one woman says. "Lot of harm she'll do."

"Let me take your names. I'll make right sure the Menagerie returns your money tomorrow—"

"With all the officials here, wreaking havoc? You'll be too busy cleaning up their mess, and you won't bother with this." The man spits at my feet. I grimace. He would hardly do that to Villiam, or even Villiam's assistant, Agni. It's easier to dismiss a freak. And truth be told, Villiam rarely assigns me any real work. My proprietorship lessons are lectures of micro-agriculture and craftsmanship; about the external structure of Gomorrah, a vast, traveling city. Never about what truly makes it tick.

"To hell with this." The man storms off.

Fine, let him leave. He'll probably rant about how lousy I am to his friends, which will return to me in whispers and stares—never anything outright rude, nothing that might risk inciting Villiam's wrath, but the kind that makes me feel like a freak show even outside the performance tent.

I stare at the small, copper coins in the tin box inside the booth—dull and tarnished but still more beckoning than starlight. It doesn't matter that I don't know these people's names. I know why they're here, same as me. For their month's earnings. For the money to make sure no one in their families has to do work on the side, like petty thievery. To ensure their loved ones have whatever they need, like medicine.

"Just need some paper," I mutter and then slip inside the ticket booth. I grab a sheet and a pencil. "I'll take your names—"

"But how will we—"

"I want my money back as much as you do. Now give me your damned names so that we can all get the hell out of here."

The woman in front huffs. "You're crass for a princess."

I hate that nickname. Real princesses are no more than pretty bargaining chips. I'm no pawn, and I gave up on *pretty* a long time ago.

"Not for Gomorrah's princess," I say.

They stop bickering, give me their names and shuffle away.

Once I'm alone, I reach beneath the counter and grab my family's forty-five copper coins. Then I slap the list of names on the table—no longer my problem—and leave.

Frice has stormed the Festival. Gomorrah has bigger things to worry about than ticket refunds.

My trusty moth illusion gets me safely from the Menagerie to our neighborhood, though I pass several officials along the path and cringe away each time. But they cannot see me, and if I concentrate hard enough, they could touch me and not know it. I stumble toward our tent, sweaty and out of breath but victorious.

Gill waits outside, and I brace myself for the scolding that I probably deserve. He swats at my moth until I drop the illusion. "Are you all right?" he asks.

"I'm fine."

"That was rash," he says. "You could've been hurt."

I jingle my pocket. "Got the money."

"No one cares about the money. We were all worried sick."

I know it wasn't the smartest plan. But tomorrow night, when the officials leave and Gomorrah has cleaned itself up, everyone will be thankful for the extra change.

"Well, I'm fine." I push past him to go inside, but he grabs my arm.

"And why was Jiafu here tonight?" he asks, for the second time.

"How should I know? Maybe he wanted to watch our show," I say, careful not to let the others overhear inside. Crown and Nicoleta also don't approve of my thieving with Jiafu, and some of them—like Hawk and Unu and Du—don't even know about it.

"Jiafu is trouble, Sorina."

"It was nothing. All's dandy." Jiafu and I have swindled enough jobs at the show to know it never affects our ticket sales.

"I don't know what you two did," he says, "but Gomorrah's in enough trouble here as it is. If rumors spread beyond

30

Frice that we've been stealing from patrons, then the other Up-Mountain cities will revoke their invitations to come. Not to mention all this chaos."

He acts as if Jiafu and I are the only thieves in this whole festival of debauchery. To the visitors, the chance of pickpockets or magical mischief accounts for half the thrill of Gomorrah.

"It was a small job. Count Pomp-di-pomp is supposed to be a bit dim, anyway. He'll probably think he lost his ring himself."

Gill rolls his eyes. "It's Count Pompdidorra. He's a very influential man."

"Whatever."

"Sorina," he says, sighing. Most of Gill's sentences are followed by a sigh. At least half of those are aimed at me. When I created Gill, I had "loving uncle" in mind, but, instead, he's more of a nuisance. Though maybe that's a bit harsh. It's not that I don't love Gill. Not that he doesn't love me and all of us. But he's certainly grumpier than in my original blueprints. If we wanted to live by all his rules, we'd go live in a religion-crazed Up-Mountain city. The only person who listens to Gill is Nicoleta, who is essentially his henchman, repeating his advice or scolding someone whenever Gill isn't present to do so himself.

"To be frank—" Gill is always frank "—you're jeopardizing the already grim reputation of the entire Festival. And if people keep losing valuable possessions during our show, no one's going to buy tickets."

I'm done with this conversation. Unless Gill can concoct a new idea for me to earn some coin for Kahina, then I'll stick with Jiafu. I'm not really hurting anyone. The patrons we select are too rich to notice a missing necklace here, a missing watch there.

"It's *my* show," I say.

"If it's all your show, you can do tricks in this tank next time. Or fit into Venera's two-by-two-foot box," he snaps. "Don't be a child."

31

"Technically, I'm older than you," I say. I created Gill when I was nine, which only makes him seven years old.

He sighs. "Of course, Sorina, you always have the last word."

This particular statement infuriates me more than anything else. I'm sorry I worried him, but Kahina is more important than the slim risk involved. And I don't understand how I could possibly be damaging the Festival's reputation when people are always whispering about assassins and drug dealers in the Downhill. Petty theft is nothing compared to that.

I turn, my cloak swishing behind me, and stomp inside.

The others sit around our foldout table, huddled together on floor cushions. By the untouched game of lucky coins and the way they fidget, I can tell they've been worried.

I toss the forty-five coins on the table, which spill out of their pouch with clatters and clangs. Venera grimly gathers them up to add to our family-stash jar. "Got them no problem," I say, knowing that I sound like an ass.

"It's almost midnight," Nicoleta says. "You took a long time."

"Is it?" Jiafu and I usually meet at midnight after jobs, but I didn't notice him waiting for me outside. I hate to leave them again, if only for a moment, but I need to talk to Jiafu.

"We can play lucky coins, now that we're all here," Unu says. He holds up the Beheaded Dame coin—the jewel of his collection—to glint in the lantern light.

"I'm not ready to lose again just yet," I say. "I'm going to keep watch and make sure no officials come near the tent. I'll be—"

"You shouldn't go outside," Nicoleta says, sighing. If one more person sighs at me, I'll tear my hair out. The bald girl who sees without eyes. What a sight.

"—just out back," I finish, waving and slipping out before any of them can stop me. There's less commotion in our neighborhood than near the Menagerie and Skull Gate. Plus, I have my illusions to obscure me. I'm not worried.

The night air is sticky, yet refreshing compared to the tension with the others inside. Thankfully, Gill has disappeared—skulked back to his tent, where he'll probably keep to himself the rest of the night, reading another one of his boring novels, where nothing exciting or romantic ever happens, and the reader always learns some righteous lesson in the end.

Lightning bugs blink within clouds of gnats, circling my face. The smoke that envelops Gomorrah utterly blocks out any view of the sky. The smoke is part of Gomorrah's legend: once upon a time, we were burned to the ground. But we did not die. Instead we kept burning, kept moving, kept growing. The smoke surrounds us, even if we no longer burn. There is no fire, but sometimes, if you catch yourself around Gomorrah's edges, the air thickens from stifling heat and the lanterns glow a little bit brighter. It reminds me of walking into the city's memory—a very ancient memory.

This section of Gomorrah is lit by white torchlights and paper lanterns, which wear golden halos in the gray fog. Everyone in the Festival seems like a silhouette, a shadow of an actual person. It makes it easy to get lost and, depending where you are in Gomorrah, never be found again.

I scan the area beside my tent—a small clearing that serves as the back of two other tents, which house a family of fortune-workers and a silk salesman. Jiafu is nowhere. We usually meet outside after jobs, so why isn't he here? If he's skipping out on me, I swear, he'll wake up tomorrow thinking there are dung beetles crawling out of his nostrils. I have a hard time believing Jiafu, the master of all crooks, would be scared of a few officials.

I sit on the grass, facing toward the thousands of tents that make up the Gomorrah Festival, the tallest being the Menagerie at the center. The family-friendly attractions—if you could call anything at Gomorrah *family-friendly*—are closest to the entrance, like games, circuses and my freak show. The majority of the Festival is in the back—private tents for prettymen and prettywomen, bars and gambling. We call that area the Downhill. Of the thousands of people who live in Gomorrah, I know the fewest from there.

Jiafu has five minutes before I get angry.

To the left, something catches my eye. A golden centipede wriggles down a tent post, and I suck in my breath and examine it. It's the size of my pinky but twice as wide, with beady black eyes and soft fuzz. I gently pick it up and let it tickle my palm with its hundred feet.

I don't remember when my bug collection began. I have over three hundred insects, gathered from various regions where the Festival has taken me, both in the Up-Mountains and Down-Mountains. A charm-worker down the way preserves them for me in glass vials, which I keep for decoration in my room—both for the aesthetics and to ensure that Nicoleta rarely comes in to nag me. Occasionally Villiam will gift me a book of local insects so I can learn about the ones in my collection. I like to consider myself an expert on all creepy crawlies. Probably because they make other people uncomfortable, but *I* see just how unique and fascinating they are. Highly underrated creatures. The bugs and I have this in common.

A horn blares across Gomorrah. Followed by screams.

"What the hell is that?" I wonder aloud. The centipede crawls up my wrist and arm, unperturbed. It sounded like a city horn from Frice. Maybe the officials are leaving.

I tiptoe around our three tents—the two where we sleep, and the Freak Show's tent—wishing I wasn't alone, in case I do need to face an official. Wishing we, like most of Gomorrah's residents, lived near the Festival's perimeter, not along a main path.

Across from the Freak Show tent lives another fortune-worker, and she—always determined to be the first on Gomorrah's lengthy grapevine—slips out down the path to investigate the commotion approaching our neighborhood. I creep near one of the torch poles to be closer to the light.

An official on horseback trots down our path. By the way he

scans the area, he's looking for something or someone. Perhaps he's rounding up the Frician citizens and marching them back to their city. The noise covered his approach, so I haven't had time to prepare an illusion. I'm exposed.

The official stares at me, his face contorted in disgust. The centipede drops from my arm into the grass, but I don't dare move to search for it. After a few tense moments, the official passes. I let out a sigh of relief.

I head back inside my tent, thinking I'll just cut through the stage area to the back. It's safer to be out of sight. And clearly Jiafu isn't coming.

The show tent is empty, all the audience chairs vacant and the ground littered with kettle-corn kernels. I squint in the darkness. There's something on the stage, but I can't tell what it is.

"Hello?" I say, in case it's a person. No one answers.

I creep closer to the stage and then climb up the steps. Something cracks under my sandal. The floor glistens. I'm standing in a mess of water and glass.

A figure lies on the floor, unmoving and limp. My eyes slowly adjust, so I can tell it's a man lying facedown. He lies on a bed of broken glass and a puddle of water in the dead center of the stage.

I scream and then root around my pockets for a match, my hands trembling. I find one, strike it and bend down to the man's body, bracing myself for my worst suspicions to be confirmed. I instantly recognize his dark hair, the grooves on both sides of his neck and his webbed hands.

It's Gill.

I scream his name and then drop to the floor and roll him over. The back of his shirt is covered in blood. I shake him a few times, but he never responds. I rest his head on my lap, and blood dribbles from his mouth down his chin. "Gill. Gill," I plead. I check his pulse, but find none.

None.

"No. No. No." This is impossible. Gill can't be dead. He's my illusion. His body, though it feels solid, is only a figment of my imagination. No one can kill him, because he doesn't truly exist.

Hesitantly, I lean him on his side and lift up his shirt, exposing the half dozen stab wounds across his back. They are a jagged, messy and oozing contrast to the smooth and translucent silver of his skin. My stomach wretches. I roll him onto his back once more and hug him closer.

I'm struck with a sudden inspiration; a flicker of hope. I can fix this. I can make him disappear. I can make him disappear and he'll come back, just like before.

I grasp for my Strings and find Gill's tethered among them. I gather them into a ball and toss them into his Trunk, a section of my mind I rarely visit except to make the illusions disappear. His Strings are lighter than usual, as if strands of hair rather than proper threads. Though the Trunk is open and full of Gill's Strings, he doesn't vanish from the stage as he should. I cry out in frustration. Why won't he disappear?

His body remains in my arms, dead.

None of this makes sense.

I run my hands down his limp arm to his fingertips, to a shard of glass on the stage floor. The wheeled platform of the tank lies a few feet away. This glass couldn't have broken by accident—it's thick, made especially for Gill's act during the show. Someone shattered it on purpose and then, afterward, stabbed him while he suffocated.

Someone, somehow, murdered him.

A wise uncle;
a good storyteller;
good at giving
advice.

FISH ARE
EASY
CREATURES
TO KILL

OBVIOUS ABNORMALITY:

GILLS AROUND HIS NECK.

WEBBED HANDS.

CAN ONLY BREATHE UNDERWATER.
STAYS IN HIS SALTWATER TANK
OR WEARS A HELMET OF WATER.

RARELY LEAVES TENT.

DISLIKES CROWDS.

OCCASIONALLY VISITS FORTUNE-WORKERS,
BUT NONE CAN READ HIS FORTUNE.

FASCINATED WITH TEA LEAVES.

CHAPTER THREE

The dampness of the salt water and Gill's blood seeps into my clothes. The sleeves of my robes. The knees of my thin pants. I tremble from the coldness against my skin, from the idea of kneeling in a pool of blood, from the image of Gill dying in this very spot. Of him gasping for oxygen, staring at the face of his killer, writhing on the stage floor among the broken glass, with no breath to call for help.

Gill's body is heavy, pressing my kneecaps and ankle bones against the hard wood of the stage. All I register is what's here. The slimy, sardine-like feeling of Gill's corpse. The dead weight of it. The smells of blood, salt and my own sweat.

My body trembles. His Strings slip out of his Trunk and fall back at my feet, one end of them tied to my ankle and the other tied to Gill's. I squeeze them until my knuckles whiten and gather them into my lap, resting them against Gill's stomach.

He's dead. He can't be dead, but he is. He won't disappear.

He's more real in death than he was alive.

Suddenly panicked, I whip my head around. What if Gill's

killer is still lurking in the darkness? I don't see anyone, but someone could be behind me, watching me. I can almost feel their breath on my neck.

Panic simmers in my gut, and the sobs burst out of me like a dam collapsing. He's dead. This is a *body*. Sickened and petrified, I push him off my lap and then wipe my hands on my robes.

I'll never have a chance to apologize for worrying him earlier.

Footsteps thump toward stage right, and Nicoleta emerges, carrying a torch. "What's wrong?" she asks and then freezes when she reaches me and Gill. I feel like one of the rare, taxidermied animals displayed at the entrance of the Menagerie, frozen and surrounded by expressions of horror.

She doesn't scream like I did at first, but she shudders. She inches forward, growing slower with each step, as if she doesn't want her torchlight to fully illuminate the scene in front of her. "Is he dead?" she whispers, her eyes locked on Gill's body.

"Yes. I came in here and found him like this. His blood…*his blood is all over me*," I choke out, my voice cracking. I scrub my hands over and over with my cloak, desperate to remove the sticky red stains on my palms, desperate to feel clean even after they've been wiped away. My lungs don't feel like they're stretching properly, like walls are crushing them from both sides. Each of my inhales grows shorter, faster. My heart pounds.

This was no accident.

"Someone killed him," I say. I sound as though I'm being strangled.

She looks at me gravely. "Get up. Come over here." As I get to my feet, she adds, "No, no, shut his eyes first." With trembling hands, I bend down and close his eyes. The feeling of his clammy skin makes me feel like vomiting. I remind myself that this is Gill. My bossy but well-meaning uncle. My family.

I hurry to Nicoleta and bury my face in her shoulder. "Take that off," she says, nodding at my cloak. "You're covered in blood. If an official comes in, what will they think? We need to clean you up and move him. Now."

"Someone *killed* him," I blubber. "He has stab wounds all over his back. Someone smashed his tank. Someone wheeled his tank *here*—"

Nicoleta grabs my shoulders and rips off my cloak. Despite everything, her voice is steady but sharpened by a terseness that I imagine is shock. "Did you see anyone? Hear anything?"

"No. It was so loud outside. I was just talking to him a little while ago. Then I went in to talk to you and the others, and when I came back, he was gone—"

"Can you make the body disappear?"

"No." And even if I could, the thought of keeping Gill locked away like this inside my mind unnerves me.

"Then we need to clean all this up, hide his body."

"I need to tell Villiam. We need to find out who did this."

She bundles my cloak in her arms. "The officials—"

"I braved the officials for some coins. You think I won't do it for Gill?" Again, I feel the urge to wipe my bloodstained hands, and Nicoleta holds my cloak out for me like a towel. My stomach flips. This is Gill's blood covering me. Blood from the wounds that killed him.

"Then go, and be careful," she says. "I'll talk to Venera and Crown."

I race out of the tent, half to put distance between me and the body and half in my urgency to find Villiam. As I leave, I faintly hear Nicoleta cry out, now that she's alone with her own grief.

Outside, a few silhouettes clothed in the white glow of the torches and encased in smoke wander through the paths that wind across Gomorrah like veins. Many of them are patrons, judging by their taffeta dresses and patent shoes. They pause at each fork in the path and waver in between the hundreds of tents. The paths do not follow any logic, as they change each time Gomorrah travels to a new city.

No matter how fast I run, I cannot escape from the scene of Gill's murder berating my mind. I try to calm myself, to prepare for speaking with Villiam. I know my father, and, despite the horror of these events, he will want facts, logic and composure in order to help. I'm not certain if I am capable of that now, but, still, I prepare my case.

After Gill and I spoke, he probably returned to the boys' tent alone and climbed into his tank, as he always does after shows and family nights. He can climb in by himself, but he cannot climb out without the help of a ladder. It would be easy for the killer to kick the ladder aside, leaving Gill helpless within the tank. We wouldn't be able to hear him scream within the water.

The killer then would've wheeled Gill to the stage. The killer must have known Gill, must have intended to kill him, specifically, and for us to find him in such a dramatic, horrible fashion, center stage.

Even from outside, I wouldn't have heard the tank smash because of all the commotion. I wouldn't have heard the violence of the killer stabbing him, which I'm sure he did to prevent Gill from shouting—all the wounds were at the top of his back, near his lungs. And I was too distracted by the passing official to notice anyone sneaking around outside our tent.

The killer had been there. Right there. And I'd missed him. How did I not see him? I should never have let Gill return to his tent alone. With his nose buried in a book, he probably wouldn't notice anyone following him.

I could've prevented this. A helplessness churns inside me, a desperation to pinch myself and pretend this was a nightmare.

Who would want to kill Gill? He didn't have any enemies—none of us do but especially not Gill. He kept to himself, rarely leaving our caravans or tents unless absolutely necessary. The other members of Gomorrah know him the least of all my illusions. Unless I was the real target…yet the killer would have had ample opportunity to attack me while I stood alone outside.

Then again, who would target me? I may be the proprietor's daughter, but I don't actually possess any power.

It's possible an Up-Mountain religious fanatic killed him. Just the thought of that makes me furious, and I curl my hands into fists. I hate the Up-Mountainers. I hate them and their hateful god.

But it couldn't have been a random fanatic. The murderer knew where Gill slept. They knew exactly how to kill him. They knew *where* to kill him.

A white-coated official storms down the path and turns to a larger road. He carries a short sword in one hand, which clangs against the massive religious chain around his neck—a sword with the sun behind it, the sun representing light and Ovren, their god, and the sword symbolizing the eternal war against the "unfaithful," or anyone who dares to practice jynx-work—who dares to exist despite the warrior god, who would have them gone. I immediately lurch back inside and wait for him to pass. I don't trust the Up-Mountain religion, which focuses more on cleansing others of sin than cleansing oneself.

He passes, and I hurry to the path, now with my moth illusion to cloak me. It is rarely this quiet in Gomorrah at night, when everyone is awake. Usually there are the rattles of dice from within the striped tents, the crackling of a thousand torches and bonfires, and the songs of fiddles and flutes. Now there are only pounding footsteps interspersed with shrieks in the distant night.

From the direction where I am heading.

I weave through the paths, and even though they've changed, I know instinctively where to head, as the central points in Gomorrah always seem to fall on the same spots.

For a visitor, after walking through the mouth of Skull Gate and past the ticket booth, you'd approach the map of Gomorrah, made of thin cow's hide stretched and bound to two ten-foot stakes. Above the map is written *The Festival of Burning Desires*.

Gomorrah is shaped like a coffin, with the entrance—Skull

Gate—at the crown of the head and the twin obelisks at the bottom corners. The top half of the coffin is called the Uphill, and its main attractions include the Menagerie, near the forehead of the coffin; the House of Delights and Horrors, located along the left shoulder; and my Freak Show, located at the right shoulder…all from the point of view of the deceased, that is.

I pull up the hood of my cloak and sprint northeast, toward the Menagerie's spire. The closer I run toward it, the louder the commotion becomes. Frician patrons drunkenly stumble their way back to Skull Gate, nearly as wary of the passing officials as I am. Everywhere is the shouting of arguments and confusion, and I imagine the heart of it will be around the proprietor's tent.

I enter the clearing around the Menagerie. Gomorrah's guards surround the entrance areas to keep the dangerous animals inside and all others out. Gomorrah officials wear all black, even over their faces, so they could blend into the Menagerie tent if not for the whites of their eyes. The Frician officials, in their tasseled, gussied uniforms, gather beneath the ruby banners in this clearing, each one depicting a different legendary animal. The officials stand straighter than toy soldiers.

Beneath the swan dragon's banner, an argument ensues.

"We haven't done anything wrong," a man shouts.

Another beside him says, "You're using pathetic excuses to shut down the Festival."

"Let her go," roar another four people.

At the center of the crowd, a young woman with fair skin wearing a red tiered vest struggles against the grip of one of the guards. I don't know her name, but by her lavish jewelry and heavy makeup, I assume she works as a prettywoman in the Downhill.

"Whore," the guard hisses at her. Her tears make her white eyeliner stream down her face.

Although the Festival's guards remain still—they would never attack without a direct order from Villiam or their captain—

a Gomorrah man rushes at the guard with a wooden staff. It doesn't surprise me that the official's insult riled him up. In Gomorrah, there are prostitutes and there are crooks. There are doctors and there are teachers. The Up-Mountainers consider us all the same—scum—so every profession, every person is given the same level of respect by other members of Gomorrah. No one here would dream of calling that woman anything other than her name.

The official brings down his sword and slices off all four of the man's fingers on his left hand. Both the woman and the man scream, and I'm so shocked that my moth illusion flickers for a moment. I swerve away from the crowd as the official throws the woman down. On her knees, she cries and digs in the dirt for the fingers of the screaming man.

I lick my lips and imagine the illusions I would conjure for those officials. I could make them feel a swarm of beetles pinching every inch of their skin or see hazy, bloody specters cutting off their own fingers. But if I use jynx-work on a Frician, I'll only cause the Festival—and Villiam—more trouble. A whole barrel full of trouble.

If that man protecting the woman had been an Up-Mountainer, the guard would've only hit him with the handle of his sword. Or simply yelled at him.

I'm so angry that it distracts me, for a moment, from why I am paying Villiam a visit—Gill's body lying limp among water, blood and shards of glass. The anger dissipates, replaced by a heaviness in my chest that I recognize as grief. I immediately miss the anger.

Villiam is the priority. As much as I'd love to send the officials fleeing for their mamas and their priests through Skull Gate, I wouldn't be helping anyone. They'd only return with more officials behind them.

And Gill would still be dead.

I skirt around the crowd to a smaller path that leads, within

47

three minutes, to Villiam's tent. I pass a number of storefronts, one selling licorice-dipped cherries, another hawking charmed lamps from the Forty Deserts, but none of them are open. Their torches are blown out, the flaps on their tents closed to visitors.

Villiam's tent is modest in appearance, a vibrant but unpatterned red, with a wooden sign hanging by the door reading Proprietor. You would hardly know it's his as you pass by it, with the aromas of licorice and the beckoning of vendors to distract you. Nevertheless, a crowd of people has managed to find it well and good. Most of them look like members of Gomorrah whose belongings were probably damaged by Frician officials. A few Frician guests linger, as well, no doubt planning to demand their money back.

Still working my moth illusion, I slip inside the tent and make my way toward the front of the line. One of the Frician officials stands guard at the door leading to Villiam's office. As if it's his to guard. He swats at the moth, narrowly missing my nose.

"Villiam will see you all in a few minutes," he says to the person in front, a boy maybe a year or two older than me. Unlike the other guards, this official has a softer face. But I don't trust appearances much. "My captain is currently speaking with him."

"I'm not in any hurry," the boy says. His voice is calm in comparison to the panic among the others in the tent. From his blond hair and his accent, he's clearly an Up-Mountainer. But he's not dressed like the patrons, all in frilly costumes the color of candy. He doesn't dress like he's here for a show; he dresses like he is a show himself. He must live in Gomorrah.

"Then maybe you should let the people behind you move ahead of you," I mutter.

He startles and looks over his shoulder. I didn't realize I had spoken loudly enough to be heard. To my surprise, he allows the woman behind him to take his place in line. He walks to the side of the tent and pulls out a journal and a pen, which he amuses himself with for the next half hour we stand waiting.

Nicoleta has probably told Venera and Crown about the murder by now. I picture her scrubbing and sweeping up the stage floor while rehearsing the words she will say to the others. I imagine Crown carrying Gill's body back to his tent and Venera cleaning it. She'll wash away the blood and change his clothes. Crown will tear up but insist over and over that he's okay, and he'll pace the tent wondering why something so dreadful could've happened to our family.

Visualizing these things doesn't make me feel better, but I can't stop. Part of me thinks that I should be there helping them. All I'm doing is waiting in line, wasting time, avoiding my family when we should be together. But talking to Villiam is more important. He'll be able to help us find the killer. And that's worth waiting for.

Behind me, several more Frician officials parade into the tent, shoving aside those in line to make room for themselves. They all have squished faces, pale brown hair and light eyes. One of them knocks shoulders with the boy, who is too enraptured with his notebook to notice them, like he comes from this region. Even his accent matches theirs.

"I'm already tired of this place," the official says to his friends. "I'll never wash the smell of these people out of my clothes."

"Three fucking pieces for a bag of cherries?" another complains.

"You could spend the three pieces on sweeter cherries deeper in Gomorrah, I hear."

"Three pieces? I wouldn't pay over half a copper for a single girl here—"

"Cheap *and* vile," the boy says, his gaze fixed on his notebook. "It's no wonder you have to pay to find company for the night."

The first official whips around. "What did you say to me?" He examines the Up-Mountain boy with a mixture of shock and confusion. He looks like one of them.

"I said…" The boy glances up from his notebook. "Ah, now

that I see your face properly, I understand it's more than just your charming personality that repels women."

With incredible reaction time, the official punches the boy in the face, slicing open his cheek with the numerous rings on his hand. As the boy falls, the others in the tent back away to remain out of the line of fire. There are several people pressed against me, though none of them seem to notice that they are pushing against what they perceive as a moth and then empty space. This is a good way to get accidentally trampled, so I nudge my way to the front of the crowd, where I have more breathing room and a better view of the show. I could use a distraction.

The boy stands up, grinning. He snaps his leather-bound notebook closed and returns it and his pen to an inside pocket of his vest.

Perhaps he has a death wish, or finds thrill in the danger—not an unusual trait in Gomorrah. But I don't recognize his face, and I study him, now that he has grown the slightest bit more interesting.

He has layers and layers of blond hair pushed back and hanging past his collarbone. He wears a jacket the color of rubies—a dye you'd usually only find in performance clothes in Gomorrah because of its price. The patterns stitched over it resemble clockwork in a variety of colors. This is paired with a white button-up, a black silk top hat, freshly polished boots and a belt lined with vials—each filled with a different liquid, some bright yellow or green, others clear—and a black walking stick. His face is young and defined by thick eyebrows, full lips and a silver stud piercing on the side of his nose.

As he glares at the official, the cut that was gushing blood down his cheek only moments ago fades. He licks his fingers and rubs away the blood. Several people in the tent gasp, even take a few more steps back. I, however, am more intrigued and tiptoe closer.

The official's eyes widen. He grabs a fistful of the boy's shirt and yanks him forward so that they're chest to chest. Though the boy is taller by a couple inches, the official is wider by several more.

"So you're a jynx-worker?" The official spits on the boy's face. Clearly, the official doesn't care that the boy is from the Up-Mountains. A jynx-worker of any origin is equated to scum. Impure, as Ovren decrees. Dirtied by magic.

"Where are your papers?" the official asks him, clearly interested to know which city-state the boy comes from.

"I lost them. It's a rather long story involving an altercation between two prettymen known as the Ebony Tower and Maximilian 'The Whip' Tarla. I found myself unfortunately caught in the middle," the boy explains.

"It's a crime for an Up-Mountain devil-worker to travel without papers."

"Not in Gomorrah, it isn't."

Another punch. Another cut. The official is holding him up so the boy can't fall over this time, and we can clearly see his wound stitch itself back together.

"What kind of jynx-work is this?" one of the other officials murmurs.

"The devil kind," the boy says. "I'm the son of a snow demon. The bastard son. *And* my mother is a prettywoman. I'm not allowed in twelve kingdoms, including the Kingdom of Ovren and the Kingdom of Hell."

Though he's clearly joking, the official pulls away from him the way a person jolts back from touching a hot charcoal. He rips out his sword and holds it to the boy's throat. A Frician lady beside me screams.

"It's no sin to Ovren to kill one such as you," the official tells the boy.

The boy very much brought this on himself, but that official probably *would* kill him if not stopped, and I don't like the idea of anyone else dying tonight.

Thinking up an illusion isn't difficult, since the boy provided me with such useful inspiration. In the eyes of the officials, he grows several heads larger, as tall as the tent's ceiling. His jaw unhinges, his mouth drops open and bits of ice pour out of it, onto their fair hair. Crimson horns sprout from his head and the sides of his arms, some as long as the official's sword.

The official shrieks and swings his blade at the illusion's head, but, of course, there's nothing there. The boy, bemused at the officials' sudden loss of sanity, backs away.

The illusion swings its arm down at the officials, but it misses—they're already running outside.

The people around me whisper in a combination of uncertainty and amusement.

The boy's sight falls on me. I was too focused on the details of my snow-demon illusion to maintain the moth one. He strolls toward me as if, moments ago, there wasn't a sword pointed at his throat. He brushes dust off his jacket.

"You're welcome," I say.

"You weren't there before," he says matter-of-factly.

"I've been here the whole time. You just didn't see me. You're rather reckless, you know."

"I wasn't about to let them really hurt me."

"No, but you're causing problems for the whole Festival." I cringe. Isn't that what Gill told me earlier?

The crowd around us has finally noticed me. "You're the freak girl," someone says. "Villiam's daughter."

Cringing, I try to ignore them and head to the front of the line. Nobody stops me from cutting in.

The boy follows me. "I'm Luca," he says. When I don't give him my own name, he adds, "That's a clever mask you're sporting. One without slits or holes. How does it work?"

"I don't have eyes," I say.

If that catches him off guard, he doesn't show it. "I've only lived in Gomorrah for a year, and I don't know many people.

Perhaps you'd be willing to show me around. I'm certain I'd enjoy your perspective on this place."

"I can't."

Villiam's assistant, Agni, squeezes past the kind-faced Frician official at the door. Agni is a lanky man in his forties who's always squinting, even in the nighttime. He squints around the tent for a few moments before realizing I'm there.

"Sorina," he whispers. In addition to the squinting, Agni always whispers. Someone once told me it's because he's such a powerful fire-worker—his voice is hoarse from breathing in all that smoke. When Agni isn't serving as Villiam's assistant, he works at the Menagerie, training rare animals to jump through flaming hoops, or participates in Gomorrah's nightly fireworks show. Everyone knows him…and everyone knows his family's tragic story.

"I need to speak to Villiam," I tell him. "It's urgent."

"He'll see you—" he raises his voice "—but everyone else should come back in another hour."

There's an uproar of protest as I climb the steps out of the tent and into Villiam's enormous caravan, muttering a quiet goodbye to Luca. Inside, the caravan is set up like a proper parlor, with two men sitting there, Villiam and the Frician captain—or general, or colonel, or whatever his title may be. The walls are layered with cabinets of books collected from all over the world. It's clear upon first entering the room what interests Villiam—knowledge. A telescope rests on a table by the window, surrounded by papers and trinkets. Villiam even commissioned an artist to paint the ceiling to resemble the night sky on the day he was born, which he claims speaks wonders about his destiny. The carpet is fur, the seats leather and the tablecloth silk.

The Frician captain tenses as I approach. His light eyes scan me, as if trying to determine who exactly I am—a young girl wearing a sparkling, beaded tunic and a sequined party mask— and what I could possibly be doing interrupting their meeting.

Even though he's sitting down, it's obvious he's tall, but his height seems to be the only characteristic that gives him any authority. His face is gaunt and unintelligent, and he wheezes as he inhales the soothing incense of Villiam's office. He does not frighten me.

Villiam smiles at me the way he always does, as if he were expecting me. No matter the situation, he makes a great effort to appear at ease and prepared. Some in Gomorrah believe that Villiam is a fortune-worker with fewer cards and crystal balls, but he isn't a jynx-worker at all—he only looks like one. The quick shifts in his dark eyes give the impression that he can read all the lies you've ever told, as though they're etched on your forehead. He has a habit of muttering to himself under his breath—usually reminders about paperwork, occasionally a sarcastic comment spoken only, apparently, to amuse himself. Even his manner of speech is unnerving. He has a skill for putting words into your mouth, steering the conversation in any direction he chooses and escorting you out of his office with a smile on your face, yet with more problems than when you arrived.

"Ah, Sorina," Villiam says. Just the sound of his voice is comforting, and I want to run forward and embrace him, but I hold myself back in the presence of the captain. "I'm just *tickled* you were able to join us." He thinks I'm here to help him with proprietor duties. The thought never even crossed my mind until now, with how distraught I've been since I found Gill's body.

I force a smile and inch my way closer to their table. "I was hoping to speak to you in private," I say.

"Of course," Villiam says. "The captain was just leaving. But first, Captain Mayhern, I'm pleased to introduce you to my daughter, Sorina. She's a captivating performer here at Gomorrah."

"Is that so?" Captain Mayhern asks. He seems unsure that I could be Villiam's daughter. Villiam has mixed Down-Mountain features from the many generations of Gomorrah proprietors in his blood. He wears his dark, curly hair long, sometimes tied at the nape of his neck, sometimes simply down. His skin is a dusty gold, with freckles along his forearms and nose. By contrast, my looks are definitely Eastern—I'm clearly not his daughter.

I am in no mood to be introduced to an Up-Mountain captain and play the charming young lady, but I try to keep the smile on my face for Villiam's sake.

"A pleasure," I say. "What brings a Frician captain to Gomorrah?" I already know the answer. To cause trouble.

"Pleasantries," he says, holding out his hand.

"Funny." I don't take his hand. "On my way here, I witnessed one of your soldiers pleasantly slice my friend's fingers off." I didn't know the man, but he was of Gomorrah. In every aspect that matters, he is a friend.

He reddens, as all Up-Mountainers seem to do whenever they are uncomfortable. I rarely see an Up-Mountainer whose cheeks aren't wearing some shade of red. "We're here to keep Lord Ovren's peace."

His god has a very different version of peace than mine.

Villiam ushers the captain out. He compliments his conversation, assures the man that Gomorrah will be out of Frice's borders by morning and other such *pleasantries*. I bite my tongue until the soft-faced official has led the captain out of the room.

"They're making us leave Frice by tomorrow morning?" I ask Villiam.

"They aren't pleased with the conduct of their citizens here. The religious officials had hoped their citizens would behave more…well, behave." He frowns. "But it is more than that. An extremely influential Frician duke has gone missing. They were here searching for him."

A thousand insults, a thousand sarcastic comments cross my mind. But I don't say them in front of Villiam. He can be quick to scold if I say something he deems out of line. Which includes most things I wish to say.

"Are you all right, Sorina? You look troubled," Villiam says. He always knows when something is bothering me before I say so. "Would you like tea? Some honey biscuits?" Villiam views food as a cure-for-all.

I run to him and press my face into his chest. In practically one, drawn-out breath, I relay him the details of Gill's murder. I talk quickly because if I slow down, I will start crying again. And I have to be strong. I need to be able to present the facts, so Villiam can work out the answers for me. Villiam always knows how to handle a difficult situation and solve even the trickiest problem.

Throughout the story, Villiam keeps a stoic expression, as if contemplating a puzzle from one of his books. I don't know how he can keep himself so contained. He knew Gill. He knows all my illusions. He examined my sketches of them before I finished them; he interviewed them soon after their creation to make sure they were suitable for performance. He knows them as *people*. Even though they are illusions, they are considered to be members of Gomorrah like anyone else.

He must be upset, but I'm grateful that he's remaining calm for my sake.

"Are you all right?" he asks. "You haven't been hurt? And the others? You didn't see—"

"I'm fine. The rest of us are all fine."

His eyes scan over me, as if searching for invisible bruises. Then his shoulders relax. He unties my mask and hands me a tissue, so that it's easier to blow my nose.

"I'm so sorry, Sorina. I'm so, so sorry." He rubs my back and then sits me down in a chair at his table. I grab a throw blanket to wrap around myself for comfort.

"I just don't understand how it's possible," I say. "Gill is an illusion."

"It shouldn't be possible," he says. "I don't understand it. I'm at a loss. None of your illusions should be able to die." He squeezes his hand into a fist until his knuckles whiten, releases his grip and then repeats, over and over. He does this whenever he is in a tizzy, as he would call it.

"We need to find out who did this immediately," I say. "I wish I could've seen more. That I'd been paying attention—"

A sharp knock sounds, and Agni pokes his head through Villiam's door. "Sir, there's a fire in Skull Market."

Villiam grimaces. "None of this is your fault, Sorina. And it destroys me that I cannot give you all the help and support you need right now. But with the problems with Frice, Gomorrah leaving at sunrise and apparently a part of the Downhill on fire, there is too much I must do. I need you to promise me something, my dear."

"What?"

"You must hurry and bury him—I'll send a few of Gomorrah's guards to help you and to search your neighborhood for anything to help us find the killer. You must act quickly. If the Frician officials see him with their duke missing, they will grow suspicious. The entire Festival could face trouble."

Packing up all of our belongings and the stage equipment usually takes several hours. If we're leaving at sunrise, we would need to get started now. This doesn't give us a lot of time to bury Gill's body, let alone to say a proper farewell.

All because one Up-Mountain politician got himself lost. He's probably somewhere in the Downhill, drunk and falling off his bar stool, and we need to pack up, forgo our grieving and move out, just to give the Frician officials peace of mind. Where is our peace of mind? I tear a loose thread out of the blanket and squeeze it in my hand.

"Sir," Agni says from outside, "the fire."

"Another minute," Villiam grunts. He kisses my forehead, where he always kisses me. Then he kneels down in front of me. "I'm so sorry, but there are ten thousand people to pack up and move in a few hours. I must focus on them first, but I promise

57

you, tomorrow—once Gomorrah is moving—we will discuss what happened to Gill."

"But the killer could be gone by then," I protest.

"There is nothing I can do right now." Villiam's voice cracks. I've never heard him so frazzled. "I'd give anything to help you, but Gomorrah is in a crisis." He hesitates. "Do you want me to send Agni with you?" Agni is always at Villiam's side. Villiam considers his advice and presence to be invaluable.

"No. I don't know what he would find in the tent that the rest of us wouldn't," I say. "But do we really need to bury him tonight? That's…that isn't enough—" I'm crying. Villiam hugs me and shushes me but still allows me to finish. I feel a hundred things at once. Grateful for the comfort. Embarrassed that I'm keeping him here when thousands of people are depending upon him. Angry at Frice. Angrier at the killer. Lost. Confused. Horrified.

Because I've been training with Villiam and learning about how Gomorrah works for years, I also know that moving the entire city is no easy feat to accomplish in several days, let alone a few hours. He genuinely does not have time for me.

"Send my apologies to our family. Tell them I'm thinking of them. I wish I could be there to help them in person. This is…such a tragedy," he says, tears glistening in his eyes. "And promise me you'll return when the commotion has died down."

The commotion won't disappear for several days, not until we reach the next city. It's hard to think that far into the future. It's hard to picture anything except the night ahead of me, of packing up the stage where Gill died, of burying him without a coffin, without a ceremony. It's impossible to think beyond saying goodbye.

Nevertheless, I mutter, "I promise."

CHAPTER FOUR

The Gomorrah Festival does not travel like other circuses, groups of wanderers, bands of musicians, thieves or markets, because it is all of those at the same time. If someone stood at the peak of the Winding Pass—the stony, barren mountains we are crossing to reach the city of Cartona—it would appear as if an entire burning city were on the move beneath them. Due to the suddenness of our departure, tents are still raised and wheeled on platforms, parties continue in the Downhill as the sun begins to rise and the white torches glimmer within the haze of smoke. It goes on for miles, with a population of over ten thousand inhabitants. Our nickname is "The Wandering City."

If that same person had watched the Gomorrah Festival travel before, they would also realize that its atmosphere feels different this morning. More subdued and downcast. There's less music, laughing and cheering since the Fricians kicked us out.

Or maybe the morning wind is cooler than usual, and it's just a chill. Gomorrah is older than anyone can remember and unlikely to be intimidated by the actions of a single Up–Mountain city-state.

Perhaps I am the only one in Gomorrah feeling the chill. Perhaps, after Gill's death, the music, laughing and cheering is quieter only to me.

Apart from Tree, who prefers to walk on his own, my family sleeps in two separate caravans when we travel—one for Crown, Gill, Unu and Du and Blister, and one for the rest of us. I sleep between Nicoleta and Venera. Hawk's feet are across from mine and sometimes kick me during the day while we rest. The caravan is packed full of trunks, the floor covered in blankets and the ground in between littered with popcorn kernels and peanut shells.

I sit up and stare out the window at the Winding Pass peaks jutting into the sky, mere silhouettes through Gomorrah's smoke. The sun has risen, barely. Gomorrah is beginning to go to bed, and I have yet to fall asleep. The memories of Gill's corpse and his brief burial a few hours ago continue to haunt me. Even though I've washed my hands over and over, removing every last trace of blood, I wipe them on my bedsheets once, twice, three times.

I replay my last conversation with Gill over in my mind. I was a jerk. Not only yesterday, the day he died, but the day before, and before, and before. I could've listened to his advice more often. Read the books he suggested. Made an effort to spend time with him, instead of avoiding his lectures.

I want to sleep until reality feels more like a dream. I want to never wake up.

But I have business to attend to and others to look after. Jiafu will still be awake in the Downhill. Even though it's dawn and no longer safe to venture outside, I'll have to take my chances for now. At least this errand will keep me distracted.

I slept in my regular clothes last night, so I crawl past Hawk and creak open the door. Then I jump out of the moving caravan into the knee-high grass of the Winding Pass.

Gomorrah can be more difficult to navigate while it's moving, but I've explored the Downhill once before during the day, when the nicest people of the Downhill—which is not saying very much—are asleep and the rest of the crooks are awake. In the Downhill, no one cares that I'm Villiam's adopted daughter. Actually, they'd probably love to skin me because of it. No one there is a star performer, a great attraction or seemingly special at all. In Gomorrah, everyone might be treated equally, but, in the end, money divides the affluent from the rest. If Villiam wasn't paying for my family's space, we'd barely be affording the Uphill ourselves.

It takes me ten minutes to walk to where the Uphill intersects with the Downhill. There's a fifty-meter gap between those two sections of caravans, and as I trudge across the small, open field, I feel eyes peering at me from ahead. People are watching me, wondering why an Uphill girl would visit them at this hour.

The wood of the caravans here rots from years of rain, with holes along the walls just large enough to toss out the contents of an ashtray or for someone to covertly slip a delivery in the gap beneath a windowsill. The ribs of horses, mules and the occasional more exotic elephants who pull the caravans are more pronounced. Their eyes burn red, and their dirty coats swarm with clouds of fleas. I worry that if I get too close, they might mistake me for the meal their owners forgot to feed them.

Thankfully, Jiafu doesn't live deep within the Downhill, and I make it there without becoming a horse's breakfast. The cramped caravan he calls home is striped purple and black, with no sign or indication of what a visitor might find inside. All of his clients already know who he is and where to find him—he doesn't need advertisements.

I knock on the dull black door and walk to keep up with it. No response. After thirty seconds of more knocking—and a man poking his head out of a nearby caravan, telling me to piss off—Jiafu answers. He grimaces when he sees me and rubs his temples, one of which has a deep scar that snakes down to his chin.

"What do you want?" he asks. His shadow dances on the grass below him, twisting into almost gruesome positions, as if trying to tear itself away from the body casting it.

"You weren't waiting for me last night," I say. "After the show."

"There were officials about. I needed to head back home and protect my merchandise."

"I want the money now. I want my cut."

"Too bad. I haven't sold it yet. I don't got your cut. Now run away, princess."

"Sold what yet?" I say, loudly and dramatically. "Oh, you mean the *priceless* ring of Count...Pomp-di-something from Frice? That's worth a fortune?"

The man who told me to piss off earlier pokes his head outside again. As do a few others. I have their attention.

Jiafu narrows his eyes and then he yanks me by my tunic and hoists me into his caravan. Inside, there are five times as many crates as in my own, with just enough floor space for a mattress in the corner. Everything reeks of burnt coffee and feet.

"You think I had a chance to sell the ring?" he hisses. "We just left Frice."

"I didn't expect Kahina to have to travel again so soon. I want the money to get her medicine as soon as we get to Cartona." Packing and traveling isn't easy on her, especially in this part of the Up-Mountains, where the roads are unpaved and hard on her bones. And now that Gill is...now that Gill is gone, ensuring Kahina stays healthy is more important to me than ever. I can't lose anyone else.

He pauses. "There *is* another job. One of my men noticed this guy carrying a big purse of change. He's at a bar now getting piss-drunk. If you could make an illusion, someone to mug him—"

"That's not how it works," I say, annoyed. I've had this conversation with Jiafu before.

"You said it takes a while to make an illusion, but I've been to several of your shows, and your act is different each time. You make it up on the spot."

I rub my temples. "Yes, *that* type of illusion is improv. But you're asking for a person. You're asking for someone you can touch, hear and smell, someone *real* like Nicoleta and the others. They take me months."

"Then get started making one. Big, preferably good with a sword—"

"The answer is no."

Even though I've technically made all of my illusions, I don't really think of them that way. They're their own persons. They're my family. I created them to be the friends I never had.

I'm not exactly the most popular person in the Festival. Who would trust someone who has the power to deceive you in every manner?

He jabs his finger in my face. "Look, freak, that job wasn't easy last night when you had the Count sitting in the front, and—"

I hold back my wince. "If you call me *freak* again, you'll think maggots are eating out your insides." I take three steps forward. Jiafu is several inches taller than me, but that doesn't matter. I can make him look like an ant. I can make myself look like a giant.

He leans back. "Hey now, 'Rina, don't be like that. We're cousins, eh?"

Jiafu plays this card a lot. He comes from the Eastern Kingdoms of the Down-Mountains, like me, so he thinks we're family. We're not even friends.

"Don't bother. I want my cut. I want my thirty percent. And I want it as soon as possible."

He collapses onto the floor mattress and kicks his legs up on a crate. "There's nothing I can tell you. I want to give you the money. Really, I want to. I want to reward all my friends." I narrow my eyes. We're. Not. Friends. "But I don't have anything. I'll sell it in Cartona. Then you get your cut."

I sigh. This is about what I expected. Sure, Jiafu probably has some money hidden inside these crates that he could give me, but that would take a bit of coercion on my part. It would take an impressive illusion to make him cooperate. What would scare Jiafu? An enraged ex-mistress? A debt collector? I didn't get enough sleep for my imagination to be at its best.

"Sorry, cousin," Jiafu says.

"You're not my family."

"Would you prefer *princess*?" He lifts his left leg and points his calloused toe toward the door. "Come back after we're settled in Cartona, and I have time for some business."

"I will." I try to make my voice sound forceful, intimidating, but I only sound broken. I plaster a smile on my face and push aside the thoughts of Kahina's snaking sickness and of Gill. Then I mutter a goodbye and jump out of his caravan.

I'm not on my game.

Outside is the sound of millions of caravans moving and horses trotting. I walk past the smell of opium teas and a sign for what I'm sure is questionable goat curry.

Sleep will be impossible, so instead of making my way home, I head toward the center of the Uphill, toward a particular caravan decked out in fuchsia drapes and murals finger-painted by neighboring children. A sign on the door reads *Fortune-Worker: Explore the Successes, Loves And Wonders That Await You.*

I knock. It's not as if she's sleeping. In all the time I've known her, Kahina barely sleeps. She stays awake most of the day watering her herb garden and stringing necklaces and belts out of forgotten coins. And worrying about everyone's futures. She should spend more time concerning herself with her own.

"I'm not done yet," she calls from inside.

"No, it's me," I say.

A pause. There's a rustle that sounds of coins tinkling together. Then she opens the door, a smile stretching across her face. "Sorina." She holds out her hand to help me into the caravan.

The first thing I notice is the purple of her veins that spread from her fingertips up her forearm in a winding, swollen web. I freeze.

She laughs and switches hands. Her right one is normal and not yet infected. I grab it and climb into her caravan, eyeing her hesitantly. Other than the dark, snaking veins, she looks *healthy*. Which almost makes the sickness crueler, convincing you she's fine until, very suddenly, she won't be. The sickness will creep through her blood, snaking through her bloodstream into either her heart, lungs or brain—wherever it reaches first. The process can take years. From there, the disease progresses quickly, attacking the organ and deteriorating it cell by cell, until it can no longer function. No one knows how it spreads, but it's common, both in the Up- and Down-Mountains.

Her long dreadlocks are pulled into a bun, full and beautiful. Her brown skin has its normal glow. Her ankle-length skirt and tunic fit her the same as always. Sometimes it's easy to forget that she's dying.

She occupies an entire medium-sized caravan to herself. Usually, that would be quite expensive, but since she has grown ill, a lot of her friends and neighbors have pulled their resources together to make her more comfortable. Kahina chose to use the extra space to add more volume to her herb and vegetable garden, many of which she makes into medicines or herbal teas. Unfortunately, none of them are rare enough to treat her own disease. The potted plants take up the majority of her home, and I brush a palm leaf out of my way as I crawl into her actual living space, which is mainly taken up by her bed, a drawer for fortune-work objects like crystals and cards, and a short table. The pots clack together as the caravan rides across the bumpy road.

Kahina lies back down on her bed and returns to the embroidery she was working on. With its red stitching and plain patchwork, it's meant for a newborn boy. As the baby ages, the empty patches will be filled with cross-stitching depicting various life moments.

"Tya is going to have a boy in January," Kahina says. "I figured I might as well start now."

Kahina's jynx-work allows her to glimpse into the future of individuals. She's accurate the majority of the time, but I've witnessed a few occasions where she's gotten a detail wrong. So it seems rash for her to make a blanket for a child that may still be born a girl. Especially because fortunes grow less certain the further into the future Kahina searches.

"You couldn't wait a few more months to start?" I ask.

"I may not have a few more months."

I pause before sitting down in the corner of her caravan. "You can't talk like that," I plead. "You can't. I'm getting you medicine. The best quality there is. I'm not going to let anything happen..." My voice cracks. "Nothing is going to happen to you." My head hurts from the build-up of pressure, and I steady my breathing to avoid crying. Damn it. I thought I could compose myself, but I am one unpleasant thought away from hysterics, no different than a few hours ago. I thought being in the comfort of Kahina's caravan would help.

"You're right," Kahina says quickly. "I shouldn't say things like that. Are you all right, Sorina?"

"Y-yes," I say. But talking makes my breathing stagger, and then I can't hold it back anymore. I cough out a sob, which turns into another and then another. There are no tears, of course, but my face reddens and my nose runs. I feel as though my entire heart has shattered.

"What has made this come on?" she asks, crawling to my side.

I bury my face into her shoulder and mumble something unintelligible.

"You're really worrying me—"

"Gill's dead. Someone killed him. Last night."

I feel her whole body go rigid with shock. "What do you mean, someone killed him?"

I tell her the entire story, just like I told Villiam last night, and it's no easier to share a second time. As I near the end, Kahina gets up to pour me a stone-cold mug of chamomile tea. "We were arguing when I last talked to him," I choke. "I... I wasn't kind."

"Arguing about what?" Kahina asks.

"Nothing important," I lie. She wouldn't like to hear that I've been working with a Downhill thief to supply her medicine. I've been telling her that the Freak Show has been booming lately. I'm not certain if she buys this, but Kahina always said I don't have to tell her anything I don't want to. Before this, I've never had anything to conceal from her.

She presses me closer to her and hands me the tea. Then she runs her fingers through my hair, the way she used to when I was a child. "I'm so sorry, sweetbug. I wish I could've seen this coming."

Kahina is unable to see the fortunes of my illusions because they aren't entirely real.

But apparently they're real enough to die.

I wish I could tell her about how worried I am about her, too. About how I feel the same anxiety, as if, even though my lungs are expanding, I'm not getting any air. And the feeling won't go away. But Kahina hates it when I bring up her health. She hates to see how it affects me.

"It's not fair," I say. "It's not fair that the Up-Mountainers get to storm our Festival and then call us the criminals. They get drunk, and they buy drugs, and they pay for all sorts of sins and call us the sinners for giving them the business they want." I wipe my nose with the back of my hand.

"I don't like to hear you talking like that," Kahina says gently.

"What do you mean? It's the truth. What they do isn't right."

"No, it isn't right. But that doesn't mean I like to hear my sweetbug saying ugly, angry things. Not my beautiful sweetbug. You're allowed to be sad. Of course you can grieve. And anger is a stage of grief. But some never move beyond that, and I worry about you when you say such things." She tugs at the ribbon of my mask until it slips off. "There. That feel better?"

Kahina always treats me like a child. She treats everyone like children, even people with more wrinkles and body aches than her. Her only child died at only two months old many, many years ago, yet she always said it was her destiny to be a mother, that every fortune-worker in Gomorrah told her that. So Kahina became a sort of mother to everyone in the Festival, quilting blankets, sending baskets of tea and keeping lucky coins for everyone she cares about.

But I'm her sweetbug.

When Villiam first adopted me, I was only three years old. He may have been my father, but, in truth, he was more of a teacher. He needed someone else to look after me while he managed the Festival, but no one was too keen to babysit me, with my freakish face, my unsettling jynx-work and Tree following me wherever I went. Only Kahina volunteered. And though Villiam and Kahina may have different views on parenting, Villiam has always appreciated the maternal role she plays in my life.

"What is Villiam doing to find the perpetrator?" she asks.

"I don't know yet. He was too overwhelmed with moving the Festival to do anything last night. He sent some guards. But they only asked us a few questions and left."

"That doesn't surprise me—last night was chaotic. I hope he doesn't involve you further in the investigation."

I pull away. "Why not?"

"Because I know Villiam. I've known him since he was a boy. And as much as he loves to involve you in all of his work, he doesn't know you like I do. He's clever and calculating—able to detach himself from a situation to view it objectively. You are not like that."

"I could be. If that's what it took," I insist. I'm going to be proprietor one day, so I'll need to be.

"Now, sweetbug," she says, continuing to run her fingers through my hair, "no one wants you to go through that. What happened to Gill is a wretched thing. But you need to promise me that you won't let the anger get to you. You have too beautiful a soul for that. You focus on love, because you still have a whole family who loves you. Don't you forget that. And drink your tea."

"A whole family I made up."

"I was made on a cold January night by a fisherman and a fortune-worker, not by you," she says wryly.

I snort. A very clogged, snotty snort.

"Yes, Venera and Hawk and all of your family may be illusions, but they still love you. And love is real. Love is a choice." She squeezes my hand, and I stare at her black veins with a mess of dread pinching at my gut. I don't know what I'd do without Kahina. "Now, you're going to take it easy right now. You're going to sleep and cry and eat or not eat as much as you want until we get to Cartona. And then you're going to perform your show and see your friends and do things again. And it won't feel better right away, but it will eventually."

Would it get better? I don't have any friends to see—the only people I spend time with are my illusions, Kahina and Villiam. Most people in Gomorrah avoid me because my face makes them uneasy. Even with my mask on, people have complained because they can't see my expression or tell if I'm looking at them. Around me, they cannot trust their own senses. I make everyone uncomfortable. It's easier to be among other misfits.

"I promised Villiam I'd go see him tonight," I say.

She purses her lips, and I prepare myself for another speech about not getting involved in the investigation.

She must know I won't take her advice. Not on this.

"Then, after tonight," she says. "You take time to yourself, okay?"

"Okay. But can you do a reading for me before I go?" Kahina often does fortune-work for me. I may have given up on aspirations of beauty, but my fantasies of romance have been kindling since Kahina told me fairy tales as a child. So I usually ask if she sees anything remotely romantic in my future. She never does.

"Of course," Kahina says. "Maybe there's a mystery man."

"Or lady," I add. When I imagine myself in Kahina's fairy tales, I tend to prefer princes and princesses equally. "I was hoping you could read for anyone connected to what happened to Gill. Through me." I sit up, my hair brushing against the leaves of a palm potted behind me.

"I don't think that's a good idea, Sorina." She only uses my name when aggravated.

"I just want to make sure that everyone else is safe," I say. "Please. It would make me feel better."

"Fine. But only this once."

She grabs a black clay jug from her table. Inside are hundreds of coins, each with a different symbol. I take the jug and shake it until one coin falls out from the opening underneath. It's a gold piece with a menace on it—a type of demon believed to live in the Great Mountains, the region between the two continents. Not a good sign.

She turns it over in her hand. "You are surrounded by confusion," she says. "It's strange. Difficult to see through. As if you're surrounded by the same smoke as Gomorrah."

I'm not sure what to make of that, but I've grown used to Kahina's vagueness after hundreds of readings.

"You can't see *anything*?" I ask.

"There's only the negative energy in your aura."

"What about any positive energy with a good jawline and broad shoulders? Or doe eyes and silky hair?" I ask it with a teasing smile, so Kahina doesn't suspect I'm thinking "ugly thoughts."

She laughs and then shakes her head. "I don't see any good jawlines or doe eyes, but, then again, I don't usually do those sort of readings with the coins. Do you want some tea leaves?"

"That's okay." Not like the tea leaves have foretold anything before, and I don't have much desire to finish my cold mug of chamomile. "I'm going back to sleep until I see Villiam."

"That's a good idea, sweetbug." She squeezes my hand. "Sleep as much as you'd like."

CHAPTER FIVE

I yank one foot after another out of the mud as I trudge my way to Villiam's caravan. This Up-Mountain road wasn't made for heavy travel in the rain. Especially not with hundreds of mules, horses and caravans ahead, tearing the ground apart and leaving a mess in their trail. With each step, I sink into the earth halfway up my shins.

The red tent usually outside Villiam's caravan is currently packed away, so the whole caravan is visible. It was painted black about thirty years ago, so now it's merely speckled with the remaining paint, revealing pale wood beneath. Fresher coats of red, pink and purple spell out the swirling letters of The Gomorrah Festival. I knock on the door, walking to keep up with the two enormous stallions that pull it.

Villiam answers. As usual, he wears neatly pressed business clothes, though I doubt he's seen anyone today, as it's barely four o'clock in the afternoon. He extends his hand out to help me up and then embraces me once I climb inside. "Dismal outside, isn't it?" he says.

"It's appropriate," I answer.

Agni is in the process of setting out a full four-course meal. In Gomorrah, breakfast is our typical supper, with the heartiest foods eaten before guests arrive. He reaches out every few moments to catch an empty wineglass knocked over by the bumps of the caravan. "Maybe the breakfast wine should be skipped today, sir," Agni says.

"Nonsense. Wine is an important component of a meal," Villiam says, ever the gourmet. "And without all the pieces, a whole structure could collapse."

Agni rolls his eyes and lets the pepper shaker tumble to the floor, spilling out onto the fur carpet.

"I didn't realize I was coming for breakfast," I say. "You just said you wanted to speak with me."

"Why? Have you already eaten?"

"I'm not hungry." Eating doesn't have much appeal. The only things that have gotten me out of bed since I spoke to Kahina this morning are Villiam's mandatory invitation to meet with him and the need to relieve myself.

"I know it's difficult, but you need to keep your spirits up," he says. "And take off your mask. Make yourself comfortable."

Difficult is hardly the word. More like *impossible*. Even if I wasn't hating myself for the way I last spoke to Gill, I'm surrounded by seven others who are grieving. The only one attempting to pull us together is Nicoleta, who brought us candied pecans and cashews, but the bag is lying untouched in the corner of our caravan, and I'm sure it was the same in the boys' cart, especially now that one of their riders is gone.

"I chose some of your favorite dishes," Villiam says, drawing me out of my morose thoughts.

With my mask off, I sit down at the table and eye the plates. Herbed lamb legs; some kind of mix of butternut squash, peas and beets; a huge dish of steaming yellow rice; and a cream curry sauce with mint. It's very colorful. And it looks delicious. But the table keeps shaking as the bumps on the road jolt the caravan. Agni runs past me—reeking of smoke, as usual—and stabilizes one of the many bookshelves.

Still, it's a nice gesture. Condolences and empathy are not my father's strengths, but he always manages to reach out to me in smaller ways. Particularly ways that involve candies or aged cheese.

Villiam sits opposite me and places his napkin on his lap, ignoring the disorder around him, even when someone knocks on the door. Agni ducks outside to answer it. It's not like Villiam to set his proprietor duties aside, even for me. He must feel guilty about not being able to help me last night.

"Will the Freak Show be performing while we're in Cartona?" Villiam asks.

I tilt my head. We aren't meeting to talk pleasantries. But Villiam adds, "Eat first. You need to eat."

My stomach clenches as I eye the huge portions on my plate. I can't possibly eat all of this. I could barely manage a nibble.

"We're planning on it," I say in answer to his question. We can't afford to stop the show for an entire week.

Villiam grabs generous helpings of each dish and adds them to his own plate. "Perhaps I will pay a visit. It's been too long since I've seen one of your shows." When I was a child, Villiam used to attend our performances at least once a week. He always sat in the front row, clapping the loudest, even if Nicoleta stuttered through her speech or I blanked when creating an illusion.

Before he can grab his fork, Agni pops his head back in. "Sir, half the Downhill is stuck in the mud. They're almost half a mile behind us."

He sighs. "Tell Skull Gate to stop moving. We'll have to wait out the rain." When Agni leaves, Villiam mumbles, "Half a mile behind. Preposterous. I should've known earlier." Villiam has a habit of talking to himself. He looks up and smiles. "The rain will stop in a few hours."

"Your fortune-worker is never right about the weather," I say.

"Timar and I have been working together a long time."

"But he's terrible. You should find a new one. There are hundreds—"

"I will do no such thing." He pops a piece of squash in his mouth. Villiam is loyal to a fault. "And none of this weather would be a problem if Frice had given us more time to leave. We could've waited out the storm."

The caravan stops moving now that Gomorrah has received the order. The sounds of utensils rattling on the table and books falling to the floor stops, and the tension eases from my shoulders. I hadn't realized how anxious all of that was making me. I decide to ignore my lack of appetite and taste the lamb, which is juicy and hot, thanks to Agni's fire-work. It's one thousand times better than Crown's grub food.

"Did they ever find that duke who went missing? The one they kicked us out over?" I ask.

"Yes. They found him dead in his parlor," Villiam says. I choke a bit on the lamb. "It appears a political rival had him killed. It had nothing to do with Gomorrah."

"Unless they think one of our assassins did it."

"Assassins? In Gomorrah? Whatever would give you that idea?"

He likes to play this game, pretending Gomorrah is the safe circus I believed it to be as a child. One day, he'll admit to the assassins. One day, he'll teach me more about Gomorrah than merely its mechanics. One day, he'll stop treating me like a child. I'm sixteen and his only heir. When will he truly train me to be a proprietor?

"We're passing several cities now," Villiam continues. "Ukarce, Meera, Thire. All denying us refuge. What if the rain worsens and it floods? What if some of our people die? Compassionate Ovren doesn't have much compassion for those on the other side of His mountains."

75

"I thought Timar said the rains would stop."

"That is not the *point*." He stabs his knife into the leg of lamb. I only meant the comment as a joke. The events of last night must have caused him more stress than I thought. "The point is that the Up-Mountainers get away with whatever they want." His words echo my own to Kahina earlier. "If we weren't forced to tour here, I'd move us down the mountains to more civilized provinces."

The problem with touring Gomorrah in the Down-Mountains is that they're not nearly as interested in us as the people are here. Fortune-workers, charm-workers, they have all those. Nearly everyone in Gomorrah comes from the Down-Mountains. We're simply the most dangerous—and oldest—festival around, one hundred times larger and grander than any other roaming carnival. The Up-Mountains—or, at least, the cities that don't shut us out—find us "exotic." They buy mundane trinkets and call them treasures. They marvel at the simplest of jynx-work, when they're not cursing it. And they keep us in business.

"If you don't mind—I do appreciate all the food—but I would rather go straight to talking about Gill," I say. I didn't come here to listen to Villiam rant about politics.

His face softens. "Of course." He leans forward and rests his elbows on the table. "As I recall, you said it was the stab wounds that killed him...not the suffocation?"

I stiffen as I picture the blood seeping through the back of Gill's shirt. "Yes."

"Perhaps the assailant only meant to scare him by shattering his tank, but when Gill cried out, he grew scared himself and attacked." My chest tightens as the scene plays out in my head. The killer kicking away Gill's ladder. Wheeling him helplessly to the stage. Smashing the tank and letting Gill fall to the floor. "You mentioned the wounds were messy, didn't you? How many were there?"

"I didn't... I didn't count. But, yes, they were messy." I clutch my stomach. I shouldn't have eaten anything at all.

He studies my face. "Sorina, we don't need to talk about this. The last thing I want is to upset you."

"No." What did Kahina say? That I couldn't detach myself. Maybe she's right. I can't simply remove myself from my emotions the way Villiam can. But that doesn't mean I'm going to give up. "I want justice."

"It was more than likely a religious fanatic from Frice," Villiam says. "I'm powerless to bring such a person to justice."

"But I don't think it was," I protest. "How would a random visitor know that Gill would be alone in his tent? And how would they know that Gill can't breathe in air?"

"Perhaps because he sleeps in a vat of seawater?"

"Someone *murdered* Gill. They killed him, on stage, for me to find. And he's not even real! I created him! They're not supposed to be able to get hurt! I didn't create a family so that they'd die!" I cover my face with my hands as I cry for the fifth time in the last twenty-four hours. It's difficult to hold back the sobs, and Villiam quiets for a minute until I bring myself back under control.

"I already began an investigation into his death, you know," Villiam says. "Not so much into the perpetrator but how someone managed to kill him. The guards last night have written me a report on what they found. I promise you I will find the answers."

I wipe my nose on one of Villiam's expensive table napkins. "What kind of investigation?"

"I'm not certain I want you involved. You and the others are grieving. It isn't healthy to be focusing on revenge. Focus on healing, instead. You're clearly still distraught—"

"I'm not *distraught*—"

"You aren't yourself. You're on edge. You look like you've barely slept. And you're only sixteen years old—"

"But I need to know who did this."

"And I will try to find you as many answers as I can," Villiam says, his voice tight. He has obviously already made his decision to leave me out of this. "We're exploring all possibilities. Questioning people near your tent. Looking into our visitors' book. Determining—"

"That isn't going to tell us *how* Gill was killed," I say.

"I was getting to that part, if you would only stop interrupting me." His deep voice booms, and I sink into my seat, holding on to my composure by a thin thread. "I'm also trying to determine if there is some aspect to your jynx-work we don't know about."

I frown. "Like what?"

"As you know, illusion-workers aren't common anymore. I've never met one. Perhaps there are aspects to your abilities that have been forgotten over the years."

I stand and walk toward Villiam's bookshelves, half to examine his collection and half to hide my face as its redness fades. "You have books all about illusion-work, though. You said you know everything about it."

"I'm sure I do, but we're investigating it, just in case," he says. "I'm not suggesting you do *nothing*. I've known you for thirteen years—you're hardly the type of girl to sit still. So perform in your show. Go out and meet more people who aren't illusions. You need to keep yourself busy. But not with this. This won't help you move on. I'm worried about you."

I only half listen and browse through his encyclopedias on jynx-work, most of which are on the floor. They're massive volumes, each bound in quality leather with golden tabs on the side, marking places where Villiam has taken notes. They chronicle the types of jynx-work that have come and gone over the past few centuries. Many abilities cycle. Some die out. Occasionally one never seen before becomes common.

"Could I read through these books, as well?" I ask.

"I assure you that I've read them all multiple times. There won't be any answers for us in there."

"But still. I'd like to read them. You're always telling me to read more. This would give me something to do." I pluck a volume of jynx-work from the Eastern Kingdoms in the last century. On the cover is a sea dragon curled into a spiral, its scales embellished with a glistening glaze. "And if you're not using books, how are you investigating illusion-work?"

"I keep detailed records on the jynx-work of everyone here, especially you." Beneath the shelves sits a trunk large enough to fit a person, which contains the records of everyone living in Gomorrah. We are not an easy people to track. Some have lineages that trace back to the earliest days of Gomorrah, but more often, our members are misfits who joined on a whim. We have Down-Mountainers escaping criminal charges. Up-Mountainers persecuted for their jynx-work. People attracted to a nomadic lifestyle, to performance, to the magic of the Festival. Gomorrah is as large as many of the city-states we visit, so the role of the proprietor is no easy task.

"There may be something I've forgotten," Villiam says. "Maybe you should revisit your original sketches for the illusions. Perhaps there was a fault in your blueprints."

"Gill's death isn't my fault," I snap, loud enough to startle him and also myself. I won't let myself think like that. The only person to blame is the killer.

"No. Of course not, Sorina. It's not your fault." He stands and gives me another hug, and even though I'm upset about not being part of his investigation, I can't help but give in to the comfort my father offers.

After he kisses my forehead and pulls away, I slide the volume back onto the shelf. There couldn't possibly be a fault in the blueprints for my illusions. If it was a building that had burned down, the question would not be whether the structural integrity was compromised but rather the identity of the arsonist. Except…these buildings were supposed to be indestructible.

Maybe it doesn't have anything to do with my illusion-work at all. Maybe the killer is the one with unusual powers. That must be how they managed to kill one of my illusions.

This idea sits well with me, easing the guilt and instead channeling it into anger. I trace my fingers along the leather bindings of the volumes, scratching them with my fingernails.

I don't mention my idea to Villiam. He already berated me about not focusing on revenge. I need to focus on "healing." But what if revenge is the path to healing? To closure? I'm not just going to sit back and go about life normally when a piece of it was ripped away.

And if Villiam isn't willing to help me, I'll just find someone else who is.

A baby brother;
likes to smile;
    rosy cheeks;
    not too much crying;

DEATH TO BE
DETERMINED

~~NO ABNORMALITY?~~
ABNORMALITY IS STRANGE &
POWERFUL FIRE-WORK; DOESN'T BURN.

WATCHES THE FIREWORKS SHOW
EVERY NIGHT WITH CROWN.

FAVORITE FOOD IS HONEY-FLAVORED
COTTON CANDY.

NAPS IN THE
AFTERNOON.

CHAPTER SIX

The performance of the Gomorrah Festival Freak Show our first night in Cartona was less than spectacular. Nicoleta forgot her lines halfway through the show, accidentally snapped her metal performance cane in two and had to apologize to the audience for her stuttering. Tree tore out one of his branches and sprayed red, bloody sap all over the floor, which Unu and Du slipped on during their dancing routine. And my illusion of giant red-horned beetles scared the audience out of their seats and out of the tent, but it was the only thing that popped into my head.

To make it worse, Villiam was there, as he'd promised. And by the end of it, he was the only person remaining, once I accidentally chased the others out. He sighed and shook his head the entire time.

It's obvious we're all a wreck.

I enter the dressing room and am immediately greeted by Blister, who gives everyone his usual round of high fives. I smile as much as I can manage. He scampers back to Crown on the other side of the divider, who beams at him and runs his hand through Blister's tight curls. Despite originally being hesitant almost two years ago when I told everyone I intended to create an illusion of a baby, Crown adores Blister, and Blister certainly loves him.

I change out of my show robes into plain black ones. No fancy shoulder pads or glittery fasteners. And I fish out my purple-striped mask, which is sequinless and the least fun—though it does have a few feathers. I'm not really in the mood to make a statement.

"Why are you dressed more somber than a nun?" Venera asks. She's applying some of her most festive makeup—red lipstick and fake eyelashes as long as her fingers. She prefers to party away her problems. It seems like she disappears to a different event every night, only to stumble in exhausted and still tipsy at eight in the morning, well after sunrise.

I worry about her.

"Just not feeling particularly fabulous." Not entirely false. No, I'm not feeling fabulous. "And I don't think nuns wear feathered masks."

The real reason for my attire is my planned trip to the Downhill tonight. I need to find someone to help me uncover Gill's killer. I don't know who I'm going to find, or how I'll find them, but I'm going to try. And the Downhill seems like the place to go. I don't know anyone in the Uphill who would know how to track down a murderer.

It's been four days since I dined with Villiam. Four days, and all I've wanted was to find the killer, but I couldn't bring myself to get out of bed at any point before our performance tonight. I ate only the butterscotch cashews Nicoleta grabbed from a vendor. I'd often wake to find Venera at my side, her makeup smeared from her nightly activities, her long black hair tangled and damp with sweat. We'd barely speak, and if we did, it was about frivolities: romantic interests, the bleak city of Cartona, the knots growing in our hair.

All I want is answers, but somehow that wasn't enough to get me out of bed. If I let myself sit down again, I probably won't go out at all. I hate myself for it.

"Here." Venera tosses me a tube of blood-red lipstick. "To keep your strength up."

I smile and then apply some in the mirror. It doesn't look as good on me as it does Venera—does anything?—but I still look pretty, nonetheless. I haven't bothered with lipstick in a while, and I rub my lips together, feeling its smoothness, and almost smile. Feels familiar. Like my life before Gill died.

I examine my dismal reflection more closely. I actually look terrible. The weather is terrible. Today was terrible. And to-morrow will be terrible, too.

I muster up my strength to force on a smile. "You're the best." I kiss Venera on the cheek, careful not to leave a smudge of red. "Don't go too wild tonight."

She grabs at her corset and hoists it up, boosting her cleavage about five inches. "Do I ever?"

I laugh but quickly stop myself. Even if it's a genuine response, it still feels wrong to laugh.

Blister reappears at my side, no longer in his performance clothes. "Boom," he says seriously.

"You're leaving to see the fireworks?" I ask him. Crown takes Blister to see them every night.

He nods. "Boom."

Crown grabs Blister's hand. "Do you want some cotton candy?"

"Yeah."

"Then we better hurry. We don't want to miss the booms."

I smile as I watch them leave, hand in hand. At least some things still feel normal.

Several minutes later, with my fresh coat of lipstick and a handful of butterscotch cashews, I head toward the Downhill. It's safer at night, mostly due to the large crowds. But I rarely venture there, even at times like this. I'm not into partying. And I'm definitely not into prettyworkers. I never have much of a reason to pay this part of Gomorrah a visit, other than to see Jiafu.

The dirt here outside Cartona is golden, same as the bricks used to construct the great wall that encircles the city and, even from here, towers in the distance. Because of the dense forests around Cartona, Gomorrah was forced to set up among trees, so the Festival feels twice as dark as usual. The leaves above are half-hidden among the smoke.

The torches in the Downhill do not burn red like regular fire. There's some kind of charm-work on them so they burn green, making everyone look a little sickly. I pass a massive tent of prettymen on my right—two stories high, created by a mess of platforms, beams and rapid reconstruction at each new destination—and a hookah and pipe vendor on my left. The air here smells sweet, almost inviting, from all the opium.

Who is going to help me? I don't have much to pay, and I doubt anyone here is willing to help me out of the goodness of their hearts. So I'll have to find something to offer. Maybe my status as Gomorrah's princess will hold some sway.

Doubtful, but maybe.

I wander around for half an hour. Past gambling dens, vendors smuggling rare animals, bars, feasts, pawnshops and fighting cages. I have no idea what I'm looking for. The Downhill is even more of a maze than the rest of Gomorrah. As I walk, my sandals crunch on broken bones from whatever meat the food stands are selling roasted on sticks, as well as syrup from coated apples and their leftover cores. The patrons in this section do not wear the usual apricot- and peach-colored dresses, arms linked with their lovers with matching bow ties. They are not here to laugh and have their palms read and buy candied pineapple. Whether the patrons in the Downhill are wealthy or not, they have a hungry look in their eyes, like animals deciding whether to attack or flee. Each one walks with a sharpness to their step, looks over their shoulders with a glimmer of fear and excitement. They're interested in the darkest of desires Gomorrah has to offer, and they've come to the right place.

What was I thinking? No one is going to help me here.

It's not as if I can do this on my own. I barely rolled myself out of bed to come here. I need someone to be objective when I—clearly—cannot. And I'm not smart, not like Gill was smart or Nicoleta is smart. Altogether proven by thinking I'd ever find someone to help me in the Downhill, or anywhere.

I stop at a strange tent on a side path, striped with vibrant Gomorrah red and purple. The fabric of the tent looks new, not yet faded from years of rain and travels. A wooden sign sticks out of the dirt by the entrance:

Gossip-worker.
Tell me your secrets and your troubles.

I've certainly got troubles. Lots of them. But I've never heard of a gossip-worker. I don't think there is such a thing. I look around to see if anyone else is venturing inside. To the right stands a small, empty outdoor stage, and to the left, a vendor selling apples soaked in bourbon or peaches soaked in sake. Somewhere ahead, in a massive tent of reds, purples and pinks, music plays—the kind meant for dancing, certainly not for telling someone your secrets and troubles.

But I'm curious, I have nothing better to go on and I also think I'm lost, so I duck inside the gossip-worker's tent.

The inside is stark, empty of nearly all decoration. A table with porcelain teacups takes up most of the room, along with a bookshelf to its right. The floor is made of bamboo shoots woven together, similar to the one in our tent, which we roll up for travel and unroll at each new city.

There is a flap in the back corner that I assume leads to another tent, probably a sleeping area.

This doesn't feel like a place for visitors. It feels like someone's home. Someone with very few belongings but, still, a home.

At the table with the empty teacups sits Luca, the boy who almost got himself killed by Frician officials in Villiam's tent. He
looks up, and I know he recognizes me. Beside him is a prettywoman, with deep brown skin and black hair braided down to
her knees. All she wears on top is a shawl tied into some sort
of covering. They appear to be—other than the fact that she is
half-clothed—simply having tea.

"You're Sorina Gomorrah," he says.

"*You're* the gossip-worker?"

"Among other things."

He stands up, adjusts his clothes and walks over. He wears the
same hideous velvet vest with clockwork stitching and the same
belt full of vials. He also has that black, silver-tipped walking
stick leaning against the table, as if his rich-boy getup needed
a finishing touch.

He holds out his hand for me to shake.

"I don't remember giving you my name when we first met,"
I say.

He smiles. He has dimples. I realize, in that moment, that I
really like dimples. I also realize that I've been holding his hand
for too long, and I'm acting like a complete fool.

I wrench my hand away. This is business. Not the time for
flings. Besides, he has a beautiful prettywoman sitting right beside him, so beautiful that I try not to gape at her slender neck,
gorgeously full lips and the curves of her chest. Between her
perfect complexion and my lack of eyes, it's not difficult to determine who would be Luca's choice. And with Luca's dimples,
it's easy to see who hers would be, as well.

Their loss, I try to tell myself.

Luca has very nice brown eyes. *Bedroom brown eyes*, an embarrassing voice in my head giggles. A voice that sounds an awful
lot like Venera. I tell that voice to shut it.

"You're that boy whose life I saved, right?" I ask. Playing it
smooth. Pretending I barely remember him—not that I did,

until this moment. I've actively tried to forget most of the details of that night.

"I hardly think I'd say that. I had it handled."

"You were about to watch your guts spill into your hands."

"Nothing I can't manage." He cocks an eyebrow and laughs. "I'm pretty durable. Quick to heal."

Luca's strange healing ability was amazing to watch, but I find it difficult to believe that he would fully heal if someone stabbed him through the stomach with a sword.

"Yelema, if you don't mind, I'd love to discuss that customer more with you at a later date," Luca tells the prettywoman. "I hope you enjoyed the tea. It's a mountain-herb blend."

"Delicious, as always," she says. She extends her hand, and he kisses it.

"I don't mean to interrupt your…" I say.

"It's fine. I know to leave when he has clients," Yelema says. "Besides, I have a client of my own in an hour." She waves as she leaves, and I ponder over her words. Perhaps Luca is more than just a client to her?

Luca points to the chair opposite him. "Go ahead," he says.

I slide into the seat. "I've never heard of that kind of jynx-work before."

"Which one? The one on the sign outside? Or the one you witnessed the other day at the proprietor's tent?"

"The healing one. But I've never heard of a gossip-worker, either."

"Gossip-worker is simply a title," he says.

"Bestowed by who?"

"By *whom*," he corrects, and I grit my teeth in indignation. I already don't like him. "And bestowed by myself. I make it my business to collect information on everyone in Gomorrah."

"Why?"

"Because the people here interest me. Because I know a fortune-worker here who claims to use the same coins his ancestors did in

Gomorrah over one thousand years ago. Because you'd never believe the intricacies involved in supplying constantly fresh food for an entire city that travels across the world. Because nobody dull runs away to join this place."

Judging by his expensive clothes, he's probably some rich Up-Mountainer who decided to run away to Gomorrah, and he thinks himself interesting and cultured because of it. He's not going to be much help if he was consorting with a prettywoman during business hours. Clearly he has other things on his mind.

"Why are you here?" he asks, not impolitely. "Doesn't Gomorrah's princess have more important places to visit than my tent?"

"I haven't decided yet," I say. I'm still curious about his healing ability, about the strange belt full of vials he wears and, if he has information on everyone in Gomorrah, whether that information could help lead me to the killer.

As if sensing my thoughts, he unclips his belt full of vials and lays it on the table. He points to each one. "Cyanide. Arsenic. Hemlock. Nightshade. Black Maiden. Belladonna. You're welcome to test one out."

"I'm not drinking hemlock."

He smiles the most insincere smile imaginable. His face makes the motions—his lips curl up, his eyes squint and his teeth show—but nothing about it appears genuine. Perhaps it is the performer in me, but it looks as if he has slipped on a mask that only I notice. "I meant pick one for me. I'll drink it. Go ahead."

"Why would I want to poison you?" I ask, both alarmed and curious.

"Most people seem to enjoy it. Or stabbing me through with their swords. Strangling me." He tips the scarlet vial from side to side with his index finger. "They pay excellent money for it, attempting to kill someone who cannot die." The vial slips off the table, and with perfect reflexes, Luca catches it inches off the floor. "I call it poison-work. Another name I've dubbed

92

myself with, since I am, to my knowledge, the only poison-worker in the world."

"How do people know that red stuff isn't just cranberry juice?" I ask.

"Because I keep a collection of cockroaches on which to test out my poisons. Cockroaches are *almost* indestructible. Just not nearly as much as me."

"It's cruel to kill cockroaches for your show," I say. Then, to my dismay, the words keep spilling out of my mouth. "Cockroaches are actually really fascinating insects, you know. They can make decisions collectively in groups. Females can carry forty eggs at one time. And they can survive over a month without food."

"It's a cruel line of work, people paying to kill you. And—" he laughs "—you are clearly more informed on cockroaches than I am."

So maybe Luca is good-looking, but I'm not into people that kill innocent creatures. Isn't that something serial killers do?

Maybe I shouldn't have come in here by myself. Maybe those dimples of his just hide terrifying intentions.

"*Most* people say they don't believe me. *Most* people say my jynx-work is impossible," he says. "You don't seem so questioning."

"I'm a trusting person, I guess," I say.

"A dangerous thing. Is that why you're here? To entrust me with something? It's unusual, as I don't get many clients from the Uphill."

"How can you tell I'm from the Uphill?" My clothes don't look any different than the ones people here are wearing. Other than my mask, of course.

"As if Villiam would allow his adopted daughter to live in the Downhill," he says.

I sigh inwardly. I'm not convinced he's going to be of any help. He seems like an ass. He's clearly an Up-Mountainer. And my gut—plus that smile of his that doesn't look like a smile at all—tells me he's hiding something.

"You're still contemplating whether or not to trust me," he says.

"You know too much about me. You sound like a creep."

"I told you—knowing about the people here is my business, the one I call gossip-work. It's a hobby of mine when I'm not being stabbed to death for sport. A hobby I'm quite skilled at." He smiles genuinely now, with the dimples, a lighthearted look in his eyes. "So, tell me, what's troubling you?"

I don't know of anywhere else I could find help, and despite Luca's strange demeanor and his Up-Mountain background, he *does* seem to know a lot about me. Maybe he knows just as much about the other people of Gomorrah. If he's as good at his so-called gossip-work as he says he is, then he might not only be my sole option but a good one.

And it's not as if I have anything to lose.

So I tell him every detail, starting from the show the other night, though I leave out the bit about working with Jiafu. Luca listens without interrupting. It feels different telling this story to a stranger than it did to Villiam or Kahina. I need to explain everything—what the illusions are, that Gill always sleeps in his separate tent, the layout of the stage. It's exhausting.

"I just don't think it makes sense that it was an Ovren fanatic," I finish. It occurs to me that Luca, being from the Up-Mountains, might also follow their religion. But I doubt it. He's a jynx-worker who ran away to Gomorrah. It doesn't matter where he's from—they would scorn him as much as me.

After a few moments of silence, Luca only says, "No."

"No, what?" I ask.

"I'm not interested."

It takes me a moment to process that he means he's not interested in helping me.

"What? Why not? I can pay you. It may take time to gather up some money, but—"

"I don't take payment. I only work if the story interests me, and, to be honest, this *does* sound like the work of a purity-crazed Ovren disciple. You haven't provided reasonable doubt, so that's my answer for you. Sorry, princess." He pulls out a golden pocket watch to check the time, as if he has better places to be.

"But I have no idea how Gill was killed at all. He's an illusion."

"Was. He *was* an illusion," Luca corrects. I lean over the table to slap him across the face, but he catches my hand and holds it there. "And I know all about your illusions. Nicoleta, for instance, had a drawn-out, tumultuous affair with a pretty-woman I happen to be acquainted with. So if your illusions can be touched, smelled, heard, and they can act on their own, what exactly is your definition of *not real*? What makes you so certain they can't be killed?"

"By definition, an illusion isn't real," I snap.

"Illusion-worker is just a title. Like gossip-worker. Like poison-worker."

I stand up. "Thanks for nothing," I snap and storm out. Who exactly does he think he is? Giving himself a fake title. Acting smarter than everyone else. He's so...so...*infuriating*. I kick down the wooden sign outside his tent. Then I kick it again after it's fallen.

My walk home from the Downhill passes in a blur. I'm so focused on my thoughts and figuring out who else would want to help me that I pay no attention to where I'm going. One moment, I'm at Luca's, and the next, I realize I'm already back at my own tent.

What makes you so certain they can't be killed?

Is there more to my illusion-work, like Villiam thought? But I create illusions. There's no debate about that. So what more could it be?

As I approach our tents, a figure runs toward me. Nicoleta. Her face is pink and puffy—our signature look, lately. But not usually for her. She's managed to stay collected while everyone else has fallen apart, at least while we've been looking. Has something happened? Or did she not mean for me to see her cry?

"Sorina!" she calls.

Nicoleta crying. Nicoleta running. Something is wrong. Something is even more wrong than before. I run toward her, my heart pounding. I push more than one Cartonian patron out of the way to reach her.

"What is it?" I ask. She nearly collides with me, and I wrap my arms around her, stiff while she's shaking.

"It's Blister. Crown found him in the dunk tank near the games area. He drowned."

CHAPTER SEVEN

Down-Mountainers wear white to funerals. I borrowed a dress from Kahina, which hangs down to my skinny ankles and is already staining with mud along the hem. Villiam stands on my left in elegant, almost priestly robes, with a starched collar and bare feet. On my right, Venera wears a simple white tunic, no makeup, no strands of beads, no flowers in her hair. She is almost unrecognizable.

All of us—my family, Villiam and Kahina—gather around the small hole that Tree dug this morning. Blister's casket, not even three feet long, lies at the bottom, wrapped in the red quilt Kahina made him a year and a half ago. There are no patches on it for significant life moments. It's blank.

I imagine the patches full. I imagine his first day of school. I imagine how dazzling his unique fire abilities could have been once he grew older. I imagine him lighting the fireworks of the show he loves so much.

Hawk sings a mourning song. Her voice sounds distinctly inhuman, more like a bird's, shrill but beautiful. It's strange to hear her sing without her fiddle's accompaniment, or to sing something so slow and deep and sad.

I look everywhere but at the casket. At the overcast sky. At the anthill a few feet in front of me. At Crown, who cries the hardest but the most quietly. Everyone loved Blister, but Crown was the one who read Blister the same stories every night, who convinced Blister to take a bath by bribing him with treats, who rocked him to sleep when he cried.

My chest tightens, and it feels as if I'm not getting enough air. I'm standing still, but my heart is pounding. I glance over my shoulder around the field, half expecting someone else to be here with us, examining the results of their handiwork. Selecting another victim.

Crown digs his cane into the dirt; his dark knuckles whiten from squeezing so hard. Circles hang beneath his puffy, bloodshot eyes. He looks broken.

I never worried about Crown's age before, but now that I know that my illusions can die, all I thought about last night was whether Crown would make it. Blister was Crown's entire world.

I can't lose another member of my family.

And I won't. My hands curl into fists and I take a long, deep inhale. Because now we know that Gill's death wasn't just a random, crazed disciple of Ovren. Not when Gill and Blister were killed so close together, both never before believed real enough to kill.

Someone is targeting my family, and I'm going to find out who, how and why.

Kahina casts me a warning glance, as if she can tell what I'm thinking. I haven't spoken to her alone since just after Gill died, but there's no way she can tell me to focus on healing now. I'll heal after we find justice.

At first, Nicoleta assumed Blister's death must've been an accident. Blister was almost two—he naturally got himself into trouble when no one was watching. But Blister hated water. He hated baths. He hated rain. He wouldn't go near the dunk tank, which is glass and obviously full of water. Not to mention tall and difficult for a small child to climb.

Someone drowned him on purpose.

He was only a baby. Our baby. I choke back a sob and wipe my face on my sleeve.

Hawk finishes her song, and Crown inches closer to the grave. He stares down at the hole blankly, as if it goes on for miles and miles. He says nothing for a few moments. The only sound is Gomorrah preparing to open for the evening a hundred meters behind us. This field outside of the Festival's fence has soft earth and wildflowers. It seemed a good, quiet place for Blister to rest.

"Blister was a happy one," Crown says, "and a star performer. He loved the attention of being on stage, especially with all of us. He clapped for all of us backstage, even when we told him to be quiet. I think we're all going to miss his high fives after the shows are over."

His voice catches, and he covers his mouth with his hand. Everyone gives him time to compose himself, and when he continues, his words quiver.

"Blister liked fireworks more than anything, so I brought one to light when this is over." Crown pulls a small red flare out of his jacket pocket. "We watched the fireworks at Skull Gate every night, just me and him."

Venera cries beside me quietly. She reaches out and intertwines her fingers with mine, and I know we're picturing the same things. Blister returning every night in Crown's arms, saying he saw the "booms." The way he said our names: "Ree-ah" and "Vu-rah." The hugs and kisses good-night.

"My sweet baby boy, you were too young," Crown chokes out. "I wish more than anything that you were here with us right now. So I'll tuck you in one last time, and maybe one morning, we'll see each other again."

Nicoleta passes me a shovel. Then all of us, except for Kahina and Crown, lay Blister to rest.

When we finish, my hands and shoulders ache, and my nose won't stop running. All I want is to sleep undisturbed, where I don't need to look at the grief on anyone else's face and I can cry in private. But my heart races, and I look over my shoulder every few moments in case someone is watching. The someone who killed Blister. Who killed Gill.

None of us are safe.

Why? Why would someone want to kill any of us, especially a baby?

I'd give anything to turn back time. To have waited one more day to talk to Luca. To have stayed home and watched Blister so he couldn't disappear. To notice the person lurking by our tent, waiting for someone to turn their back for a moment while Blister wandered outside.

"Does anyone have a match?" Crown asks. "I...forgot to bring some."

We rarely needed matches. Blister lit our candles and charcoals for us.

"Here." Villiam pulls a brass matchbox out of his pocket and hands it to Crown, who thanks him quietly and bends down to position the firework in the dirt.

It shoots off in a streak of gold. I wince at the sound of the explosion.

Boom, I hear the echo of Blister's voice.

Tree gathers up the shovels and thuds back toward the Festival. Hawk spreads her wings and flies into the distance to be alone. The rest of us linger. And when we do begin to tread back to our tent, Crown lingers still.

I walk beside Villiam, the hot summer wind whipping my hair across my face and the grass against my ankles. "Why would anyone do this?" I ask.

He frowns. "Nicoleta told me that Blister's death was an accident."

"She's in denial. First Gill and now Blister, barely a week apart? That's too much of a coincidence. And Blister never would've gone near a dunk tank on his—"

"It's not proper to speak of such things at funerals," he says. "Let's go—"

"Then when do you want to talk about it?" I snap. "Because all I could think about the whole time is that we're out in the open, that the killer could be here watching us and we'd never notice. Who has to die next before you realize that these aren't random—"

"Sorina." He puts his hands on my shoulders, and I'm so rigid and anxious that I have to hold back the urge to shrug him off. I want space and air and for my heart to stop pounding.

"I... You're right. Of course you're right," Villiam says. He leans down to kiss my forehead, but I pull away. I don't want him or anyone else to touch me. "The timing of these two tragedies is unusual and terrible. I can't imagine what you must be going through. I am looking into Blister's death, as well. I'm doing..." His voice cracks. "I'm doing everything I can."

"Are you? I don't want you to just *look into* it. I want a full-scale investigation, and I want to help. I want to make sure my family is safe."

"Sorina... I really don't think this is a good time for you. You know that I like to involve you with my work, but this is a decision I've made as your father, not the proprietor. Trust me to do my job. I'm trying to protect you."

"How can I trust you with this when you think Blister's death was an accident?"

His expression looks wounded, as if I've insulted him. Maybe I have. Of course Villiam is doing everything he can. He has a hundred things on his plate at the moment, all dire. "I will begin the 'full-scale investigation' you want. I will question everyone in Gomorrah if that protects our family. Of course I will. I'd do anything for you. But you need to promise me something."

Why is it that every time I ask someone to do something reasonable and necessary, they always ask for something in return? At what point do my requests stop being opportunities to teach me some kind of lesson? I'm not acting like a child. Whether or not I'm an adult, I'm allowed to be scared. I'm allowed to be worried. It isn't some fault in my character that I demand the right to ensure my family's safety. The childish thing to do would be to dismiss the facts in order to avoid a truth you don't want to face. I'm facing the truth head-on. Even if it hurts.

"Promise you what?" I don't mean for my voice to sound so harsh, but it does.

Villiam winces and then hesitates before he answers. I swallow my guilt in a dry lump.

"All right. If you want to be part of my investigation, you can."

My mouth drops open in surprise. Villiam never changes his mind.

"But," he says, "the investigation methods will not be as you think. Based on a few interviews with your neighbors and a lack of evidence to the contrary, I'm starting to suspect the perpetrators are trying to get to me through you."

"Perpetrators? You think there's more than one person behind this?"

Villiam glances at the others walking ahead of us with sad eyes. He lowers his voice. "Tomorrow evening. Come to my caravan like you normally would for your lessons. There is much to talk to you about."

"Like what?"

He embraces me, and I am overcome by his familiar scent of cologne and white tea. With his breath close to my ear, he says, "I wanted to wait until you were older, eighteen, before formally beginning your training as proprietor. But the burden of

our legacy has reached you earlier than I ev[...]
he pulls away, his eyes glisten. I don't kno[...]
never seen Villiam shed a tear.

"I'll meet you tomorrow night," I say, t[...]
entirely certain what he means. Why would[...]
illusions to get to Villiam? Who are his en[...]
But I'm too taken aback by his emotion to ask any more questions, especially out here in the open. "I love you," I say.

"I love you, too."

The rest of us silently return to our tent. There won't be a show tonight.

Kahina cooks us couscous and lamb, and though she's outside at the fire pit, we can all hear her hacking coughs, a symptom of her snaking sickness, from inside.

She could die next. Or Hawk. Or Unu and Du. Or Nicoleta. Any of us.

I lean my head on Venera's shoulder and stare at one of Blister's toy tops lying on the table. Each time I finished making one of my illusions, Villiam gave me a gift for them from him. A birthday gift, of sorts. This is what he gave to Blister, and it always was Blister's favorite toy. I grab it and spin it. The purple-and-pink-painted swirl spins in a never-ending spiral. Until it stops.

Venera strokes my black hair and twists it around her finger. "Do you think Kahina will mind if I don't eat anything? I'm not very hungry," she says.

"She won't care." I spin the top again. "Are you going out tonight?"

"I think so. I need to escape for a bit."

I press my finger on the top's handle until it slows to a stop. "Be careful."

"Always am."

After Venera leaves, Unu and Du gather everyone around for a game of lucky coins to keep us distracted. We clear off the e to make room for our play. The game is mostly luck with a hint of strategy, but, by far, the surest means of victory is a hefty wallet to purchase the best coins. Unu and Du, who save their allowances specifically for this, own the strongest collections. The Beheaded Dame has a nearly indestructible defensive bonus. And the Iron Warrior has no attack penalties. The only one with a collection formidable enough to defeat either of them was Gill.

Halfway through our third game, only my weakest coins still defend my playing field, leaving me wide open to attack. Someone clears their throat outside.

We all pause. "Who is it?" Nicoleta calls.

A man's silhouette appears by the entrance of our tent. He is a member of Gomorrah's guard, wearing all black. Villiam must have assigned him to watch over us tonight.

"There's a boy out here who wants to speak with Sorina," the guard says. "He calls himself a poison-worker."

Luca? What would he be doing here? I'm not sure if I am more confused or annoyed that he'd have the gall to pay me a visit.

"What's a poison-worker?" Hawk asks.

"Just wait here for a minute. I'll be right back."

"But the game isn't finished," Unu yelps.

"I was going to lose anyway."

I slip outside to find Luca waiting for me behind the tent. He wears a grim expression. After one look at his hideous, quilted vest and his uncombed blond hair, I am reminded of the details of our conversation last night, and how his words so easily manage to be even more offensive than his clothing. I'm already dreading whatever he has come here to say.

The guard leaves to give us privacy.

"What are you doing here?" I snap. "You made it quite clear yesterday that I wasn't worth helping."

"I was wrong," he says. "I heard about Blister. I'm so sorry, Sorina."

I cross my arms and turn away. Now he decides that my case is interesting to him? I shouldn't have sought him out in the first place. Had I been home, maybe I would have noticed Blister wandering off. Instead, I'd been wasting my time.

"You should leave," I say.

"Please. I want to help you. How are you doing?"

"Are you only being nice because you're *interested* now?" Luca reddens. Last night he was all wit and calm and I-have-better-things-to-do, but now he fidgets and avoids my gaze. I'm making him uncomfortable. Oh, well. It's not my job to keep him at ease.

"No. I'm being nice because you look like you need it," he says. "I have thoughts about what happened. Just hear me out."

I can tell he won't leave until he's had his say, so I let him speak.

"So it could still be a disciple of Ovren, I suppose," he says, his gaze focused on the grass. "But whoever they are, they do seem to be targeting your...family."

I shiver at the thought that someone out there, for whatever reason, wants more of my family dead. I'm not sure I can protect them.

"The big question is why," Luca says. "You're the proprietor's daughter, which could be the reason. But how well does Villiam know your family?"

"Well enough." That sort of thing is private. I'm not about to share our family business with him.

"They don't seem close."

I purse my lips in annoyance. "They do not spend as much time with Villiam as I do, but they are still family. Not that it's your business."

"So if the killer did this to get to Villiam, they're not doing a very good job, are they? Villiam hardly seems affected. So the killer must have a different motivation."

I squeeze my fists until my knuckles whiten. There are kinder ways to say something like that. My father isn't as dismissive as Luca seems to believe. No, he doesn't always invite my family to dinner, but he helps provide for them. He buys presents for all of their birthdays. He asks about them whenever he sees me. He's devastated for me.

Luca looks over his shoulder in case anyone is eavesdropping, but it is still early enough in the afternoon for the paths to be quiet. Even the nosy fortune-worker who lives beside us is still asleep—the best gossip is witnessed late in the night, when drunk patrons stumble back to Skull Gate or when her friends flock to her door to share the latest news.

"And there is still the question of how the killer is doing this," Luca says. "You're convinced the illusions are simply illusions. And since you're the only illusion-worker I've heard of in the past few centuries, I'm not inclined to question your judgment on the matter. I'm thinking the killer might have an unusual sort of jynx-work. The kind that might be able to kill someone who isn't real."

"You didn't say anything like this yesterday," I say.

"I was thinking it. But it seemed unlikely. I thought Gill was probably killed by an Up-Mountainer—however, most Up-Mountainers suppress their jynx-work, so the perpetrator is statistically less likely to be from there. But now we have a proper killer on our hands. Someone with jynx-work who *does* know how to use it. Where is there a large collection of jynx-workers nearby? Here, in the Festival. Which also makes sense, as it seems odd that someone outside the Festival would target you so specifically. You're not that important." He speaks so quickly I almost grow dizzy.

"You're wrong," I say.

He furrows his eyebrows as if he didn't understand my words. "What?"

"I am important. I'm the proprietor's daughter, destined to be the next proprietor."

"Is that what Villiam thinks the killer's motive might be?"

"Yes."

"Is that what you think?"

I hesitate. Like Luca said, no, my illusions aren't particularly close to Villiam. He grieves for them more because he grieves for my own pain. Plus, Luca repeated my thoughts earlier about the killer having an unusual form of jynx-work. Maybe the answer is not in my blueprints but in the killer's abilities. At least someone is validating my opinions, even if he has less tact than a swarm of desert hornets.

"We can work together," he says. "I'll start profiling the type of jynx-work that might be able to kill an illusion. We could find them together in Gomorrah."

"I'm already working on an investigation with my father."

"Do you or do you not believe the killer is targeting Villiam through your illusions?" He digs his walking stick into the dirt.

"I... I suppose I can't be certain," I admit.

"Good. We'll meet tomorrow night. At ten."

"To what?"

"To begin," he says. "You can continue your investigation with Villiam—" his tone seems to indicate that his own is more important "—but *we* can investigate everything you and Villiam aren't. It will cover every aspect of what happened to Gill and Blister. Between all of us, we'll find who did this to your family."

"And you're doing this why? Out of the kindness of your heart?" I don't trust that he'd just show up here and change his mind. He's an Up-Mountainer, not Gomorrah-born. He probably wants something. A favor from the proprietor's daughter, perhaps.

"I was rude to you yesterday. I feel like I owe you."

"You don't owe me anything."

"All right, then, yes, out of the kindness of my heart." He watches me seriously with his brown eyes, and for a moment, he reminds me of Villiam. Like he can see right through me. He knows I'm going to say yes. If it's an opportunity to protect my family, I'm going to take it. Even if it means swallowing my pride.

"Fine. Tomorrow. At ten." I turn around and head back to my tent.

Neither of us bothers to say goodbye.

CHAPTER EIGHT

Nicoleta doesn't look up from her washboard as I approach. She dunks one of Hawk's shirts into the suds and scrubs the dirt out of it so hard the material tears. She hardly seems to notice the damage as she wrings the water out onto the muddy grass at her feet.

"I need to talk to you," I say.

"You shouldn't be working with Jiafu. *I* think so. *Gill* thought so. *Crown* thinks so."

The fortune-worker across the path looks up from her knitting to eavesdrop. I am tired of her nosiness. But she did bring us a box of roasted goat legs, for our loss. I think Unu and Du already managed to eat them all.

"I don't want to talk about Jiafu," I say.

"All right, then who was the boy who visited you last night?"

"Could you lower your voice?" I ask. Even though it's late and most of Gomorrah's visitors are leaving, there are still people wandering. The fortune-worker may be harmless, but I don't want word to break out that we're concerned a killer is after us. There would be panic in all the tents in this neighborhood.

She raises her eyebrows and then reaches for one of Unu and Du's shirts—with two holes for their heads—soaking in the bucket. "What were you talking about?"

I step closer to avoid being overheard. "We were talking about Gill's and Blister's deaths. He thinks that someone is targeting us."

"Sorina, do you hear yourself? Why would anyone target us?" She tucks an oily strand of brown hair back inside her favorite hairpin and crosses her arms. Despite being only twenty-two, her face appears older. She looks old and frazzled and tired.

"I'm not sure yet—"

"Blister's death was an accident. And there's nothing we could do about Gill's."

I almost don't know what to say. Is she willfully trying to remain ignorant? That's dangerous for everyone involved.

"You know as well as I do that Blister would never go near the dunk tank," I say. "Someone took him."

Her face reddens. "No one was here. I would've seen. Because… because I was the person watching him when he wandered off. I would've seen or heard if someone came near."

I wince. I didn't know that. No one had told me Nicoleta was responsible for him when he disappeared.

"Maybe he wandered off and they took him—"

"Why are you saying these things? Sometimes bad things happen. And there's nothing we can do about them, and no one we can blame."

"But what if this is someone targeting us?" I grab her shoulders. "How would you feel if we're burying someone else in the next city? Or if we're burying you? Or if someone else gets into an *accident* on your watch?" Her eyes widen, and I know I shouldn't have said that. But a small part of me feels better blaming someone else for Blister's death, since it's so easy for me to blame myself. "I'm sorry. I shouldn't have said that. All I'm saying is that we need to be careful. I want us to start sleeping in the same tent and not to go out alone."

"Who is this person who said these things to you?"

"His name is Luca. He's smart. And he knows—"

"Luca von Raske? You shouldn't be talking to him."

I fume. I am not a child or someone she can just order around. "Why not?"

"He's dangerous. He's friends with a lot of seedy people in the Downhill. And he's an Up-Mountainer."

My mind jumps to Luca's unnerving, insincere smile, but he doesn't seem *dangerous*. He just seems like an asshole.

"Well, how do you know him, then?" I ask.

"Adenneya knows of him," she says. Adenneya is a pretty-woman who works in the Downhill. She and Nicoleta broke up about a year ago, back when Nicoleta still knew the meaning of the words *fun* and *relaxation*. Mentioning her name around Nicoleta has become taboo. "He hires prettywomen and pretty-men, but he never touches them. They say he's...strange. That he isn't interested in *that*."

For a moment, I don't understand what she means. Then her words sink in, and I blush.

"I couldn't care less about Luca's personal life," I say, a little defensively. Sure, he might be nice to look at but only until he opens his mouth. "All I care about is that he's interested in helping me look into Gill's and Blister's deaths."

"I thought Villiam was investigating."

"Villiam and *I* are investigating. I'm about to go meet with him tonight." I try to keep the pride out of my voice. My family knows how long I've wanted Villiam to take me more seriously. "Anyway, I'd like to have the family sleeping in the same tent from now on. As a precaution."

"And you want me to tell everyone so you don't have to," she says bitterly.

I swallow down my annoyance. She doesn't have to act like such a martyr. "If it's such an inconvenience, I'm happy to—"

"You want to tell Hawk and Unu and Du that you think someone is out to kill them? Because, yeah, I think that might be a problem." She grabs another shirt—one of mine—from the pile and throws it into the soapy water.

"I thought you could think of something. You have a way with words." I smile my best performance smile, which doesn't amuse her. "The worst that could happen from all this is we all have to smell Crown's feet."

"Fine. But I think you're making a mistake with Luca. Does Villiam know you're looking into this behind his back?"

"No, but only because I haven't had a chance to tell him." I glance toward the sunset. "Which I am leaving to do now. Goodbye, Nicoleta."

That evening, Villiam wears a ruby brooch on his waist jacket. An heirloom from his mother, a poor woman from the Land of the Forty Deserts with half-Up-Mountain and half-Down-Mountain blood who ran away to Gomorrah. She died in childbirth with Villiam's brother, whom he hasn't seen in years. His father was the brother of Gomorrah's proprietor, from the ancient Gomorrah family rumored to have been the rulers of the Festival when it originally caught on fire two thousand years ago. His father gave her the brooch when he learned she was pregnant. She gave birth to Villiam in the third month under the warrior constellations, the ones painted on the ceiling of his caravan.

"You don't wear that very often," I say.

"Today was my mother's birthday. I've been feeling senti-mental."

Of course. I hadn't remembered, though that's hardly surprising, considering everything that's happened this week.

"We're going for a walk today," he says. "You and me."

"Do we really want to be discussing the investigation in public?" I ask.

"We'll remain discreet." He turns to Agni, who is stamping Villiam's wax seal on letters on his desk. "Stay here and take care of anyone who knocks. We'll be back in an hour."

"Of course."

While Villiam searches for his jacket, I stare at the world map above his desk. The Up-Mountain continent reminds me of a hand with an incredibly large thumb to its west. The most dominant city-states in the Up-Mountains line the coast of the thumb, made powerful by their impressive navies that allow them to terrorize the rest of the world, even from their rather remote locations. Much farther east, along the peninsulas that make up the fingers, are the Yucatoa lands, which, though different in culture and climate from the rest of the Up-Mountains, also share the Up-Mountain belief in Ovren and penchant for greed.

The region of the Great Mountains, located immediately below the thumb, connects the Up- and Down-Mountain continents. The Down-Mountain continent is six times larger than its northern counterpart, and it is made of many different nations: the Forty Deserts, the Vurundi Lands, the Eastern Kingdoms, and the Southern Islands, each with their unique cultures, religions and histories. The Up-Mountains invaded in the name of religion but in search of wealth. With prayers on their lips but greed in their hearts, they stripped the Down-Mountain leaders of their power and installed their own merchant governors. The Up-Mountains believe their rule a divine right, an absolute bestowed upon them by their god, but they know nothing of the strength of our peoples.

This is common knowledge, but I wish I knew more specifics, particularly about what Gomorrah's role has been all this time. For every major war, every conflict, it seems like Gomorrah was at the center.

"Are you coming, Sorina?" Villiam asks, tearing my concentration away from the map.

"Yes." I wave goodbye to Agni and follow him outside.

Villiam leads me to the left, toward the direction of Skull Gate. Because Gomorrah hasn't opened yet, the only others on the roads are merchants setting up their displays. The air is rich with the smells of food being prepared—cotton candy, kettle corn, roast lamb, licorice cherries. Villiam pauses at a nearby food cart and purchases an extra-large bag of candied pecans and then pays the vendor double his selling price.

As we eat, he surprises me when he fishes in his pocket and pulls out—of all things—a lucky coin. It's the Harbinger, a rather common coin with low defensive stats, but fairly decent for the offensive-focused player. The depiction on the coin is a man wearing a long cloak with his arms extended, as if casting a terrible charm on someone beneath him.

"Do you know who the characters on lucky coins represent?" Villiam asks. When I don't answer, he continues, "They are the proprietors of Gomorrah."

"Really? Who was the Harbinger?"

"My uncle. Rather pitiful stats, aren't they?"

Villiam's uncle was the proprietor before him, and though I've never met him, I know he and Villiam were very close. When Gomorrah was traveling in the Forty Deserts, the Festival found itself caught in the Eighth Trade War, a series of disputes when the Down-Mountains rebelled against the cruel Up-Mountain slavers and governors. Villiam's uncle was killed by a crossbowman on a visit to a desert caliph.

"Was he a charm-worker?" I ask.

"Yes. He unleashed a terrible curse on the local Up-Mountain governor by attaching it to his crown—can't imagine how he managed to get his hands on it in the first place." Charm-workers can cast enchantments through objects, particularly ones that

114

hold value to an individual. "All of the governor's children died when he touched them."

"That's horrible," I say.

"It only activated after the governor had my uncle killed for his alliance with the caliphate. They killed my father, as well." Villiam wasn't particularly close with his father, who preferred improving the strength of one's body over improving the strength of one's mind. "That's why the minters depicted him like this."

"That's why they called him the Harbinger?"

"Yes, because his death brought the Eighth Trade War."

We approach Skull Gate, its great mouth gaping open as an archway. The views from the entrance and the exit are identical, so even on the Gomorrah side, we still get a view of its eyes, covered in black shards of glass that glitter and reflect the images of anyone below it a thousand times, like in the eyes of a fly. The rest of it is painted white, stained gray by the smoke around Gomorrah and peeling from its constant exposure to the elements.

Villiam and I sit on a bench beside the Festival of Burning Desires sign.

"Until now, I have been teaching you only the mechanics of the Festival, without revealing to you the true nature of the role of Gomorrah's proprietor," Villiam says. He sits up straighter and admires the Festival around him with regality. "Two thousand years ago, Gomorrah once stood in the Great Mountains, and, for most of history, it sought to maintain peace between and within the two continents."

"Then where did it pick up a reputation for depravity?" I ask.

"Well, that reputation came later, when Gomorrah became more festival than city." He grabs a fistful of pecans. "But it has always been our responsibility, as the people and city who are from nowhere, who are from everywhere, to fight for a peace that was lost to Ovren's conquests."

I turn the Harbinger coin over in my hand, studying the proprietor's might. It's hard to dissociate the historical figure from the character in the game. It's hard to fathom Gomorrah as more than simply a grand carnival.

"How do you 'fight for peace'?" I ask.

"We secure alliances between distant kingdoms by becoming their mutual friend. We travel to the doorsteps of wherever we must be. We supply information, refuge and—sometimes—manpower." He pops several pecans in his mouth. "In short, there is a lot a city can see, hear and experience by traveling the world. Thus, we manage to mingle in the affairs of virtually everyone, and we gain enough intelligence from each destination to pull some powerful political strings."

He shoves another handful of nuts in his mouth, and I turn over his words in my mind. He speaks of intrigue and politics and history, but that would make him a king. My father, though intelligent and hardly a man to underestimate, has never struck me as more than a teacher, a lover of simple luxuries and one with deep-rooted opinions.

"The Beheaded Dame," he says. "That's Unu's favorite coin, isn't it? She was a proprietor in the eighth century. Beheaded right here in Cartona, in their public square."

We both look up over Skull Gate at the golden wall of Cartona in the distance, which feels more ominous now that I know its role in our family's history.

"The proprietors sound more like martyrs than leaders," I say. "Is that how you're planning to die? Killed by some Up-Mountain executioner?"

"No. I like to think I'll live to be an old man, so I can spoil my grandchildren." He throws a sly grin at me, and I snort at the idea of my having children someday. I can't imagine myself as a mother.

"But then what about me? Is that how I'm going to die?"

"You don't have to become proprietor, Sorina."

"But I'm your daughter."

"It's not a monarchy."

"But you are a king."

The last glimpse of the sunset disappears in the west, and the white torchlights ignite around us. The voices of visitors murmur from behind Skull Gate, eager to enter and explore.

"I am no regent. We do not live lavishly like Up–Mountain lords," Villiam says. "A better term would be *commander*."

That unsettles me even more than the idea of the Gomorrah family as monarchs. The word *commander* elicits thoughts of battle, of violence. I am not fit for such a role, and I never imagined my father would consider himself comfortable with that position.

"Who decided that the proprietors would be what they are?" I ask. "That *Gomorrah* would be what it is? Why can't you simply be a proprietor, and Gomorrah simply be a festival?"

"These things were decided before either of us were born. Before anyone alive today. Gomorrah was a city before it was a festival. Two thousand years ago, there was no Freak Show. No House of Delights and Horrors. No Menagerie. There were only people who had seen the world and sought to change it."

The first patrons enter. A family: husband, wife and child. Wearing sage, apricot and raspberry, each like their own kind of candy. I watch as they pass us to admire the map of Gomorrah and all the attractions we have to offer. Sometimes, when I observe the patrons, I admittedly think of them less like people and more like potential sales, money to be made. How does Villiam see them? The political playing field?

He hands me the bag of candied pecans. "Here. I've had too many. Agni's wife keeps telling me I should watch my waistline."

I smile slightly, despite the seriousness of our discussion. Agni's wife isn't wrong.

Villiam watches the family in their candy clothes pass. "It's hard to feel at ease in these cities, where, apart from clothes or accents, I can never tell if I'm looking at the face of a friend or one of Ovren's disciples." He studies the family as they point at the Festival map, as if trying to pick out the details that mark them as being from the Up-Mountains rather than Gomorrah. To an untrained eye, it's difficult to tell.

"Why are you telling me all of this?" I pull the drawstring to seal the bag. I'll share them with the others when I return to our tent later.

"Because this is your legacy. If you want it to be. I can teach you everything you need to know. The history of each lucky coin and the illustrious people who came before you. The art of writing letters to foreign dignitaries. The parts of Gomorrah you have never seen. If you want this, that is."

"That isn't what I meant," I say, purposefully avoiding his unstated question. I don't know if I want this. I've always been satisfied being a performer, my aspirations involving love and family more than power and leadership. Nor do I think I'm capable enough to handle such a position. "I thought we were going to discuss the investigation."

"This *is* the investigation, Sorina. I have enemies right now just beyond Skull Gate, maybe even within it." We both reproachfully watch the patrons as they pass through the entrance. "I am almost certain that the perpetrators are after me. After both of us. We've interviewed people in your neighborhood, in the games neighborhood, anyone who we imagine could be responsible. But we should be looking outside Gomorrah, not within."

"But there have been murders in two different cities now. Unless you think the killer is following us?"

"No, I don't think it's one killer. I believe it to be organized beyond Frice, beyond Cartona, throughout the Up-Mountains. My most powerful enemies live in these cities. I brought Gomorrah here searching for ways of destroying them, and, instead, they were the ones to make the first moves."

To our left, a woman begins to perform on a harp. Its box lies open before her with a few coppers inside to invite donations. The song sounds jovial, meant to welcome patrons into our gates, with a fast rhythm to quicken everyone's steps and lighten their hearts. It occurs to me that this is a terrible choice of place for my father to share this information with me. Now I cannot help but see the Festival as a farce. We are putting on a show, but I had always believed that was because Gomorrah is a city of performers.

Turns out, we are a city of liars. I suppose one could call them the same thing.

"I need your help, Sorina. I wish I could provide you with a simple solution, a single perpetrator for you to bring to justice. But I fear the battle will be not so easily won."

"I don't think I can do that. I'm not..." Smart enough. Strong enough. Brave enough.

"When I met you thirteen years ago, I saw the potential in you. Three years old, rebelling against slavers. You rode Tree to battle the way a general rides a stallion. I knew you were a warrior."

"That was a long time ago." I don't remember being that child. Villiam makes the story sound like a fairy tale, when truly it's a horror story in real people's lives. And his words make me uncomfortable. I am no warrior.

"I don't want to pressure you, but this is what I have to offer."

I lean back and press my shoulder blades into the firm wood of the bench. When Villiam proposed to include me in his investigation, I expected interviews, paperwork. I wasn't anticipating this sort of responsibility. I was hoping for clearer answers.

But haven't I always wanted Villiam to take me more seriously as the future proprietor? For thirteen years, all he's taught me is record-keeping and moving agriculture. Not strategy. Not politics.

If I say no, I can continue my investigation with Luca in Gomorrah. But Villiam doesn't believe the killer will be found within our walls, and I'm inclined to agree with him. If I want to protect my family, helping Villiam is my only option. Becoming a true proprietor is my only option. Even if it eventually means leaving the Freak Show behind.

"When do we begin?"

Villiam smiles and then wraps his arm around my shoulder and squeezes. "Immediately."

On our return trip to his caravan, he details his plans for my upcoming education. Rather than meeting with him twice a week, as I always have, I will meet with him five or six times. There will be reading, and studying, and a number of assignments, already piling up in the back of my mind with a lump of anxiety. I'm not a fantastic student. What if, after all of this, Villiam doesn't think I'm good enough?

I remind myself I'm doing this for Gill and Blister. And maybe a little for myself.

Back in Villiam's caravan, Agni remains hunched over the desk. Villiam pulls various volumes off the shelves. "This is a history of all of the proprietors. This is a list of historic places in Gomorrah. This is a history of all eight of the Trade Wars." He slips them all in a messenger bag and then hands it to me. "Oh, and one last thing."

He reaches into his cupboard and pulls out a glass box. Inside is a scarlet cricket, as red as Villiam's brooch. It's petrified from the use of charm-work, perfectly preserved within the glass. "This is a rare Cartonian Cricket. They're considered a delicacy here, served with bay leaves and paprika. I thought you might want to add it to your collection. A piece of memorabilia from the city."

I don't want anything to remember Cartona by. I'll already remember it forever as the place where Blister died. Still, I take it, because Villiam means well. He loves spoiling me with gifts.

"Thank you," I say. The cricket has three eyes. Probably a deformity. Rather fitting, for someone like me.

"Do you like it?" he asks.

"Absolutely."

He beams and slaps my shoulder. "Great. I'll see you soon, my dear. Take tomorrow to read and spend time with your family, and then come visit me the day after that. That's when the real fun will begin."

organized;

motherly;

hard-working;

good at laundry;

good at cleaning;

ROOM FOR CREATIVITY

LOOKS LIKE
    AN UP-MOUNTAINER.

 ABNORMALITY IS STRENGTH,
BUT IT'S INCONSISTENT.

TRAVELS ALONE TO RUN ERRANDS
SEVERAL DAYS A WEEK.

 SHOW MANAGER.

   PREFERS WOMEN.

PROBABLY WOULD NOT BE MISSED.

CHAPTER NINE

When Gomorrah is standing still, a three-foot-tall fence separates the Downhill and the Uphill. The stakes are painted black and sharpened into points, and trinkets and trash hang along their entire length, from top to bottom. Empty bottles stuffed with cigarette ash. Animal bones from food picked clean. Broken charms. Flyers advertising attractions and services, such as a short-term moneylender in Skull Market, where you could find anything from stolen jewelry to pickled lizard eyes for charm-work. Occasionally, there is a white ribbon for memorial of someone passed.

I haven't decided what I'm going to say to Luca. Villiam is convinced the killers are from outside Gomorrah, so convinced he is allowing me to train as proprietor two years early. I am inclined to agree with him. Before meeting with Villiam today, I intended to tell him about Luca's proposition, but it didn't seem to matter by the end. I'll find Luca and tell him thanks, but no thanks. The thought of doing so thrills me a little. He rejected me once; now I can reject him.

To my left, a man missing his left eye sharpens a machete on a stone block. He holds it up to glint in the green torchlight. Behind him, a vendor sells rice and meat that he claims is lamb, but I'm fairly certain it's either horse or rat, judging from the tough-looking exterior. Farther down, a woman nearly six and a half feet tall sits on top of a group of cages. They're exotic animals, she says. Some better than hunting dogs, others the warmest of pets. But that dragon snake, with its horns and spiked tail, only looks half dragon snake. Most of the animals are mutts, a little bit what she claims but mostly descended from rodents or pests found wandering the Festival during our travels.

Someone taps my shoulder. Reflexively, I whip around and shriek. It's an older woman, her skin covered in age spots, and she cringes away in the face of my outburst.

"I'm sorry," I say.

She grumbles something unintelligible and holds up a strand of vials full of a pink liquid. "Someone so jumpy shouldn't be in the Downhill," she says. "Maybe you're looking for something sweet? A little love juice? Just a drop in that special someone's tea, just a dab behind the ear—"

"No, thank you," I say. That sounds like the sort of thing Unu and Du might slip into Hawk's drink to give her hives. Besides, I like to think that when I eventually find love, it won't be from a charm. That is hardly fit for fairy tales, and I don't intend to settle for anything less.

"It's from Madame Lamoratore, an experienced charm-worker—"

"I'm not interested." I brush past her and hurry down the path, retracing the route to Luca's tent.

Cheers cry out from my right. I turn and face a crowd gathering around a platform, one I realize I've seen before—while it was empty, anyway. An enormous man the size of two or three people is strangling someone beneath him. I can't make out the other person, except for a hint of blond hair and the fact that the victim is much smaller than the giant attacking him. After another fifteen seconds, his arms go limp, and he slumps against his stool. The larger man turns and throws a fist in the air. The crowd cheers louder.

I didn't realize killing was now a sport in the Downhill. I'm about to turn away in disgust when the smaller, dead man with blond hair stands up. It's Luca—almost impossible to recognize out of his usual, obtrusive clothes. He coughs up a bit of blood and spits it onto the stage.

An Up-Mountain woman next to me blesses herself. "That's devil-work," she says. "Cursed are the demon-workers, for they will return to the depths."

The large man swivels around. "What?" he roars. "You were dead. I killed ya."

"And now I'm back." Luca smiles his insincere smile. "That was a remarkable attempt, sir, but I think we should let someone else take a turn."

After some cursing and grumbling, he leaves, and another man climbs onto the stage. He has a wide nose and dark, beady eyes. He reminds me of a cockroach.

"What's your name, sir?" Luca asks.

"Garrett."

"I have poisons, knives, rope…you can take your pick—"

"I'll use my own sword, thanks," Garrett says. He pulls it out of its sheath. It's jagged but appears sharp enough. "You don't mind if I use my own sword, do ya?"

"Not at all."

Before Luca can ready himself, Garrett swings his sword straight through Luca's neck. His head thumps to the stage and rolls off and onto the grass at my feet. I cover my mouth with my hands and fight back the urge to vomit. Red blood stains the dirt. Luca's bedroom brown eyes look very dead.

I sway and put my hands on my knees to regain my composure. It doesn't matter if I didn't like him. Too much blood.

Too much death. My chest tightens, and the anxiety from earlier returns in full force, as if it had never left at all. I back away so the blood doesn't touch me.

"I killed him," Garrett shouts. "I killed him. So I get the four hundred gold ones."

A middle-aged Southern Islander woman looks hesitantly from the bag of winnings to Luca's limp, bloody body on the stage. "I'm not sure—"

"He's dead, bitch," Garrett says. He rips the bag out of the woman's hand.

Below me, Luca blinks his eyes and stares up at me. I scream. He mouths something, but no sound comes out. I suppose, without lungs, he wouldn't be able to speak.

Revolted, I gently pick up his head and lift it to my level. A bit of blood dribbles onto my tunic.

Luca's eyes dart around until he notices his body. One by one, his limbs move on their own. He stands up, headless. Garrett turns around and shrieks as Luca's body tackles him at the feet of the Islander woman. Garrett doesn't put up much of a fight, and Luca stands, the bag of winnings clutched in his hand, blood spilled all the way down his clothes. He walks to the opposite side of the stage, toward me, and reaches down. I hand him his head, my stomach performing somersaults.

He screws it back on as if he's a doll, flesh reattaching to flesh.

"That ain't right," Garrett yells. He clutches his religious necklace. "You're some kind of demon."

Luca grins and stuffs the heavy bag of winnings in his vest. "I think that's it for the night." He hops off the stage and lands at my side. "Thanks, princess," he says. I'm too stricken to bother correcting him for using that nickname. "I usually have a block ready in case someone beheads me. I don't like to get myself dirty." He licks his hand and rubs some dirt off his chin. Around us, the crowd dissipates and moves on to a new attraction.

"That was repugnant," I say.

128

"I usually do better the bloodier it is," he says. "Some people put money in without even trying to kill me. They just get a kick out of watching me die."

Maybe that's because you're an ass, I want to say, but then feel ashamed of the thought. These people don't know him. They're merely cruel.

"Doesn't it hurt?" I ask.

"Only for a moment." He taps my mask. "I like your mask today. Very sparkly."

"Thanks." My mask is silver and covered in glass fragments, smoothed by a translucent coating. Its reflections shimmer green from the Downhill's torches. "Why do you let them do that?"

"The money, of course," he says, his voice hollow. "Even demon-workers have to eat."

What a pitiful way to survive.

"I didn't intend for you to witness my gruesome spectacle," Luca says. "You're early."

"I said nine."

"And forgetful." He studies my messenger bag. "What are you carrying?"

"Some books," I answer.

He swiftly snatches a book out of the bag, nimbler than a pickpocket. "*A Complete List and History of Gomorrah Proprietors*?"

I grab it from his hands and return it to its place. It's no secret in Gomorrah that I'm Villiam's heir, but I don't want anyone overhearing clandestine information.

"Can we talk in private?" I ask.

"Yes. Let's take our discussion elsewhere. Away from prying ears." I peek over my shoulder, and there are others watching us. Children crouching behind the stage or tents, wondering if the seemingly blind girl would make a good target to pickpocket—as if they can assume anything about me simply from one appraisal. Some of Luca's audience members, lingering for any additional entertainment.

Luca avoids their stares and leads me to his tent next door. The gossip-worker sign I kicked down the other day has been put upright. He must think I'm such a child. How embarrassing. I take a seat at the table while Luca pinches at the fabric of his shirt, damp from blood. "Would you like something to drink?" he asks.

"I'm fine."

"Gin it is," he says. He sets two glasses on the table, pours them a quarter of the way full and then slides one to me. "Here. Drink some. Compose yourself. I'm going to change into something more comfortable."

He disappears into the other, more private tent. While he's gone, I take a sip of the gin and then immediately spit it back into my glass. I untie my mask for the moment, to release some of the pressure on my forehead and my sinuses. All the crying in the past week has turned me into a mess. And Luca's show outside managed to agitate my anxiety. But gradually, my heart rate slows. I tap my fingers against the table to the rhythm of the Freak Show's opening song to avoid thinking about Luca's blood on my tunic.

Then Luca returns, so quietly I hadn't heard him approach, and I freeze. My nose is running, I'm sweating and I'm maskless. He pauses, studying my face, and I brace myself for an expression of disgust or discomfort. But it never comes.

He sits across from me. "Are you all right?" he asks.

"I'm managing." I fiddle awkwardly with the mask in my lap, tracing over the glass shards with my thumb. I rarely remove my mask and never in front of near strangers.

I'm still beautiful without my mask, I tell myself. Nevertheless, I tie my mask back on and hate myself the entire time I do it. My face shouldn't matter. I shouldn't care what he thinks. But I do. And it's hard enough to sit here, salvaging what remains of my pride after asking him for help, and talk about Gill and Blister.

He takes a generous sip from his glass.

"Should you be drinking?" I ask.

"It makes me nicer," Luca says.

"Then drink up."

"I wanted to thank you for helping me earlier. That man could've run off with a lot of money, and I'm not quite as rich as I used to be. So…can I get you anything else?"

"I'd rather we talk about Blister and Gill."

"Of course. I—"

"I don't think we should work together."

He sets his glass down on the table with a *clunk*. "Does your father disapprove?"

"I haven't even told him—"

"Good. I doubt he'd like to know his only daughter is spending her nights in the Downhill."

"Anyway," I say with annoyance, "Villiam believes the perpetrators are from outside of Gomorrah, looking to shake him. I agree with him."

"Didn't you tell me the other day that you didn't believe that? Someone *knew* Gill slept alone in the other tank. Someone *knew* how to kill your illusions. You think a group of Up-Mountainers, however cunning Villiam believes them to be, could accomplish that?" Luca stands, abandoning his drink, and begins pacing his tent. "It has to be someone inside Gomorrah. Someone targeting your family, not Villiam. If they wanted to target Villiam, they would have simply killed you. That would have been easier and more efficient."

"Why don't you have more of that gin?" I mutter.

"You agree with me, don't you?" He stops pacing to examine me.

"I… I don't know what to believe." Both he and Villiam make sense. I wish I were smarter, able to weigh each perspective equally. One argument from Villiam or Luca is enough to sway me, and I am rocking back and forth like a seesaw.

"It doesn't matter," Luca says. "You don't have to decide.

But it makes sense to research both ways of thinking. Just... stay. Hear me out."

"Why are you so eager to help me?" Doesn't the gossip-worker have better things to do? If he is right about the killer being in Gomorrah, I don't want to abandon the opportunity to find him by only investigating Villiam's political enemies. But I wish I understood Luca's motives better. Especially if we're going to become partners.

"This is a fascinating puzzle," Luca says.

"I'm glad you find the murders of my family so fascinating."

"What did you think I would say? That I'm a saint? That I love coming to the rescue of damsels in distress? We both know that I'm no hero and you're no damsel. Sorry, princess, this isn't that sort of story."

I purse my lips at his condescension. Luca is hardly my idea of a fairy-tale hero.

"Fine. I agree with you—the killer could be in Gomorrah," I admit. "We can be partners. We don't have to be friends." My voice is biting.

He hesitates. I can't possibly have offended him after that speech of his. "Fine." He resumes his pacing. "It strikes me as odd that Nicoleta is the only one without any strange abilities."

I suppose the pleasantries are over.

"Nicoleta does have abilities," I say.

"But she doesn't have an act."

He's certainly done his research.

"That's because she's terrible at performing. We need a stage manager, anyway," I say. "Nicoleta is much stronger than she looks. She could probably snap iron, if she wanted to. She just... isn't *always* strong. Only when she's upset or scared, so it's hard to work something like that into the show."

"And you didn't plan the abilities, right? They were, um, born that way?"

I wonder how he could possibly know this and hesitate before giving my answer. "Yes."

"What is your inspiration for each illusion?"

"I wanted them to be my family."

"In theory, could you recreate Gill or Blister if you tried?"

I grimace at the idea of trying to replace them. That wasn't what Luca was implying, but that is what his words conjure, nonetheless.

"No. I could, I suppose, create people *similar*, but much of their personalities—and their abilities—weren't in my original plans. I could make up, for instance, another two-year-old boy, but he may or may not turn out to be like Blister, regardless of how much I try." I picture Blister in my head, his sweet face and big, brown eyes, and the anger and grief settle in my stomach, heavy and hollow. "And usually before creating that sort of illusion, I feel, I don't know, a spark. Inspiration, I guess."

"You just said your inspiration was family members," Luca says.

"I don't know how I do it, exactly. But the idea comes to me somehow. To make a sister. To make an uncle. I wake up picturing them in my head, and there is a *need* to create them, like an empty space in my mind that needs to be filled. It's the same space they go when I make them disappear. The locked Trunks."

There's a pause. "Maybe you could elaborate—"

"It's hard to explain. Why does this matter?"

"I like having the whole picture."

"But it's not an exact science. It's an art."

"You're not a thinker, are you?" He runs his hand through his chin-length blond hair while I seethe at the insult. "*I've* been doing a lot of thinking about jynx-work," he says, sitting on the floor and motioning for me to join him. "About all the different sorts. Where I come from, people only spoke about them as if there is one type: demon-work."

He slides into a seat at the table, and from this close, I can smell his sandalwood soap. "Where are you from?" I ask.

"The city-state of Raske," he says matter-of-factly. I'm surprised he even answered at all. He seems the sort who'd be private about himself. Or maybe I only think that because he's so different from everyone else in the Downhill, all clean and polished. "Very minor city. In the northeast. The one with the clock tower."

"I've never heard of it," I say.

"You've never heard of the Tower of Raske?" Now that he says it...maybe. In one of Villiam's lessons.

"Isn't *von Raske* your name?" I recognize it from when Nicoleta was talking about him.

"I just go by Luca now." He drums his fingers against the bamboo floor. I remember that we're not friends; he has no obligation to share anything about himself with me. "So, jynx-work. It appears to me, from the time that I've spent in Gomorrah, that there are three extremely common types: fortune-work, charm-work and shadow-work. Seems like eighty percent of jynx-workers here practice one of them."

"Are you just going to ramble the entire time?"

"Yes, I am. It's not like you're paying me. The least you could do is listen to me ramble."

"Do you do this to all of your clients or just me?"

"What would give you the impression that you're special?" He lies down on his back so that I can't see him because of the table between us. Always moving. It's hard to keep track of him. "There are also a few less common forms of jynx-work that are still well-known. Like fire-work and mind-work. I'd put illusion-work in this category, because almost everyone has heard of it, but you're the only illusion-worker I've actually met."

"There isn't another illusion-worker in Gomorrah," I say.

"So I assumed," he says. "Now, there's one last category of jynx-work. The abnormalities. The ones that only one person is known to have, particular to that individual. Like my poison-work." Luca's words begin accelerating beyond the point of comprehensibility. I wonder if he's even talking for my benefit or simply to hear the sound of his own voice. "I want to focus on the possibility that these incidents have nothing to do with your illusion-work and everything to do with the jynx-work of the killer. Assuming that your illusions are, in fact, entirely il-lusions, and unable to be killed without the use of jynx-work."

"Do you always do this?" I ask.

"Do what?" Luca asks.

"Talk *at* someone rather than *to* someone. So fast I can't keep up. Then *I* end up looking like a fool."

"I always just assumed you *are* a fool," Luca says from the floor. I open my mouth to retort, furiously, but then hear him chuckle softly. "Joke. I was joking. Don't look at me like that. *Sometimes* I make jokes. I'm not a total freak."

The word *freak* makes me tense. It's not a word I associate with many others except myself and my illusions, so it's strange to hear it from someone else's mouth in reference to themselves. Luca may be an Up-Mountainer in Gomorrah—a rarity—and have a rather unusual jynx-work ability, but is that worthy of being called a freak?

"Did you leave Raske because you were a jynx-worker?" I ask.

"Why the personal questions?"

"You don't have to answer. I was just curious." I look around his tent, which lacks any personal possessions besides a few books and essential furniture. Even when misfits run away from home to join Gomorrah, they take a few things with them. If *I* were going to run away somewhere, I'd take my bug collection. Judg-ing from his home, Luca doesn't have anything he truly values. If he could only take one item with him, he'd probably reach for his bottle of gin.

"No, it's fine," he says, in a way that makes me think maybe it's *not* fine. But I don't bother stopping him, as he's already started talking at a hundred words per minute again. "For most of my life, I didn't know I was a jynx-worker. I left after the last of my family died. I didn't have any reason to stay. And if the people in the city found out what I was…they'd probably have burned me at the stake. Sometimes I amuse myself by thinking about what they would have done after I *wouldn't* die."

"Is that a joke, too?"

"No. Yes. I don't know. I suppose my jokes are rather morbid."

He smiles his full smile, the one with the dimples, and I catch myself smiling back. I immediately stop. It's not fair to my family to be smiling when everyone else is grieving. It's not fair to Gill and Blister. Not so soon after their deaths.

"Back to where we were before," Luca says, as though he never paused his initial thoughts. "You say your illusions can't die. For the moment, let's assume you're right. So who can kill someone who can't die? Well, someone with a unique ability to do so. The common jynx-work, like fortune-work and charm-work, hardly seem capable of that. Nor do some other well-known kinds, like mind-work or fire-work. It seems the best guess is that whoever did this has a unique ability, one like mine."

Luca turns his head and assesses me coolly, as if examining a rabbit turning over a spit. I dismissed Nicoleta when she claimed Luca was dangerous. He's only a few years older than me, with less muscle tone and far less tact. But there is an emptiness in his expression that makes me doubt. Because it's not empty—he's too intelligent for that. So what truly lies behind his blank stare?

"What?" I ask.

"I was waiting for you to guess that I'm the killer. *I* have a unique ability."

"For getting *yourself* killed. Not other people," I say.

"Glad that isn't an issue." He rubs his hands together. "There are eight in Gomorrah, excluding your illusions, who are, well, freaks and don't count." He pauses. "You don't suspect any of them, do you?"

"Of course not," I snap. "Besides, they were all together when Gill died. And mostly together when Blister disappeared."

"Even Tree?"

"You know the names of my illusions?" The only ones I've told him about so far are Blister, Gill and Nicoleta.

"I know everyone in Gomorrah," he says simply. I find that difficult to believe. Villiam doesn't even know a third of the people in the Festival by name.

"Well, first off, Tree isn't as violent as people assume," I say. "And you think in an area as busy as the games neighborhood with the dunk tank, no one would notice a half man, half tree walking around?"

"I was simply asking. Tree would be strong enough to smash the glass of Gill's tank."

"So would anyone with a proper weapon," I hiss. Tree may be prone to tantrums, but he wouldn't hurt anyone, least of all Blister and Gill.

"So it wasn't Tree." Luca sits up in one graceful motion and spends a few moments counting off on his fingers. "I think the unique-ability idea sounds like a better option. So those eight people in Gomorrah are our suspects. Seven, excluding myself."

"You want to question them and figure out who could've killed Gill and Blister?" I ask.

"Well, yes and no. The problem with people with unique abilities is that no one knows for certain every aspect of their jynx-work except that person. It would be easy to hide something. It's smarter to try to determine if any of them would *want* to kill your illusions."

"But that line of thinking means someone else in Gomorrah could also be hiding an ability," I say. Unease prickles down my neck. Anyone in Gomorrah could be hiding their powers from us. And their motives.

"Yes, it does," Luca says. "If all seven suspects seem innocent, then we'll have to move on. Then we can think of anyone, jynx-work or not, who would have a reason to attack them. But that's broad. The seven are a better place to begin."

He pulls his golden pocket watch out of his vest and checks the time. It's a beautiful watch, with ornate engravings all over its case. If he sold it, he wouldn't need to perform that ghastly show of his. But maybe it has sentimental value. Strange—Luca doesn't strike me as a sentimental person.

"Tomorrow we can visit the first suspect," Luca says. "Are you free?"

"Yes. Later tomorrow night." We won't have any shows for the rest of the week in mourning of Blister, but I imagine I will be spending most of tomorrow with Villiam.

He stands. "Excellent. Tomorrow." He grabs his black top hat off the books I brought him and then pauses. "Would you like me to walk you home? The Downhill gets dodgy this late at night."

"You look like you have a place to be," I say.

"I was going to have tea and biscuits with a prettyman known as the Leather Viper, but that can wait until you're safe back in the Uphill."

"The Leather Viper?" I smirk.

"Maybe I should just call him my friend Ed," he says. "So how about that walk? I have time to spare."

"Are you really that good of a bodyguard?"

"Truthfully, no. I usually just save myself the trouble and let them kill me."

At home, such a morbid joke wouldn't sit well at the moment. But I'm not at home. I don't feel like home Sorina.

"Fine. You can walk me back to the Freak Show tent."

We step outside into the green light of the Downhill. It's roughly three in the morning, the high point of the night for business. The air smells of torch smoke and sweat, even though

Cartona's forests provide cooling shade. Rhythmic music plays from somewhere behind us. It sounds like a party Venera might attend. There aren't quite as many people on the paths as there were earlier, as most of the visitors have found their ways into the tents of prettywomen or taverns by now, where they will remain until Skull Gate closes at dawn.

"Do you *actually* know everyone in Gomorrah?" I ask.

"No. Maybe a fifth or so directly, and about half through information."

I smirk. Not quite as impressive as he makes himself seem.

"And you get all your information from...prettymen and prettywomen?"

"A lot of information but not quite. I also make friends with everyone who sells necessities, like food, water, the tax collector. Because if you know them, you'll have a connection to everyone in Gomorrah."

"I suppose that makes sense. But why bother with any of this? Why are you a gossip-worker? You don't get paid for it, like you do for your shows."

He shrugs. "Like I said, the people here interest me. They're nothing like the people at home, who are bound by the rules of Ovren and *purity*." The bitterness gives his voice a sharper edge. His walking stick clacks against the shards of a broken beer bottle, and he kicks it. "You know, now that you've seen one of my shows, maybe I should see one of yours. When is the next one?"

"Probably once we reach the next city." No one feels in the mood to perform without Blister or Gill, but unfortunately, we'll run out of money if we're not generating ticket sales. William gave us the rest of the time in Cartona off, but once we reach Gentoa, we'll need to put our performance smiles back on.

We pass a bordello tent nearly five stories tall, leaning to the side and looking like a strong wind could blow it over. The tent is entirely bright pink, and dancing outside the door is Yelema, the prettywoman who was having tea with Luca when I first walked into his tent. She waves at him, and I try not to stare too much at her dancing, even if I'm a little transfixed by her suggestive routine.

Luca waves back with barely a passing glance.

"I've heard there's a man at your show whose hair is made of nails," Luca says.

I pull my gaze away from Yelema's hips. "That's Crown."

"Now, I don't know a lot about how illusion-work is done, but I'm assuming you came up with that idea. My question is… how?"

"Not exactly. I imagined all my illusions in vivid detail before creating them, but I never imagined them to be, well, freaks. That part is beyond my control. I don't know why. Villiam thinks it's my subconscious."

"Your subconscious?" he asks.

"I'm a little unique." I tap my mask. "So I tend to like people like myself, apparently. And it's hard to run a Freak Show if we're all normal."

"I can see the sense in that. People who are different—freaks, as you say—tend to enjoy the company of those like themselves."

We near the stake fence at the edge of the Downhill, with all its trash and charms. Lightning bugs blink throughout the Uphill, gathering around the glowing paper lanterns or along the dewy grass. Luca reaches out and cups one in his hand.

"I used to put them in jars as a kid," he says. "Don't worry. I let them out afterward. I recall your sentiments about cockroaches."

"There are huge lightning bugs in the Great Mountains called blinking beetles. They're the size of hummingbirds."

Luca lifts up his cupped hands and peeks at the lightning bug inside. "Another bit of information I'll never need to know." He lets the bug go, and it hovers between the two of us, blinking.

"As if spying on people and learning every detail of their lives is somehow *useful information*."

"I do not *spy* on people," he says haughtily.

"Then what do you do?"

"I…" He pauses. "I also do other things, besides my gossip-working and being publicly killed. I like stargazing. I know quite a bit about stars."

We pass through the clearing and enter the Uphill, where most of the activities are winding down for the night. Everything closes here much earlier than in the Downhill. Residents clean up the food wrappers and trash littered throughout the grass outside their caravans. Some take their laundry off the lines or throw tarps over their tents in case of rain.

"Like what?" I ask. The only things I know about stars are the nonsense Villiam tells me.

"Right now, it's the constellation of the lion." Luca points to a pattern in the night sky. "Once a year, the moon will position itself directly behind the lion's head like a mane. It's said that on that day each year, a king is either made or falls."

"When is it?"

"It already passed a few days ago. I don't know about any kings coming or going, though. It's just a story the town loon used to tell."

We approach the Freak Show tent, with its black and red stripes and shimmering glass ball at its peak. Tree stands beside our sign, slouched slightly but not quite sleeping, and blending into the forest scenery. He watches us approach, particularly Luca. "A bit fancier than my little platform," he says, then startles. "Oh, I didn't see him there." He eyes Tree up and down and then extends his hand.

Tree doesn't move.

Luca moves the hand away and shoves it in his pocket. His eyes narrow as he inspects Tree, as if making sure he's awake. I stifle a laugh. No one seems to understand Tree besides me. "So," he says awkwardly, "I'll see you tomorrow, then."

Both of us pause, and I'm not sure why. Perhaps because this walk has felt very casual, that a lot of our relationship feels casual, when it is centered around the deaths of my uncle and baby brother. It was somehow surprisingly easy to forget that fact when I was at his tent, bickering about things that don't matter, but now we're here, in front of *my* tent and the grief it houses.

A few minutes ago, I was someone else. Someone distanced from the despair here.

But now that I'm back, I'm Sorina again.

"I'll see you tomorrow," I say. "Thanks for the company."

He doesn't say anything but simply nods and walks down the path.

I decided earlier we weren't going to be friends. But as I watch him disappear into the smoke, I suppose I could warm up to him. This partnership won't be a complete disaster.

I turn to Tree, who leans down over me so that his leaves itch the back of my neck. One of them falls at my feet. "You're shedding," I tell him.

He pokes my cheek with one of his twigs, which scratches me. He forgets which parts of me tickle and which do not.

I tickle him under his arm, and his laughs make his leaves shake as if a wind blew through him. "You're not usually in the Festival at night. Are you keeping watch?"

He nods. His eyes are wide. He's worried. He's missing Gill and Blister.

I rub behind his ear. "We'll protect them, don't you worry."

CHAPTER TEN

While we're gathered together in our sitting room, seated on the floor among peanut shells and junk that no one has bothered to clean, Nicoleta tells the group that she thinks sleeping in the same tent together will cheer everyone up. I, unwilling to participate and be the bearer of bad news, focus on my book. Neither Crown nor Tree seem to care much one way or the other, but Hawk and Unu and Du complain about it until nearly sunrise.

"Du has morning breath. I'm not sleeping next to him."

"Hawk snores."

"Unu sleep-talks. It's terrifying."

"Then sleep at opposite sides of the room," Nicoleta snaps. She rubs her temples, and I brace myself for the complaints I'm bound to hear later about one of her stress headaches. "Hawk, you can trade places with Crown."

"But his feet—" Du starts.

Nicoleta grabs him by his ear. "If I hear your voice again in the next ten minutes, I'll shave you both bald in your sleep."

Both of their jaws drop in expressions of horror. Unu and Du's impressive manes of brown hair are their pride and joy.

Nicoleta takes a deep breath to compose herself. Her hair has fallen piece by piece out of her bun, and she scratches at the dry skin on her arms, leaving streaks across her biceps. "Venera, you can sleep in Sorina's room to make room for the others."

I look up at the mention of my name. Villiam likely expects me to have the reading finished for when we meet again the day after tomorrow, but Venera would be a welcome distraction. I'm currently skimming the book about Gomorrah's proprietors, though the stories are rife with bloodshed.

Hawk digs into her pouch of lucky coins. Earlier today, she and Unu and Du traded some of theirs in the gambling neighborhood.

"Look at the one I got, Sorina," Hawk says. "I'm not interrupting you, am I?"

"No," I say. I need a break. I don't have the attention span to read an entire book in one sitting.

She hands me the coin. It's the Necromancer, a rarer coin than even the Beheaded Dame. Unu and Du are probably seething with her finding this. I flip through the pages of the book until I find the Necromancer.

"She was a proprietor of Gomorrah shortly after the city burned. She's credited with the charm that keeps the city burning. Legend goes that she bound the souls of the dead to the city walls, who, eternally smoldering, cloak the city in its smoke."

Her eyes widen. "*That's* why there's smoke?"

"It's just a legend."

"All legends in Gomorrah are true," Unu says devilishly, having overheard pieces of our conversation. Hawk whitens.

"Don't you two have chores?" I ask them. "Shouldn't you be taking care of the horses?" The animals are Unu and Du's only job.

They skulk outside, leaving Hawk to stare nervously at her new lucky coin.

"It's not real," I say, even though it might be.

She nods slowly. "You missed Kahina. She stopped by earlier and brought us all caramel rice cakes."

"How did she look?" Her most recent supply of medicine is probably running low. I will have to pay Jiafu a visit later. He has had ample time to sell Count Pomp-di-pomp's ring in Cartona.

"She looked about the same. Do you want a rice cake?"

"That's all right. I'm still full from Crown's kebabs."

I close my book and head back to my room, sectioned off from the rest of the tent by a tapestry. It's mainly full of pillows and the specimens of my bug collection, which Venera doesn't particularly mind. She follows me back there, lacking her usual makeup, her brown hair braided down to her waist. "Mind if I join you?" she asks.

I sit down and scoot over to give her room. "This is your room now, too."

Venera sits, a stack of papers on her lap. She manages all the books and financials of the Freak Show. The rest of us can't handle working with so many numbers, but Venera can not only do all the math in her head, she seems to enjoy it, as well. She finds the repetition and mindlessness comforting. I don't find it mindless at all, probably because I'm not half as smart as her. I wish other people knew Venera as I do; our neighbors merely view her as a party girl, leaving every night with a face full of makeup and returning each morning at the early hours of dawn.

"Why do you think Nicoleta has us on lockdown?" she asks.

"No idea," I lie.

"I think she's shaken up about Blister. She was supposed to be watching him." Venera's voice is steady, as if we were discussing the weather, not our dead baby brother. Venera has always had a talent for distancing herself from anything unpleasant. Apparently it's a skill I need to develop, as well.

"I don't mind us all being here," I say. In the other room, Unu and Du bicker about who gets the last caramel rice cake, somehow already finished caring for the horses. Nicoleta snaps at Hawk—no, she hasn't finished the laundry. She has a pounding headache.

"Let's talk about something different." Venera sets her papers aside and leans back into the pillows. "Any special someone in your life?"

I smile at the familiarity of the conversation. As if our lives are still normal.

"If there was, you'd be the first to know," I say. "What about you? Anyone you're off seeing when you leave after the shows?"

She rolls to her left so that her back faces me. "I don't know."

"What do you mean, you don't know?"

"I mean that I don't know. No one is interested in someone who isn't even real."

Her words linger in the air for a few moments and then she continues.

"Men like me. I mean, I can bend myself backward, twice. Then I discover the next day they don't want to see me again. They say, 'I just wanted to know what it was like. It's a better version of jerking off.' I'm just a fantasy they can touch." Venera curls herself into a ball, and I don't know whether to hug her or not. She has never mentioned anything like this to me before. I don't know what to say. I wasn't prepared for such a sudden outpouring of emotion. "I'm sorry to tell you all these things. Out of the blue."

"Who said these things to you?"

"It doesn't matter."

"It does to me. I'll show them another illusion they can touch. One with claws. And horns—"

"I don't want you to go after them," she says.

"Why not? You are *not* one step above jerking off. You are the smartest person with numbers I know. You could give a pep

146

talk to a man chin-deep in quicksand. You're funny and sincere and a joy to be around, and they tell you you're a better version of jerking off? How would they like to be jerked off by a horseshoe crab?"

Even though I can't see her face, I'm sure she's smiling.

"I don't want you to do that," she says.

"Well, what do you want?"

"I want to find another job for when I'm not working at the Freak Show, something to keep me busy besides parties. Maybe I could handle Gomorrah's books like I do for the show, if Villiam will let me," she says. "And I want to meet someone who sticks around. I want kids, if that's possible. I want to know how to go through life not being really alive."

I can't think of anything to say to that.

Our first suspect is a man named Narayan who lives at the edge of the Uphill, on the opposite side of the Festival from the Freak Show. This explains why I've never seen him before. During the early hours of the night, he works for an attraction called the Show of Mysteries, in which a man uses mechanical contraptions to make it appear as if he has achieved the impossible. Like turning pigeons into butterflies. Or sawing a beautiful woman in half.

"Narayan is the only actual mystery in the show," Luca says. He wears an outrageous puffed-sleeve shirt that I assume he had before joining Gomorrah, since no one I know would be caught dead in it. The fabric is shiny and expensive, with silver strands woven into the sleeves and faux diamond buttons. During all his time spent at the Festival, he has somehow managed to keep it stainless and pure white.

"In his act, Narayan enters a coffin standing up in the center of the stage. Then the magician inserts swords inside. Narayan has the ability to lose his solid form, so that he can walk through the walls of the coffin and the floor without the audience knowing. He calls it ghost-work."

The two of us pass the Menagerie tent. I glance at the swan dragon banner under which a Frician official hacked off that man's fingers last week. The air smells of licorice cherries, a scent I've come to associate with the comfort of home.

But it doesn't smell comforting now, on our walk to uncover a murderer.

"I know Narayan because he holds a second job working in the Downhill for a man named Jiafu, a ringleader of thieves. Perhaps you know him, Sorina?" Luca asks, then looks at me pointedly.

How does he know about Jiafu?

"I might be acquainted with him," I say. I expect Luca to reply with a statement of judgment, but he doesn't.

"I picked Narayan to visit first because you have this common acquaintance," he says.

I've never met one of Jiafu's other cronies, and though it's not impossible, I doubt that Narayan's work with him would translate into any sort of a motive. What would he stand to gain? I'm not Jiafu's favorite crook, by any stretch. I've worked a few minor jobs. None worth killing over.

"I've already arranged for Narayan to speak with us," Luca says. He swings his black cane through the air in a loop. "So he'll be here."

"How did you manage that?" I ask.

He shrugs. "I paid him."

"You didn't have to do that," I say. Working the way he does, money must be precious to him. Though I find myself surprisingly pleased that he would choose to spend some on helping me.

"Consider it a gift." He hesitates when he sees my pursed lips. "Is something wrong?"

Besides the amount of reading I crammed into my brain earlier today, I'm still uneasy after my conversation with Venera.

I had no idea she wanted a family. Can she have one? When I created my illusions, I always thought about who they would be for *me*, not the independent lives they would lead. I have created living, functioning people. Is that normal for illusion-workers? Villiam said he's done as much research as possible into my abilities, but surely my family isn't normal?

I'm interviewing a suspect in mere moments. I can't be distracted.

"No, I just have a lot on my mind," I say.

"Understandably so. Take a deep breath."

I do.

"Hold it."

I do.

"Now picture someone annoying in their underwear."

My mind naturally goes to an image of him. I'm so startled by this command and mortified at my own thoughts that I let out of bark of nervous laughter.

"Feel better?" he asks. "It's what I do before my shows."

"Um, yes," I say, my cheeks growing warm. "Let's just get this over with."

We step inside the tent to the Show of Mysteries. It's overly decorated, in my opinion. Chairs painted with purple glitter. The stage torches each burn a different color—the result of the same fire-work that keeps the Downhill's torches green and the Uphill's white. Black-and-red-striped tape lines the stage.

Narayan sits on the stage, his skinny legs dangling off it. He has deep brown skin and wears his hair in one long braid that reaches his tailbone, and his pointed eyebrows are dyed silver. He looks to be in his midtwenties, maybe older. The intensity of his eyebrows overshadows any further impression of his other facial features.

"Hello," Luca says cheerfully, as if we've come around for tea. "I hope we haven't inconvenienced you by meeting so soon."

"Not at all," he says. "I needed a break, you know? My girl

back home is ready to pop—" he makes an exaggerated circular motion over his stomach "—and you know how they get. Driving me mad. All she does is order me around while she sits back, complaining about her mother or her sister. I need a breather." He reaches behind him and pulls out a beer bottle.

"Well, he's a talker," Luca mutters beside me.

As we walk closer, Narayan gets a clearer view of us. He studies Luca's expensive clothes and walking stick briefly, but his eyes rest on me. "How do you see out of that thing on your face?" he asks. I'm surprised he doesn't immediately know who I am, and Luca's words from a few nights ago enter my mind: *You're not that important.*

"I manage," I say coolly.

"That's a woman for you. Eyes on the back of their heads."

"You remember why we're here, don't you?" Luca asks.

"You're going to ask me questions." He sets his beer bottle down, leaps off the stage and staggers for a moment before collapsing in an audience seat. "Ask away."

Luca doesn't make eye contact while asking his questions. He examines the bottom of his walking stick and then taps it against the toe of his shoe. "We were curious about your ghost-work. It's not very common, is it?"

He jabs his thumb at his chest. "You're looking at the only one."

"I've seen your act before," Luca says. "I imagine you simply use your ghost-work to fall right from the coffin through the floor, right?"

"Yep. There's space under the stage. I keep snacks down there."

Luca smirks. "What kind of snacks?"

"Beer."

This man doesn't seem like he could have killed Gill and Blister. Not only does he lack a motive, I doubt he's smart enough to have committed two murders and thrown suspicion off himself each time. And his ghost-work doesn't seem to be the kind that would make illusions killable. Not that I know what that jynx-work might be, but this one doesn't feel right.

"Have you been busy lately?" Luca asks. "The show performs every night, does it not?"

"Every night. I usually get one night off a week, but lately I've been staying on. Babies are expensive. So my girl keeps telling me."

"So were you working two nights ago?"

"Yep. Working every night except when we were traveling." He finishes off his beer. "Gets me away from my woman."

"Uh-huh," I say with disgust, thinking of Venera's troubles. People like him are the reason I have trust issues. "So do we get to see your ghost-work?"

"Sure, if you want." He holds out his hand. "Shake it."

I reach for it but swipe only at air. I wiggle my fingers in the empty space that appears to be Narayan's wrist.

"Almost like an illusion," Luca says. He grabs my arm and pulls me back toward him, and then he leans down to my ear. "What do you think of his jynx-work?"

"He's not smart enough," I whisper back.

"That's not his jynx-work."

"And he has an alibi that we can verify with the manager of the Show of Mysteries."

Luca sighs. "You're not much of an outside-the-box thinker, are you? He could be lying. There could be something to his jynx-work we don't know about."

"He's a drunk, Luca."

"I'm certainly not disagreeing with you about that."

Narayan points between us. "You're both jynx-workers?" We nod. "What kind?"

"Poison-worker," Luca says.

"What does that mean?"

"It means I can't die, even if you kill me."

"No shit? Can I try to kill you? Uh, if you don't mind—"

"I have a show in the Downhill. Pay up and you can."

Narayan nods enthusiastically. "Yeah, I think I will. Sounds fun. No offense, but you look like you'd be fun to kill."

"What do you mean?"

Narayan makes motions over the top of his head. "Your hair. It's too everywhere. It annoys me."

"Well, that's rather harsh." Luca turns around, twisting a blond strand around his finger. "Does my hair annoy you, Sorina?"

My face warms. Why is he asking me? As if I cared about his hair. "Your hair is fine."

"I think that's all of our questions," Luca says. "Thanks, Narayan. I know you're a busy man. I'll send your wife a gift for the baby."

His face softens with a loopy grin. "Our fortune-worker said it's a girl. She'll be a pretty one, like her momma."

When we leave the tent, I say to Luca, "You're awfully formal to a drunk."

Luca shrugs. "So what are you going to get his daughter?"

"Me? I didn't agree to that."

"It's polite," he says.

I mutter a curse under my breath. I suppose I could ask Kahina to make the baby a life quilt. She loves making those.

"We'll go see the next person tomorrow," Luca says. I almost demand to know why we're not seeking out anyone else tonight but catch myself, remembering that Luca has a whole life of his own outside this investigation. He probably has a prettyman to share crumpets with or something equally as absurd to do later. And I can't expect progress to be made overnight.

"Same time?" he asks.

"That's fine. But I'm not leaving yet. I'm following you to the Downhill. I need to talk to Jiafu."

We pass through the food market at the back corner of the

Uphill that caters to Gomorrah residents, not to visitors. It's been months since we've been in the Down-Mountains, so most of the food is local. Fresh apples and pears. Beef, poultry and deer meat hang from wooden stakes, rubbed with salt for preservation.

Luca waves to a few of the vendors and calls them by name. I grimace. I've come here my entire life to shop for food, and I don't know any of their names. Luca's lived in Gomorrah for less than a year, and he's managed to make friends with half the Festival. How am I supposed to be proprietor if I don't know anyone?

"What do you do for Jiafu?" Luca asks.

"Don't you already know?"

"Yes. I do. I'm just making conversation. Does Villiam know that you help Jiafu steal from patrons during your shows?" His voice lacks the judgmental bite I'm used to from Nicoleta and Gill about my side work.

"Villiam doesn't know," I say.

"Ah, Gomorrah's princess doesn't have as clean a nose as Villiam believes." Luca smiles the way our fortune-worker neighbor smiles when hearing a fresh piece of gossip. It occurs to me that Luca is simply a paler, younger, male version of her—the local gossip, only with more entitlement. "Why do you need to meet with Jiafu?"

"He still owes me my cut from the last job. It's time for me to collect."

"That sounds quite amusing. Would you object to me spectating?"

"Go ahead." Usually Jiafu isn't difficult about paying me, but I've never had to ask for it so long after the job. An audience could be advantageous. Jiafu is uncomfortable being the center of attention.

We pass the fence between the Uphill and the Downhill. Above us, the crescent moon glows dimly over the mountains.

In a little over an hour, the birds will start chirping, and the sun will rise, and drunks will skulk outside in the Downhill.

I lead Luca in the direction opposite the path to his tent, where Jiafu's caravan is parked in between a brothel and a tavern. Black paint covers every inch of it, so it practically blends into the darkness. Appropriate for a shadow-worker. Having a flashy caravan would be bad for business, when business hinges on not being noticed.

I knock on his door. "It's me," I say. It's early enough that Jiafu will be awake but not out and about.

"'Rina?" he says from inside. "What'd I do to have to see your ugly face again?"

I wince. Maybe having Luca as an audience wasn't the best idea. "You didn't pay me."

"Yeah, I did."

"Don't shit with me." I knock harder on the door. "Open up."

He swings open the door. On the ground below him, his shadow twists and curls in the torchlight, marking him as a shadow-worker. His left eye is sporting an impressive shiner.

I smirk as I climb inside, Luca behind me. "Who gave you that?"

"I gave you your money two days ago. I handed it right to you." He flicks my forehead. "Don't tell me you lost it, cousin."

"Lost it? You never gave it to me!"

He grabs fistfuls of hair in each hand and yanks his head back. For a shadow-worker, he has quite the dramatic flair. "It was two days ago. In the late afternoon. You were coming back with your whole lot of illusions from the baby's funeral. I put it in your hand. I offered my condolences, and I left. Are you mental now or something?" He glances at Luca. "And who's this Up-Mountainer? Your boyfriend? Come to convince me to pay you twice? He's not much of a muscle, 'Rina—"

"You're lying," I say. "You're never awake that early."

"How would I even know about the funeral thing if I wasn't there?" He points at the door. "Get out. You're a lunatic."

I flinch at the insult, my hands shaking. I would remember it if Jiafu paid me after the funeral. It's not as if I would've forgotten. Which means he's lying and trying to make me second-guess myself. It's a pretty poor attempt. And it's embarrassing in front of Luca, who might be starting to think that I really am crazy.

I rack my brain for an illusion terrorizing enough to make Jiafu piss himself. Venomous moths come to mind, the golden ones from the rainforests in the Vurundi Lands.

They appear one at a time, buzzing inside the cart.

"Don't you pull this shit," Jiafu says.

More moths appear, their eyes black, their stingers sharp and as long as my thumb. My Strings vaguely appear around my feet from using so much illusion-work, and I step aside so as not to get tangled up in them.

"I'm not kidding. Stop this." He backs away from the moths toward the opposite wall of his cart. "You don't want to fuck with me, 'Rina."

The moths attack him, swarming as he swats at them and screams. While Jiafu falls to the floor in a fit, I reach into his pocket and pull out his coin purse. Then I jump out of the caravan. I'll make the moths go away in a few minutes, once we're far gone.

"Was that wise?" Luca asks. "He's a criminal, who is acquainted with other, scarier criminals."

"I'm pretty scary, too."

In the caravan opposite us, an old man peeks his head outside to figure out where the screaming is coming from.

"What if he sends one of these criminals to your place tomorrow morning to threaten you or the others?" Luca asks.

I swallow. Maybe it *was* a reckless move. But I need the money for Kahina. He should've paid me what he owed me. "I have this friend who is half tree. He's seven feet tall. He's made of bark, the sharp kind—"

Luca rolls his eyes. "Don't act like you thought that through one bit."

Where does he get off thinking he can act like my father? He's not exactly responsible, allowing people to kill him all the time. What if something happens, and his head rolls off the stage, but he never wakes up? Does he even know what kind of fire he's playing with?

But his company is growing on me, and he *is* helping me, so I'm not going to yell at him. Not over this. Instead, I change the subject.

"Do you want to go into Cartona with me tomorrow afternoon? I know that's rather early..." I say, holding up the coin purse. "But I have some shopping to do."

His face darkens. "Is it wise to go into Cartona?"

"Of course it is. I've been in plenty of cities before."

"This far north in the Up-Mountains? They won't take kindly to someone like you."

I straighten my mask. Someone like me. Someone *deformed*. "I've dealt with unpleasant people before. I can handle myself." I shake my head. "Never mind. Forget I asked."

He opens his mouth to say something and then abruptly shuts it. "Then...enjoy your trip."

sister;

beautiful;

sassy;

likes

makeovers

and

clothes.

CATCH

HER

DRUNK

UNNATURAL FLEXIBILITY.

BEAUTIFUL.

WEARS OUTRAGEOUS CLOTHES
MEANT TO DRAW ATTENTION.

FREQUENTS DOWNHILL PARTIES
AND REGULARLY LIES WITH
STRANGERS, DRINKS TO EXCESS.

EASILY BORED;
WANDERS GOMORRAH ALONE
DURING THE EARLY MORNING.

CHAPTER ELEVEN

There is a palpable sense of grief throughout the golden city of Cartona. The pedestrians walk as if wandering aimlessly, rather than traveling to a destination. The vendors don't bother to greet any passersby. Even the apricot in my hand tastes unripe and sour.

The most unsettling sight in Cartona is the colors. Black shrouds cover every door, every window, blocking the sunlight from each home, church and shop. The Cartonians wear all white, which reminds me too much of Blister's funeral. Strange how Ovren's disciples associate white with purity and we associate it with death.

Naturally, I am wearing dark clothes and black-and-pink-striped tights, so I stick out like a raven among a flock of doves.

I hurry through the streets, searching for a bazaar where I can find an apothecary. Cartona is a city of gothic architecture and merchants. In what's considered to be Ovren's holy city, churches with flying buttresses tower over the skyline. The air smells of humidity, the spices they obtain from Down-Mountain traders and the reek of city dwellers. Everyone here has an exotic item from somewhere far away; everyone has something to sell.

As I pass a vendor showing off mosaic pottery and jewelry, each shard stained a different color and glimmering, the vendor shouts at me, "A necklace for your girl?" It startles me, as everyone else is so quiet. He holds up a massive strand of iridescent glass beads. At first I'm confused, since I'm alone, and I glance over my shoulder to find Luca standing behind me, dressed all in white and carrying a separate white tunic, which he throws at me.

I'm so shocked by the sudden projectile, Luca's appearance and the vendor calling me Luca's "girl" that I shriek and fail to catch the tunic. It falls onto the dirty, golden street.

"The idea is to blend in," Luca says.

With his fair features and white clothing, Luca fits in with the Up-Mountainers in Cartona, but not as much as I would have expected. His hair is much too long. His nose piercing glints in the sunlight. And the smirk on his face hardly matches the somber expressions of those around me. Despite his past and his looks, there's definitely more Gomorrah in him than I'd noticed before.

The vendor continues to berate us and show off the necklace. I redden and wonder if Luca will say something, but he just ignores him. Did he not hear him? Or is he avoiding giving a reaction to my being "his girl"? It's useless to overthink something like this, but I like the idea of being somebody's girl. It makes me sound desirable. Not like a freak with no eyes. And Luca, though irritating, is hardly terrible to look at.

"You've been following me," I say.

"Are you angry?"

"Yes." I hold up the white tunic. It should cover most of my clothes, judging by its length. It looks to be one of Luca's shirts. "And also no. Thank you for this."

"I'm glad I came. Cartona's archbishops have a reputation for cleansing mania. The white clothes are meant to refer to a person's purity." He nods his head to the right, where black smoke billows into the sky. "Vanity burning."

"What's that?"

"It means the city is doing one of its cleanses, burning everything from secular books to makeup." I glance at the women around me and notice for the first time that none of them wear rouge, lipstick or even a hint of glitter. How dull. "I've never seen so many in white, though, as if it's a law now. Something must've happened here."

"I don't intend to stay long."

"Good."

Jiafu's coin purse jingles in the breast pocket of my cloak. I cross my arms as I walk, in case of pickpockets. I've been in enough Up-Mountain cities to know the poor and the homeless perch on every corner, waiting to seize an opportunity in the form of an unwary shopper. Though Gomorrah has its share of petty crime, our thieves are less desperate, and no one would risk mugging and injuring a patron.

"There's an apothecary symbol on that building over there," Luca says, pointing to our left. A green cross hangs over the door.

The shutters on the top two floors are bolted closed, but the door is ajar, and an Open sign dangles from a rusted nail on the pane. The vendors outside the building sell produce and seeds, normal-looking stands run by normal-looking people. But the apothecary shop looms and casts a shadow onto the street, jagged like teeth from the broken thatches on its roof. Like a monster waiting to snatch you from behind.

"That looks like a good place to get murdered," I say.

"It's the only place we've found," Luca says.

"Easy for you to say. You can't die."

"How about this? You wait out here. I'll check it out and give it the all clear."

While Luca slips inside, I inspect the apples at a nearby vendor. From far away, I didn't notice their bruises and discoloration. I wouldn't be surprised to find each of their cores eaten out by worms.

"You, Down-Mountain girl," someone hisses to my left. An elderly woman crouches underneath the vendor's stand, her skin sagged and hanging off her face, as if she's shedding one layer at a time. "How dare you come to Cartona? We don't need whores or thieves like you in our holy city. A disgrace." Her voice trails on the *s* sound. "After the death of the baby prince, the poor baby prince—"

"Excuse me," I say to the vendor, "there's a woman hiding beneath your stand."

The man frowns and lifts the cloth over the table. "Bitch! What do you think you're doing?" He kicks her, and she groans and crawls out from underneath. "I could call the officials and have you thrown into the Pit!" I take several steps back to get out of the way as the woman flees around the corner, reeking of sweat and piss.

The vendor turns his attention to me. "Would you like an apple? They are the freshest in the city. So juicy…" He lifts up a browned slice from a sample and holds it to my lips. "Take a bite. You will want to buy more."

"No, thank you," I say. "What did the woman mean? About the prince?"

"The crown prince died of pneumonia earlier this week. Ovren can be cruel even to the most innocent." He looks over my clothes, which, though simple and unassuming, do not entirely match the white attire of everyone around me. My tights peek out from underneath. "You are not from here." His eyes light up. "You're a Gomorrah girl. I hear the Gomorrah girls will lay with a man for next to nothing."

He grabs my hand and tightens his grip, even as I try to squirm away. "And you're blind. You shouldn't care. You aren't worth as much as other girls."

A scream rises in my throat, but that would only cause a scene. All that matters is buying Kahina's medicine and leaving.

"I can see the blistering sunburn on your nose," I say instead. "And your fat gut. And each of your nose hairs." With one hand braced against the table, I push myself away from him and walk toward the apothecary, despite how decrepit it appears from the outside. The repugnant man continues to call after me, but I ignore him and duck into the shop.

Luca stands near one of the shelves. "It smells good in here. Like mint."

I hug my arms to my chest. The homeless woman's words about the prince echo in my head, and in an instant, I've switched from Sorina-with-Luca to regular Sorina, the one whose baby brother and uncle just died. The Sorina who knows her face makes her worth less than other girls.

"Are you all right?" Luca asks.

"I'm fine."

"You're not fine."

"How can you tell? It's not like my half face gives anything away."

"Because your whole body is rigid and tense, and you usually walk as if you're floating."

I uncross my arms. I like the idea of floating high above everyone else, where no one can touch me. Does Luca really think I look like that? "I'd rather not talk about it," I say truthfully. Venera can best remind me that I'm beautiful and worth ten times more than that man could ever dream of. Luca doesn't need to hear about all my problems. Besides, I'd rather forget about it.

Luca doesn't ask any more questions, but I can tell he wants to by the way he keeps glancing at me and frowning. He points to one of the shelves full of vials. "They have an impressive collection of poisons. I'm thinking of buying a few for my show."

"Don't you think it's dangerous to play so many games with death?" I say.

"Not if I never lose."

"What do you think that means for you? Will you just go on living…forever?"

He picks up a vial full of gray powder and holds it up to the light of the crooked candelabra. "Maybe. I don't know. I don't really think I'm immortal." He returns the vial to the shelf and inspects a new one. "I have a theory about a way to kill me."

"Chop you into pieces and bury your body parts in different locations?"

He opens his mouth to say something and then pauses. "You've given this thought?"

I laugh. "I guess so."

"Hellfire," he says. "That's my theory."

There's some sense to that. Hellfire is an everlasting fire created by skilled fire-workers, which glows a brilliant gold. Since his immortality is jynx-work, it seems logical that a different sort of jynx-work could counteract it and prevent him from rapidly healing or resurrecting.

He reaches into the pocket of his pants and drops several tiny trinkets into my hand. "I keep charms sewn into my clothes— usually my vest—to protect from Hellfire, in case a fire-worker were to take a chance at my show."

There are three charms. One looks like an animal fang wrapped in wine-soaked thread. The middle one is fabric with an embroidered image of the sun, and the last is some kind of dried herb inside a glass bead.

"The sun protects from Hellfire. The other two protect from harm," he says. "Made by the charm-worker who lives behind me."

"I'm glad to see you take a bit of precaution in your work."

"I'm perfectly safe."

"I'm just worried that one of these days your head will roll and your body won't get up to retrieve it."

He laughs without any mirth. "Doubtful."

The medicines are displayed on the opposite end of the shop, next to the body creams and ointments. The elixir for snaking sickness is the same deep purple as the disease itself and thicker than molasses. Kahina claims it tastes like crushed-up centipedes.

I find the vial on the shelf and hand it to the shopkeeper, who, like most others in this city, wears white. "Three spoonfuls a day. With food. Should last about three months," he says. I pay him fifteen of Jiafu's gold coins, enough to buy my entire family food for two weeks. The elixir doesn't come cheap, but it's a small price to pay for Kahina's health and comfort.

Luca narrows his eyes at our transaction. Once the apothecary's back is turned, he whispers, "This medicine isn't proven to do anything."

"It slows the progression of the disease."

"That's conjecture. The snaking sickness takes who it will."

"It's helping Kahina," I grit through my teeth. "Do you think I would go to such extremes for something I didn't believe would work?"

"I believe you would go to any extreme to help your family."

I seethe for a moment, deciding whether or not to snap at him again. Luca isn't the first person to tell me that the elixir is merely a gimmick. The snaking sickness takes thousands of people every year, Up-Mountainers and Down-Mountainers, rich and poor, elixir or no elixir. But that doesn't mean I won't try. I can't just do nothing.

After we exit the shop, Luca says, "Let's leave sooner rather than later. The sound of church bells, in my experience, is a warning to people like us."

It's not as if people can tell we're jynx-workers just by looking at us. The only one who sticks out is me, in my eyeless violet-sequined mask. I'm the freak.

"I'll be happy to leave this city behind," I say.

In less than a week, Gomorrah will pack up and move to the next city-state, Gentoa, farther up the Up-Mountain's western coast. It will take six days of travel through the valleys between the sea and the mountains. In Gentoa, we'll start performing the Freak Show again, and we'll be a hundred miles away from the place where Blister died. His small grave will remain here, in a place that meant nothing to him or to his family, just as Gill's remains in Frice. I hate to think of both of them alone, where no one will visit them until Gomorrah's smoke passes over the horizon once again.

As we leave the bazaar, a group of Cartonian officials approach from down the street in white coats with black mourning bands around their arms. They each brandish a sword. Passersby duck out of their way as they run toward the bazaar, almost in a stampede. Several voices cry out. Doors slam all around us.

"What's going on?" Luca asks.

"I can't tell."

The crowd runs in three directions: behind us, to the left and to the right—everywhere except the direction where the officials were headed. Luca grabs my hand, and we race toward an alleyway. We slump against the stone wall of a church.

"We've got to get out of here," Luca says. "You in particular. Ovren's disciples believe He marks the impure with physical ailments and abnormalities."

"Thank you for telling me what I already know," I snap, my chest tightening in that awful, all-too-familiar way. That's the reason William originally thought a religious fanatic murdered Gill. "Freaks" are easy targets for those hunting the impure. "As if I'm not anxious enough already."

The officials walk in a shoulder-to-shoulder line, forming a wall from one end of the street to the other. There's no way to get past them without running through side streets. Their strides each fall at the same moment, so it sounds like a giant stomping down the street, rather than twenty men.

"What do you think this is all about?" I ask.

Screams ring out from the bazaar as the crowd stampedes through.

"I don't intend for us linger long enough to find out," Luca says.

The church bells above us toll a deep and hollow sound, and it warns all those not welcome here. *Get out, Get out.* With our fingers still intertwined, Luca and I slip through the alley, following several others who do the same. There are eight of us in total, and we crowd together in front of a gate at a dead end. Luca's shoulders press against mine, and his touch is a small comfort when my pulse throbs in my chest and gut.

"They won't turn down this way," a woman says.

Someone shushes her. "You don't know that."

The footsteps of the officials approach.

I focus on the gate behind us, on its iron spires twelve feet high and on the royal crests engraved on its locks. Then, as usual, I return to my most trusted illusion—the moth. There are eight moths, hovering around the mud at the corner of the alley. Eight moths, no people, I tell myself. Eight moths, no people. I shove the illusion out of my mind and suspend it in front of us.

"You aren't from here," a man says to my right, nearly breaking my concentration. "You're jynx-workers. You're deformed." I flinch. "You mustn't let the officials see you."

"What are they looking for?" Luca asks.

"Sin. They are looking to purge sin from this city." The man's teeth are rotted, and several are missing, so he whistles when he speaks.

"It's why the baby prince was killed," the first woman says. "Punishment for the city."

"Or, if you believe the rumors, the royal family of Frice killed him. They're looking to start a war."

Why would Fricians kill him? Frice and Cartona are allies.

The officials in their white coats glance down the alley, and all of us hold our breath. I focus on the illusion of the moths and the iron gates, and the officials pass without suspicion. I relax and release Luca's hand.

"A miracle," a woman gasps. I roll my eyes. If she knew the truth, she'd just as quickly call it devil-work.

Once the officials are out of sight, Luca and I sprint down the alley back to the main street, my heart thundering worse than a summer storm, and then turn and make straight for the gates outside the city. The impressive wooden drawbridge is wide open, stretching over a stagnant pool covered in algae below.

"That was smart," he says. "The illusion. I saw you concentrating."

"Just because I'm not immortal doesn't mean I'm entirely helpless."

He shakes his head. "Shit. That was actually terrifying."

Because my chest is so tight there is actual pain, pain like I could have a heart attack, I snap, "It's not like you had anything to worry about."

"Of course not." He grimaces. "I only stayed up late to follow your sorry ass into Cartona to keep an eye on you and give you the white clothes I knew you'd need. But I can't die, so what could I *possibly* have been worried about?"

His sarcastic remark startles me. I didn't realize he cared so much about my safety. All of this time, I haven't known whether Luca was merely a partner or more my friend. I know I should apologize, but I don't. I'm too focused on escaping this place, which makes me feel disgusting and unclean. I need to bathe and wash everything about this city off of me.

I make up my mind to apologize later.

A crowd forms around Cartona's gate. We mustn't be the only ones trying to flee the city. Concealed by my illusion, Luca and I push forward.

Until we see the actual reason for the crowd.

In the center, a priest in white robes clutches a sun and sword medallion in his hands. He blesses a man in front of him, who, rather than accepting Ovren's grace, cowers. "You cannot expect Ovren's forgiveness if you do not accept His punishment," the priest tells him.

All I can think about is the Beheaded Dame, potentially executed in this same public square hundreds of years ago. The fate of Gomorrah's proprietors. Fear gnaws at my stomach as I study the priest's robes, the crowd and Cartona's golden walls.

"Look away, Sorina," Luca whispers.

The priest's assistant hands him a knife. The priest dunks it in a basin of water.

"Sorina, you don't want to see this."

I turn away just as the priest raises the knife, but I don't have time to cover my ears to block out the noise of the man screaming. The crowd around me winces, but no one looks away, as if they are forcing themselves to watch.

The man falls to the ground, his face sliced open and covered in blood. The tip of his nose dangles by a small strip of skin.

A cold sweat breaks out over my forehead. "What was his sin?" I ask.

"Withheld vanities, I think. I don't know what kind. That's why there is a crowd. He's an example."

Luca tugs me away by my arm. My illusion keeps us from the notice of the guards who stand watch around the crowd. If that is the punishment for vanity, what is their punishment for stealing? Blasphemy? Jynx-work?

After leaving the city behind, we have a mile-long trek back to Skull Gate. It stands at the edge of the road, twenty feet tall, its mouth gaping open as an archway. It beckons us home.

We enter the black tunnel of its mouth, lit by white lantern light. The ticket booth stands at the end, blocking off the entrance to the Festival. Several Gomorrah guards gather around it. They don't wear uniforms like the Up-Mountain officials, but they wear black sashes tied across their shoulders to their waist and around their hips, and their faces are always concealed.

"You're not the first people we've seen running back from Cartona," one tells us. "You should get back to your caravans. We're leaving early, by dusk."

"That's the second time in a row we're just packing up and leaving a city," I say. "How much money is that losing us? We're leaving because of a little commotion?"

The guard shrugs. "This time we're choosing to do it. The proprietor was just attacked."

CHAPTER TWELVE

I am no fortune-worker, but during my race to Villiam's tent, I cannot shake the feeling of doom. One by one, this killer will rip my family away from me, and after all the horror is over, I will be alone. The certainty of it weighs in my soul like a stone lodged in my throat.

I cannot breathe.

Gomorrah's guards circle Villiam's tent, looking like a flock of ravens. Many members of the Festival crowd around them, still in their sleeping clothes, whispering to each other. I am not accustomed to seeing so many people in the Festival in daylight. Even with the smoke to shield the sun and the cover of forest, the brightness makes the dirt on our skin and clothes more pronounced.

Gomorrah holds no glamour before sundown.

I push my way to the front of the crowd. "What happened?" I yell at the closest guard. "Is he all right?"

The guard startles and then, realizing who I am, pulls me out of the crowd. The onlookers chatter more behind me. "The proprietor is okay," he whispers. "His leg is broken. We aren't announcing anything yet."

"How did this happen?"

"Trampled. Someone spooked his horses and the caravan ran right over him."

The sort of attack that could look like an accident. Like what happened to Blister barely three days ago. Could this have been the same person?

"Have you found out who did it?"

"Yes, we have, but I haven't been informed of the attacker's identity yet." He approaches the tent, where four guards stand outside. One of them leaves to find Agni. While we wait, the guard rests his hand on my shoulder, which I imagine is meant for comfort, but I'm so tense that I wrench myself away.

"Sorry. I'm sorry," I say.

"Don't be."

I hug my arms to my chest and search around the area. Is this where it happened, right outside of his tent? Or was he attacked somewhere else? I know his horses, and they aren't jumpy creatures. Gomorrah animals are accustomed to loud noise and strangers.

Agni appears at the tent's flap. "Sorina."

"Is he all right?" I ask. I move to pass Agni to enter the tent, but he blocks my path.

"He's fine. No permanent harm done. But he doesn't want to see you right now."

"What? Why not?" He must know how worried I am, how much I need to see him.

"He's embarrassed. He needs to collect himself—"

"No, no," my father's voice unmistakably bellows from inside the tent. "Do not go near my horses. I've had Nahim and Wilhemina for over five years. You'd be spooked, too, if I held a torch underneath your legs."

"He sounds fine," I say, relieved but also doubly annoyed he

174

doesn't want me to visit him. And what does he mean about a torch?

I create a simple illusion of myself, standing in front of Agni, while the true me slips around him, inside the tent. It only takes Agni a moment to see through the illusion before he clears his throat and follows after me.

Villiam leans back on a chaise with his leg propped up on an ottoman, wearing a brace and a serious expression. A wineglass rests beside him, mostly empty. His jacket, though mud-stained, is neatly folded on his right.

I let out the breath I was holding. He's perfectly fine.

Villiam's eyes fall on me, and he frowns. "Who sent for my daughter? Agni? I specifically said I didn't want her to see—"

"This wasn't my doing—" Agni says.

"No one sent for me. I found out on my own," I say. "And why wouldn't you want me here? You were attacked! Of course I'd want to be here."

He waves his hand. "I'm fine. Had a fright, is all. Absolutely dandy."

"You won't be walking for six weeks at least, sir," the doctor mutters from behind him.

"I heard the man who did this was apprehended," I say. "Is that true? Is he..." I swallow the rest of my words. *The man who murdered my family?*

"No, he isn't the same one. But we believe he's somehow connected," Villiam says. "We don't know much, other than that he's Cartonian. He entered last night and never left."

"Why would a Cartonian man attack you?"

The room silences. I wonder at first if I've said something offensive, and then I realize, by the way everyone exchanges looks, that clearly they know something I do not. I understand that Gomorrah is not popular in the Up-Mountains, but attacking the proprietor is practically an act of war. The Cartonian leaders would never condone such an action.

"Have you done your reading?" Villiam asks.

"Yes," I lie. I've done…most of it. "But what does that have to do—"

"We'll still be meeting tonight, as we planned," he says. He slaps the thigh of his bad leg. "I've had worse. It'll take more than a runaway caravan to bring me down."

"Why can't we talk now?" I ask. The men in the room exchange more glances, and I get the feeling that I am wasting their time. They're waiting until I leave to discuss what's actually important.

I thought Villiam was including me in his work. Turns out all I've been given is homework, busywork.

"Because there are still some facts we don't know but will know soon," Villiam replies. "We'll have the answers tonight. Besides, it's nearly ten o'clock. You should be asleep."

"Sleep?" I snort. "You think I'll be able to sleep? Let me see the man who attacked you. You said he's connected to the man who killed—"

"He's already dead." Villiam tosses an empty vial on the floor with only a few drops remaining of a dark liquid. Poison. "Have a guard escort you back to your tent. There's no point in discussing anything until we have more information. Go help our family pack their belongings. Gomorrah will be leaving by dusk."

Unsurprisingly, I barely slept more than a few hours. I roll my sleeping pad up and fasten it closed, and then I toss it into our caravan. Even though Hawk and Unu and Du are still sleeping in the next room, I don't bother being quiet. I'm still seething from my conversation with Villiam earlier, when he essentially sent me off to bed in front of all those people. He made me look like a child.

Or am I merely acting like a child? They obviously had important matters to discuss, and there was no reason for me to be there. I would have nothing to contribute. I would only impede their progress by asking more questions.

But I have a right to ask questions. My father was attacked. My brother and uncle are dead.

I wish I had a chance to speak with Luca before meeting with Villiam in an hour, after Skull Gate begins to move. But Luca is likely either asleep or packing up his own tent—I shouldn't bother him. After we returned to Gomorrah from Cartona, I don't even remember if we said goodbye. I heard about my father, and I ran. I can't snap at him all morning, not bother to say goodbye to him and then expect his help whenever I want it.

I should have thanked him for coming to my aid in Cartona. Had I been caught in that vanity burning alone, dressed in crow-black, I don't know what I would have done. I also wish I could thank him for helping me in general. Regardless of whether he finds my illusion-work intellectually interesting, there are hundreds of unsolvable puzzles in Gomorrah. He has chosen to concern himself with mine, and for that I am grateful. I want to tell him that I consider him my friend. That I appreciate his concern. That, apart from my family, he is the only person I trust, who doesn't seem uncomfortable around me, even after seeing my face. That I like that he thinks of me as floating—

My thoughts stutter to a stop. Do I...do I *like* Luca? I mean, he's attractive. That's obvious. But he's also arrogant and condescending sometimes, and I cannot stand listening to his Up-Mountainer accent, sounding so posh and above everyone else. Am I only thinking like this because he's nice to me? Trust me to develop a crush on the first person who doesn't think I'm a total freak.

I ball my blanket into a fist in frustration. I'm pathetic.

Something slips out of the blanket and clinks to the roll-out bamboo floor. I pick up a small sack of coins and count them. Fifteen gold pieces. Exactly what Jiafu owed me. Where did this come from?

I walk into the main part of our tent, where Nicoleta softly tries to shake Hawk awake. Hawk moans and pulls her pillow over her head. "Nicoleta, did you remember seeing Jiafu the other day after Blister's...in the evening?"

"No," she says. "I thought you were going to stop working for him."

"I never said that."

"It's what Gill wanted."

"Yeah, well, I probably *am* done with Jiafu now, anyway."

Nicoleta doesn't say anything. She slams the table closed so hard that it cracks in the corner. Hawk and Unu and Du all startle awake at once and, chastened, Nicoleta gently lays the table down on the floor. "I don't understand why we're staying in this part of the Up-Mountains. These cities...they're huge. They're powerful. And they clearly don't want us here." Her voice quivers. Nicoleta's voice never quivers. "I just want to stay in one place for a while. To relax for just a moment." She starts rolling up the bamboo floor. "Why are we still going north?"

I'm not prepared to see Nicoleta cry. Nicoleta rarely cries, and if she breaks down, I might, too. My heart still hasn't slowed since running from the officials in Cartona earlier today as they began to cleanse the city of sin. She's right. They don't want us here.

"Do you need any help?" I ask her, hoping she'll say no. She always says no.

"No," she snaps, though not unkindly. She needs to be left alone.

I squeeze the pouch of coins in my hands and return to my room. It doesn't make sense that both Nicoleta and myself wouldn't remember Jiafu giving me the money after Blister's funeral. But where did the money come from? No one would simply leave coins in my room. It wouldn't be the first time I've lost things within my pillows, but it *would* be the first time I've ever forgotten an entire interaction.

Jiafu is probably still lying. The coins must be from a while ago.

And after yesterday's incident with the venomous moths, I doubt he'll want me to work with him again. But I don't know of any other way to pay for Kahina's medicine. Stealing from him was foolish. He'll never take me back now.

Maybe if I give him time to cool down, he'll change his mind. I've never lost him a deal. I'll ask him when we get to Gentoa, where he'll be excited about new visitors and new victims. He'll change his mind.

I need him to.

Villiam's door is open, and Agni sits outside on the caravan's ledge, smoking a cigarette. Earlier, there were dozens of guards. Now only two pace around the caravan as it moves. "Hello, Sorina," he whispers. "How are you?"

"I'm well. How are you? How's your wife?"

"Well enough." He stares at the sunset. It was this time of summer nine years ago when his son was kidnapped by slavers. It's a sad story that everyone in Gomorrah has heard—Agni, being Villiam's assistant, is well-known throughout the Festival. Sometimes, when I look at him, I can only see his story. His loss follows him like an extra shadow.

I say something pleasant but meaningless and step into the caravan. With his leg propped up on the seat next to him, Villiam smiles as I empty out the books from my messenger bag. Though he seems cheerful, it's obvious from the dark under his eyes that he hasn't slept.

"I'm impressed," he says. "Have you read them all?"

"Yes," I say, because I finished the last one before I slept earlier. "Does this mean I pass? Am I *allowed* to learn why my father was attacked? About how the man who did it is connected to the man who killed my brother and uncle? Or do I need to read a few more books before I'm qualified to hear some answers?"

He doesn't grace my fury with a proper response.

179

"What I'm about to share with you is strictly between the people in this room." Behind me, Agni closes the door and snuffs out his cigarette in the ashtray. "For now, I'd like for you not to share this with your family."

Finally, answers. Not entirely appeased—I wish I was given these answers earlier—I take a seat across from him and cross my arms.

"After our discussion and your reading, you understand more about the role of the Gomorrah proprietors, of Gomorrah in general. Now you need to understand who we are up against, and who I am certain is responsible for the deaths of Gill and Blister, who sent the man who attacked me earlier."

He turns to the map over his desk and points out several northern city-states along the thumb of the Up-Mountains. First, Frice, known for its powerful colonies in the Forty Deserts. Ukarce, the navy stronghold. Cartona, the holy city of Ovren. Gentoa, the capital of a trading empire. Then Sapris and Leonita, who I already know are responsible for most of the evils that Down-Mountainers face in our homelands. Last are Teochtia and Ximia, the two largest cities in the faraway Yucatoa Region, whose zealous armies patrol the world searching for relics and hunting demons.

"These are the Up-Mountains' most powerful city-states," Villiam says. "Do you know why that is?"

"Wealth?" I say.

"Unity. Several hundred years ago, these city-states united themselves, both under Ovren and under a major, secret political alliance." He nods to Agni. "Why don't you explain to Sorina the exact history of it? I want to get our files." He reaches for the two crutches beside him.

"Let me get them, sir," he says.

"No, no. I am perfectly capable." He grunts as he hoists himself up and balances on one leg. "I'm big-boned. The fracture…

it's merely a chip. My great-great-grandfather *lost* his leg and still managed to fight in the Seventh Trade War."

I smirk. "He was a powerful mind-worker. He didn't even have to leave Gomorrah to fight."

"Very good, my dear. There's no more hoodwinking you, it seems." On the crutches, he hobbles to the door and manages to climb to the ground without injuring himself. "Just a jiffy." He closes the door.

"He thinks he's a warrior," Agni says, "but I don't know of any warrior who eats quite so much and sleeps with so many pillows."

We both laugh. Agni stands and points to various cities on the map.

"There was a prophetess born in Cartona, where we are now, almost four hundred years ago. At this point in history, the Up-Mountain cities all had colonies in the Down-Mountains, but they were sparser and less terrorizing. This prophetess foretold the First Trade War."

He points to Leonita in the far north and Cartona in the central thumb region. "The lord of Leonita at the time, who was a cousin to the lord of Gentoa, decided to arrange a marriage between this prophetess and his cousin. It would solidify the many friendships that were already blooming in the city-states."

"So that's it? We're up against...friends?" I ask.

"No, there's more. On the eve of the wedding—the prophetess, by the way, was likely a fortune-worker—the Gomorrah proprietor at the time arranged for her to be murdered. The proprietor is now known as the Beheaded Dame."

"Like Unu's lucky coin. She was executed in Cartona, wasn't she?"

"Exactly. Found guilty of the future princess's murder, she was beheaded in the public square. However, rather than preventing major war, this resulted in the Up-Mountains fashioning their dead princess into a martyr. The alliance, no longer a public marriage, became private: the Alliance of Cyrille, named after the prophetess. After that, the Up-Mountains launched their expansions south, disrupting the peace the Down-Mountains had so long enjoyed and devastating our people."

So the decisions of Gomorrah's proprietor can affect the course of history for generations. I don't think I'm capable of that sort of responsibility. It should be someone smarter than me. Like Venera. Or Luca. Villiam may see me as a warrior, but I'm only a performer. However, like Agni said, Villiam isn't much of a warrior himself.

Agni continues. "The Alliance of Cyrille is still an active collection of powerful individuals among these city-states who work to ensure the Up-Mountains' continued dominance."

"And you and Villiam think the Alliance is responsible for the murders?" I ask. "And for the man who attacked Villiam?"

"We've been distrustful of them ever since they invited us to return to their cities. We thought they were planning something."

"And why don't you think the man who attacked Villiam is the same who went after Gill and Blister?"

"Because, since Gill's death, we've been monitoring the patrons in Gomorrah more closely. We know that he entered yesterday, three days after Blister's murder. We also have intelligence on him before then, placing him in the city. He wasn't here to commit those crimes."

I collapse into a chair at the table. Villiam and Agni thought the Alliance would strike at them? If they knew they were planning something, they should have prepared better. Even now, they only keep two guards outside their caravan. The Festival can be confusing when moving, but with all the chaos, wouldn't this be an easier time for someone to sneak inside?

"Then we should turn around," I say, "before others are killed or hurt."

"On the contrary, I think this is exactly why we should progress farther. Cautiously, of course. Villiam has Gomorrah's guard keeping watch over you and the Festival at every hour of the night and day. They're currently stationed entirely around Gomorrah's perimeter. But wars are not won through retreat." His voice rises, and I can sense the personal stakes he holds in this mission. If the Alliance of Cyrille is as powerful as he claims, they are at least partially responsible for the kidnapping of his son.

"What if your own past is clouding your judgment?" I ask.

He raises his eyebrows. "I've never heard you sound so much like your father. You wouldn't normally ask so direct a question."

It takes everything in me not to show my pride at this statement. "I'm trying to protect my family. I don't want to risk them on a personal crusade."

"The Alliance has *personally* murdered your family. This is your crusade, as well."

I hadn't thought of it that way. I stare at the map on the wall and the various cities Agni pointed out to me. The Alliance, even if they are responsible, seems faceless. More difficult to picture than Luca's idea of the killer, lurking within Gomorrah. Even if the Alliance did attack Villiam, I don't know how Agni and Villiam can prove they're also responsible for what happened to Gill and Blister. It's likely, of course, but it isn't certain.

Villiam returns, carrying a bag full of notebooks and struggling with his crutches. Agni quickly helps him into the caravan. "I have the list of notes from our spies. Has Agni finished explaining this to you, Sorina?"

"Yes," Agni and I say simultaneously.

"Good." Villiam spreads the notebooks out over his table. Each one appears to be detailing people in different cities. "For the past several years, Agni and I have been trying to compile a list of names of active members of the Alliance, and in particular, identify the most influential of those members in each city. It is our belief that if the Alliance falls, the Up-Mountains would be paralyzed long enough for the Down-Mountains to initiate a Ninth Trade War and, this time, find victory."

I didn't realize we were hoping for another war. I always thought we'd be trying to avoid one.

As if reading my thoughts, Villiam adds, "Hundreds of years of conflict will not be ended by peaceful revolutionaries, Sorina."

He's right. I'm being naïve.

"According to our spies," Agni says, "there is a leader. We believe he's in either Sapris or Leonita, but probably Sapris."

Gomorrah will be in Sapris in a few weeks. It's only two cities away on our itinerary.

"As if a nod to history, there is a marriage occurring in Sapris when we will be arriving. The princess will be marrying her father's advisor, an influential duke. We suspect this wedding will draw out a number of people in the Alliance and, in particular, the Alliance's leader. If all goes according to plan, we could kidnap the leader at or just before this event. His information would be absolutely invaluable. This is what we were discussing today when you weren't here. Our informants have only just brought us the information we needed."

"Isn't that playing rather dirty?" I ask.

"Gomorrah is a Festival of Sin, Sorina," Agni says. "A city of antiheroes, at best."

"That is mainly the Downhill."

"The Downhill *is* Gomorrah. The Uphill is merely a business front."

I frown. Maybe my entire impression of my home has been childish. Maybe I know no more about the Festival than the average visitor.

"I realize this is rather new to you," Villiam says. "I raised you in Gomorrah's most sheltered neighborhood on purpose, to protect you. I didn't want to see your childhood end as early as it has. But this is the nature of the world, and we're going to need your help."

Now I feel even more like a fool. I didn't ask to be sheltered.

"What do you need me to do?" I ask.

"Use your illusion-work. Agni and I are still gathering intelligence on the wedding and finalizing our plans. But, in the meantime, I want to prepare you. I want to introduce you to the arsenal that Gomorrah has to offer us, because your illusion-work is hardly going to be our only weapon."

"Do you mean the Downhill?"

"Exactly."

The corner of my mouth curves into a smile. "Will you admit now that there are assassins in Gomorrah?"

Villiam's eyes glint. "I have no idea what you're talking about."

CHAPTER THIRTEEN

"The Downhill isn't safe in the daylight," Villiam says, buttoning his jacket. I don't understand how he isn't stifling in the September heat. He eyes a knife sitting on his desk. I never realized previously that my father owned a knife, but there it sits, with a bronze handle, gleaming on a stack of papers as if freshly polished. It's curved—definitely not meant for opening letters. I wait for him to take the knife, but he merely stares at it and then turns away. "But you and I will have nothing to worry about."

I'm not sure I believe him. Villiam is sporting his nicest double-breasted coat and fine leather shoes. A masked criminal might take advantage of our vulnerability and Villiam's overly luxurious fashion sense. Not to mention that I'll be pushing him in a wheelchair, and I doubt we would be able to outrun an assailant in such a position.

"Where are we going in the Downhill?" I ask.

"To meet with the captain of the guard."

I've seen the captain of the guard from afar and overheard him speaking to Villiam in his office. Unlike the regular guards, he wears a burgundy sash over his uniform, though, in the dim smoke of Gomorrah, the deep red is as equally difficult as black to perceive within darkness. While the Up-Mountain officials like to preen in their flashy medals, Gomorrah guards would prefer to dress as chameleons rather than peacocks.

Hobbling on one leg, Villiam steps down from the caravan and collapses into the wheelchair. "What are the three occupational roles a person can play in Gomorrah?"

"Well, in the Uphill, there are performers and vendors. People who cater to visitors," I say, turning the wheelchair in the direction of the Downhill. Villiam is heavier than I anticipated. "Then there are the people who oversee the upkeep of the Festival. Teachers, doctors, merchants, gardeners." I pause, trying to come up with the last profession. "All that's entering my mind is criminals, but I doubt you mean—"

"That is precisely what I mean."

"So the third: thieves, prettyworkers and assassins." To my slight thrill, Villiam doesn't bother to argue that there are no assassins in Gomorrah.

"These criminals, as you call them, are as vital to Gomorrah as any of the others. The nature of the Downhill is our arsenal, Sorina. *Sin* is our arsenal. It is through the very depravity of Gomorrah that we fight wars of righteousness." He speaks with a hint of excitement in his voice. I don't know if it's over the subject matter or the fact that he's sharing this information with me at last. "Thieves can be hired to steal documents outside of Gomorrah. Prettyworkers overhear valuable information from clients. Assassins, trained from birth, are always at our disposal. The people of Gomorrah first and foremost work for themselves, but they also work for us."

The mention of prettyworkers and information sends my mind to Luca. This afternoon, shortly after waking, the guard stationed outside our caravan handed me a note from him. All it said was "Ten o'clock. Wear something festive." I don't know what to expect, so I wore all black clothes but brought my most colorful mask, stowed away inside my robes for after I finish with Villiam. We're supposed to be interviewing another suspect, but I'm no longer certain we're following the right leads. If the Alliance of Cyrille is responsible for orchestrating the murders, then we should be seeking out a spy within Gomorrah, not established—albeit suspicious—residents. Then again, even if the Alliance is a real threat to my father, there's no proof they're the ones responsible for Gill and Blister.

I'm anxious to hear Luca's thoughts. I think he avoided seeking me out yesterday because he wanted to give me time with my father, but, truly, I wish he'd paid a visit. I like when he thinks out loud, so that I don't need to. Lately, too much thinking has led my mind into dark corners.

Villiam and I slowly approach the fence of the Downhill. I've never crossed this border with my father. He passes it with confidence and ease, as he probably has hundreds of times before.

"I don't believe you and I have ever discussed the guard," he says. "The guard has its soldiers, those who protect Gomorrah. Shadow-workers, mainly. But it also recruits a number of thieves and assassins, those who are bred in families who make crime their expertise. It has one rule, and one rule only. Can you guess it?"

"No."

"All members of the guard have lived their entire lives in Gomorrah. Anyone from outside cannot be trusted."

I try not to show any outward reaction to his statement. This goes against the Gomorrah philosophy, that any misfit or outcast can find a home within its smoke. It reminds me of what Nicoleta told me a few days ago, that Luca was not to be trusted. I suppose I thought this at first…but not anymore. Gomorrah has found a way of interweaving itself in Luca's character. He passes no judgment on the prettyworkers he befriends, as many

Up-Mountainers have done. He dresses like any performer in the Festival—though with terrible taste.

"Chimal will be excited to meet you," Villiam says. "He's been hearing about you for years."

Villiam's voice momentarily pulls me out of my reverie, but I realize with mild mortification that no matter how much I try to focus, my mind keeps returning to Luca. I'm growing uncomfortably aware of how much I think about him. Kahina always says that no one can choose whom they fall for, and even though I consider myself a romantic, I don't want to cause myself unnecessary heartache. I'd rather squash the feelings before they begin—after all, how could Luca possibly be interested in someone like me?

"Chimal began his life as a thief," Villiam continues. "As he will probably tell you, there are a number of established families in this section of the Festival. Although the Uphill is associated with wealth, the oldest families reside in the Downhill. Families as old as Gomorrah itself."

To our left, we pass a house of pretty women. The two-story caravan has its shutters closed so its residents can sleep during the day. A garland of brightly colored glass bottles clunks against the wood as it moves, a sound like long nails clicking against a hard surface. One woman tends to the elephants by washing them as they walk.

I'm immediately embarrassed to be walking beside a brothel with my father, no matter how common a staple of Gomorrah they might be. Despite everything I know about Villiam, he's never told me if he's had a lover. I've never seen him with either a woman or a man, but I don't think it's because they don't interest him. Venera once said it was probably because he puts his duties as proprietor far above any bodily needs. It hardly seems fair that his job has stripped him of the opportunity for romance, since proprietors in the past have had spouses and proper families.

I know there are sacrifices I must make when I become proprietor, but I've spent years daydreaming of the princes and princesses from Kahina's fairy tales. I won't give up on my own romantic happily-ever-after, not even for the Festival.

As we leave the brothel behind, my thoughts drift to Luca's beautiful prettywoman friend, Yelema. Nicoleta mentioned that Luca was not interested in the services prettyworkers had to offer, but she's never actually met Luca. Probably never even seen him. He's handsome, and, regardless of the rumors, I would be surprised if Luca had never pushed his "friendships" with prettyworkers beyond the realm of simply friends.

Luca and I, we are friends.

But lately, I'm finding that I want us to be more.

"You seem rather distant. Is something troubling you?" William asks.

"No," I say quickly.

"Certainly you've been in the Downhill before. I don't need to know every detail of my daughter's life, but I imagine—"

"I have. I guess I'm just tired from all the packing earlier. Not so much sleep."

"Yes, unfortunately, leaving Cartona so early has given us less time to prepare for the wedding in Sapris."

"Is that what this is about?" I ask. "The wedding?"

"Yes. But I don't want to discuss it now. Let's wait until we meet with Chimal."

Chimal lives at a deep corner of the Downhill, far beyond Luca's tent, far beyond any place where I have ventured. I had always envisioned that the deeper one travels into the Downhill, the seedier it becomes, but evidently the opposite is true. This neighborhood is wealthy. Caravans freshly painted. Beautiful stallions pulling their carriages. Full gardens on top of their carts. But, still, there is a hint of the Downhill. The smell of incense. The unnerving quiet.

One caravan in particular, painted in deep scarlet, stands out from the others. It's more of a cart than a caravan, with no wooden walls or ceiling, only black fabric. When we near it, Villiam uses the crutch on his lap to pull himself standing. He cumbersomely climbs inside without bothering to knock or call out Chimal's name. I fold up his wheelchair and rush to follow him—anyone could be hiding in there, waiting for the proprietor to arrive. In his state, he would be unable to defend himself. He thinks, because he's the proprietor, that he is untouchable. It's only taken him a matter of hours to forget the event that resulted in his broken leg.

As I enter the cart, I receive my first glimpse of Chimal. He's a shockingly tall man while sitting down, but after observing his stumpy legs by the light of his candle, I deduce that he probably doesn't reach six feet when standing. His features are a mixture of Yucatoan and something else. Perhaps Vurundi. Perhaps Eastern. More than likely, a variety of peoples from the melting pot that is Gomorrah. He wears the face and expression of a man who has seen heartache and has allowed it to harden him on the inside, rather than the outside. A warm face and cold eyes.

"Sorina," he says. He smiles, showing a gap in his front teeth that makes his otherwise threatening demeanor less intimidating. "How pleasant to meet you at last."

"A pleasure indeed," I say. My words strike me as sounding very much like my father, who has always been a master of pleasantries. I wish we could jump immediately into the heart of the important conversation we need to have—my father has been attacked by enemies beyond Skull Gate, enemies who potentially killed Gill and Blister. We must decide how to retaliate.

However, Chimal doesn't seem eager to rush things. "I am told you can create a man using merely your imagination."

"That's right."

"An act worthy of a god, don't you think?"

"I wouldn't know. I wasn't raised with much faith."

"I thought you followed the stars, Villiam?" Chimal asks.

"My mother did."

191

"Well, as it turns out, I'm not a believer myself. The only god I worship is the god of death."

He smiles, and the gap in his teeth seems more sinister to me than before.

"The man we seek," he says, "he is not a man easily identified. In the letters we have intercepted from the Alliance, he has written under pseudonyms, and several. Nor are we certain where the letters are originating from."

He means the leader of the Alliance. The man Villiam intends to kidnap. The man who has orchestrated so much suffering.

"It will be heavily guarded. Even with your illusion-work, Sorina, slipping past the entrance won't be easy. But I do have ideas regarding my men." He leans forward, close enough that I can smell his breath. Sweet, like corn. "Your illusions have powers unlike anyone else in Gomorrah. These could prove an asset to us. I'm particularly interested in the girl who can fly."

"Hawk? She's only thirteen," I say with dismay.

"And you're sixteen. There isn't much of a difference."

I watch Villiam, who doesn't seem perturbed by these comments. Perhaps Chimal has discussed this notion with him before, when I was not included. "I won't put Hawk in danger," I say.

"Would she be able to carry both you and a man during flight?"

"I doubt it—"

"It wouldn't be far—"

"I don't think—"

"It would be the surest method of slipping you safely inside the wedding. From there, it would be simple to lure the man away using your illusion-work."

"I'm not comfortable asking her," I say, with more strength in my voice. "Too many of my family members have already been murdered by the Alliance. I don't want to risk another."

"Surely she would be more than willing to help the cause, considering the tragedies that have befallen your…family."

Of course Hawk wouldn't object. But that's what I'm afraid of.

"Her willingness is beside the point. I don't want her involved," I say.

Villiam clears his throat. "Chimal, my daughter has all of the weapons of Gomorrah at her disposal. Surely there's another way of executing this without endangering anyone beyond those in this cart and those who already serve the Festival."

Only now do Chimal's words dawn on me. I'd been so concerned with Hawk's involvement that I hadn't paid attention to my own. He wants *me* to be the one to lure the leader away from the wedding? I don't perform well under pressure. I could be killed and jeopardize all of Gomorrah in the process. Is my father truly at ease with that?

"What are our other options?" I ask, fear obvious in my tone.

"You sneaking into the wedding from ground-level," Chimal says.

"I hardly look like an Up-Mountainer." Chimal, with such Yucatoan features, looks more Up-Mountainer than me.

"You would need to disguise yourself the whole time, with illusion work."

Chimal has no idea what level of concentration that requires. I can maintain my moth illusion for a few minutes, at best, but something more complex than that? Something to disguise me and then later lure the leader of the Alliance away from his guards? My routine in the Freak Show is ten minutes long, but it requires a different skill set, as the illusion is always moving. Fixed illusions are more challenging, like holding a weight with an outstretched arm.

"Are we even certain who the leader is?" I ask.

"We have a few theories," Villiam says. "We suspect it's an archduke of Sapris. He has the money, the name and the connections. But it could also be the crown prince of Leonita, the future heir of the city. Or a lesser-born merchant from Frice, who commands an empire of wealth."

"Do you intend for me to kidnap all of these men?" I ask.

"No. We're placing our bets on the archduke. His name is Dalimil. He'll be your target. If he turns out not to be the leader, he will still provide valuable information. There's no doubt that all of those men are high-ranking members of the Alliance."

"You're gambling an awful lot on this theory of yours," I say.

"Yes," he says seriously, "we all are."

"Villiam, would I be able to speak to you alone for a moment?" Chimal asks. The way he looks everywhere but at me, I don't anticipate he means to compliment me in my absence.

"Of course," Villiam says. "Sorina can wait outside."

I climb out of the cart with a swift, indignant leap. I've been kicked out of their club. When I lean closer to the fabric of the cart to eavesdrop, I hear nothing. It must be charmed to be soundproof.

Does Chimal think I'm being uncooperative? I'm not thrilled by the idea of kidnapping anyone, regardless of what they may or may not have done. Do I need to make a decision now? Gomorrah is swiftly approaching Gentoa and, after that, Sapris, where the wedding will take place. A quick decision is needed, but I don't feel ready to decide. I wish I could speak with Luca first. I haven't told him everything Villiam has shared with me, but I have a feeling he already knows. With all the prettyworkers he's spoken to, he probably knows more about Gomorrah than I do, even though he's only lived here for a year.

After a few more minutes of waiting, Villiam steps outside to join me. I help him onto the ground, and he balances himself with his crutch. We remain still as Gomorrah drifts around us.

"I will get straight to the point," he says, resigned. "Chimal doesn't trust you. He doesn't think your heart is in this. I have worked with Chimal for over seven years, and if he doesn't sense complete and utter loyalty, he won't work with you."

"Of course my heart is in this. The Alliance may have murdered two members of my family. What more does he want from me? Should I kneel? I don't need to agree with him to know we are on the same side." I curl my hands into fists. I'm completely and utterly loyal to Gomorrah, but not to him. We only met a few minutes ago; he hasn't earned my trust yet.

"He wants you to speak to Hawk."

"He seems unwilling to compromise." The salty winds from the nearby coast blow my hair against my face, and I hold it back and wrap my cloak tighter around myself to keep warm.

"As do you."

"Surrendering is not the same as compromise."

"Chimal is the man planning the details of this mission. He won't include you in his plans if he doesn't trust you. He's the captain of the guard—he is essential to this. He's been essential to Gomorrah for years."

I hear the words he has left unspoken. That I'm inessential to the protection of the Festival. The thought of this stings more than a little.

"Then I will help the effort in some other way," I say at last.

"There are no other illusion-workers in Gomorrah."

"I thought you said the Downhill was our arsenal, and I thought I was a future proprietor. Not Gomorrah's finest weapon."

"Your skills are necessary. Do you think I would ask this of you if they weren't? I've already had the argument with Chimal that you're having with me now."

"Why didn't you tell me you brought me here for this? I thought I was getting a tour."

"I didn't know he wanted to use Hawk until just now. He's only mentioned you in passing before this."

"I don't want Chimal to *use* anyone. Not me and certainly not anyone else in my family." I turn to leave. I have other things to do today, like finding Jiafu to return the extra coins and meeting with Luca to interview another suspect. I don't want to stay here long enough for Chimal and Villiam to convince me. Not before I have time to think everything over, and maybe talk to Luca.

If Chimal is so *essential*, he can push Villiam home.

"You have a day to think about this," my father says from behind me. "If you want, we can all talk to Hawk together."

I ignore his comment as I walk away. No one is talking to Hawk; I don't want her to know we even had this conversation. If I decide to help them, that's one thing, but I won't allow them to put any more of my family in harm's way—not even for justice.

Younger sister;
adores me;

plays
fiddle
for
show;
cute.

SNAP
HER
NECK.

MOSTLY HUMAN,
BUT WITH <u>DISTINCT</u> BIRD FEATURES.

PREFERS TO HUNT FOR FOOD
    AND EAT IT RAW.

EXTREMELY KEEN EYESIGHT.

    SOMETIMES SINGS AND PLAYS THE FIDDLE
NEAR SKULL GATE FOR COIN.

SECRETLY VISITS AN ORPHAN BOY
    IN THE GAMES NEIGHBORHOOD.

OFTEN <u>ALONE</u> OUTSIDE OF GOMORRAH'S
LIMITS, SEARCHING FOR FOOD.

CHAPTER FOURTEEN

The overcast sky obscures the few stars visible through Gomorrah's smoke, so the only light in the Downhill comes from the green-fire torches, flickering from the heavy coastal winds. Several of the torches have blown out. Everything is green and dark and hushed, and, despite becoming accustomed to the Downhill after visiting it so much with Luca, I'm acutely aware of how little I know about these neighborhoods of Gomorrah, which are not nearly as nice as Chimal's. The person who lives in the tent beside me could be a killer. Or a shadow-worker could be skulking about between caravans, waiting for an opportunity to grasp my shadow in the green light, like I'm a rabbit walking into a snare. Villiam said that I would have nothing to worry about, as the future proprietor, but I don't believe him. I don't feel like a proprietor. I feel very much like a girl, far too young to make the decisions ahead of me.

Jiafu isn't in his caravan, even though it's only five o'clock and he rarely rises before eight. I wait for him, my right hand in my pocket, gripping a concealed knife. My illusion-work prevents me from being noticed, but, today, even being invisible doesn't seem like enough to keep me calm.

Jiafu returns forty minutes later, whistling, and I lessen my illusion-work as he reaches his cart. "Holy shit," he curses, when I appear out of nowhere. "'Rina, what the hell were you thinking? You look like a monster in that mask."

I lift a hand to my violet mask, which doesn't pair well with the green lighting. I'm going to assume that's what he meant and not that *I* appear to be a monster.

I throw him his coin purse with the fifteen gold coins from the other one added to it. "I don't know if you were lying, but I'd still like to work with you, if you don't mind."

"You have a lot of balls calling me a liar," he says. "And you have even more balls to be coming back here after the other day."

"I thought we were cousins."

"Fuck you, princess." He spits on my shoes. "You're lucky I haven't sent someone to beat your freak ass."

"Don't be like that. We work well together."

"Yeah, like a lion and a gazelle. And you keep forgetting that I'm the lion. And that you need to watch your back."

I smirk. "You didn't seem much like a lion the other day. Bet they heard you screaming all across the Downhill."

"You want to say that again, freak?" He pulls a knife out of his pocket. I'm fairly certain that Jiafu is an empty threat. He wouldn't hurt Gomorrah's princess. He's not that reckless.

But that doesn't mean I'm going to stick around to find out if I'm wrong. So much for repairing our business relationship.

"Careful," I whisper. "How do you know I'm actually standing here? This could be an illusion. I could be behind you right now, and I could gut you through your back."

And I do just that—without the gutting part. The image of me stays put in front of him, while the actual me, unnoticeable, tiptoes away into the darkness.

"This isn't you, bitch. You're not breathing or moving," I hear Jiafu say from behind me.

"Go to hell," I say. It's a sound illusion. Jiafu hears it to his right, and he whips around, his knife out. But there's no one there. I'm gone, running through the moving Downhill to Luca's caravan.

Luca sits at the edge of his caravan, his feet dangling. He taps his walking stick against his door with one hand and checks his golden pocket watch with the other. He doesn't look up as I approach, so I get to study him for a moment. His blond hair rustled from the wind. His pristinely white shirt. His angular features.

He looks up and smiles with his dimples. My heart does a little twirl.

I've never had a crush on someone. I may have admired from afar but not like this. When the fairy tales spoke of butterflies, I didn't anticipate it feeling more like hornets.

"How are you?" he asks.

"Good." My cheeks are warm and flushed, and I might just die of embarrassment.

"I hear Villiam is well enough."

"He is."

"You're not usually so quiet." He hops off the caravan. "Do you have news? I heard his attacker killed himself. Cyanide. Not particularly elegant."

I have a million things I wish to say. That, though not certain, it's seeming more and more likely that the Alliance is behind my family's murders. That training to be proprietor means potentially putting myself in danger. That I'm scared. I'm scared of what Villiam is asking of me. I'm scared of the Alliance, of what they have and may have done. I'm more scared that Luca is right, and the killer is from Gomorrah working on a separate agenda. How many enemies do I have? Who might be lurking in Gomorrah's smoke?

Luca's contemplative expression appears all the more serious in the green torch light. "You don't have to say anything."

"Are you still certain that the killer is in Gomorrah? That we're not wasting our time?"

He raises his eyebrows. "As certain as ever."

If I ask why, that will lead to an entire debate of theories. Of Villiam's attacker versus the one who attacked Gill and Blister. Of the Alliance's agenda or something else. Maybe to Villiam and Luca, that debate would feel more like simply words. A battle of logic. To me, all I can see is how little we see, how dense the fog is that covers our enemies. We have no idea what we may be up against. Any theory could be right. Any person could be suspicious.

"Let's just go," I say.

I don't know how I've never noticed before, but Luca walks everywhere as if he is bracing himself to run through a brick wall. He keeps his shoulders locked, his head down and, at full walking speed, could outrun the average horse. He barrels through the Downhill, all one hundred and fifty lanky pounds of him, and I follow awkwardly in his trail.

By the time we reach our destination, I'm sweating in every conceivable place I could sweat. I take off my mask for a moment to wipe the droplets off my forehead and nose.

"So who are we meeting tonight?" I ask, panting slightly.

"Her name is Tuyet," Luca says, his voice steady and his breathing normal, despite our near run to reach here. "She's not as harmless as Narayan. If you're looking for someone cold enough to kill a baby, Tuyet is a respectable guess."

Goose bumps prickle up my arms. Regardless of whether this is the woman who murdered Gill and Blister, the idea of facing someone so cold-blooded unnerves me.

Luca leans forward so that I can feel his breath on my cheek. I have the urge to pull away at his closeness, but I don't want him to think that I'm acting strangely. Or know that he's plagued my thoughts all afternoon. "Tuyet has two types of jynx-work. Rare, but when it happens, the two kinds of magic often blend together. Tuyet is both a mind-worker and a fortune-worker. She can hear what you think before you think it. The average mind-worker needs to touch you to use their jynx-work, but Tuyet can hear your thoughts as if you're speaking. This makes her one of the most successful assassins in Gomorrah."

I stiffen at the mention of assassins, as it reminds me of my conversation with Villiam and Chimal earlier today. Something to ask Luca about later.

Luca continues, "She's also rather famous for not possessing a heart—literally, I mean."

"What do you mean, she doesn't have a heart?" I ask, mystified. "How is she alive, then?"

"It's a mystery. She has no pulse, and yet her blood pumps."

A mystery. That's how everyone describes me—I have no eyes, and yet I see. The Girl Who Sees Without Eyes.

I never thought I would have something in common with a killer.

"I advise you not to speak," Luca says. "Forgive me, but you're not good at keeping your thoughts quiet. Even I can tell what you're thinking half the time, and I'm not a mind-worker."

"What should I do, then? Just stand there?"

"I'll do the talking," he says.

"Can't she hear your thoughts, too?"

"Probably." He smiles. "But not for certain."

I'm about to open my mouth to tell him he's not half so smart as he thinks he is, when he says, "Just trust me on this. I'm trying to help you, remember?"

I nod hesitantly.

"Good. Glad that's settled." He disappears inside the open caravan.

I take a deep breath and climb in after him.

The caravan is decorated in a similar manner to my own and

to every other caravan in Gomorrah. A low, fold-up table. A collection of pillows, tapestries and candles sold from any vendor in the Uphill. And, since Gomorrah is traveling, a number of trunks stacked in the corner. It's so remarkably average that I wonder if we're in the wrong home.

"You expected it to be more morbid? Perhaps with some skulls, with gemstones for eyes?" a woman's voice says to my right, chorusing my own thoughts.

Tuyet sits in the corner, playing with a deck of cards. Not fortune cards, which are compiled in a deck with various trump cards depicting each animal of the constellations. It's just a regular deck. She turns the ace of spades over in her hand, her pointed fingernails clacking against its edges.

She has olive skin made darker by the tattoos along her forehead, neck and arms. Upon closer examination, I realize it is one giant tattoo of a flower with drooping midnight-blue petals, drawn in the gentle brushstrokes of the Eastern art style. The intensity of the color and the details within the lines are so fine that it's difficult to believe they could be drawn in such a way on human skin instead of paper.

"That's a black maiden flower," I say. Its essence is in one of Luca's vials on his belt.

"Which you know because it's a famous poison," she says. "That's what you were thinking. And you're not supposed to speak, which is what *he* was thinking. He's right, you know. It makes your thoughts louder." She nods to Luca, who stiffens. "Actually, it isn't a black maiden flower. Though it appears so in the dark. In full light, you can see the color of the petals better, a more vibrant blue. The maiden's daughter, it's called. Perfectly edible."

She stands, and she's the tallest in the room by at least three inches. She looks me up and down. "You're Villiam's adopted daughter," she says.

"How do you know that?" I ask. Luca and I are standing in

the shadow of her caravan—she cannot see my face. "I wasn't thinking it. Or about to think it."

"Because you *are* thinking it, whether or not you realize it. Everyone has dozens of thoughts jumbling around in their head, and almost all of them are what I call static. You think them so often you stop listening, even as they repeat over and over. I can hear you thinking *I am Sorina Gomorrah*—which is the loudest of the static, yet the one you ignore the most. Your identity. And then there are thoughts like *Gill Gill Gill* and *Blister Blister Blister*. The people—no, illusions—you wonder if I could have killed."

Luca sighs. "Conversations with you always get right to the point."

"But you're not really interested in how I'm doing, or the weather or the nutty politics of all these cities we keep coming and going from. You're not here for small talk."

"Can we at least sit down?" he asks. "I'm rather fond of formalities."

The corner of her lip twitches. It's not exactly a smile, but it's close. "Why not?" The three of us sit around her table. In the light, she momentarily examines my eyeless mask. Then she looks away, much in the way adults tell children not to stare at deformities.

"Why do you think my jynx-work would be able to kill illusions?" she asks. There's no hint of annoyance in her voice at being accused of murder. "Because guilt doesn't pinch as hard as hunger pains." She eyes me. "Your thoughts are very loud, dear. You need to sharpen your mind."

"What are you suggesting?" I ask, even though I know exactly what she meant. I clench my teeth.

"*You* don't think you're smart, either," she says. "Being smart isn't everything. Right, Luca? You've certainly learned that the hard way."

Not a single expression crosses Luca's face.

She examines him. "But, even so, your thoughts are difficult for me to hear. Not like you're covering them, like a mind-worker might. Like your static is in knots."

"That can't be good," Luca says, not sounding particularly concerned.

She laughs more genuinely than I imagined an assassin could. She lives in too average of a home. All this directness unnerves me. No matter what we say, she will always know the meaning behind our words. She will always be the one in the position of power. It occurs to me that, if she can hear all of my thoughts, she already knows of my feelings for Luca and about my conversation with Villiam and Chimal today. How easy it must be for her to unravel secrets. I wonder if I should leave before she discovers something else, but the damage is probably already done.

"I didn't kill the two illusions. I had no reason to. I'm not the only assassin in Gomorrah, but I'm the best. No one is going to pay me top dollar to drown a baby. You could pay anyone to do that."

"Not everyone would do it," I counter.

"But someone would. Someone mad, probably, to go messing with the proprietor's daughter. It seems to me you want someone who doesn't make it their living to kill people. None of us are trying to be on Villiam's bad side. We don't mess with the guard."

"That's not much of an alibi," I say.

"If it takes jynx-work to kill your illusions, mine doesn't even make sense," she says. "And if it doesn't, no one is going to pay a lion to kill a caterpillar when a pigeon would do just fine."

I whip toward Luca with a *This is bullshit, right?* kind of expression, but he has his eyes closed, as if concentrating.

"That makes sense," he says.

"Any liar can make *sense*," I say. She could've been hired by the Alliance. She could be a spy. What a brilliant spy she would make.

At this, Tuyet barks out a laugh. "If the Alliance was seeking out a traitor, they wouldn't choose Gomorrah's most famous assassin. They're much craftier than that. If it's a spy you seek, then you should concern yourselves with those closest to you."

That would narrow our scope to Kahina, Villiam and the illusions, and none of them have the means or motive—or such cruelty in their hearts.

Luca stands and straightens his posh Up-Mountain clothes. "We're leaving."

"That fight brewing in your head," Tuyet says, "take it outside."

Luca grabs my hand, and I think it's meant to be reassuring, but it only makes my heart hammer. He pulls me outside before I can say anything, and he crosses his arms as if bracing himself for the storm coming.

"She still could've killed Gill and Blister," I say.

"She had no reason to," Luca says. "No motive. In fact, she had a better reason not to."

"Unless someone paid her."

"She already made two excellent points about why she is not the woman for such a job." Luca sighs. "If you're so certain that woman killed them, then we can come back after we figured out who paid her to do so. But I don't think you believe she did, anyway. You're just in a sour mood. What was Tuyet talking about, anyway? What did she mean about a traitor?"

"I'd rather not discuss it here," I say. I'm not convinced that we're out of range of Tuyet's strange jynx-work yet.

Luca swivels on his heel and walks down a path to the left. "Then let's discuss as we walk. We're on our way to a party. I did say *festive*."

"I *am* festive."

I have to nearly run to keep up with him. I lean in close so that no one can overhear us. "My investigation with Villiam isn't much like ours," I start. At first, I hesitate about whether to tell him. Villiam told me not to trust anyone not born in Gomorrah. But Luca has never given me a reason to suspect him, and I desperately want his advice. "Have you heard of the Alliance of Cyrille?"

"Yes."

I should be surprised, but nothing Luca knows surprises me anymore.

"Before I came to Gomorrah, I knew a man who was involved in it. I've also heard people speak of it here," he says. "Villiam believes they killed your illusions? Why wouldn't they simply kill you, or his assistant, or people closer to him?"

"They could simply be trying to shake me. I am Gomorrah's future proprietor."

"And I suppose Villiam has told you what it means to be a proprietor."

His words sting. Was everyone aware of this truth except me? If Villiam was purposely trying to keep me sheltered like he said, he really did an extraordinary job.

"I'm aware of what that means," I say. "They think the man who attacked Villiam worked for the Alliance."

"He probably did. Cartonian. Hiding out in Gomorrah during the day. Carrying a vial of poison to kill himself when necessary. That feels a lot like their style. But the one who killed your family? Who knew exactly how to disable Gill? Who turned no heads when he was with Blister? We're looking for someone established in Gomorrah for more than a few hours. So it doesn't make sense for that person to be working for the Alliance. If the Alliance simply wants Villiam dead, they wouldn't bother with your illusions. They would send a man to spook Villiam's horses."

My head hurts from spinning around so many theories, all of which make sense. If Luca is right, my family is still in danger.

I fill him in on the details of my conversation with Chimal and Villiam today, particularly the bit that involves Hawk. "They've given me a day to speak with her, but I don't want her involved in this."

"Then don't work with Chimal. You said Chimal gave you an ultimatum."

"I... I have to be a part of this. There is still a chance that the Alliance could have killed my family. And Villiam wants me to take on more responsibility as a proprietor." *And I don't want to let him down.*

"If you have to be a part of it, then you don't have a choice. You'll have to speak to Hawk. But Hawk can still decline, can't she?"

"She won't. I know her. She'll want to help."

"If you consider this a family matter, I would discuss it with your whole family. Maybe Hawk will listen if more people than you tell her no."

I didn't think of that. Nicoleta has a talent for persuasion. We could have a family meeting tonight. Villiam and Chimal cannot be disappointed in me if Hawk refuses.

"What sort of party are we going to?" I ask, my spirits now considerably lighter.

"The sort with classic Gomorrah debauchery. There's a tent behind mine that often hosts them."

So he means the kind of parties Venera attends wearing her black lipstick and skintight, striped dresses.

"Why are we going to this party?" I ask.

"There's someone I need to speak with there. Another client. You don't have to come, but I thought you might like to."

"I've never been to a party."

"I don't know how your father could possibly give you a working knowledge of Gomorrah without sending you to one."

He leads me to the tent behind his packed-up caravan, a tent which is a massive expanse of various tarps sewn together, nearly the height of the Menagerie in the Uphill, all rolling on a platform charmed to move on its own. The air smells like a summer night and rum and fever, and just breathing it in makes my steps feel lighter. We each pay two copper pieces to enter.

Inside are at least one hundred people, maybe two hundred. Wearing the most outrageous clothes I've ever seen in one place. Suit jackets made of taffeta. Dresses with more layers than a wedding cake. Hats with brims full of ragweed. Shoes with platforms six inches high.

A fire-worker stands in the center of the dance floor surrounded by a fence, juggling three balls of flames that burn purple, red and pink. The musicians play a Vurundi dance with a beat that pulses throughout the tent, beckoning dancers closer with its hypnotic rhythm. The bar is opposite the musicians and quite crowded.

I notice Yelema, the prettywoman who was having tea with Luca when I first found his tent. She's dancing and is as mesmerizing as always. She waves at me, and I wave back. Then she waves at someone else in the room, and another. As if she knows everyone here. The only two people I know well in the Downhill, which makes up more than half of the city, are Luca and Jiafu. If I'm going to be proprietor, that needs to change.

Luca sits on a stool and speaks to the bartender, their heads so low it looks like they're talking into their glasses. I slide in beside him, but they keep their voices almost too low for me to hear.

"...yesterday morning," Luca says. "Nearly certain he's a shadow-worker."

"Who is?" I ask.

The bartender eyes me cautiously. "She's with you, von Raske?"

"Do you mean do I care if she overhears, or is she *with* me?"

"Both, I suppose."

"I'd rather she not overhear. She's a client for a different matter," he says.

Before I can ask what's going on, the bartender says, "I thought you weren't the physical type?"

It takes me a moment to process what the bartender means—that he thinks I'm here with Luca as a date. As a possible lover.

I force myself not to look too pleased, not to hope too much, as I hold my breath, waiting for Luca's response.

"Everyone seems to have opinions on my *type*, don't they?" Luca rolls his eyes and then turns to me. "Give us a moment."

I feel a shrivel of disappointment.

"Fine," I say and then creep my way to the other side of the bar, hoping for someone to talk to. I search for Venera in the crowd but don't find her. Instead, I bump into a woman with a five o'clock shadow and hands twice the size of my face.

"I like your mask, dear," she says to me.

"Thank you. I like your shoes." She wears glittery purple heels that pair perfectly with the frills of her dress. "Is it always this crowded?" I ask.

"They're all celebrating the Up-Mountain war that hasn't happened yet," she says. "But everyone thinks there will be one because some fortune-worker said there'd be. The fortune-worker's name changes with each story. They think a war here will bring the Down-Mountains more freedom." She raises her eyebrows. "Wishful thinking."

"War in the Up-Mountains? Why?"

"People keep dying, I think. Important Up-Mountain people."

I think back to the young prince in Cartona, the one who died of pneumonia, but people really believe he was murdered by Frice. Then there was the Frician duke. Villiam didn't mention anything to me about a possible war, and I'd believe him over any fortune-worker.

Luca reappears at my side. "Sorry," he says. "I only needed to speak to him for a moment."

"About what?" I ask.

"A private matter." His face is serious and cold, and, for a moment, I have the urge to take a step back. He's definitely hiding something important. This isn't some meeting with the Leather Viper.

213

Or maybe I'm just on edge, with all this talk of war and the Alliance.

There's a pause. I can feel the thrum of the music in my fingertips. Luca shifts almost awkwardly next to me.

"Do you want to dance?" he asks suddenly.

"With you?"

"I mean, I invited you here. Unless you have someone else with whom you'd prefer to dance."

I look him over and try to keep myself from flushing once more. His dark eyes that deeply contrast with his pale hair and skin. His angular features, his broad shoulders, his slender frame. If Venera was here, she would tell me he's attractive and that I should definitely dance with him. That I should seize the opportunity, even at the risk of making a fool of myself.

He's probably just being nice. We're friends, after all.

I take his hand anyway.

Luca is a marvelous dancer. His feet seem to guide him more than his head, as if his body remembers a song his mind doesn't. It's the sort of skill that comes from teaching, and I wonder about his life before Gomorrah, his wealthy family who all passed away. Did one of them teach him to dance?

He grabs my hands and twirls me around quicker than Blister's top, and I'm spinning too fast to remember to be sad. At one point, he dips me so low that my hair brushes the floor. He makes quite the show of waltzing me around the dance floor. I should've known he had a flair for the dramatic—he's a performer, after all.

After several songs we stumble outside, dizzy with exhilaration. The night air feels like a sigh against my skin, though the atmosphere here isn't peaceful. The Downhill paths are trafficked with wanderers, some drunk, some just looking for trouble.

We take a few steps behind the tent, halfway to Luca's caravan. And I think about how close this tent is to where Luca sleeps, which I'm suddenly very aware of. Luca takes a deep breath of the night air and stretches. He laughs, a sound I realize I've rarely heard before. "You're a terrible dancer," he says.

"Am not."

"Yes," he says, grinning his dimpled smile, "you are." He runs his fingers through his hair so it's pushed out of his face. "That was fun."

"More fun than spying and gossiping?" I say.

"Yes."

"Are you going to tell me what you were talking to that bartender about?"

"You're awfully nosy," he says. He steps closer and lowers his voice, so that no one around can hear us. I instinctively lean into him. "Why are you so curious?"

"Because I'm curious about what you do when you're not with me. Because...because I've heard rumors about you, and I—"

"What rumors?" he asks sharply. He searches my face, and I wish I knew what he was thinking. His expression is always unreadable; he may as well also be wearing a mask. What does he think about my appearance? Does it bother him like it does everyone else?

"Nothing in particular," I say.

He takes a step closer, so that we're nearly chest to chest. There's a rustle to our left from those passing us, but I'm too distracted to care.

"I know you're one of those people who never talks about themselves," I say. "I can tell. You don't. But you can tell me. We're friends, you know."

"Friends?"

"Well, I'm not just your client. We're clearly friends." I've hoped this is true, but his tone is starting to make me wonder if he feels differently.

"Because we do friend things, *clearly*. Like interrogate people and...flee from tumultuous cities."

I gesture between us. "But...I listen to you ramble. I tried your gin because you like it—even though it's disgusting. I even had Nicoleta wash the white shirt you lent me. That's something a friend would do. I say we're friends. We're...we're at a party together."

I don't know whether it's because I'm so far from my tent, from the depression that hangs over it, or if it's because I'm feeling brave or desperate for human connection. But, for whatever reason, I press my lips against his. I didn't dwell on this decision before I made it. I didn't think at all.

His lips are soft and the skin around them is smooth from a recent shave. I inhale the scent of his sandalwood soap while pressing a hand against his vest. Maybe Kahina was wrong about romance in my fortune.

He stands absolutely still, tense. His eyes are closed, but he's barely opened his mouth. Even though I've never kissed someone before, it doesn't take an expert to realize when someone isn't kissing you back. I pull away, mortified.

"I'm sorry," I say. "I'm not sure what I was thinking." Even though I know exactly what I was thinking. That maybe he saw past my deformity. That our relationship had extended beyond business.

He doesn't say anything.

"I'm sorry. I'm sorry." I have the urge to hide my face in my hands and run.

He studies the silver handle of his cane. "No. Don't apologize. I'm not usually...put in this *position*. Can we talk about this tomorrow? I need to think."

"You need to *think*?"

"*Yes*. I need to think," he says, suddenly flustered. I've never seen him so uncomfortable before. "Because I think about everything, over and over, and I think myself into things, and I think myself out of things. And I need to think. Are you...are you upset?"

"No." I cross my arms, forcing my face into neutrality. "I'm fine. It's fine. We're fine. I'll see you tomorrow."

He pauses once more to examine my face, his eyebrows knit together. Then he turns on his heels, straightens rigidly and disappears out of the green torchlight of the Downhill.

Someone giggles to my right, and I whip around, my face flushed with embarrassment. Who was watching us? Well, they certainly got quite the show. I cover my face and mask with my hands. The last thing I need is for someone to recognize me and make me the laughingstock of the whole Festival.

"Don't be rude," someone hisses. I realize that it sounds like Hawk.

"Unu? Du? Hawk?" I say.

The three of them appear in the torchlight, their eyes wide from being caught.

"How long have you been there?" I ask.

"You *kissed* him," Du says. He makes kissy noises.

"You spit in my ear," Unu mutters. He yanks on a piece of Du's hair, making him curse.

"None of you should be in the Downhill," I say. I grab Unu by his shoulder and Hawk by her wing, and then I drag them down the path with me. "You'll be grounded if Nicoleta finds out. And since you were so rudely stalking me...I might just tell her."

"We wanted to see where you go to every night!" Unu blubbers. Unu hates getting in trouble. "We...we were worried about you."

"You're a terrible liar."

I glance between the three faces. I can tell they're all embarrassed, not so much at being caught, but because I doubt they intended to witness such an awkward scene while spying. That doesn't make me any less annoyed.

"You each owe me three bags of licorice cherries," I tell them. "Unu and Du, you count as two people."

They gape at me. That's a decent amount of money. But if I tell Nicoleta, they won't be allowed out of the tent for a week. Hawk won't get to practice her fiddle with those kids in the orphan tents she visits. And Unu and Du won't be able to gamble away their allowances in the games neighborhood.

"And say you're sorry," I say.

"Sorry," they chorus.

I flick their cheeks, now more amused than angry. "Yeah, you are."

CHAPTER FIFTEEN

The next afternoon, Nicoleta is the first to rise, as usual. As per her morning ritual, she throws on clothes, climbs out of the caravan and seeks out a vendor to buy everyone breakfast. Usually, Crown cooks for all of us but not when the Festival is traveling. Instead, we subsist on fruit, sugar-coated nuts and various candies until we reach the next city.

Once Nicoleta jumps onto the road, I wrap myself in my cloak and follow her. She is already far down the path on her walk, and I run to catch up. I tap her on the shoulder, and she screams.

"Sorina! I didn't hear you. It's so early—what are you doing awake?"

"I wanted to talk to you. It's important. I need your help."

"Is this about Luca von Raske? You told me you would tell me how the investigations were going, but you haven't said a word."

"It's not about him. It's about my investigation with Villiam." As we walk, I am careful to keep my voice low as I explain what I have learned over the past two weeks to Nicoleta. "Chimal wants Hawk involved in the wedding that is happening in two weeks."

"Absolutely not. Honestly, I'm shocked that Villiam would stand by Chimal's suggestion."

"He gave me a day to think it over, at least," I say.

Nicoleta turns the copper coins over in her hand as she thinks. "They don't have any evidence to support their claims that this so-called Alliance is responsible. I'm worried that Villiam is simply pulling you into his political affairs."

"Whether or not the Alliance *is* responsible, these affairs will one day become my own. I want to help him. I just don't want Hawk involved."

Nicoleta ponders this. "Why is he so set on Hawk?"

"He said the Up-Mountainers will be prepared for normal forms of jynx-work. Obviously, Hawk's abilities are unique."

We approach a small vending cart, only now opening its shop. The vendor, a young man with a birthmark on his cheek, smiles as Nicoleta approaches. "I gave you some extra licorice cherries this time. I know how you like them."

"They're for my brothers, actually. That's very kind of you."

Nicoleta fishes in her pocket for some extra coins, but when she hands them to the man, he shakes his head. "They are a gift." He smiles a second time, and Nicoleta does her best to appear gracious. He must not know that she has never been inclined toward men.

She takes them, looking more than a little uncomfortable. I wonder if she still misses Adenneya. Their relationship ended nearly a year ago, and, unlike Venera, Nicoleta avoids all discussion of her private life. I should ask Luca how well he knows Adenneya. And if she misses Nicoleta, as well.

As we leave, I realize with mild annoyance that the man never paid me a moment of attention, not even to inquire who I am. I suddenly feel very much like the ugly sister.

"He always gives me gifts," she says. "He won't let me refuse. I'd go elsewhere, but he's the closest vendor in the neighborhood…" She shakes her head. "Petty problems. We need to figure out what to tell Villiam. I don't want Hawk learning of this. She would jump at the opportunity for a little thrill."

"We could find someone else." I think of Narayan, the so-called ghost-worker. But even if his abilities would be extremely valuable to Chimal, he's a drunk. We couldn't possibly trust him with the importance of this mission. Luca wouldn't be much use, either. Faking his death won't help us sneak in and out of the event.

"What about me?" Nicoleta asks.

I pause. Is she serious? "Chimal might be interested. But your abilities aren't that reliable."

"It's worth a shot," she says strongly.

"It's going to be dangerous. That's an awful lot to gamble on."

"I don't know whether the Alliance is responsible for what happened to Gill and Blister—I don't have any idea what happened. But I want to help you. We'll tell Chimal that this is your best offer." She holds her head higher, as if readying herself for a battle, even if she has never been in one. I don't know what Chimal will think of commanding our show manager, but I, like Nicoleta, figure it is worth a shot.

"We'll talk to them tonight."

"The medicine is working, sweetbug," Kahina says, resting her purple-veined hand against mine.

"You don't seem better," I say, swatting one of her plants out of my face.

"I'm not worse."

I avoid looking at the sickness crawling across her skin. Not worsening isn't progress. I try not to think about how we might be only stalling the inevitable, but the thought remains, whispering at the edges of my mind.

"Nicoleta tells me that you've been going out at night, that you sometimes return later than Venera," Kahina says. "Now, I love Venera dearly, but I don't like the idea—"

"I'm not partying," I say, though I don't tell her the truth, that I've been sneaking out to question suspects with Luca.

My memories of last night send flutters through my stomach. I have the urge to squeal like a child, and an equal urge to bury myself in a mountain of blankets and hide from the world. *And* to smack Hawk and Unu and Du silly. I humiliated myself. How am I going to face Luca in a few hours?

"Is the investigation with Villiam too pressing for you? I didn't want you involving yourself with his work until you were eighteen."

"Villiam *and you* decided that?" I say.

"When you were young. Villiam wanted to start you earlier, but I didn't think it was the best idea. He eventually relented."

When I was younger, I remember Kahina and Villiam consulting each other, but now they speak so rarely. It isn't so much that they had a falling out, but they no longer need to discuss me like they did when I was a child. I'm really the only thing they have in common, after all.

"If you're not partying, may I ask what you *are* doing?" Kahina says.

"I've made a friend."

"A nice friend?"

"Yes. A nice friend," I say, smirking. I begin the story with the truth, that I met Luca in Villiam's tent that night in Frice. The story quickly transforms into a jumble of lies about how I sought out Luca's show, how we spend our time learning the secrets people tell him. The words taste oddly sweet on my tongue. It's a pleasant story. Much more pleasant than the truth, that we spend our time searching for a murderer within Gomorrah. That I spend all my time finding justice for my family.

"You say Luca is an Up-Mountainer?" Kahina asks, a bit warily. "Sorina, you cannot trust new Up-Mountainers in Gomorrah. They come to take advantage of people here and then they leave."

"I don't think he has any intentions of returning home."

"They always say that, in the beginning. Until they grow tired

222

from moving city to city. Until they travel below the Mountains and are confronted with the evil of their people face-to-face."

It's true that Luca has not traveled with Gomorrah long enough for him to reach the Down-Mountains. It's difficult to picture him wearing anything but his structured, crisp Up-Mountain clothes. I smile at the image of him roaming the Forty Deserts in his velvet vest.

Nevertheless, I also cannot picture him leaving, and I don't feel like continuing this discussion with Kahina. "I was wondering if you'd do a reading for me," I say.

"About your new friend, perhaps?"

"Yes." It was only a week and a half ago that Kahina saw nothing in my romantic future, but that seems to have changed. Would she see Luca's name written in my tea leaves now?

"I'll grab the coin pot," she says, though it's across the room on one of her shelves.

"No tea leaves?"

"I have a good feeling about the coins."

"I'll get it." I stand and pluck it off the shelf. It's covered in glossy black paint and red symbols that match those on the coins inside. It rattles as I hand it to her. I love the sound of the coins, of the anticipation of what might fall out.

Kahina rubs the bottom of the jar in circles. "Your friend Luca? It's hard for me to picture him. Perhaps because I've never met him…" she says and then gives it to me hesitantly. "Picture him and give it a go. But I can't promise the reading will be detailed. He seems quite cloudy, in my mind."

I shake it a few times before turning it over. A single dark coin falls out, barely the size of my fingernail. On one side is a wolf's claw and on the other, the three streaks made from a claw tearing through earth or flesh. I don't have the gift of fortune-work, but, even to me, the coin feels cold and dead.

Kahina takes the coin hesitantly, as if not wanting to touch it. "You were thinking of Luca when you shook the jar?"

"Yes."

"There's no hint of him on this coin. I cannot see him in your fortune at all." Her face softens as she watches mine. "I'm sorry. Were you hoping I would?"

"I'm confused, I guess," I say. The kiss aside, I've been with Luca the past several nights, and I'll be with him again for many more. How could his fortune be so distant from my own?

"This coin means impending doom," she says. "The Were's Claw."

My heart stutters for a moment. "You don't think...another illusion—"

"It's difficult to say when everything is so cloudy. You know I cannot tell fortunes for your illusions. Perhaps the Were's Claw references the wars brewing around us. Or perhaps it does refer to Luca, and I'm having trouble seeing it."

I frown. If Luca is about to encounter trouble, the chances of it being associated with me are low. He spends his free time befriending assassins and the like, and I can hardly be the only person his personality has—at some point—rubbed the wrong way.

"Do you see anything more?" I ask her.

"It's unclear. Perhaps the vision is clouding because Luca is an Up-Mountainer, and the entire fate of this area balances on the edge of a knife. It feels as though Gomorrah cannot move fast enough to outrun what will happen if the Up-Mountain city-states are no longer united. It could mean a war here."

"Luca isn't mixed up in any of that."

"I'm not certain," she says. "But you should be concerned about his safety. The fortune in this coin feels very imminent. Tell him to be wary. The Were's Claw does not simply warn of danger. It promises it."

When Nicoleta and I visit Villiam that evening, Chimal and Agni also await my arrival inside his office. The atmosphere, even just upon entering the room, is tense, as though they were

224

in the middle of an argument before we arrived. Cups sit in front of each of them, filled with red tea that has long gone cold.

"Sorina," Villiam says, his gaze shifting to Nicoleta questioningly, "we're hoping you have reconsidered your decision about Hawk. The more I've spoken to Chimal, the more it seems that Hawk would prove invaluable—"

"I'm not changing my mind about that." I pull up the fourth chair at the table and take a seat. They all watch me with apprehension. "But I have a compromise. You say you need someone with abilities the Up-Mountainers won't expect. I propose Nicoleta."

"The stage manager?" Chimal furrows his thick eyebrows and inspects her skinny frame. "Forgive me, Nicoleta, but I didn't realize you had any jynx-work."

"She's stronger than ten of your men combined," I say for her.

"But not reliably so," Villiam adds.

"True, I've been known to get stage fright," she says. "But, from what I understand, this is hardly the sort of job that would elicit an audience. Besides, you wouldn't be sending a child into battle." She lifts her chin higher in self-righteousness.

"I think that is a very viable idea," Agni says.

Villiam drums his fingers on the table. "With no disrespect, Nicoleta, how can we depend on you?"

"I will show you what I can do." Nicoleta bends at the knees and picks up Villiam's chair in her right hand and lifts him with ease. He grips the edges of his seat so as not to slide off. With her left hand, she lifts Chimal, who raises his eyebrows in interest.

"I look Up-Mountainer," she says. "We may have to enter through the front door, but you could easily make me look the part. Only Sorina would need to remain hidden."

"Can you replicate the accent? Walk like a dignitary?"

"I'm a performer. Of course I can." She sets Chimal and Villiam down. The teacups rattle.

He crosses his arms. "It will be dangerous."

"I imagine so," Nicoleta says.

Their words remind me that by making this compromise to ensure Hawk remains out of the conflict, I have lost my opportunity to escape myself. I wish I was braver, but the thought of walking directly into an Up-Mountain crowd terrifies me. As much as I want to please Villiam, I'm scared. So much is depending upon me—my survival most of all.

What if the doom referenced by the Were's Claw is my own?

"It'll require preparations every day until we reach Sapris," Chimal says.

"I'll make arrangements." She leans over the table. "I know that you were more interested in what Hawk had to offer, but I believe you'll be making an altogether safer decision if I accompany Sorina. If you are dissatisfied in the future, you can change your mind. But you won't get Hawk. It's me or nothing."

Chimal purses his lips like a child who's lost his toy. "Fine. We start tomorrow."

CHAPTER SIXTEEN

An hour before Gomorrah reaches Gentoa, I slip away to the Downhill to pay Luca a visit. His caravan is empty, though nothing appears out of the ordinary. As I walk back to the Uphill, I tell myself over and over again not to worry. All of Gomorrah is about to unpack, which means people are scrambling about, preparing to set up their tents and belongings. He's probably on errands. Or at one of his tea parties with his assassin and pretty-worker friends. Not in danger, like Kahina predicted.

Still, falling asleep that night poses a challenge.

When I do drift off, I dream of Luca. I dream of him in such detail that it even embarrasses my dream self. The pout in his lips. The angular shadow cast by his brow bone. The slopes where his neck blends into chest, then shoulder. My imagination roams to other places, and I am more than a little humiliated at the level of intimacy. In the dream, I know every line of his body. I know every memory behind his brown eyes.

It all feels familiar.

I wake with Venera's knee jutting into my back, her drool

staining my pillow, the details of the dream already becoming distant and hazy. I shake Venera awake.

"Hmm?" she says, her eyes closed.

"I want to talk to you about something. A boy."

"'Rina, you know I'm always ready to talk about romance," she mumbles, "but did you have to choose ten in the morning to ask?"

"Never mind. Go back to sleep."

She rubs her eyes and sits up. "No, it's fine. I'm all ears."

"According to Kahina's fortune-work, there isn't any romance in my future."

"Fortune-workers don't know everything. Tell me about him. Why are you thinking romance?"

"Because I kissed him," I whisper.

Venera squeals and squirms closer to me. "How forward. I'm so proud."

I hush her, not wanting to wake the others. "No, you don't understand. I kissed him, but he didn't kiss me back. And now I'm worried. He wasn't in his caravan earlier. Maybe he's avoiding me. Or he got himself into trouble—"

"One concern at a time," she says. "How about you just tell me about him first?"

I squeeze my pillow to my chest. "Last week, I ran into him during one of his acts. He calls himself a poison-worker. People pay to kill him, and he always comes back alive. I watched him get beheaded."

"How romantic. Your special someone sounds like some kind of demon."

"I think he'd take that as a compliment," I say.

"You should tell him you think he has nice eyes."

"How do you know I like his eyes?"

She snorts. "Because you have a thing for eyes."

I flush slightly but can't help being a little amused at the irony. "His name is Luca. He calls himself a gossip-worker. And—"

"Wait, *that* Luca?" she says. "Luca von Raske? The Up-Mountainer? Sorina...I heard he isn't interested in...romance."

"What do you mean?"

"Well, half his friends are prettymen and prettywomen, yet he never shows interest in them. He's totally apathetic to that stuff."

"To what stuff? My stuff? Or any stuff?"

"Any stuff. Apparently."

I think back to last night, to how he tensed, to how he claimed that he needed to "think." That makes much more sense now. Maybe he's just inexperienced. Maybe he really does have to *think*.

But think about what? Our relationship? My face?

"Well...that isn't what I was expecting," I finally say.

"What did you think it was? Your appearance?"

"Of course I thought it was my appearance!"

"Has he ever commented on it? Has it come up before? You've spent a lot of time together, haven't you?"

"Yes. He's seen me without my mask on, if that's what you mean, and he didn't even flinch." I roll over, press my face into a pillow and groan.

Venera rubs my back in circles. I feel childish, but her touch is very comforting. "Well," she says at last, "you know my advice is always to go after what you want, with all the confidence you may or may not have. Because you're so powerful that you can make grown men run in fear. And you're imaginative enough to have thought up me—and I'm, I mean, perfection." She tosses her hair at this, smiling at me, and I can't help but laugh a little.

"And you're helping to hold this family together even after... everything. If he's half as intelligent as I've heard, then he recognizes all of these qualities in you."

I sink deeper into my pillow, dreading seeing him tomorrow. Even with Venera's kind words, I cannot help thinking I've ruined whatever friendship Luca and I have managed to create.

229

★ ★ ★

Our first night in Gentoa, we open the Freak Show after what seems to be years of nothing. It's strange to see each other in our usual costumes—all pink glitter and black stripes and fake smiles. Without Gill's and Blister's acts, we had to lengthen each of our own to keep the show forty minutes long. I haven't thought about what I'll add to my performance—I usually improvise, anyway.

All I think about is that Luca might be in the audience. He promised he'd come see one of our shows once we reopened. Though he probably didn't mean the first night, the thought of him watching gives me the jitters of stage fright. And I'm never nervous about performing.

"You're awfully jumpy," Venera says. Her white-painted face appears spooky in our candlelit dressing area. The effect is even more dramatic on stage.

"Luca might be here," I say.

"You have black lipstick on your teeth," Venera says, and I scramble to fix it before pulling up the curtain.

The performance does not begin well. Tree goes into a tantrum during his act, forcing me to take control before he starts tearing out his branches, which Venera works so hard to keep trim. Crown never smiles once through his entire performance. Unu and Du hiss at each other during their dance routine loud enough that the people in the first row definitely heard Unu call Du a "growth worse than toe fungus," which will earn him one of Nicoleta's tirades after the show.

During my act, I scan the rows for Luca but don't find him anywhere. My stage smile falters a bit, but I regain my composure enough to produce the illusion of a giant bird, the size of the tent and more. Every person in the room rides on its back through thunderclouds that light the sky in blinding flashes of violet. It all runs smoothly until I trip on my Strings and fall, tearing a sizable rip down the side of my cloak.

After the show, Blister isn't there to give out high fives.

"Luca wasn't there?" Venera asks from her usual perch at her vanity.

"Is that the *boy*—" Hawk starts.

I flick her on the forehead, and she clamps her mouth shut. I'm already so nervous that my stomach is cramping up. "It doesn't matter. I'm going to see him now." My words sound brave, but it's all a farce. I wipe off my rouge, and it smears pink down my cheek. I look like a clown.

"A date?"

"Sure," I lie. If you can call hunting down the murderer of your uncle and brother a date. Nothing we've done has ever been even remotely romantic. Even the party was a business rendezvous for Luca.

"Make sure he comes tomorrow night," Venera says. "So I can decide if he's worthy."

I decided to leave on my black lipstick from the show to remind Luca—without needing to tell him outright—that the Freak Show has reopened. When I enter his tent, relieved that he is indeed all in one piece, I catch him staring at my lips from where he's sitting on the corner of his bamboo floor, and he quickly shifts his gaze to his hands.

My stomach churns.

"How was reopening night?" he asks.

"Not so dandy," I say. "Tree was on his absolute *worst* behavior, and Unu and Du's language made a few audience members gasp."

"I'm sure your act was mesmerizing," he says. "And I'm sorry I missed it. I intend to catch tomorrow night's show."

I mentally decide to wear my scarlet mask, which Venera always tells me is alluring.

"Should I start wearing makeup for my show, too?" he asks.

231

"I could paint my lips blue, like a corpse." He smiles at his own morbid joke.

I wince. The memory of his head rolling off the stage to my feet now seems more like a nightmare than a dark parlor trick.

I sit beside him. As soon as I open my mouth to speak, he rises to pour himself a glass of gin. I watch—impatiently—as he finishes the whole glass.

"I've been thinking," he says.

"Is that a good thing? You told me you drink gin to make yourself nicer."

He white-knuckles his glass. "Have you heard what people say about me?"

"I don't know what you're talking about," I lie.

"You're missing eyes, Sorina, not ears."

I cross my arms. Yes, I've heard the rumors—from both Nicoleta *and* Venera now—but I don't know what to think of them. If I even believe them. "Is there something you want to tell me? Because I'd rather hear it from you." I probably don't have any right making demands of him, but I really want to hear what he has to say.

"As I told you, I've never been in this position."

"What position?" I snap. *I* initiated the kiss. *I'm* the one who feels completely mortified. What position could he possibly be talking about?

"*This.*" He gestures wildly between the two of us. "I spend my free time investigating people, studying people. Every single aspect of their lives. And half of my information comes from prettyworkers. I know people's desires and the most intimate details of their relationships. And I've never understood them. I've never wanted or needed *that* in my life."

"And what is *that*?" I ask.

"The thing you're asking for. The thing everyone expects."

"I'm not asking for anything." I've never seen Luca get this worked up. Not about assassins, not during the havoc in Cartona...but apparently one kiss is enough to cause a breakdown.

This is altogether mortifying. I wish I hadn't kissed him at all.

"You're asking for things that I can't give you," he says. "I can't promise to give you everything that you want."

So Venera was right. Luca isn't interested in any sort of romantic relationship. But then why doesn't he just come out and say that?

"Well, what do *you* want?" I ask.

"Things I never thought I would." He runs his hand through his hair. "But, mostly, time."

My chest lifts from a tug on my single strand of hope. "I can give you time."

"Thank you." He takes a seat at the table. "You don't have to keep sitting on my floor." He holds out his hand, and I grab it and slide into the opposite seat. When I envisioned this conversation in my head, this is not how I pictured it—Luca, across the table, fidgeting in his chair and looking everywhere but at me. We sit at a respectable distance apart, our postures rigid. Like a business meeting.

"Is your family all unpacked?" he asks.

So this is what we're doing. Small talk. "Yes. And the show was decent, and how about this weather?" I smirk. "If we're going to change the subject, I actually have something I want to discuss with you."

"Go ahead." He refills his glass of gin. "Do you want some?"

"No. That stuff is vile," I say. "Yesterday, I visited a fortune-worker. And she told me to warn you."

"I don't put a lot of stock in fortune-workers."

"She's a good one. I've known her for a long time—"

"I know whom you're referring to," he says. "Kahina. The one with the snaking sickness."

"I can't decide if I prefer it when you pretend you don't know everything about my life, or if it's convenient that you do."

"I'll admit that I didn't know all of this when I first met you. I *may* have asked around after we started working together."

"I'd rather you not pretend to be all-knowing."

"There's little fun in that. So, tell me about this warning," he says, sounding bored.

"It was imminent doom."

"Naturally."

"You should take these things at least somewhat seriously," I say. "Since, you know, I wouldn't like to see you meet imminent doom."

"There's a fortune-worker several tents down who drops to his knees whenever I pass and foretells of my upcoming demise," Luca says. "As he's been doing for about three months now, this Saturday. Forgive me if I'm not immediately convinced."

"You're impossible," I say.

"So said my mother, many times. Then I ran away to join the circus. And you're not half as scary as her." He takes a swig of his gin. "Well, I've spent most of today and yesterday interrogating the rest of the people in Gomorrah with strange abilities."

"You questioned them without me?"

"Yes. You were getting too personal with it. Too sensitive."

"And did you let them all go after hearing their made-up logic?"

He leans his head back, as if asking the heavens why he has to tolerate someone as annoying as me. Well, he doesn't. He doesn't have to help me if I'm tormenting him too much with my concern. I can't help it if I can't detach myself from what we're doing—we're searching for whoever murdered members of my family. I'm not sorry for caring. And I'm not weak for doing so.

"I thought we were going about this as a team," I say. "Partners."

"I felt it was more efficient to go alone. You're busy with Villiam, anyway."

"Is this about efficiency or you being uncomfortable? Because it's pretty shitty and high-handed of you to do all of this without me. This isn't a game. I'm trying to protect my family."

"Which is why you'll want to hear out my theory," he says calmly.

"No. I want to hear about the other people you talked to."

"That's not necessary—"

"It is if you'd like me to keep my composure."

He sighs and twirls his finger around the rim of his glass. "No one was worthy of note. There was a man who could perfectly imitate anyone's voice—to be honest, I'm not entirely certain that's actually jynx-work. A woman who can turn gold into lead but not back. Not particularly useful. Another man—he was more interesting—had two types of jynx-work. Fire-work and charm-work. He's the one who makes the torches in Gomorrah glow white and green—in regular charm-work, fire is not considered an object and it can't be manipulated. He was not someone who could kill an illusion, but we had a good conversation. He's missing an arm, his left arm. Yet he can pick things up if they're close by. They look like they're floating. It's very bizarre. He calls it a phantom limb."

"You said he had two types of jynx-work?" I say.

"Yes."

"Tuyet had two types. She's missing her heart, yet her blood pumps. He's missing an arm, yet it's as if he has one. And I'm missing eyes…yet I see."

Luca considers this. "I've never heard anything to suggest having two types of jynx-work alters your body in such a way. But it's possible. That amount of magic could have physical repercussions."

Do I have two types of jynx-work? I would know if I did, wouldn't I? I can't see the future. I can't bless charms.

But maybe this is the missing piece of my jynx-work. In those books I borrowed from Villiam, nothing I read about illusion-work mentioned anything like my family. Maybe they aren't proper illusions at all.

I mention this theory to Luca. "And if they're not illusions," I say, "then what if we're going about this the wrong way? What if it doesn't take any special ability to kill them? The killer could be *anyone*."

I have the urge to kick something. And then cry, but kicking something would be less embarrassing. "One moment," I say, then step outside his tent and, as hard as I can, kick Luca's Gossip-Worker sign. It flies across the air and lands in the grass with a satisfying thump.

Luca stands at the entrance of his tent. "Feel better?"

"Not really," I say. "Because all the work we've been doing up to this point might have been pointless. And because maybe anyone can kill the illusions, which means our suspect list has grown from eight to every person in Gomorrah."

"First of all, it wasn't pointless," he says. "We wouldn't have come up with this theory in the first place without meeting Tuyet and the other suspects. And, no, not every person is automatically a suspect. Not every person has a motive." He grabs my shoulders and turns me to face him. I'm so startled by his touch that I freeze. The last time we were this close, I kissed him.

"You need to take deep breaths and calm yourself."

"Right," I squeak. I'm not taking deep breaths. I'm barely breathing at all. The air in the Downhill is too sweet, too smoky and Luca's sandalwood smell makes me a little light-headed. "Do you think I'm right about this? About my jynx-work?"

"I think you might be. It hadn't even occurred to me until now, but I see the sense in it." He pauses. "I feel I really should tell you about *my* theory now."

"Go ahead," I say dismissively. I'm still caught up in my potential discovery.

"We know that Gill died in Frice, and Blister died in Cartona. Now we've reached a third city, and if the killer is operating under some sort of pattern, he may strike again extremely soon. I think you need to protect the illusions while we're in Gentoa."

My stomach sinks. "The best way to protect them is to make them disappear. I can do that, but it's difficult. They reappear the moment I break my concentration. Including while I'm sleeping."

"We're going to be in Gentoa for a week and a half," he says. "You can't keep that up."

A shiver runs down my spine that has nothing to do with the night breeze. He's right. There's no way I can handle that for so long. "They'll also have to be out during the Freak Show. And…this will involve telling them that I think they're in danger. I never make them disappear, especially not all at once."

That won't go over well. Crown has still refused to consider Blister's death as anything more than an accident. Hawk and Unu and Du will be terrified at the idea of being targeted. Tree will be in a constant state of panic, which is dangerous for everyone around him.

"I don't know how I'm going to do this," I say. "I can't just not sleep for eleven days."

"Why don't you just command the guard? You're the proprietor's daughter."

"Villiam doesn't know I'm working with you."

"Why haven't you told him?"

"I… I don't know. It didn't come up at first, and now I feel like I've been lying to him." Now that I know Villiam's, Agni's and Chimal's true feelings regarding those born in the Up-Mountains, I'm even more reluctant to reveal my relationship with Luca to my father. I don't want him to feel betrayed. "I may be able to ask the guard tomorrow. We're just arriving in Gentoa. I can say the new city is making my family anxious. But I don't want to wake them now and make them suspicious. It's already so late."

A man approaches us carrying hundreds of cheap hookah pipes for sale. I'm about to snap at him—simply to snap at *any-*

one—when Luca pleasantly waves him away. I wish I could be so cordial.

I need to lie down and take deep breaths. I need a glass of water. I need fresh air not polluted with ancient smoke.

"Jiafu's cronies could be paid as bodyguards," Luca says.

"Jiafu and I aren't on the best of terms at the moment." Considering he pulled a knife on me last time I saw him.

"That doesn't matter," he says. "I know what will convince him. You and I can go visit him tonight."

He leans down and whispers a secret into my ear.

Younger brother; full of energy; will drive Gill bonkers; plays drums for show.

CUT IN HALF

SECOND, SEPARATELY
SENTIENT HEAD,
BUT SINGLE SPINAL COLUMN.

NOT IDENTICAL,

PRONE TO TANTRUMS.

REGULARLY BICKER AMONG
THEMSELVES; FIGHT FOR
CONTROL OVER THEIR SHARED
LIMBS; EASILY DISTRACTED.

CHAPTER SEVENTEEN

As predicted, Jiafu isn't happy to see me waiting for him at his caravan with Luca. His eyes bulge, and he walks toward us, stumbling in a zigzag pattern with the smell of the tavern on his breath.

"I told you not to show your freak face here again," he spits out.

"Nice to see you, too, cousin," I say. "This is Luca."

Luca leans lazily against his walking stick, but I can tell he's upset because of how tightly he grips it. He examines Jiafu the way a tarantula might inspect a fly already caught in its web. Even though Luca's skill with fighting begins and ends with him getting killed, he has managed to appear intimidating without needing to speak a word.

"Kudos to you, freak, for managing to find someone even freakier than you are. Yeah, I found out who he is," Jiafu says, as I startle slightly. "You don't seem the type to hang out with an Up-Mountainer. What would Villiam have to say?"

I expect Luca to react to the accusation, but his face remains impassive.

"I have a favor to ask of you," I say.

"Like hell I'd do anything for you."

"Well, it's not exactly a favor. More like blackmail."

Jiafu raises his eyebrows. "If you turn me in, we both go down."

"Oh, I'm not talking about that," I say lightly. "I'm talking about the boy who works at the Menagerie. The boy named Zhihao."

He's been very careful, Luca told me earlier. *His half brother, Zhihao, works cleaning out the manure in the Menagerie, and he lives in one of the orphan tents in the Uphill. He's ten years old and probably the only person who matters to Jiafu. Jiafu won't want anyone finding out about him, because anyone associated with someone in Jiafu's business could be in danger.*

Jiafu stiffens as if something has grasped his shadow. "I don't know who you're talking about."

"Ten years old," I say. "You have the same mother, don't you?"

I told Luca that, as much as I dislike Jiafu, I wasn't prepared to expose his ten-year-old brother and thus put a kid in danger. But Luca assured me it wouldn't come to that. Hopefully Jiafu won't figure out that this is all an empty threat.

"We can talk inside," he grunts and then slides his key into the door of his black caravan. Luca and I climb inside. It still smells of burnt coffee and feet.

Why can't Jiafu just work a safer job if he cared about his brother so much? I asked Luca.

Because, he said, *he loves his job. He lives for the danger of it.*

"How did you find out about Zhihao?" Jiafu asks once he shuts the door. "He hasn't been telling people, has he?"

"It doesn't matter how we found out," I say. "I have a favor to ask you. I need some bodyguards tonight."

"Are you paying me?"

"No."

"Then how am I supposed to pay for men?"

"I don't know. You pay them," I say. "I definitely don't have any money at the moment. I may be able to get you some later but no more than ten gold pieces."

"That's not enough."

"It's all I've got."

He narrows his eyes. "What do you need bodyguards for?"

"Because someone has been killing my illusions. Two are already dead," I say.

"I heard. How do you kill illusions?"

I glance at Luca. Should we be telling Jiafu this much? I wish Luca would take over—he always chooses his words better than I do. But he only nods for me to continue. "We're not sure," I say, "but we're starting to suspect that it's the same way you could kill anyone else."

"I can't get any men so soon. It's already so early. I can give you some starting tomorrow...for the ten pieces."

"I need them today."

"I don't know what to tell you."

When I sleep, the illusions will be vulnerable. But it's only for one day. I don't have to sleep. Tomorrow, I can get the guard. I'll stay up all day and keep them locked away, protected, in my head. I know this plan is working under the assumption that the killer is operating with the pattern of one illusion per city—when that may not be the case—but if there's any chance my family is in danger, I need to protect them.

"Thanks, anyway. Sorry to bother you."

"Don't tell anyone about Zhihao," he says and then jabs his finger into Luca's chest. "Not a word."

We climb down from the caravan into the darkness of the Downhill. There are three hours left until sunrise, which gives me just enough time to gather up the illusions, explain what's happening and brace myself for staying up all night.

"So your plan is to keep yourself awake all day, alone in your tent?" Luca asks.

"Yes."

"That's ridiculous. You could easily fall asleep," he says. "I'll stay up with you."

"At my tent?"

"That's where the illusions are, is it not?" He bites his lip and digs his walking stick into the dirt. "Besides, I know you have questions to ask me. I can see it all over your face."

"I'm wearing a mask."

"Yet I *still* find you rather easy to read."

I consider this. I *do* have questions to ask Luca, about his life before Gomorrah and why Nicoleta thinks he's dangerous. Not to mention continuing our conversation from earlier. We've moved rather quickly from Luca needing time to him staying with me, alone, all day.

Regardless of how awkward that might become, the idea of staying up all morning in our tent by myself, waiting for the killer to pay a visit, sounds terrifying. Even if Luca is a better target than a swordsman, just having another person there will reassure me.

"Thank you," I say. "You don't mind skipping sleep this morning?"

He shrugs. "I'm not from Gomorrah. I'm still somewhat accustomed to staying awake while there's sunlight."

The walk to my tent is quiet, and my head swarms with dozens of different thoughts and emotions. Making the illusions disappear requires me to tell them that I think they're in danger. That Blister was definitely murdered.

Then I can't help but imagine what follows, after Luca and I are alone. I think back to his words earlier, that he wants things with me he never thought he would want. I want to be patient. I want to give him the time he needs. But our entire conversation was so vague, and I'd still like some more concrete answers.

I'd like to know if he thinks of me the way I think of him, even if that means telling me with words rather than showing me through action.

When we reach my tent, everyone is home except Venera, who Hawk said dressed for a good time and left three hours ago. Usually she returns home by sunrise.

The rest of us gather together in the tent, including Luca, who sits off to the side, stiff with all the eyes on him. With his expensive clothes and pale features, he looks like an audience member we've allowed backstage.

"This is awfully formal to be meeting some boy," Hawk says. "Do you really like him or something?"

"Um, this isn't about that," I say, reddening. "It's about Gill and Blister."

The room sobers immediately. Nicoleta peers up at me with round, warning eyes. I know this might start a panic, but I can't help that. The best way to protect everyone is to make them disappear, and, for that, they need to be informed so they won't be constantly fighting me to get out.

"I've been working with Luca for a while, trying to figure out how Gill and Blister died, as well as with Villiam," I say. "Because of some things we've discovered, we think it'd be best if, while in Gentoa, we keep you protected. And the best way to protect everyone is to keep you locked in my head."

"The entire time we're *here*?" Hawk screeches. "I have things to do."

"Like what?" Du says.

"*Things.*"

"What is significant about being in Gentoa?" Nicoleta asks.

"Well, Gill died in Frice, and Blister died in Cartona," I say, stumbling over my words. I wish I could explain things as logically as Luca. "If there *is* a pattern of some sort, we want to take precautions. It's better safe than—"

"So you're saying Blister was murdered?" Unu nearly wails. "You're saying there's someone after us?"

"I'm not sure," I lie. "But it's still better to be safe, isn't it? You'll be out for the shows, and during the morning so you can sleep. Other than tonight, anyway."

"You can't just lock us up for everything but our performances," Hawk snaps.

"I'd like everything to at least *appear* normal. And it won't be like that. After tonight, you'll be under the watch of the guard. Your time locked up will be minimal."

"Normal is Unu and Du playing the drums until sunrise. Normal is Venera yelling at me while trying to comb my hair. Normal is chaos," Hawk says. "Everyone will notice if we're being quiet."

"Everyone would probably be grateful," Nicoleta mutters.

"You're not going to let her do this, right?" Unu asks Nicoleta, the unofficial mother of the group. You'd think it would have defaulted to Crown because of his age, but this entire time, all he has done is keep his head down.

"I think Sorina's right. Better safe than sorry," she says. "How would we all feel if we woke up tomorrow morning and found you two cut right down the middle?" She means it as a joke, but the morbidity does not suit the situation. Unu pales.

"At least I'd be free of him," Du grumbles, earning a slap in the face from Unu.

"Then it's settled," I say. "While we're in Gentoa, you all get some extra sleep."

One by one, I concentrate on them disappearing. To accomplish this, I have to locate each of the illusions' Strings, the thin bonds between them and my mind. I untangle one illusion's Strings from the jumble and then reel them in like a fisherman with a fresh catch. The Strings and the illusion go into a Trunk, a mental compartment where they're safe, which makes their physical form disappear. They each vanish one at a time, leaving the room empty, except for me and Luca. My head feels heavier, and there is a constant knocking on each of their Trunks like the pounding of several headaches.

"This is going to be exhausting," I say. And Venera isn't even here yet.

"I have faith in you," Luca says.

It's strange to see him sitting at our table, where Unu and Du's lucky coins are spread out across everything, including dirty plates and brushes for stage makeup. "Do you want something to eat? We have kettle corn and..." I glance into our food trunk. "Kettle corn." Guess Crown hasn't been feeling up to cooking or buying more food since we've gotten to Gentoa.

"Go right ahead," he says. I fill up a bowl and place it on the table.

"I'm sorry I don't have any gin."

He smiles. "I'll manage."

"Is this the part where I get to ask you questions? Where I get to find out the gossip-worker's secrets?"

"I've made up my mind to tell you anything you ask." His tone is light, but the expression in his eyes shows the weightiness of this statement.

I blush and look down. "You don't have to share anything."

"No. I want to," he says. "I've been living in Gomorrah for almost a year now, collecting other people's secrets, and not once have I told anyone mine. I'm not usually comfortable enough to do so."

"I make you feel comfortable?" I'm absurdly pleased at the thought but try not to show it.

"Yes." He pauses. "And no."

I sigh. "Before you start getting vague and confusing again, I'm just going to ask my two questions," I say. He nods. "What was your life like before Gomorrah?"

I expect him to wait a moment before launching into his story, but he doesn't hesitate. He wasn't kidding about telling me everything. He does, however, talk at his usual breakneck pace that's difficult to follow. I wonder if he's been practicing this speech.

"My life before Gomorrah seems so long ago that it's almost hazy. I lived in a small city known as Raske, and my family was the wealthiest in the town. We owned the clock tower, the church beneath it and the library. My father was an engineer, and he taught me about clockwork, about everything behind the face that makes a clock tick. He had—and I have—a similar approach to people. He had to figure out everything beneath someone's surface before he felt comfortable enough to trust them."

My hand is lying palm up on the table between us, an invitation to hold it, if he wanted. An invitation that feels terribly dangerous. At first, I'm not sure if he hasn't noticed it or is ignoring it, but then, to my surprise, he slides his hand into mine. The rushed way he does it doesn't feel natural—it feels forced— but his smile looks genuine.

He pulls out his pocket watch. "This used to be my father's." He turns it over in his hand wistfully. "My father knew I was a jynx-worker for years. I hurt myself badly once when I was young but healed instantly. He wasn't a particularly religious man, not like my mother and the rest of the town. But it didn't occur to him then it was jynx-work. He just thought I was blessed." Luca laughs. "Gomorrah visited my town once when I was ten, and I remember thinking then how much the people fascinated me. The jynx-work that my town refused to acknowledge because it was unordinary. And I started to wonder if that's what I really was—a jynx-worker. Or a devil-worker, as my town would say.

"My family lived on an estate outside of town, and when I was seventeen, it was struck by lightning and burned to the ground, with my entire family and all of our servants inside."

He squeezes my hand. I squeeze back.

"Naturally, I survived. With no burns or injuries, despite

being dug out of the rubble. The rumors spread around town that I had come back from the dead, that I'd made a pact with the devil. So I grabbed what remained of my family's possessions in our clock tower and fled. I found Gomorrah several weeks later. Bought a caravan. Conjured a performance. And figured out a way to make money to survive."

"You could have chosen dozens of different jobs," I say. "You're brilliant. Villiam would hire you to help him run Gomorrah. You could help with—"

"I asked him, when I joined," he says. "I don't know whether it's because I'm an Up-Mountainer or if he genuinely disliked me, but the only space he would sell me was in the far corner of the Downhill where I now reside."

"I could talk to him." Even if I have no idea what I would say.

"I like my show, believe it or not. I like the thrill of it."

"The thrill of dying?"

"The thrill of horrifying my audience. The thrill of being a freak."

Normally the word would bother me but not from him. He went from being an outcast in his city for his jynx-work to becoming a sort of outcast here because he's not as lustful for Gomorrah's sexual pleasures as others. *Freak* may be the only word to describe a misfit in an entire city's worth of misfits.

There are footsteps outside the tent. I instinctively lean myself closer to him. "I wonder if that's Venera." It's past sunrise. She should be back by now. Venera out, alone, partying in the Downhill has never been a safe endeavor. But now, if there really is a pattern to these killings, she could be an easy target.

The footsteps disappear down the path.

"I could go find her," Luca says. "But I also don't want to leave you here alone."

"I'd rather you didn't, but...what if she's—"

"I'm sure she's fine," he says.

"You don't know that."

"No, I don't, but I don't think getting worked up is going to solve anything." He scoots closer toward me until our shoulders touch. I work up the nerve to lean my head into the curve where his neck meets his shoulder, and I wonder how many times a sword has sliced through this area to decapitate him. Surprisingly, he doesn't tense at my touch, and he doesn't let go of my hand.

"Do you have any other questions?" he asks.

"Only one." I'll give Venera a few more minutes before my worry grows. "Why does Nicoleta think you're dangerous?"

He laughs. "Probably because I know a lot of assassins. That's not much of a stretch. Dangerous by association."

"Then what were you talking to the bartender about last night?"

"He wanted me to track down a woman he met once."

"You're joking."

"I'm entirely serious," he says. "He gave me her description, and I found her. She's a shadow-worker, lives in the Uphill, helps manage an orphan tent. Quite personable. Too good for that man." Even though I'm not looking at him, my head is against his shoulder, and I can feel his cheeks move into a grin. "I could tell you a lot about Gomorrah's estranged lovers and family drama."

"How interesting."

"I think it is. I've always found people's romantic lives rather baffling. Like everyone was gushing about a song that I've never been able to hear."

"You've never felt interested in…anyone?" I ask.

"Not really. Nothing beyond a passing thought. Then again, I wasn't close with that many people as a child. And I don't have any acquaintances whom I could truthfully call a friend."

I smirk. "Not even Ed, the Leather Viper?"

"We occasionally have tea, but I've found most people I meet with prefer to tell me their problems simply because no one else will listen or no one else cares. They tend not to reciprocate. Ed normally rambles on about a man he's in love with who barely knows his name."

It would be difficult, in my opinion, to not notice someone who goes by the name "The Leather Viper."

"I guess I don't just look at someone and think...attraction," Luca says. "It takes, I don't know... I have to care about the person first." His gaze flickers to me, and I'm amused to see that his cheeks are red. He clears his throat. "That's probably everything important about me that you didn't know. Unless you have further questions."

"No. I'm good."

He moves his thumb in circles on the inside of my palm. "Is there anything else we can do to pass the time until Venera gets back? Now that I feel so very exposed?"

I rack my brain for something to do. What does my family do for fun? Mainly bicker with each other and complain about there not being enough food around. Or practice our acts. Lucky coins is more of a fierce competition than simply *fun*.

"I can show you my bug collection," I say.

"Is that a euphemism?"

"I have over two hundred different species from all over the world. Including a Giamese tortoiseshell moth."

"You have me convinced. A 'Giamese tortoiseshell moth,'" he says. "Am I supposed to have heard of that?"

"It's very rare. Legends say it can produce an elixir of youth from its venom. That isn't true, but the venom does make the skin puffy and hard. Ladies sometimes put it around their eyes to get rid of wrinkles."

I stand up and lead him to my section of the tent, made up of my bed, some clothes strewn about—both mine and Venera's—and the chests full of my bugs. Luca glances around, particularly at my bed.

"Are you *positive* 'bug collection' isn't a euphemism?"

"I'm starting to think you want it to be."

"Hey, I'm quite interested in this moth. I swear."

I lift open the first trunk and find the Giamese tortoiseshell moth on the top.

Luca peers into my crate of preserved insects. "I thought most girls collected jewelry." He narrows his eyes. "Did that one just move?"

"Of course not. They're frozen," I say, though there have been times when I swear I've seen some move, as well. "I like bugs because you can learn something different about each one you have, and they're specific to different regions—"

"Like, I don't know, dried flowers, perhaps—"

"I can remember each city we've visited because of an insect I've found while there."

"You are a complete hypocrite," he says.

"What are you talking about?"

"You yell at *me* for killing cockroaches for my performance, and yet you sleep next to a giant chest full of dead bug carcasses that you keep for your own viewing enjoyment."

"They're not dead," I say. "They're petrified. They never felt a thing."

"Nor will they ever again. So much for the nectar they could've eaten or the wind they could've felt between their little wings—"

There are footsteps in the main part of the tent. My heart leaps into my throat. Is it Venera, or someone else?

Luca puts his fingers over his lips and then peeks his head out of my room.

Venera shrieks.

"There's no need to scream," he says. "Honestly, you're the one wearing green lipstick."

"You must be Luca." Venera pushes aside the tent flap and peers in. "Where is everyone?" Her gaze falls to the moth in my hand. "And, really, Sorina, there are more creative things you could be showing off back here besides your bugs."

"The Giamese tortoiseshell moth is quite a sight," Luca says.

She smirks. "I'm sure it is. Now, where is everyone else?"

"We had a family meeting. While in Gentoa, everyone is getting locked up in here." I tap my forehead. "Except for shows. For protection."

"You're joking, right?"

"Just trying to take precautions."

"And who's going to protect you? Isn't this the one whose head you caught rolling off a stage?"

"So she's told you about me," Luca says, clearly amused.

"Just for tonight," I say. "I have bodyguards coming tomorrow and for the rest of the time in Gentoa."

"I have a *life*, Sorina," she says.

"I realize that."

"I don't think there's anyone after us."

"It's better to be safe."

She pouts her green-painted lips. "But the *parties*."

"There'll be parties when we get to Sapris."

"*Beach parties—*"

"Oh, just give it up," I say. Before she can whine more, I hoist her Strings into my mental Trunk and lock it. Her defeated groan lingers in the air for a moment before she is entirely gone. "She's such a baby."

"It's better that she's safe," he says. "You've made the right decision, keeping them locked away while in Gentoa."

"You think so? I feel like I'm only going to start a panic. And I'm worried about Crown, who's been coping with Blister's death by convincing himself it was an accident," I say. "After all this time looking for the killer, I feel like we haven't made any progress. I feel like I haven't protected my family at all."

"Sorina," he says, and the force in his voice quiets me. "You have gone above and beyond to protect them. I promise that the two of us will find out who is responsible. I will do anything I possibly can to help you. I don't... I don't know your family very well, but I care about you quite a bit."

My heart skips a beat. "I care about you 'quite a bit,' too," I say, imitating the posh way he speaks.

I don't know which one of us moved first, or if I ever made the decision to move at all. One moment, we were at least a stride apart, and then the next, my chest is pressed against his and his arms are around my waist, our lips meeting with urgency.

This isn't anything like the last time we kissed, when I was the only one involved. Luca's mouth opens and his hands press hard into my back. He seems to want this as much as I do.

I squeeze the Giamese tortoiseshell moth vial in my hand, unwilling to drop it, but not knowing what to do with it. After a few minutes, when Luca makes it clear from his tugging on my hand that he wants to move to the floor, I pause for a moment to return the precious insect to the chest.

"It's an interesting bug," Luca says.

"You're lying," I say, kneeling beside him. "You don't think it's interesting."

"I think you're interesting."

I pull him closer to me by his vest. His poison vials jingle. In my head, the knocking on the Trunks of the illusions grows louder. My head aches, but I ignore it. "You're making it difficult to concentrate," I say, kissing him again.

"Let me know when you want to stop, then," he says, his lips moving to my neck.

"Are we moving too fast?" I ask suddenly.

The knocking sharpens.

His fingers trace their way down my back. "Maybe. This is all rather new territory." When I begin to pull away, he adds, "But I'm all right with exploring for a few more minutes."

He reaches up and unties the back of my mask and slips it off. While I frequently remove my mask around my family, this feels more intimate than if he lifted off my shirt. He presses our foreheads together, and we're both warm and sweating in the September heat.

I slip his vest off his shoulders and inch myself closer to him. There seems to be no space left between us.

My head pounds harder, and I wince.

"Are you all right?" he asks.

"It's difficult to concentrate while we're doing this," I say.

"Do you want to stop?"

"No, but we probably should." I collapse next to him and adjust myself so that my head rests against his chest. I can hear the rapid *thump thump thump* of his heart.

"You're not going to fall asleep, are you? Lying like that?" he asks.

As much as I'd like to continue lying against his chest, he's right. It's entirely too comfortable, and I'd drift off in minutes. The Trunks would fly open. I sit up and push my hair out of my face. "You're right."

"There are about ten hours until the Freak Show," he says. "Another six before people are up and moving about. So we have time for some of *my* questions."

"You have questions for me? I thought you already knew everything about me."

"I'm deeply, passionately curious," he says, smiling in a way that tells me he's lying, "about your bug collection. And I'd love for you to go through each one and tell me all about them."

I rub my aching forehead and laugh. "I thought you'd never ask."

CHAPTER EIGHTEEN

We survive the first night in Gentoa. The following afternoon, Nicoleta and I walk to the Downhill together. We're mostly silent until we pass the twin obelisks. I'm exhausted, and a little loopy from it. I munch on kettle corn for the much-needed sugar.

Nicoleta keeps her head high and her walk brisk. A slight smile plays at the corner of her lips. If I didn't know Nicoleta better, I'd say she was excited. I've forgotten about her wild side over the past year.

Gentoa is a coastal city, with long stretches of white, rocky beaches and salt winds that tussle my hair. It's beautiful. Even the weather is perfection, I realize, as we pass through Gomorrah's smoke into clean air and blue skies.

One hundred yards behind Gomorrah, a single tent is situated on the dunes.

"Why don't you want Villiam to know that you're working with Luca?" Nicoleta asks. "I don't think it's wise to keep that from him. It seems awfully suspicious. I can't see him being an overly protective father type."

"It's not about that," I say. "I was going to tell him, but then I decided I was just going to tell Luca to call it quits, so I kept quiet. Then Luca and I kept working together. Then I found out how much Villiam and Chimal distrust people who weren't born in Gomorrah." That came out as a mess. The whole situation is a mess.

"I just don't want to make him angry," I finish.

"What are you doing with Luca that's different from your investigation with Villiam?"

"Luca believes the killer is within Gomorrah. Not related to the Alliance."

"Then it seems like Luca's theory provides better means but less motive."

Nicoleta has voiced exactly what I have been struggling to put into words. "Exactly. I don't know which theory I believe more," I say. "When I'm with Villiam, I agree with him. And then the opposite is true when I'm with Luca. I'm easily persuaded, I suppose." I wait for Nicoleta to voice her own opinion, but she doesn't. "Do you think I should be working with Luca?"

"I think both theories are valid, and I also think you would wound Villiam by telling him now. Temporarily keeping Luca a secret is not a terrible idea."

"You've never been an advocate of sneaking around."

"The past few weeks have been terrible. I think we've all changed our tunes a bit."

As we approach the tent, the guards outside come into view. They're dressed all in black, with swords tucked into their sheaths. Menacing, tall and muscular—these are the men I want protecting my family while I cannot.

Inside, we find Chimal, Agni and a few other men I don't recognize. It seems my father has yet to arrive—probably because

---

he insisted on walking by himself this time. Chimal straightens when he sees us and leaves his conversation with Agni.

"Sorina, Nicoleta, these are the men and women who will be assisting you next week." Chimal introduces each of the individuals, but I forget their names almost immediately after he says them. There is a woman who is an expert in Up-Mountain politicians. She'll be able to give us information on the people we might encounter. There's also an apothecary to supply us with the drugs we'll use to knock out the Alliance's leader.

"Agni will be helping, as well," Chimal says. "We're hoping to take advantage of his fire-work to serve as a minor distraction to any officials there."

Even though we've been planning this for several days now, it hasn't felt real until this moment, when the men and women who will be working with us stand before me. Nicoleta and I are going to kidnap an Up-Mountain archduke. I shiver at the idea of returning to an Up-Mountain city, considering what happened while Luca and I were in Cartona. If all goes well, no Up-Mountainers will notice me. I will be merely a moth. But I've never needed to maintain an illusion for so long under pressure.

Then there is the question of whether Nicoleta's abilities will pull through. We're all counting on her.

Chimal rests his hand on my shoulder. "Sorina, why don't you go with Villiam and practice maintaining your illusion-work? I know you said you're concerned about how long you can maintain the image of the moth. We want to have a good sense of your limit."

I whip around to face my father, who stands in the doorway leaning on his crutches. Despite his injury, his strong posture and confident smile make it clear that he's in his element. He's not simply a proprietor. He's a general.

Before I leave with him, I turn to Chimal. "I want to ask something of you," I say.

"Anything," he answers.

"My family is restless now that we have arrived at a new city, as new cities have lately brought tragedy. I would appreciate it if you could spare a few members of your guard to watch over them. More than there already are."

"Of course. We have a few men stationed in your neighborhood, but I can absolutely add more. Escorts, too."

"Thank you."

I follow Villiam outside, onto the uneven ground of the dunes. I feel almost naked being out on the beach, unprotected by Gomorrah's smoke. Anyone traveling from far away would spot us as two dark flecks on the shoreline.

"Is it safe to be out here, in the open?" I ask him.

"No one will notice one man walking along the beach."

"There are two of us."

"That person would have to have spectacular vision to notice a moth from such a distance."

I take that as my cue to concentrate on my illusion. I've used this image so many times that it appears naturally, the way muscles remember repetitive motions. The two of us walk closer to the water's edge. It froths white along the sand and shards of broken shells. What a peaceful spot to plot a battle.

"Your footprints are showing, Sorina," Villiam says.

"The wedding will take place in a church, won't it?" I ask. "I won't need to worry about sand."

"It's not about that. It's about the concentration. Any jynx-worker improves through practice."

I begrudgingly cast illusions to cover my footprints. As we walk, the images become more difficult to conceal. The weight of the jynx-work makes my thoughts trip, as if I'm drunk.

Within moments, my exhaustion takes a toll on the illusion. The fluttering of the moth's wings fades, and gradually, more details disappear. The smell of me—smoke, like everyone in Gomorrah—returns.

"I can see your silhouette. It's barely been three minutes," Villiam says. "That's unlike you."

"I slept terribly last night. It's difficult to focus."

"If there has ever been a time to focus, now is it."

"I know. I'm sorry."

He shakes his head and then kisses my forehead. I wait a moment in shame under his questioning gaze. Then, to my surprise, he says, "It's fine. I am more concerned about Nicoleta than you, my dear. You're always spectacular. A born performer. Why don't you go home and sleep?"

"Will Chimal mind?"

"Chimal is focused on Nicoleta. He probably won't notice." As I turn to leave, he adds, "But, Sorina, you must be more prepared tomorrow. Half-heartedness simply won't do."

Later that day, fresh from ten hours of sleep—thanks to the new guards stationed around our tent—I slip down my neighborhood's central path to see our local charm-worker, Agatha. In my pocket, a jar with holes the size of needle pricks contains a rare northern cicada, which I found crawling over my pillow this morning, as if it were a present. I haven't personally added a new bug to my collection in a while. It feels comfortingly normal.

Agatha is setting up her stand of charms and trinkets. Most of them are hand-crafted jewelry with charmed stones, some for peace of mind, some for strength or power or meditation. I scan the bracelets for one Venera, or even Nicoleta, might like.

"Sorina," she says. She appears not a day over thirty due to one of her beauty charms, yet her frail voice hints at her true age. "I was wondering when you'd come back. It's been almost a week."

"A week? I haven't seen you in a month," I say, confused.

She furrows her eyebrows. "You came last week, with the

butterfly. Probably one of the prettier of the disgusting insects you bring to me. Have you come with another?"

Last week? A butterfly? Maybe Agatha is growing senile in her old age. But then she produces a small glass vial, and within it, a perfectly preserved butterfly, its wings a vibrant purple.

"Are you sure I gave this to you?" I ask. "It wasn't…a gift or anything?"

"Villiam had me charm that cricket, but that was a while ago. You gave me this butterfly." She feels my forehead. "Are you feeling all right?"

"Dandy, as always," I lie. Perhaps I didn't sleep as soundly as I thought. Or maybe Agatha is just senile and doesn't remember Villiam giving this to her instead of me.

I pull the jar with the cicada out of my pocket. "Here's the cute little critter."

Agatha grimaces, as she always does. "My daughter collects rings. I wish you'd find yourself a different hobby."

I slide the jar toward her and lean against her stand.

"Here's two copper pieces," I say. The usual payment.

Agatha nods and ushers me inside her tent. The inside contains even more charms than on the outside. I sit on her floor cushion while she pulls the cicada out from the jar. To my left, resting on a table, is a handmade doll that resembles Agatha's daughter.

"What's that?" I ask.

"It's a charm doll," Agatha tells me. She cups the cicada within her hands and then kisses her thumb. "There's magic in a kiss."

When she opens them, the cicada is frozen, petrified. She roots around for one of the glass vials she uses to store my bugs. Once she finds one, she slips the cicada inside and hands it to me.

I take the cicada and then run my fingers through the doll's hair.

"You shouldn't touch it," Agatha says. She gently takes it from me. "Charm dolls are linked to a person. This one is linked to my daughter. Whatever I do to the doll, she will feel."

"How are they linked?"

"It's very simple charm-work—it only requires a small item from my daughter, something important to her. I sewed the item inside it, and then I give the doll its life." She holds the doll up to my ear, and I hear a heartbeat.

"What do you use it for?"

"Oh, all sorts of things. If I pinch the doll's arm, my daughter knows to visit me. If I bless the doll, my daughter is blessed. But charm dolls do not have the best of reputations. Without proper protections placed on the doll, someone could use one to cause another harm. Even kill them. They are simple but powerful jynx-work."

A shiver runs down my spine. The doll looks like a toy, yet it could become a deadly weapon.

"Thank you for your work," I say. "The cicada is beautiful."

"If you say so."

Luca walks me to the edge of Gomorrah, his hand in my mine. We have not kissed since that first night in Gentoa, but hand-holding has become our normal. His hand feels warm and steady. Something I could grow used to.

"We should stop here," Luca says as we approach the edge of Gomorrah's caravans. Once again, the Festival is on the move. "I know you don't want Villiam seeing me."

I suppose I should introduce Luca to Villiam properly at some point. Not as someone helping me investigate my family's murders but as my friend. Well, more than my friend, really.

Maybe after all of this blows over.

"This is our last day here," I say. I squeeze his hand tighter. I'd be lying if I claimed I wasn't nervous. This is more than the greatest performance of my life—it's my first role as a Gomorrah proprietor.

"Do you want me to meet with you before you leave for the wedding?"

"I… I don't know." In my head, I'm simply picturing this as a performance. It's the only method that doesn't leave me panicking from anxiety. Before a Freak Show, our only pre-show rituals are tolerating the bickers of Unu and Du and the sounds of Hawk tuning her fiddle. Or Blister's high fives.

"I won't be offended if you don't want me there," he says.

"I don't want to make a big deal of it."

"It's sort of a big deal."

"But I want to pretend this is normal. That this is what I do. I am the Girl Who Sees Without Eyes. I can make an illusion. I can fool them all."

He nods, but, from his expression, I can tell he doesn't understand. He gives me a hug, and I press my nose and mask into his shoulder. "Be careful," he says.

"Always am."

"Break a leg."

"Naturally."

He pulls away, his face stern and shadowed. I don't want him to worry about me. Nicoleta and I will walk out of that wedding alive and with the leader.

"I'll see you tomorrow," I say. "Afterward."

"Tomorrow."

The limit of my illusion is nine minutes and twelve seconds.

"You will need to enter the cathedral quickly and find a place to conceal yourself while Nicoleta finds Dalimil," Chimal says.

Nicoleta nods. I'm accustomed to seeing her fatigued, with dark circles under her eyes, complaining of a headache as she hunches over to do our laundry. But this week, she holds her head high and is fueled solely by excitement. I wish I could enjoy the thrill of this as she does. As much as I adore performing, I prefer when I have control. But the success of this mission depends on too many random factors.

"You'll be entering with the other guests through the main

265

entrance, but they will only see Nicoleta. The guards outside will ask you to produce your invitation, and we have a copy of one here." Chimal slides Nicoleta a piece of golden parchment. "Your name is Lady Michala, the daughter of a distant count. The real Lady Michala has the snaking sickness, so she will not be attending."

Nicoleta hands me the parchment, and it's nearly impossible to read the intricate Up-Mountain calligraphy. An embellished yellow sun of Ovren glints at the top of the page.

"Sorina, once inside, you will conceal yourself somewhere and give yourself time to recuperate. Because of this, we think it's best if you are dressed as a nun, someone who, if seen, will still escape notice. It'll also allow you to keep most of your face covered."

I don't love the idea of dressing up as an Up-Mountainer. I don't want to wear their clothes. I don't want to look as if I belong in such a terrible place.

"Dalimil will likely be seated near the front. Repeat again what he looks like."

"He's six foot two, approximately sixty years old," Nicoleta says, barely hesitating a moment to think. "Fair features and a crooked nose. His most notable characteristic is his one blue eye and one green eye."

"That will require Nicoleta to get rather close," I say.

"You'll have several opportunities to do so. First, when he is entering. Second, in Up-Mountain weddings, every member of the congregation must throw flower petals into the water the priest shall bless. And third, while leaving." Chimal studies me. "Sorina, you'll need to cast an illusion to conceal Nicoleta when she makes her move. Then you must quickly get the three of you *out*. Dalimil is a large man, but Nicoleta should have no difficulty carrying him. There will be a carriage waiting for you outside."

I stare at the blueprint of the cathedral in front of us on the table. The congregation appears massive, easily several thousand people. I don't have that sort of range. Or endurance.

"I have a horrible feeling that this isn't going to work," I say.

"Three fortune-workers have already prophesized that we will be victorious."

As Luca would say, you shouldn't put too much stock in fortune-workers.

"We cannot lose, Sorina," Chimal says.

"We cannot lose," I echo. I certainly hope he's right.

Grandfather; quiet; sweet.

PRY OFF NAILS.

NO HAIR—ONLY FINGERNAILS, EVERYWHERE; HIDEOUS.

UNLIKE TREE, HE IS CAPABLE OF SPEECH AND EMOTIONS, AS IF A REAL PERSON.

PREFERS SOLITUDE; OFTEN TAKES LONG WALKS IN THE UPHILL.

UNOFFICIAL CARETAKER OF BLISTER.

ENJOYS PEOPLE-WATCHING.

CHAPTER NINETEEN

The two-hundred-and-four-story Cathedral of Saints Dominik and Zdena is fabled as the tallest building in the world. Constructed of solid black stone, it towers over the skyline, not unlike the spires of the Menagerie. It appears like a giant spindle, though it is meant, when the sun is positioned directly over its peak, to resemble a torch. I now understand why Chimal was so eager initially for Hawk's help, as Hawk could easily enter from above and descend the likely thousands of steps below, completely unnoticed.

It's difficult to imagine that, in a mere hour, I'll be in that cathedral.

Four of us approach the city from the hillside road, our carriage freshly painted to appear more regal than anything owned by Gomorrah. Chimal has shed his normal red and black captain uniform for the clothes of a passing peasant. Villiam wears his usual suit, as elegant as any of the other wedding guests. The many layers of Nicoleta's gown take up nearly an entire seat in our carriage, leaving me only a foot of space in the corner. With the peach fabric, the peachier rouge and her pale complexion, she resembles any Up-Mountain patron who visits Gomorrah. Her transformation is nearly unnerving, especially when she speaks in her practiced accent.

Where Nicoleta is all beauty and elegance, I look—as Venera would say—frumpy and old. The black clothes of a postulant cover every inch of my skin, complete with gloves and heavy leather boots. I'm thankful I told Luca not to come. I feel ridiculous. But at least the absurdity of the costume makes the situation feel lighter.

We're about to risk our lives.

In the distance, toward the city, a hillside fire clouds the sky with the smoke of Agni's jynx-work, meant to distract the guards as guests arrive. That, too, is a comfort, even if it's blacker than the smoke of Gomorrah behind us.

Villiam kisses my forehead. "Be strong."

"I will be," I say.

"I love you so much. And I'm very, very proud of you."

His praise strengthens my resolve, and I smile at him. "I love you, too."

Even as we grow closer to the city, the cathedral's tower still seems far in the distance. I don't believe in Ovren or any Down-Mountain god, but it feels as though a higher power is observing us from that tower, aware of our ill intent. I am no fortune-worker, but I sense doom.

The carriage pauses so that Villiam and Chimal can leave. I hug my father once more, but I don't say anything. I want to appear strong. I am Sorina Gomorrah, daughter of this city, and this is my destiny.

We abandon them on the hills.

Our driver, a member of the Gomorrah guard, says nothing. He has instructions to remain in the vicinity of the cathedral and await our return, no matter what.

We enter the city gates. They aren't as impressive as the gates of Cartona, yellow and gleaming. Just as Cartona was the golden city, Sapris is gray, blending into the stone of its hills, silent and shrouded. Even with all our preparation, I'm not certain what awaits me there.

"You look tense," Nicoleta says. "You need to relax."

"I'm trying to," I say.

"It's just another performance."

"A performance? My job is to be invisible." I fiddle with the edges of the nun sleeves, which, on close inspection, are the darkest shade of navy, rather than true black. I hope it will go unnoticed. "Nothing about this is certain. We aren't even sure that Dalimil is the Alliance's leader."

"We're mostly certain. And if he isn't, he'll have information. It will be of value, nonetheless." She peeks out of the window. "We're nearing the cathedral. It's best to remain silent. I'm supposed to appear alone in this carriage."

It's impossible not to dwell on what's coming as the voices grow louder. A church organ plays a somber ballad that sounds inappropriate for a wedding. Other than the musical accompaniment, the atmosphere reminds me of the moments just before a Freak Show. The hushed whispers and chattering of anticipation. I imagine the feeling of our tattered velvet curtain in my hands, the voices of my family behind me.

Our carriage pulls to a stop.

Nicoleta nods to me.

The show is about to begin.

I cast my moth illusion as soon as the liveried attendant opens the carriage door. "My lady," he says, his eyes on Nicoleta. She grasps his arm for support as she descends to the cobblestones. Just as her foot touches the ground, she makes a show of losing her balance and then, with her other arm, braces herself by keeping the carriage door open. I climb out, invisible, into the city.

"My lady, are you all right?" the attendant asks.

"My shoe merely slipped," she says, her accent lilting heavily from practice. In the Freak Show, her lines required constant repetition. It took her months to perfect her persona. Here, she seems a natural. I suppose she performs better than me under pressure. They say pressure can turn even a grain of sand into a pearl under the right circumstances.

As Nicoleta joins the queue of pastel-colored guests, I follow in her shadow. My form is gone. My smell, gone. The sound of my footsteps is replaced by the slight flutter of the moth's wings. I am a ghost.

The tower above us extends endlessly into the overcast sky, turning my stomach even as I admire it. This tower has stood for hundreds of years, and it will likely remain for hundreds more in the same spot. I can imagine why such a landmark would appeal to people: such a rigid sense of home. But then I turn behind me, where the Gomorrah smoke is slightly darker than the afternoon clouds, and the spire of the Menagerie is just barely visible, the flag above it a speck. For the common people of Sapris, that represents excitement. Something new.

I've always preferred change to tradition.

After three minutes, the fatigue of the illusion is already setting in. I fix my gaze on Nicoleta's beaded slippers in front of me to keep my focus.

Nicoleta presents her invitation to the attendant, who allows her to enter the cathedral. I squeeze in past her, careful not to brush shoulders with any of the guests who cannot see me.

Once we enter the cathedral, I immediately adjust my illusion to expand to the crowds and adapt to the dim lighting. Candelabras glow from the edge of every stone pew, and it almost reminds me of the flickering torchlight of Gomorrah. Nicoleta speaks her name to an usher, who directs her to her seat. It's early enough that the pews are only a quarter of the way filled, and we have nearly a half hour before the ceremony will begin.

While Nicoleta walks to her seat, we both scan the front for someone matching the description of Dalimil. There are many blond men in the crowd. Many tall men—Up-Mountainers are shockingly tall, or at least they seem so to me. I feel like an ant roaming unknowingly in their midst. Nicoleta shakes her head nearly imperceptibly. He isn't here.

Next I scan the room for other nuns, but there aren't any. It's been nearly seven minutes; I need to find some place to conceal myself, somewhere I can still see Nicoleta. Along the edges of the cathedral, behind a row of columns, are individual prayer rooms separated by a gate. Each features a unique piece of artwork, all depicting the artistic prowess of Up-Mountain prodigies: warrior saints cleansing the world of the jynx-work, through such choice weapons as fire, sword or rope.

Sneaking inside proves a complicated task. Not only do I need to continue to conceal myself, I need to make it appear as if the gates are not moving at all. Once inside, I slip myself within the shadow in the corner, angled away from the wandering eye.

And now we wait.

The air smells of incense, which I associate with Gomorrah's mehndi tents or fortune-workers. Here, however, it doesn't feel sacred, warm or safe. Despite the summer heat, the inside is kept cool from the thick stones walls of the cathedral. It feels sterile.

Minutes pass as I scan the entering crowds for Dalimil. I briefly make eye contact with Nicoleta, and it's clear from her expression that she hasn't seen him, either. What if he doesn't show? What if all of this danger was for nothing?

With a handful of moments to go before the ceremony begins, Nicoleta temporarily excuses herself from the pew by saying something to the man beside her. I take this as my cue to follow her, and I rush to slip out from the prayer room. We walk side by side, though I am concealed again. She should not gamble with my endurance. I need my illusion-work to last us.

"I don't see him. There are so many men," she says. "When everyone forms a line to bless the couple, you will need to be close. You'll need to find him, if he's here."

"I can't get so close to the altar. Someone could notice my silhouette."

"We need to find him, Sorina. Gomorrah needs him."

I sigh. "Fine. But I don't want to die in this church."

Nicoleta returns to her seat, and I to my prayer room.

The cathedral doors open, and the wedding procession begins. The bride, a young girl not many years older than myself, wears rose-pink. Her dress trails out nearly three meters behind her, and there are more flowers on her head than there is hair. The groom is nearly two decades her elder, with a beard already touched with gray. He smiles at her in greeting rather than with love.

People have joked and called me Gomorrah's princess before, but I'm not a political pawn like this girl. I'm not a prisoner of my role. I'm a warrior, at least in this moment.

The priest opens one of the five books of Ovren to begin a reading about how the union of two souls brings them closer to Heaven. Love cleanses one another.

I've never heard a religious text of Ovren lacking the usual fire and brimstone.

After the reading, the couple exchanges their vows. It's then that the procession begins.

I slip out of the prayer room and hurry to the front of the cathedral. It's so large that it takes me nearly a minute to reach the altar. The line grows behind me as every individual finds a place, and I keep to the steps, facing them. They are an endless line of lemon and apricot and lavender. Men, women and children. I've never seen so many Up-Mountainers directly in front of me, without the darkness of Gomorrah behind them. I'm horribly out of place. I don't belong here.

I look straight at them, but they do not see me.

While in the seating area of the church, I didn't see the construction of the ceiling above the altar. Directly above us is the tower, which is hollow and black and endless. The tip of the tower must be glass, as a pinprick of light shines down from above, like a single star. It's horribly eerie, as if I'm staring into the eye of Ovren Himself.

The altar is a simple wooden desk, but the mural behind it catches my eye. A saint of some sort—perhaps St. Dominik, one of the patrons of this cathedral—stands on top of the body of a man, whose face appears disfigured. Bile rises in my throat as I realize how determined the Up-Mountain artist was to depict the man's ugliness: his blotched skin, his broken limbs.

To Ovren's disciples, he is impure. Deformed. A freak.

Like me.

My heart races as each of the Up-Mountainers pass through to pick up a flower petal from the basket. One by one, they toss them into the basin. I nearly hold my breath as I struggle to maintain the illusion. I crouch on the white steps, close enough to the passersby to feel the wind of their dresses swishing past. Though I'm invisible, I feel exposed.

I falter for a moment as one man approaches. He wears the white uniform of an officer, ornamented with tassels and medals. He's almost taller than Chimal told us—six-five, perhaps, and broad, taking the space of nearly two people. His one blue eye and one green eye stare over me into the distance of the church, and he doesn't look to see if the petal he tosses lands in the basin.

It does.

This man is responsible for the deaths of Blister and Gill, I tell myself. I'm not sure if I believe that, but it will help me to focus in this moment. This man is evil. A sort of fury stirs in my gut.

Dalimil walks past me, and my gaze follows him so I can find his seat. His pew is at the edge of the church, much farther to the right than Nicoleta and I had anticipated.

I search for Nicoleta in the line, and she's approaching the front. I run to her side as she returns to her pew and then tug on her sleeve.

"He's here. In the sixth pew on the far right. We must catch him as he leaves."

I'm out of breath, practically panting. My head aches from all the focus, the constant pushing, the constant creating. I scamper to the edge of the cathedral, to the comfort of the shadows, and gradually release the illusion. The pressure in my mind eases, but my brain feels flimsy, like a muscle overworked. I don't know how I'll manage to cover the three of us while we escape.

Now comes the most difficult stunt of our performance: finding an opportunity to lure Dalimil away. It's unlikely, even if Nicoleta beckoned him, that he would come to her. She's a stranger. I need to think of something appropriate.

Because I'm in a church, I could play on the surroundings. He could see candles going out, prayer doors opening and lights shining from above. But would he attribute this as an act of Ovren, or would he run?

I could conjure the image of a child alone. If he saw the child, wouldn't he feel obligated to ensure he found the child's parents? I remind myself that this is the man who could be responsible for Blister's death, so perhaps not.

Then I think of the simplest thing. Calling his name.

As soon as the organ plays its final notes and the newly wedded couple exits the church, Nicoleta finds me. Fortunately, Dalimil is in no hurry to leave. He talks to the man beside him, also dressed in a white military uniform.

"Archduke Dalimil," I call, using a sound illusion to conceal my voice so that only he and I can hear it. It's such a simple illusion, but the effort of it hits me with a jolt of dizziness. I use what strength I have left to conjure my moth, and then I lean against the column to catch my breath. Every part of me is tired.

He glances at us, or, rather, simply at Nicoleta. She curtsies to him to show her respect, but her calling out to him would not be considered particularly gracious. Still, he says goodbye to the

other officer and strays toward us. The crowds of those depart-
ing walk behind him, away from our secluded space.

Nicoleta freezes, trying to come up with something to say,
I imagine.

"It has been…a while since we last spoke, Your Grace," she
says.

"Forgive me. I don't recall our last meeting—"

He doesn't even see her move. To him, seeing my illusion, she
is still. Nicoleta slices him on his forearm with a knife, coated
in the diluted juice of the black maiden flower. Without a viable explanation for the sudden pain, he merely stands there in
stunned silence. The next moment, he collapses to the ground,
silent and now invisible to the rest of the congregation.

My head pounds. "Let's go. I'm dying. Pick him up."

Nicoleta nods and then reaches down to lift all three hundred pounds of him. He doesn't budge. She groans and tries a
second time, but it's useless.

"Shit," she mutters. "Shit. Shit."

"What's wrong?" She hasn't had an issue all week with her
abilities.

"It's not working. I'm not strong." She gives a third heave
but to no avail.

"Don't hurt yourself," I say. "You need to move him. I won't
last more than another minute or so."

"Sorina, I can't," she snaps. "It's not working. I'm not working."

I curse under my breath. When my illusion fades, if I'm found
out, I won't be treated with mercy. Nicoleta, perhaps, can flee.
She looks like an Up-Mountainer. Her abilities aren't so read-
ily apparent on her face. I am the obvious freak, and I am des-
ecrating a sacred house of Ovren.

We both grab one of his arms and pull him over our shoulders to drag him. The massive weight of the man on my back

strains everything I have left, even with his feet dragging across the stone floor behind us.

"I can't do this," I grunt.

"It's not that far."

It's all the way out of the church and then to the carriage. It's far enough to fail.

We make it halfway across the church before I need to stop. When I let Dalimil fall to the floor, it is only a half rest. I still need to maintain the illusion. The weight of the constant pushing presses against my mind, and I feel as though I am drowning, too exhausted to fight against the currents.

"The breaks won't help," Nicoleta says. "You're only extending the illusion."

She's right. I'm depleting our time.

We hoist him up again. This time, we make it out of the cathedral's doors and into the packed square. People dart around us, searching for their respective parties. They don't see us. They don't see the man we carry, though more than one person trips on Dalimil's ankles and mistakes them for a cobblestone.

I spot our carriage among many others huddled together at the street's corner. The sight of the end propels me forward and, despite my blurring vision, I quicken my step.

As we cross the street, a carriage darts out in front of us. Obviously, the driver does not see us, and we're directly in the path of his horses. "Push," Nicoleta pants, and we both lunge forward. The wheels of the carriage, however, nick Dalimil's shoes and roll over his ankles with loud cracks I'm not prepared to conceal. We stumble and fall, Dalimil landing on top of us.

For a moment, the illusion flickers.

"What was that?" the driver calls. He stops the horses and jumps out of his seat.

"Sorina," Nicoleta hisses, "I think I've sprained my ankle."

The driver comes closer, not realizing he's about to walk over us. I let out a long curse and cast an additional illusion, a bird swooping down in front of his horses. The effort feels like I'm stretching my muscles to the point of tearing. The horses shriek, pulling the driver's attention away.

"Get up," I snap. I'm ready to scream or cry; I don't know which. "Get up. We're nearly there."

We hobble the rest of the way. I have no strength left, but still I manage to move forward, to maintain the illusion. The strain comes at the expense of breathing. I nearly collapse against the carriage door and then gasp as I release the illusion on Nicoleta.

"Hirohito," she says to the driver, "help us."

He startles at her sudden appearance and then leaps to our aid. He, Nicoleta and I push the limp body of Dalimil into the carriage, and we collapse in afterward.

We have succeeded, but we don't waste time on self-congratulation. Hirohito snaps the reins, and we exit the gray city toward the comforting smoke of home.

CHAPTER TWENTY

Villiam embraces me, and I allow myself to relax, inhaling the warm scent of his cologne. I'm in Gomorrah. Safe in my father's office. Back in my regular clothes. The tower of the Cathedral of Saints Dominik and Zdena is behind me, and it cannot see me through Gomorrah's smoke.

"I'm so proud of you," he says. "And so, so relieved."

"I felt like such a…" I search for the word, but that feeling of helplessness and ugliness I felt in the church is difficult to articulate. "A bug. An ant." Like, if they saw me, they could squash me at any moment, without the slightest bit of thought.

Villiam smile softens. "Who has carried more than her fair share of weight, as I understand." He brushes my hair behind my ear. "You have never looked more beautiful."

I don't feel beautiful. I don't even feel victorious. Only tired.

In the corner of the office, a healer braces Nicoleta's sprained ankle. She doesn't wince as he pulls the fabric tighter. Her gaze is fixed on the floor, and I can tell she's troubled. She wears the sort of expression she usually has before snapping at Hawk that she has a headache.

"When will you and Chimal speak to Dalimil?" Nicoleta asks.

"This evening. But I don't wish to concern you two with that. Your roles in this matter are very much completed, and you deserve a rest."

Part of me wants to insist on being there, however gruesome Chimal's interrogation methods become. That man potentially orchestrated the murder of two members of my family. But even though the fury over their deaths remains, I struggle to connect it to his face. Dalimil may not be a good man. He may even be an evil one. But when I looked into his eyes, even if he didn't see me perched on the marble steps of the church, I didn't sense I was before Gill's and Blister's killer. And I would know, wouldn't I? The soul should recognize those who have wounded it.

Once the healer finishes treating Nicoleta, we say our good-byes and head to our tent.

"I'm sorry," Nicoleta says. "I nearly got both of us killed."

"It doesn't matter."

"Of course it does. I was useless."

"Had you not been there, I wouldn't have been able to carry Dalimil out on his own," I say, trying to ease her mind. "It's over. We did it. That's all that matters."

Outside our tent, Luca is bent over a table, playing a game of lucky coins with Hawk and Unu and Du. His face sags with relief as we approach, and he abandons the game to come to my side.

He wraps his arms around me. "Did we win?" he asks.

"Yes."

"Are you all right?"

"Yes." I press my forehead against his. "I'm going to sleep."

"Of course."

That evening, after a much-needed rest, I don my best mask and some bright red lipstick. Luca has promised me a night of fun.

I don't know what to expect. Luca's idea of fun is tea-partying

283

with prettyworkers and telling morbid jokes. But, regardless, I could use some fun. I could use a distraction from my thoughts, which keep drifting to Dalimil and what Villiam might have learned from him by now. If he really is the leader of the Alliance, anyway.

In my excitement, I race to Luca's tent. The Downhill is abnormally quiet for this time of night, and the weather has grown chillier over the past few days. I had to dig my thicker cloaks out of storage. The guests have also changed their clothes, shifting from pastel oranges and salmons to rich sapphires and emeralds. I don't know why anyone would wear their best clothes to Gomorrah, but our audience members, without fail, are always gussied up in pearls and satin gloves and sweeping up-dos. Begging to be pickpocketed.

I find Luca waiting outside his tent, leaning against the silver-tipped cane that does nothing but make him look pretentious. He smiles when he sees me, that smile with the dimples that makes my insides flutter.

"Where are we going?" I ask. I try to hide the giddiness from my voice, because I've never been on a date and I'm starting to think that's what this is. A real date. He's probably going to make it a surprise. Somewhere enchanting or exhilarating, a part of the Festival only he knows.

"I'm taking you to Skull Market," he says. "I know you've barely explored the Downhill."

"You weren't supposed to tell me," I say.

"What?"

"It was supposed to be a surprise."

He furrows his eyebrows. "I hate surprises."

"That's because you're serious. And bor—because you're so deliberate."

He flicks my forehead, on my mask.

"What was that for?" I ask.

"You were going to say *boring*."

He pulls me forward by my hand and leads me down a diagonal path, deeper into the Downhill, where I've never ventured before. Within a minute, we reach one of the two obelisks that mark Gomorrah's end. They are twelve feet tall, black and identical. Their stone is so solid that no one has been able to carve into them, and, despite constant exposure to the elements, their surface remains forever smooth and matte.

"The other obelisk is…maybe a mile away," Luca says. He points his cane to the left, toward the twin obelisk. "Legend says that to walk between them brings misfortune."

"Everyone knows that."

"Well, excuse me. I didn't mean to *bore* you."

I smirk and let him take me farther down the paths. We turn to the left and, nearly immediately, are struck by the noise and heat of hundreds of people together in a small space. The paper-lantern lights that usually dangle above tents and caravans are decorated with various expressions of sorrow, terror and fury in black paint. Skull Market is a maze of hundreds of vendors, thousands of smells. It sounds of coins jingling, the bells of auctions, the squabbles of haggling. There's something to see around every corner. I can hardly believe the size of the place. It must be two or three square miles, made up entirely of stalls. They aren't set up in a grid pattern to make it easy for the customers. Instead, vendors have constructed their tables and stalls wherever they please. In the middle of paths, adjacent to each other, in clusters that you practically need to crawl into in order to view the merchandise. The market is a mess of hiding places, and I have the itch to explore.

"The fabric seller here can spin thread out of nearly anything and turn it into something worthwhile," Luca says. He points to another stall. "That red sign means it's a trading booth. You barter. I've seen the owner take one man's trash and sell it to another as a treasure."

He has spiels prepared for nearly every stall, putting on a show for me.

"As huge as this place is," Luca says, "I doubt anyone is selling rare and exotic bugs. Unless they're covered in chocolate."

"I don't know…this place seems to have anything you could want."

"The Market covers a huge area of the Downhill, and it's got quite a few landmarks. There's a haunted caravan, apparently full of spirits. A cursing well. The famous pillar of salt in the heart of the Downhill."

The smells of the spiced wine and candied cashews from a nearby stall make my stomach rumble, and my coin purse is growing warm and eager in my pocket. Before Luca can object, I buy us two mugs of the wine.

"What is this?" an Up-Mountain girl asks me, pointing at the mugs in my hands. She wears a brown cloak covering all but her pale face. She doesn't seem like the type to visit the Downhill. She's too…delicate.

She also looks rather familiar.

"Wine," I say. "It's warm. They put spices in it."

Her eyes twinkle and she mutters something to the man next to her, who nearly jumps at her touch. He doesn't seem the type to be in the Downhill, either. After some eye rolling, he fishes in his pockets for coins and hands them to the girl.

"Your mask is beautiful," the girl tells me. "The colors are so vibrant."

"Thank you," I say hesitantly. I'm not used to being complimented by a visitor. It also bothers me that I cannot figure out why I recognize her.

"And that boy there. He's beautiful, too, no?" She giggles and takes a sip of her wine. At the taste of it, she squeals with delight and turns back to the man with her.

Then I recognize her. The bride from yesterday. I'm certain of it. She's less recognizable without her trailing pink gown and the flowers in her hair, but it's definitely her.

I return to Luca's side. "That girl over there. She's the bride from the wedding this morning," I say. I point her out to him. "What do you think she's doing in Gomorrah?"

"Can't have been much of a honeymoon, if she's here without her husband," he says jokingly.

I watch her pass with the man beside her—probably a bodyguard. As jarring as it may be to see her here, I won't stop her. She deserves some fun.

"I can't believe I've never come here before," I say to Luca, turning my back on the princess. "This place is so *alive*." I sip my wine, and it warms me all the way down. "Where should we go first?"

The wine turns Luca's lips a deep burgundy. "I thought I had to make that a surprise," he said.

"See? You're catching on."

He wraps his arm around my waist, and I'm surprised by our closeness and the firmness of his grip. We haven't been this close since almost two weeks ago, when he stayed the night to help keep me awake and the illusions locked away in their Trunks.

We walk through the paths, and within a few minutes, I realize Luca has no idea where he's going. Not that I blame him; Skull Market has clearly been constructed for visitors to lose their way—and their money—within it.

He tucks a strand of hair behind my ear, and for a few moments, I forget to breathe. "Come on. I want to show you the pillar."

"Do you even know where you're going?"

"Of course I do. It's just this way." He points to a mere crevice in between a few tents. We squeeze through it, the tent material brushing against us on all sides. Soon the Market vanishes behind us, and we are in a tunnel of pink, purple and red. Luca stops walking, and he turns around so suddenly that his blond hair falls out of place and into his eyes.

"Why are you stopping?" I ask.

"There's no one around," he says. His eyes travel from the silver tip of his cane to me, and he watches me as if I should have expected this comment, as if I should know what's coming, as if I should keep up.

And then he kisses me.

Since we have only kissed a few times, it still shocks me when it happens. It only lasts for a few moments, but it's tender, and I'm breathless when he pulls away. He slides his hand around my waist and holds me there, our faces only inches apart. The material of the tent beside us presses against my hair.

"I know I haven't told you, but I like having you around. I like what we have," he says.

I laugh breathlessly. "Did you bring me here just to kiss me?"

"Did I surprise you?"

"Yes."

He smiles a wide, boyish smile that makes my heart melt. But it disappears, replaced by hesitation. "I know I'm not impulsive or spontaneous, but I like what we are. I've never had this. And I want you to like what we are, too."

I kiss his cheek. "I promise I like…what we are. As long as you do."

"What I said before was true—this is very new to me. I've rarely had close friends, let alone anything close to a romantic relationship. And I still doubt I'll ever be a person who looks twice as I pass the House of Delights. But I'm not breakable— you can touch me. I'm a big boy. I can tell you what I want and what I don't, if I want to stop, if I want to keep going. You have my consent to…touch my neck." He brushes my fingers against his neck. "Or step close enough that we're touching." I inch a step closer, until there is no space between us. "Or kiss me, whenever you want."

I know this is an invitation to kiss him exactly the way I've wanted to for so long, but I'm so amused by his use of *big boy* that I giggle.

"What?" His face reddens. I've probably embarrassed him. That was a very serious speech.

Once I have my laugh at his expense, I kiss him the way I want to, the way he wants me to. I wrap my arms around his shoulders and pull him so close that the buttons of his vest press into my stomach. I slide my tongue over his bottom lip, and he runs his fingers through my hair. And after at least a minute of this—maybe two, maybe five—I kiss my way along his jaw, my lips only brushing his skin.

I want to move. The tents are so close that it's growing claustrophobic and almost uncomfortable, so I say, "Maybe this isn't the best place for this."

"I was going to suggest relocating, as well."

We slide our way out of the tunnel to the other side, free at last. "I'd like to show you the salt pillar," he says. "Unless you'd rather we go back somewhere else."

I interpret this as going somewhere private. "What, to your tent?"

"If you'd like." The words are loaded. Not with the promise of sex—at least, I don't think so—but of taking this further.

"I feel like you have this idea of me as someone who is walking around in a permanent state of lust," I say

"I envision that of most people, actually. It's not only you. And this is based purely on observation."

"You observe prettyworkers, Luca," I say, snorting. "Believe it or not, I'm not a walking mess of urges. And a lot of this is new to me, as well, even if it's in a different way." I blush a little to admit this. "Do you mind postponing your offer for another time? I'd like to see that pillar of salt."

It's more than that. I'd still like to have my date. I'd still like to hold his hand and walk in public as an item. Me, the girl without eyes, and him, beautiful in a way that makes me feel beautiful just to stand beside him. I still want that private night, even if it's just lying on his chest. But I want this first.

"Not at all," he says. He links his arm with mine and walks us down the path. "And I don't *actually* think of everyone as if they're in a permanent state of lust." He laughs. "But you know what they say about Gomorrah girls."

"Careful, that's your girl you're talking about."

As we turn down the path, we bump shoulders with the princess. She clutches at her bodyguard's arm but never looks at him, as she's too preoccupied with the sights around her. She glances at me and then recognizes my face. "Oh! It's you again." Without hesitating, she links her second arm with me, and I'm so taken aback that I tense. Luca shrugs beside me. "We're looking for the pillar of salt. It's supposedly famous."

"It's cursed, Your... Reia," the man says.

Luca raises his eyebrows but says nothing.

Reia ignores him. "I heard it was once a woman," she says to me. "Is that true?"

"So the story goes," Luca says.

She smiles at him, and I grip his hand tighter, a bit possessively. "Do you live here, too? You don't look like you do."

"My tent is only a short walk from here."

"That's marvelous." She sighs as we approach a clearing with a statue in its center. "I'd love to travel more." She pauses when she sees the statue. "Well, this must be it!"

The white statue appears to be of a woman, but her salt features are so weathered down that her form is barely recognizable as human. Her head is turned, as if she's glancing over her shoulder. When Luca mentioned the statue to me, I expected it to be taller. Instead, it's about my height. Life-size.

I let go of the girl's arm and creep closer to it, to see if there's an expression on the woman's face. There isn't. If there ever was, the years have worn it away. I run my hand along the woman's nonexistent facial features.

Someone chokes behind me.

I turn around just as Reia raises both of her hands to her

throat, which is spurting out blood. Her eyes widen in terror, and she crumbles to the grass, facedown.

I scream and grasp for Luca, several feet away from me. The man with the princess lunges toward her body and swiftly turns her over. He tears off a piece of his shirt and ties it around her neck to stop the bleeding, but it's clear she's already gone.

"Who did this?" the man shouts. The people around us begin to notice what has happened, and they shriek and step back.

"I didn't see..." Luca says. "I'm not sure what I saw."

"But there's no one around," I say. "It was only us."

"It looked like..." Luca hesitates before continuing. "It looked like her throat sliced open on its own."

The man stands over her, ushering the crowd back. "No one move. If anyone saw anything, anything at all, you'll be questioned. In the name of Ovren, come forward." His voice sounds more frightened than authoritative.

The people around us whisper.

"The princess," one says.

"I saw it. Her throat just slit open. There was no one near her. Like she was attacked by a spirit."

"Maybe a Frician assailant we didn't see."

Luca squeezes me against him. "We were just talking to her," I stutter. "How did this happen? And how did anyone else recognize her?"

Luca shakes his head. "I don't know." I can't blot her panicked face from my mind. She was young. Barely twenty. With the sort of beauty befitting a princess. Yesterday, she was married. Isn't she supposed to be living a fairy tale?

"We should get out of here. There will be trouble later." He pulls me away from the gathering crowd. "I'll take you home."

He squeezes my hand comfortingly, and I try to pretend that seeing the princess so gruesomely killed hasn't shaken me, only moments after speaking with her. I've spent the last month talking myself out of panic attacks. I can't let this death of a random Up-Mountain princess cause me to utterly break down, no matter how kind she'd been. I have to be stronger than that.

But it's hard to convince myself of this when I can't help but think that my family isn't okay, even if everyone is safe and under the protection of Gomorrah's guards. Two people I loved were murdered, and we still don't know who did it, or how, or why. Nothing about that is okay.

Luca said her throat slit open on its own. It just doesn't make sense.

"I want to go back to my tent," I say. There's a lump of dread in my gut.

We don't speak on the way there, where members of Gomorrah's guard stand outside speaking with Nicoleta, whose back faces us. Since it's only a little past midnight, it doesn't seem like anyone else is home yet. Unu and Du aren't running around the yard outside. Hawk must be on her usual hunt for a midnight snack. And Crown on one of his walks. All of them are accompanied by their guards, but, still, I cannot help but worry.

Luca hugs me and presses my face lightly into his chest. "I'm sorry. You've seen too much death lately."

"I can't get her face out of my mind."

"I imagine. I… Do you want me to stay with you tonight? You don't have to stay here. Or I could stay here. If you—"

"Sorina," Nicoleta shouts. She whips around, and her eyes are bloodshot and puffy. Unlike the last time I saw her this way, I don't make a move toward her. I'm frozen. Last time she cried, we learned Blister was dead. Rather than my heart pounding and urging me forward, I feel as if it's stopped.

As Nicoleta runs for us, Luca squeezes my arms, as if bracing me for what I might hear.

Nicoleta throws her arms around me. "You're back. We're waiting on the others. The guard and I have already sent some men to find—"

"What happened?" Luca asks for me. My voice is gone. I'm petrified, shaking.

"You need to sit down. Sorina, look at me. You're trembling. Sorina—no! Don't go in there!"

But I'm already running to our tent. I don't want to hear Nicoleta tell me that another member of our family is dead. I need to see it myself. I need to make sure this isn't some terrible dream repeating itself over and over until everyone I care about has been taken from me.

I halt as soon as I cross the threshold.

The throat of the body on our living room floor is slit, blood staining her black-and-white-striped clothes and pooling around her on the floor. She appears untouched, except for her neck. There's no evidence of her backing away or of a fight. It seems the killer attacked her from behind, and she crumpled to the floor, the shock rigid on her face.

I wail at the sight of her and grasp Luca's forearm for support once he and Nicoleta enter. "Sorina," he says, trying to pull me toward him, away from Venera's body, out of the tent, but I squirm away and rush to her side.

There's no point checking her pulse. No person could survive that amount of blood loss. But I do it anyway. I check on her neck. On her wrists. I press my ear to her chest and listen to nothing within it.

Unlike with Gill's or Blister's death, there is no shock. Maybe because I've been afraid this would happen for weeks now, bracing myself for another loved one to be ripped away. The pain of it seems to tear me in two.

My best friend. My sister.

The anger, the grief and the suddenness feel as if a screwdriver is jutting out of my chest and turning, twisting my insides together.

"I found her like this," Nicoleta says, sobbing. Even though she's standing, her posture makes it seem like she's trying to

293

be as small as possible, to sink into herself. "The guard outside didn't see anything, but someone could've snuck in when his back was turned. He wasn't paying attention. He didn't realize Venera was here." She hugs her arms to her chest. "Why would someone do this?"

I don't have an answer for her. After a month of working with Luca to protect my family, we've come up with nothing, and I've failed them again.

"Luca, can you stand outside the tent and make sure no one comes in?" Nicoleta asks. "Let me know if someone comes. Sorina and I are going to clean her up. I... I couldn't do it on my own."

Luca opens his mouth as if to speak but says nothing. I doubt he is used to obeying someone else's commands. He nods and moves to go outside.

Venera. And the Up-Mountain princess. Their two beautiful faces blur together in my mind, and I'm overwhelmed with the horror of it all. Two identical deaths.

Suddenly, it all clicks together in my mind.

Venera and the princess.

Blister and the baby prince.

Gill and the duke.

"We need to talk to Villiam," I breathe. I grab Luca's hand and pull him toward the tent's exit.

"Where are you going? How can you leave right now?" Nicoleta asks, her voice high and squeaky. She tears a strip of fabric off of her tunic and ties it around Venera's neck, just below the cut. This is not the first body she has cleaned.

"I've thought of something," I say.

"The guard has already gone to notify Villiam." She grabs a handful of white towels and lays them on the puddle of blood, sobbing silently as they stain red.

"They're connected," I say, and my voice speeds up in panic. "The princess from the wedding was in the Downhill today. She died the same way as Venera and around the same time.

Then there was Blister and the baby prince in Cartona. Gill and the duke in Frice."

"That doesn't make sense. How could they have been linked to those people?" Nicoleta says. Beside me, Luca keeps a straight face, thinking.

I remember my visit to Agatha's tent a few days ago. "Have you ever heard of a charm doll?" I ask.

"Yes," Luca says, just as Nicoleta says, "No."

"It's a doll that is linked to a person," Luca says. "Through charm-work. Whatever happens to the doll, happens to the real person."

"But you're not a charm-worker," Nicoleta says. "Or…do you mean the killer is?"

"Either is possible." It's just like I guessed before. I must have two types of jynx-work: illusion-work *and* charm-work. Because I'm missing my eyes the same way Tuyet is missing a heart and that man is missing an arm. Never mind that I don't know the first thing about charm-work. It fits.

But I never knew the princess existed until three weeks ago. I'd never heard of the Cartonian baby or the Frician duke. How could I have linked them? It doesn't make sense.

There is the possibility, like Nicoleta said, that the killer is a charm-worker. There are at least a thousand of them in Gomorrah. But the similarity in the "phantom" body parts is too difficult to ignore.

The tent flaps open, and Unu and Du poke their heads inside. Their four eyes wildly scan the room, hopping from Nicoleta to me, to Luca, and then, lastly, to Venera on the floor. "W-what happened?" Unu asks.

"Outside, outside," Nicoleta says. She lunges toward them, rests her hand on Unu's shoulder and leads them away. It's quiet except for the sound of them wailing.

"I'm so sorry, Sorina," Luca says. He stands three feet away, the way someone would from a stranger. His face, as always, remains expressionless. I wish he would show emotion. I wish he would scream or cry or, at the very least, frown. To make it *seem* like he cares about the world and about me.

Then he turns around and kicks the leg of our table so hard that coins and kettle corn spill off of it.

When he faces me again, I see the failure in his eyes. The anger. Moments ago, I didn't want to be touched, but now I run to him and bury my face in his chest. I squeeze my nails into his shoulder.

"She was my best friend," I choke out.

"I know," he whispers. He rubs his hand down my hair.

"She's gone."

"I'm sorry," he says.

I lift my gaze to his, suddenly determined. "We need to find out why."

Villiam arrives as we all huddle outside around a fire, where Crown cooks lamb kebabs that no one is going to eat. Villiam wears a pin-striped suit and a brown turtleneck, as if dressed to meet someone important, and Agni appears wearing his pink-and-red-striped uniform from his job at the Menagerie. The people who live in the tents nearby watch Villiam as he passes and stray over to see the commotion.

My strength seems to return to me the moment I see him, but only in a single form: fury. Nicoleta and I underwent the entire trial of this morning to protect our family, and for what? I hop off my seat and march toward him. "Venera is dead," I say. "Someone slit her throat."

The people nearby inch closer until a small crowd is gathered to see the drama of Gomorrah's freaky princess.

"That's three deaths in a month," I say, which gets people whispering. "What has he said?" *He* meaning Dalimil, of course.

"We know he is not the leader, as we'd hoped."

"Then who is?" I snap.

"He won't say."

"My sister is dead."

Villiam holds out his arms for me to embrace him, but I don't. Not at first. I pound my fist against his chest, not hard enough to hurt but enough to make me feel better. Then I let him wrap his arms around me and hold me. I feel three years old again, exhausted and scared. It is awkward, him trying to support me while his crutches support him.

"I think I understand now," I say. "I understand how this is happening."

I search behind me for Luca, who nods. Villiam's eyes fall on him, as well, and then narrow as Luca approaches.

"This is Luca von Raske," I say. "He's been helping me look into Gill's and Blister's deaths. I was going to tell you, but...it's complicated."

It's dead quiet, except for the sizzling of Crown's lamb and Agni telling the spectators to return to their caravans, though with little success.

"I know who he is," Villiam says quietly. He and Luca perform a staring contest of sorts. "Sorina, I think we should talk."

"I think so, too. We all should. I understand why—"

"No, just you and me." He turns away, and I'm too stunned to reply. Luca gives my hand a comforting squeeze, but his face is rigid. Villiam raises his voice so anyone around us can listen. "Everyone in this neighborhood will be questioned tomorrow about what they saw, so I advise you all to think clearly about the faces that passed you today. One of them belonged to a murderer."

CHOP DOWN.

AGE IS UNCERTAIN. SEVEN FEET TALL.
INCAPABLE OF SPEECH; BEASTLY.

REQUIRES SUNSHINE AND WATERING.

ACTS AS A GUARD DOG; GRUNTS AND
GROWLS AT STRANGERS.

PRONE TO SELF-INJURY.

CHAPTER TWENTY-ONE

Villiam and Gomorrah's guards escort me to his caravan. I do my best to hold my head up, but I'm only moments away from tears. Venera is dead, and only now am I beginning to understand how. My family has always been inherently different than my other illusions. They're more than a mirage, more than a trick. They *live*. And that's because they're connected to other living people.

They're dead because of what I can do, because I don't fully understand my own jynx-work. I never question what I don't need answers to. I never stop to think. And my willful ignorance is the reason my family members have been murdered.

As we pass the Menagerie, even the vendors seem to understand something is wrong. Normally they would call out to us to admire their collection of lucky coins or sample a piece of kettle corn. But they don't bother the guards, in their intimidating, all-black uniforms with swords at their hips. They don't bother the proprietor and his daughter. Instead, they duck away and whisper words like *murder* and *freak*, and I squeeze Villiam's hand for support.

"You and me alone, Sorina," Villiam says firmly once we reach his caravan. Venera, my best friend, my beloved sister, is dead, and yet I feel as though I'm about to be scolded. I cross my arms and follow him inside.

We sit down, and Villiam takes my hands. "How much have you told von Raske?" he asks.

"He knows everything, because I trust him."

"He's an Up-Mountainer."

"So? You don't even know him," I snap.

"I'm not angry with you," he sighs. I hate when people sigh. "You're only sixteen—this is exactly why I wanted to avoid you taking on responsibility. You're too young. It's not your fault that he has clouded your—"

I rip my hands out of his. "My judgment is fine."

His frustrated expression makes it clear he disagrees. "I want you to tell me how you met and what you have been doing."

I consider not saying anything at all, but I know that would be immature. Still, I didn't come here to be scolded like I'm ten years old. My sister just died, and my father is supposed to have the answers, supposed to support me. Instead, he's letting bias cloud his own judgment, letting his own prejudices distract him from what's really important. At least Luca would listen to me. At least he wouldn't treat me like a child.

But I talk. Not for Villiam's sake but Luca's. I don't want the guards to cause him trouble. He's there to help my family when I'm not. And I care about Luca too much to allow my father to hate him. I'll make him understand what Luca means to me.

The story doesn't take long. I'm careful to emphasize how Luca's entire philosophy differed from Villiam's, and that I was never certain which theory I believed more. I still don't know which is right. Because I'm speaking at length, I also tell Villiam about my theory of charm-work and how my family could be linked to Up-Mountainers.

When I finish, Villiam no longer appears angry—only sorrowful. He places his hand on my shoulder, and his voice, once edged with annoyance, has become hesitant and careful.

"Dalimil has spoken of one thing: a spy within Gomorrah," Villiam says.

My breath catches in my throat. After everything I've told him about how Luca has been helping me, can he really believe that *Luca* is the spy? It could be hundreds of different people!

"You say that Luca was determined to interview people with unusual types of jynx-work. Did it never occur to you that *he* possesses such a rarity himself? A boy who cannot die. What if he can use those same abilities and reverse them? Your illusions should not be able to die. Have you never thought to question him?"

I shrug his hand off my shoulder and lean back into my seat, arms crossed. "He was with me when Venera was murdered."

"But you were both with the princess when she was. Were you watching her when she died?"

"No—"

"Did you *see* her throat being slit?"

"No, but—"

"What if Luca did it himself?"

"He didn't!" My voice cracks, and I'm crying. This is too much to absorb in too short a time. I was with Luca. I wasn't watching him in that moment, but I was with him. He didn't... He wouldn't...

"Don't you find it suspicious that he spends his time prying into other people's business, seeking out information? That he knew everything about you the first time you met?" He lifts my chin up so that I'm looking at him. "Luca must've been feeding this information to the Alliance's leader."

"No. That's impossible... Luca would never..."

But now that the seed has been planted, it's difficult to think of Luca without considering Villiam's words.

Luca interviewed the rest of the suspects without me. Did he interview them at all? Or was it just a farce, a show, as our conversations with Narayan and Tuyet must have been?

He knew about our mission to find Dalimil. If he was a spy, wouldn't he have tried to stop us? But Dalimil isn't the Alliance's leader. It wouldn't have been worth giving up his position.

When he found that shortcut earlier today, did he only use it to bring us closer to the princess again? So that he would have his chance? I wasn't watching him when the princess died. I was examining the statue.

Who else could be the spy, if not him? Luca is an Up-Mountainer, an outsider in Gomorrah. He told me himself that he came from one of the wealthiest families in Raske.

"I don't… He wouldn't do this to me. He cares about me."

But my denial sounds weak even to my own ears.

Once again, the questions were right in front of me, and I didn't ask. I didn't think. All this time…

Villiam hugs me, and I cry on his sleeve. "I'm so sorry, my dear. None of this is your fault."

"I want to speak with him."

"You will. I will send my guards to bring him here."

"I meant Dalimil. Let me see him." I need to know more about this spy. I need to know the truth before I face Luca again, before I accuse him of the unforgivable. "Where are you keeping him?" Gomorrah doesn't have a prison.

"The Menagerie."

Dalimil lies within an animal's cage. His shirt has been removed, and his back openly bleeds from fresh lashes. On each hand, he bears matching burns, fresh and oozing.

"Back so soon?" he hisses, hearing the sound of my footprints rustling the hay. This back room is dark, lit merely by the lantern in my hand. We are alone.

My heart pounds, but I manage to keep my voice steady, to put on a show. "We have never properly met."

He lifts his head at the sound of a female voice. "I was expecting the fire-worker." His voice breaks. When he struggles to sit up to face me, I can tell how weak he is. Chimal and Agni have not been kind. Still, he lifts his head higher. "I haven't been broken. Not by them. And I won't be by you. You're only a girl."

I rest my lantern on the floor and then sit a few feet away from him, cross-legged. The metal bars of the cage are all that separates us. I can see the stubble on his chin and the dark circles beneath his eyes. I can see the hatred blazing in his eyes.

This man did not kill my family.

But he is all that stands between me knowing who did.

I untie my mask and let it fall into my lap.

He grimaces when he sees my face. "They have brought a demon to me. Whatever devil-work you have prepared, I will not break. The strength of Ovren burns in me. My mind doesn't submit to the mind-worker. My soul doesn't tremble at the pains of the fire- or shadow-worker."

"You're going to tell me the name of the Alliance's leader, as well as the Alliance's spy within Gomorrah."

His voice is weak. "As I told the others…I don't know the name of the spy."

"I guess we shall see."

When I perform a show, my mind isn't necessarily with the audience. In order to conjure illusions, I must turn my focus inward. I must project and create. During the Freak Show, it's the audience, the stage and all of my surroundings that fade into the back of my mind. The illusions are the reality. I'm more aware of the rushes of conjured wind and scents of imagined forests than I am the heat of the tent, the aromas of kettle corn and candied sweets.

It's a blessing and a curse, so easily losing myself in my thoughts.

I seek out that unconsciousness now. The illusions burst forth, one by one, but I sink deeper into my own thoughts. I don't want to feel what I am creating. I don't want to witness this performance. I crouch in a corner behind my subconscious, allowing it to do as it will and as it wants.

I don't have to hear the screams. I can tune those out. But as easy as it would be to entirely remove myself from reality, I need to be present enough to hear what I'm waiting for: the name.

Twenty-four minutes later, I hear it.

Dawn approaches outside, but I'm not tired. I drum my fingers against the table in Villiam's caravan while I wait for Luca's arrival, my body numb. I do not think. I do not dwell. Since my conversation with Dalimil, I haven't truly strayed outside the confines of my mind.

I hear the footsteps as they approach. Agni nods at me, but I'm already standing. All at once, the numbness fades, and my mind fills with conflicting images of Venera's body, of Luca's lips, of my knees drenched in water and blood on the Freak Show stage, of Luca's hand in mine, reassuring and steady.

No matter what Villiam said, this cannot be true.

Outside, the guards have forced Luca to his knees. His hands are bound behind his back, and he wears an impressive bruise on his cheek.

My stomach clenches in anger, both at the guards and at myself. "He's been hurt," I say to Agni. "This is too much. I thought you were just going to ask him questions."

"He resisted coming. He tried to run."

Why would he do that? Did he think I would stop the guards? Should I have?

Why would he run?

"Sorina," Luca says. His brown eyes widen as I approach him. My instinct tells me to help him to his feet, clean off the dirt from his clothes, kiss him. But I can no longer trust my instincts. "You can't possibly believe this." His voice is panicked, and I turn away from him. I don't want to see him like this.

"I don't know," I say.

"I wouldn't do this to you. I would never hurt you. I wouldn't kill anyone," he says. I want to believe him. I want to trust him and walk away with him and never let him go. But I don't know if I can, nor do I know if I've ruined any chance of the relationship that could have been between us. Either way, I have lost a second person important to me today.

"I don't know," I whisper.

"How could I have known about the charm-work? You didn't even know yourself. It doesn't make sense. You *know* this—"

"Haven't you heard me? I *don't* know."

He flinches as if I've slapped him. When he opens his eyes again, they're vacant. They don't shine when he looks at me. He turns away. "Then I suppose my only guilt is being a freak."

My lip quivers, but I don't want to cry in front of the guards.

I clear my throat, prepared to apologize, to plead forgiveness. But at that moment, Villiam returns and behind him, Chimal. I leave Luca's side and hurry to my father. He'll question Luca, and we'll prove his innocence. Luca will be free to go, and I will follow him.

"I heard you coaxed words out of Dalimil," Villiam says, the surprise obvious in his voice.

"Prince Exander Kyrannos, of Leonita," I say. "He's the Alliance's leader. Dalimil doesn't know the spy's name."

"Exander is too young. That's why we ruled him out before," Chimal says. "How do you know Dalimil wasn't lying?"

"He wasn't." Hearing my hollow tone, they don't press me for more.

"These are the things he was carrying when we apprehended him," Villiam tells me. He hands me a bag full of Luca's belongings. His cane, with a blade concealed inside. His belt of poison vials. A handkerchief. Some copper coins. His golden pocket watch.

Hesitantly, I pick up the pocket watch and open it. I remember there being an engraving inside. It has been scratched out, as if someone purposefully tried to remove it. But the words are still visible. *E. Kyrannos.*

"This belongs to the prince," I say in a shaky voice.

Villiam puts his hand on my shoulder to comfort me, but even with his steady grip, I feel as though I'm falling. Why would Luca possess something belonging to Leonita's prince if he wasn't working with him to murder my family? This can't be coincidence.

I let the watch fall to the grass and wait for the closure to come. I have my answers, but my grief only feels heavier, and I'm suffocating in a truth I never wanted. In a truth that breaks my heart.

Luca doesn't resist as the guards take him away a second time.

CHAPTER TWENTY-TWO

After the funeral, Gomorrah's guards dismantle our tents for us. The Freak Show tent caves in on itself and sinks to the earth in a heap. I put my arm around Hawk's shoulder as my family gathers in a circle to watch strangers pack our belongings away.

Agni supervises them, taking notes on his clipboard and occasionally introducing us to a guard who will be assigned to watch over us from now on. "Villiam told you that you could go buy food."

The coins Villiam gave me for licorice cherries and kettle corn remain in my pocket. "We're not hungry," I say.

Agni nods, a knowing look in his eyes. He's no stranger to grief.

Two guards work together and pull the Freak Show's sign from the ground.

They're moving our tents to be beside Villiam's, where we'll be under his watch at all times. I've been told there will be guards stationed at every entrance of our tent, from now until we are entirely certain of Luca's guilt. It's as if we are under quarantine. Though no one in the family cares, except for me. None of the illusions wish to participate in the investigation or even venture outside our tent. They sit inside—even Tree, who hates feeling so cramped—and watch time pass.

It's only a short move. Still, I turn away to avoid watching my home fall apart.

The Gomorrah Festival's Freak Show has been closed for twelve days during the height of the investigation and as we traveled from Sapris to Leonita. Over one hundred people who live in our neighborhood of the Uphill have been questioned and, under Villiam's reproachful gaze, have detailed every person they saw that night, from the usual passersby to any particularly suspicious visitor.

"Are we moving there forever?" Hawk asks. "I like our neighborhood."

"Only for a little while." Until we are certain this nightmare is finished.

"Du said that Luca is the one who killed Venera, Blister and Gill," Unu says.

"Where did you hear that, Du?" I ask, my voice sharp.

"I heard the guards talking. Why did you kiss him, then?"

"I don't want to talk about this." I walk away, half expecting them to follow me, hoping they won't. My Strings gather like the train of a gown, and I begin gathering them to me as I walk. My family will be safer inside my head, where no one can reach them. Even if Luca, the supposed perpetrator, is locked away in the Menagerie in a cell beside Dalimil's, I don't want to make assumptions. It's been over twelve days, and I still don't want to believe his guilt.

Nothing has been proven. Villiam has reached out to his own spies to search for confirmation. We could learn the truth at any moment. After all, we are mere hours away from Leonita. He could still be exonerated.

But the truth might condemn him, as well.

"Hey!" Du shouts. "We don't want to—"

His protests disappear as he and Unu vanish inside my mind. Hawk, Nicoleta, Crown and Tree follow. I'm not taking any risks tonight.

But I don't want to wait for our arrival in Leonita alone. I don't trust myself to play nicely with my mind, and Kahina already offered to have me stay with her. But, first, Villiam has invited me to dinner. Food has always been his favorite solution for soothing a grieving heart.

Once I arrive at his caravan, I pull the book he lent me from my bag. I spent last night poring over theories about jynx-work. "I have those books of yours," I say. I slide the encyclopedias into his shelf.

"Did you find anything in those?" Villiam asks. He pours us each a glass of wine.

"No, but I keep thinking..." I say. "The killer could be the charm-worker, not me."

"I thought you were convinced the charm-work is what gave them their lives?" He pushes the cork back in the bottle. "Or is it because Luca is not a charm-worker?"

"There was no motive behind this realization," I say. "It was merely a thought. And I'm not really in the mood for wine."

"You come from a long line of Gomorrah proprietors. Wine is one of our legacies," he says, ignoring the tension in my voice.

"I'm not against wine, but your taste is so dry. I'd prefer something sweet."

"The tastes of Gomorrah wine are bolder. They suit you."

"I don't feel bold," I say. Maybe I once was. I remember the first night in Frice, before Gill died. My family had gone to the Menagerie, but the officials stormed the Festival. It was dangerous for anyone to be out, let alone a deformed jynx-worker. I should've gone home with them, not strayed away and left myself vulnerable. I shouldn't have let my family worry, especially over something as useless as money.

"You *are* bold," Villiam says. "You're a warrior."

"But I'm not. Not really."

"What you're going through is a war in its own sort of way, and I hate to see how it has affected you. But I know you. You're strong. And you will make it through." He watches me fondly, and I don't know how he can manage such an expression. Perhaps he thinks I'm still the same young girl who rode on Tree's back to escape from slavers. But I'm merely a fragment of who I was then.

"I've barely been any help to you since Venera—"

"I hardly expected you to help me with such gruesome matters, considering what you're going through," he says. "Besides, the matter of the Saprish princess has been cleared."

"I'm surprised Sapris didn't storm the Festival like Frice did."

"I was worried they would," he says. He takes a sip of his wine. "But that's why I needed to act quickly. I met with the right people. Sapris didn't want it known that their new princess was in the Downhill, and we don't want her death to have any association with us. I won't let a war break out in the Up-Mountains with Gomorrah in its center. Not until we're gone."

"Would the Alliance allow a war to happen?" I ask.

"The Alliance, once we reach Leonita, will fall. Now that we know the Alliance's leader is the crown prince—who, at any day, will inherit his father's throne—it's easy to strike."

An assassination attempt. In revenge for killing my family. For allowing the Up-Mountains to spread their prejudices across the world. Still, murder is not an easy thing for me to swallow.

"We should turn around quickly," I say. "If there's going to be war, we need to get Gomorrah out of here."

"I agree with you, but we cannot turn back. There's already war breaking out behind us. My plan was to travel to Leonita and from here head east, far from these cities. We could follow the Great River south, where it will be safer for us."

So this will be our final stop before we leave the Up-Mountains. "What is Leonita like?" I ask.

"Leonita is arguably the most powerful city in the Up-Mountains, or at least it was. Leonita's lord has suffered from the snaking sickness for many years. His son—Exander—has been looking after the city, and he isn't merciful or sympathetic to those unlike himself. From the rumors I've heard, he is intelligent but very cruel. He wants nothing to do with Gomorrah. We won't be staying there for long."

His eyes wander over me, and then he stares at the fur rug on his floor. "I can't help but feel the weight of your family's deaths on my shoulders. I was so certain capturing Dalimil would be the end—that is why I pushed you into going into Sapris as I did. I thought being Gomorrah's proprietor in its time of need was the most important thing, but I neglected even more important duties—being your father during yours."

"No one *knew* Dalimil wasn't the leader," I say. I can't help but comfort him because, even if it's true that he was distracted, the deaths weren't his fault. I blame myself much more than I blame him. When no attack occurred in Gentoa and it proved the killer didn't have a pattern, I relaxed my guard too much, and Venera paid the price for that.

"True, I'm no fortune-worker, but I wish I'd only realized… Dalimil's kidnapping could have angered Exander into retribution. Venera didn't deserve that." He sighs. "Sometimes I forget how much you've grown. You're hardly a child anymore."

I don't respond to this, though I definitely agree with him. I don't feel like a child. I never did, really, but when I reflect over the past several weeks, I can't help but remember my old self as childish.

How could I possibly lead Gomorrah when I can't even protect my family? When my anxiety threatens to send me into a panic every night? When I hardly know anyone in this Festival?

Throughout our years of training, Villiam and I've never spoken about the obvious elephant in the room. I'm a freak. The proprietor has a responsibility to correspond with city leaders, to meet with them to organize Gomorrah's travels, as well as to lead the city and the thousands of people in it. Who's going to listen to me? The sight of me makes everyone uncomfortable. No matter how much I learn of Gomorrah, of history and of leadership, all that knowledge is lost if I'm unwanted.

"It's growing late," I say. "Don't you need to open Skull Gate?"

"You're right. It's nearly sundown. I hadn't even noticed that we've stopped moving." He stands and approaches me. I think at first he's going to kiss my forehead, as he often does, but instead he gets to his knees so that we are—theoretically—seeing eye to eye. "I don't think I can in good conscience conceal this from you. Our informants returned this afternoon."

My heart skips a beat. "What did they say?"

"I'm afraid Luca is the spy. He's been corresponding with Exander through messengers. We believe he recognized your jynx-work for what it is, before even we did. Or, as you said, he hired a charm-worker to complete the links between your family and Up-Mountain politicians. We have evidence Exander selected all of the victims himself. He intends to break the Alliance and conquer the Up-Mountain cities."

Despite everything else Villiam just said, I can only hear one piece echoing in my mind: *Luca is the spy.*

"I'm sorry," he says, "I know you were hoping—"

"It doesn't matter."

"Of course it does. It—"

"I'm going to see Kahina," I say.

Villiam's face falls. "If you want to talk to me—"

"It's not you," I say. I just don't want to spend another second in this caravan. I don't want to think about Luca and what he did to my family. I hate him like I've never hated anyone before.

I befriended him.

I kissed him.

I thought, for a few precious moments, that I could love him. More important, I thought he could love me. The only person in my life besides Villiam and Kahina whom I didn't imagine into being.

Everything was a lie. One betrayal followed by another. My stomach knots.

"You haven't eaten anything," Villiam says.

"I'm not very hungry." I gather my bag and head to the door. "What will happen to him?"

"He's going to be executed. Once we've determined how to get around his jynx-work."

I nod. Of course. But the thought of him dying, for good this time, pains my heart more than a little bit.

"Sorina," he says. He kisses my forehead. "I'm sorry."

"Me, too."

"I love you."

I smile weakly. "I love you, too."

Kahina opens her door with a sorrowful expression on her face. "Oh, sweetbug. I haven't seen you in days."

"It was Luca," I sob. "He murdered them."

She opens her door wider for me to climb inside her caravan and then pulls me into a long embrace. The inside smells of freshly potted mulch and tea. After we split apart, she wraps a quilt around my shoulders, and I take off my mask and lie down on her bed.

"Do you want to talk, sweetbug?" she asks. "Or do you want to sleep?"

"Talk." If I go to sleep, my family will reappear. I want to wait until we are inside our new tent, surrounded by Gomorrah's guards. Even if the killer is locked away, I don't feel safe. I might never feel safe. "You were right, you and Villiam. You told me not to trust Up-Mountainers."

"I never thought it would come to that," she says. "I'm hardly happy to have been right." She runs her fingers through my hair. "Where's your family?"

"Locked away." I wrap the quilt tighter around myself. "Can you talk for a few minutes?" My voice sounds weak and broken through my sobs. "I just want to listen."

"Of course, sweetbug. Did you know Villiam has begun sending me the medicine? You don't have to burden yourself with that anymore."

I'm surprised. She never wanted me to ask Villiam for money, even when I suggested it when she first grew ill. She said it would come from Gomorrah's public funds, which helps everyone here. She'd rather die than inconvenience someone else. "You're not a burden," I say. "You've never been a burden."

She shows me her arm, the one covered in veins. "Do you see this? They used to snake all the way up to my shoulder. Now they're barely past my elbow." She massages my scalp. "I'm getting better. It's taken years and an awful lot of medicine and worry on everyone's parts, but you don't have to fret about losing me. I'm not going anywhere."

At last, the crying stops. I try to sink deeper into her blankets. To relax. But all I can think about is Luca's execution. How will they manage to kill someone who cannot die?

I remember that conversation with him at the apothecary in Cartona. He believes Hellfire would do the trick. But I haven't told that to anyone, and I don't think he has, either.

Should I have shared his theory with Villiam?

Suddenly, there's a shout from outside, and running, and the sound of doors slamming. I instantly think back to the Menagerie, to the time the Frician officials stormed the Festival. To the night Gill died.

Kahina peeks out her window. "People are packing up their displays. We've barely opened." She leans out farther. "There's smoke ahead. Darker smoke than usual. Something is burning."

She pulls away, her expression grave. "I don't think we're welcome in Leonita."

I wipe my running nose and pull my hair out of my face. Anything to distract myself from my heartache. I'm with Kahina, who is *not* going to die of the snaking sickness. My family is inside my head, and they're *not* going to die, either. I won't let them. It doesn't matter what's happening outside.

I'm in control.

"What is going to happen to Luca?" she asks.

"They're executing him. Probably tonight." I roll over onto my back so that I face her ceiling, covered in hanging plants. "I don't want to go back to my tent."

"You don't have to," she says. "But I was wondering if you'd want to hear my suspicions. I was waiting until the verdict was announced, because it's about Luca. About the Were's Claw."

"What do you mean?"

"I'd never met Luca before, until Venera's funeral," she says. "When we shook the coin pot for him, I remember the fortune being foggy. The Were's Claw felt distant, disconnected." She grabs the coin from where it rests on her shelf and turns it over in her black-veined hand. "Once I met him, I knew there was something strange about him."

"What do you mean?"

"I mean there is a cloud of nothing around him. I see absolutely nothing in his fate."

"You weren't touching him or doing a proper reading."

"I don't think I would see anything then, either," she says. "This is a nasty business, sweetbug. Terrible." She grabs her jar of coins off the table and shakes it. A red coin pops out beside the Were's Claw. "The Coin of Falsehoods. Something we know isn't true. Something is wrong with what we know."

What is she suggesting? That Luca is innocent? Our informants told us that he is the spy, that he is the killer.

I've already made up my mind to hate him.

"What's wrong?" I ask. "What don't we know?"

"I'm trying to see into your fortune, but it's blurry." She closes her eyes and leans her head back, almost moaning. "There's nothing around Luca at all. There's nothing around any of your illusions." She opens her eyes and squeezes the Coin of False-hoods. "What is Luca's jynx-work?"

"Luca is a poison-worker," I say.

"The boy who cannot die," she says. "No one cannot die, sweetbug. No one who truly walks this earth."

"What are you saying?"

"I'm saying that could be the missing piece. Luca could be an illusion," she says. "A freak."

Impossible.

"That doesn't make any sense. I never created him."

"You cannot always trust your mind," she says. "Memory can be the clay of mind-workers. Memory changes each time you look back on it. Memory fades. *If a worker looks into your mind, then pieces will be left behind.* So the song goes."

I consider the time with Jiafu, when he swore he paid me, yet I didn't remember it. When I stole his coins and later found my payment from him in my bedsheets. I think about the un-known origins of the purple butterfly Agatha preserved for me, and how she insisted I was the one who gave it to her.

"I wouldn't forget," I say. "I wouldn't forget making him."

But my words falter. Could I have? What if the killer is a mind-worker, who has been peering inside my head all along? Tuyet is a mind-worker, and certainly not the only one in Go-morrah. Anyone with that ability could see inside my thoughts, my memories, and figure out how to mold them.

And if I *were* a charm-worker, they could be molding me.

"If he's an illusion—which I'm positive he's not—then I can make him disappear," I say, trying to sound confident, like Ka-hina's words haven't shaken me. "I can lock him in a Trunk, if I'm close enough."

And if he is an illusion, he could be a target like the others. If he is an illusion, he isn't safe. Poison-worker or not.

Not that I believe Kahina's words. I don't know any mind-workers. I couldn't possibly forget creating an entire illusion. But her suspicions are still enough to worry me. If what she believes is true, Luca could face execution for a crime he didn't commit.

I have to find him. And once I do, I'll make sure he doesn't leave my side. I'll tell Villiam our suspicions. Luca will be set free. We will all make progress. We'll learn the truth. Together.

My determination falters for a moment, remembering what Villiam told me. "But the informant…he said Luca was the spy," I say.

"The Coin of Falsehoods, though vague, is a reliable fortune," she says.

Luca could be innocent.

And I let the guards take him.

"I need to find him," I say.

"It's dangerous," she says.

"I know. But I'll be back. I'll come back with him, and you can read him again. You'll see he isn't an illusion. And if he's not…" He would still be guilty. "I don't know. I don't want him to die."

If they figured out how to kill him, he could already be dead.

CHAPTER TWENTY-THREE

I sprint as fast as I can to the Menagerie, my mind in knots. Usually on our first night in a new city, the Festival bustles with activity. But Gomorrah is strangely empty, smelling of kettle corn and roasted cashews, waiting for patrons. An uneasiness hangs in the air that I can't simply be imagining. The fortune-workers and other attractions of the Uphill don't have their signs out, either because they aren't expecting any visitors or because they don't want any. I turn around toward the smoke Kahina mentioned, billowing black and ugly into Gomorrah's dark sky. It's coming from Skull Gate.

Everywhere, people close the windows and doors of their caravans. They pack up, as if preparing to leave. Did Villiam give the warning to flee? I haven't heard a horn.

The commotion near the entrance to the Festival only makes me more anxious. I can't help but picture Luca the way we found Venera, his throat slit. Or his back and chest riddled with stab wounds, like Gill.

But Luca can't die. If someone tries to kill him, he'll just come back.

Villiam said he murdered my family. So doesn't he deserve to die?

I don't know what to believe. I haven't known what to believe, what to do or anything since I held Gill's lifeless body in my arms a month ago.

I try to think about the idea of Luca being an illusion logically, to remove my emotional perspective, the way Villiam or Luca would want me to. But I can't. Luca *can't* be an illusion. Every illusion I've created has taken months of work, sketches and blueprints. How could I forget all of that? How could I forget creating him?

A painful stitch develops in my side, so I half walk, half jog the rest of the way to the Menagerie. The slow pace grates on me, only adding to my sense of anxiety and urgency.

My heel crunches on something in the grass. I bend down and pick up the pieces of three charms, which look as if they were broken even before I stepped on them. Someone ground them into the dirt.

Suddenly, I recognize them. They're the charms Luca had made to protect him from Hellfire. He had them sewn into that atrocious vest he always wears. Maybe Agni found them in his shirt, brought them out to show Villiam and then smashed them beyond repair.

Fear boils in my stomach. What if Luca really is an illusion? What if he's the next target, linked to another political figure? What if someone has discovered the secret to killing him?

I run around the Menagerie to the main entrance, toward the clearing that leads directly to the Festival's entrance. The Menagerie, being at the dead center of Gomorrah, is also the dead center of trouble.

I run directly toward the chaos.

Up-Mountain officials swarm around the clearing, iron masks

concealing their faces. In front of them, members of Gomorrah protest. A few of them have swords of their own, but they don't have them brandished. They seem to be in a standoff with the officials, not willing to attack in case it causes a full-out brawl. The officials would not hesitate to kill them if that happened.

Skull Gate is burning in the distance. A crowd points at the Leonitian officials who stand behind it, their torches raised as they push into the Festival. They carry short swords pointing out, daring anyone to approach them. A few people turn and run. The others are more defiant. Members of the guard untie their jackets and reveal their black uniforms beneath. They pull on masks that cover all but their eyes.

"We're looking for the proprietor," one of the officials says.

Well, they're certainly going to get his attention by burning down Skull Gate.

I wonder if I should step forward. I could take over as the proprietor here, try to bring the situation under control. If Villiam were here, that's what he would tell me to do. Gomorrah comes before anything else, even family.

But suddenly I realize that I can't do that. I never could. As much as I love the Festival, I would abandon this life in a heartbeat if it meant keeping my family safe. And maybe that means I'll never be the sort of proprietor Gomorrah needs.

That's what Villiam would say.

Or maybe it means I'm simply kind of heart. That's what Kahina would tell me.

One of Gomorrah's guards approaches the official. "We've already sent someone for the proprietor. In the meantime, we ask you to wait outside. You're distressing our residents."

"We have orders from our new lord to make this Festival of Sin leave," the official says. "Thanks to the sin and impurity your Festival has brought to our land, our previous lord has been consumed by his snaking sickness, may he rest in peace."

"We don't give a shit about your lords," the guard says.

The official makes a move to smack him across the head with the handle of his sword, but the guard catches it and yanks the official off his horse.

The old lord is dead? That means that the new lord is Exander, the leader of the Alliance. A shiver of dread trickles down my spine as I realize that the most powerful man in the Up-Mountains now leads its most formidable city-state.

Someone bumps into my shoulder as they run past, knocking me to the side. Others follow, fleeing from the officials. They haven't come here with peace on their minds. Who knows what devastation they could cause before Villiam gets here?

With my moth illusion to conceal me, I slip around the crowds to the Menagerie's entrance. The taxidermied animals, many of them knocked over, stare at me as I enter. I cannot shake the image of a dead Luca out of my mind. Dead like these old Gomorrah performers. Even if he can't really die.

In more ways than one, it makes sense that Luca could be an illusion. His poison-working is an anomaly, maybe just as bizarre as Crown's nails or Hawk's wings. And Kahina cannot see anything in his fortune. Tuyet struggled to hear his thoughts.

But what does that say about me? That I may have fallen in love with one of my own illusions, someone I *created*?

No wonder Luca, with his handsome face and strange abilities, fell for someone like me. The only person who could love a freak is another freak.

I step inside the empty main show room, lit by five torches near the center ring. The Menagerie tent is massive. There are dozens of tunnels, hundreds of hiding places. I search around the room for one of those tunnels and choose a small, concealed one, probably meant for the performers to enter the backstage area. This is where they were keeping Dalimil, but he's no longer here.

The inside is barely lit, and it reeks of animal droppings. There don't seem to be any actual animals here right now, thank goodness. The last thing I need is to run into a chimera.

I peek through the next few rooms and make my way back to the main area of the tent, full of stands, the trapeze and the circle where the circus master reigns. Entirely empty. My memory from my night with Dalimil is cloudy. Purposely so. That isn't something I wish to remember.

I turn down another hallway, bracing myself to encounter a loose animal. All it contains is a cage. But instead of a chimera, or a dragon, or a unicorn, I find Luca.

Luca.

He's unconscious. I kneel beside the cage where he lies. "Luca," I hiss. "Luca, please wake up."

He doesn't.

But it doesn't matter. If he's an illusion, I can make him disappear now that I know where he is. I find that place in my mind with the Trunks, the place where all my illusions are locked away, safe. I pass Venera's empty Trunk, and Blister's, and Gill's. And I keep walking, past the other Trunks, until I'm entirely in the dark. The air here is thick, almost like sludge, and my pace slows as I fight against the heaviness of it. It's exhausting. As if something is trying to stop me from going here.

But I keep pushing. It feels like I'm a magnet walking toward another one, repelled with each step. I place my hands on the wall to feel my way forward. And at last I reach a Trunk and then a handle.

When I touch the handle, my mind fills with Luca. I see his brown eyes. I see the vest he always wears. I see everything. The images flash before me, too fast and blurry to properly make out. But they are there. The memories, though muddled, are there.

This is his Trunk. He *is* an illusion.

And he must be innocent.

I swing it open.

Luca, however, doesn't disappear. He remains in the cage,

though the Trunk stands waiting for him, sucking the air out of me like a vacuum. Why doesn't Luca disappear? After a few more moments of waiting, I shut the Trunk and take three deep breaths.

Then I notice the charms hanging inside the cage. Maybe they're preventing Luca from leaving.

But the only person who would think to put those in the cage would have to know that Luca is an illusion. And there are only three people who have access to Luca: my father, Chimal and Agni. The only person capable of creating Hellfire—a fire-worker—is Agni. He would've recognized Luca's charms for what they were.

My stomach fills with dread. Has it been Agni all along? He could've lied about the informant. He could've fed lies directly into my father's ear. Villiam trusts him more than anyone.

I need to get Luca out of here, and fast. If Agni is behind all of this, then even Villiam could be in danger. Then I think back to the incident with the horses and realize that he might have been in danger since the beginning.

Desperate for a solution, I open the other Trunks. First, Unu and Du and Nicoleta. Unu and Du appear beside me, and they stumble as their legs hit the ground.

"Where are we?" Unu asks.

"Smells like shit," Du says.

"Language," Nicoleta hisses. She materializes behind me. "We're in the Menagerie tent." Her eyes fall on Luca. "What's going on? Why are we here with him, Sorina?"

"I think he's innocent."

"How can you—"

"He's an illusion, Nicoleta," I say. "I don't know how. My mind... I don't remember creating him. It doesn't make sense, I know, but he *is*."

I expect her to argue with me, to claim that I'm breaking down under too much stress. For days now, we've all begun to believe that Luca is the killer, that he's the Alliance spy. That he's dangerous.

Nicoleta looks at me, wide-eyed, for a long moment. But she doesn't argue.

"I need you two to be lookouts," Nicoleta says to Unu and Du. "We're going to figure out how to get Luca out of this cage."

The four of us exchange glances. If Venera were here, this would be easy. Venera could bend through the bars and throw the charms out, and then I could make Luca disappear. But the situation isn't entirely hopeless. Nicoleta has her strength, after all, even if her abilities come and go.

"I need you to bend the cage bars," I tell her. "Please."

"I don't know if I can." She holds her hands behind her back. "I… I messed up the last time. I failed you."

"But no one else can get him out," I say.

"But I'm not strong enough—"

"*Please*," I beg her. "Please *try*."

Nicoleta takes a deep breath, nods and then walks to the cage. She grabs two rungs with each hand and pulls. Nothing happens.

"Nicoleta—"

"Just give me a minute," she snaps. "I'm not talented like the rest of you, I know. But I can do this. I can do this." Her voice quiets, as if she's only talking to herself.

She pulls again. The bars give a little, but not much. Not enough.

"Why is it that everyone else is special and I'm the useless one?" she says, nearly in hysterics. I've never seen Nicoleta like this. She always wears a mask of composure. The effort of bending the bars must be draining.

I place my hands on her shaking shoulders. "You're the least useless of all of us," I say gently. "You're the one who holds us all together. You're the one keeping everyone sane."

"And who's keeping me sane?" she snaps, tugging on the

metal bars. They screech and bend some more. "Who's taking care of me?"

"I..." I don't have an answer for that. This entire time, I've been leaning on Nicoleta for help. While I've been gone with Luca, searching for the killer, Nicoleta has been repairing the mess at home. Buying food, even if no one eats it. Doing the laundry. Setting up and packing up. Ensuring that our lives go on. She has managed to simultaneously run our family and, when I asked her, to help me capture Dalimil. Maybe I have been asking too much of her.

She groans and pulls more on the bars. Slowly, they give way, barely enough for me to reach my arm through and grab the charms near the top of the cage. I reach inside and rip them off, and then I drop them to the dirt and grind them into pieces with my heel.

"Now what?" she asks.

"Now I make him disappear," I say.

I return to the Trunks in my mind and reach for that last one, the one hidden within the haze of forgotten memories. I unlatch the lock and reach out for Luca's Strings. They're there, taut and binding him to me. How did I never notice them? I've never thought to look for them before, of course, but I can't believe that they've been invisible to me all this time.

I gather the Strings in my hands and throw them into the Trunk. Luca disappears from inside the cage and enters the Trunk in my head. He's safe.

I throw my arms around Nicoleta. "Thank you," I breathe. "Thank you."

She squeezes me until my chest hurts. "We're going to get out of this. Even if it means leaving Gomorrah, we're going to escape."

If leaving Gomorrah will keep my family safe, then so be it. But it may not come to that. If Agni is the killer, then everything would be solved. The investigations would end, and my family could stay here.

But he might not be.

"Well, I guess this means Luca is definitely an illusion," Nicoleta says.

"Yes." It takes me several seconds to manage the word. Because *yes* means that something is wrong with my memory. *Yes* means that all of this makes less sense than it ever did. *Yes* means that I fell for someone I made up. *Yes* means I made up someone to fall for. And for him to fall for *me*.

The two of us walk to the doorway out of the room, where Unu and Du sit on the ground and wait, muttering to themselves.

"There's been no one here," Unu says.

"Not a soul," Du echoes.

Nicoleta looks around the dressing room and then turns to me, her voice hushed.

"Your mind must have been tampered with," she says. "A mind-worker."

"I don't know any mind-workers," I say. I mean, I technically do. I know Tuyet, though her mind-working isn't normal and might not be able to alter someone's memories. And there are several other mind-workers in Gomorrah, but no one I associate with.

"That doesn't matter," she says. "There has to be a mind-worker involved."

"Do *you* know any mind-workers? By name? Who would want to hurt us? Who would know anything about us?"

"No, but if Agni *is* involved, he can't be acting alone. He must have a mind-worker answering to him."

Footsteps crunch the hay somewhere in the next room. I act before thinking and shove Nicoleta and Unu and Du back into their Trunks. Unu and Du are only twelve—how could they help with an official? And Nicoleta, well, maybe I should've kept Nicoleta out, since she looks like an Up-Mountainer.

The tent flap parts, and there's a flickering light, cast by a flame. The flame dances over the outstretched hand of Agni, casting an eerie mix of glow and shadows over his angular face.

"Sorina," he says, a hint of surprise in his tone. Now that he's seen me, it's too late to use an illusion to hide myself. But maybe I could make a dummy to fool him like I did during my argument with Jiafu.

"What are you doing here when there are officials out? You should be safe in your tent. They're causing quite a havoc."

"I was out when they arrived. I came in here to hide from them," I lie.

He raises his eyebrows. "We both know that you could hide yourself with your illusion-work. Why come in here, alone, in the dark?" At this, he dims the light of his fire until it is no bigger than a match flame. I try not to whimper. These are just theatrics to scare me. "Were you talking to Luca? Sorina...that isn't a good idea. Not after what he has done."

I am brave, I think to myself. I am brave enough. All I need to focus on is making it back to Kahina, now that I have Luca and the other illusions safe inside my head. I need to protect them.

"I think he might be innocent," I say.

"Don't let him trick you, Sorina. You can't trust an Up-Mountainer. Look what they're doing to the Festival just as we speak. Look what they've done to your family. To my son." He shakes his head. "Don't let your feelings for one boy ruin our crusade."

I have known Agni my entire life. During every meeting or dinner with Villiam, he has been present, though silent. It's difficult to imagine him trying to hurt me.

"I know he's an illusion," I say boldly.

The sympathetic smile on his face morphs into a scowl. He

takes a step toward me, the fire above his palm glowing brighter. "I didn't expect you to figure it out."

My heart freezes into a hard lump of ice. I hold back a scream and force out an illusion of myself, so fast I don't bother with the details. It's so dark in here that all I need is a silhouette to stand here—so I can run.

Agni is the killer.

This entire time, he's been watching from the background behind Villiam, learning about my abilities. Maybe he's a mind-worker, as well. That would explain how he knew Luca could be killed with Hellfire and how I'd forgotten about creating Luca. Villiam usually helps me create my illusions, but Agni is always with him. He'd have opportunity to mess with his mind, as well.

"I'm not trying to hurt you," he says. "I've known you a long time. You're a nice girl. But this is much bigger than you and your little family. You have seen for yourself what we are up against."

I inch back, deeper into the darkness, the illusion of myself only a few feet from Agni.

"You're not fooling anyone," he says. He shakes his jacket, which jingles with glass and metal clacking together. "I had charms made to counteract the effects of your illusions." He takes a step forward, and I take another back, keeping him at least ten feet away. Even if he can see through my illusions, there's still the safety of the darkness.

"The Up-Mountainers need to pay for what they've done to us. We can put an end to the way they've treated us for centuries. Don't you want to help, Sorina? You were a slave once. Where would you be now if Villiam hadn't freed you?"

I don't answer. I'm sad for Agni's loss, truly, but I'm now ter-rified of being alone with him. Terrified of the way he looks at me, as if my past is etched on my skin. I might share pieces of Agni's story, but I cannot feel the way he feels. Maybe I should.

But however justified his ends, the means will only see more innocents murdered.

"I'm curious," he asks. "How did you find out about Luca?"

I don't answer. I don't owe him any explanations.

"You're rarely this quiet. In fact, Villiam can hardly get you to stop chattering on." He shakes his head and then the flame over his hands goes out, and we're in nearly complete darkness. All I see is the outline of his body coming closer. "Answer me, Sorina."

Still, I say nothing.

"I haven't wanted to hurt you, but you're forcing my hand. If you don't make the Up-Mountain boy reappear, I'll kill you in order to kill him."

Then his fire returns, all at once, but ten times as large and ten times as bright. It glows pure gold, and the entire room is illuminated as if we're within the core of the sun.

Hellfire.

I dash for a tunnel and make it into the main circus room, where I trip on a balance beam. Agni sprints toward me, and I look around frantically. I need to get away, out of the reach of him and his fire.

Hawk appears beside me before I even call to her. Just as Agni is an arm's length away from burning me, she grabs my leg with her talons and flies me up to the high trapeze. I dangle upside-down and scream as the entire perimeter of the tent becomes engulfed in golden flames.

All except for Agni, who must be wearing charms like Luca's. The Hellfire parts for him as he walks.

"We need to fly out of here," I tell Hawk.

"The doors are covered. I don't think we can fly low enough to get out without getting burned," she says.

Agni twists the flames into something else, sculpting it like melted glass. He makes a bow and then points one long shining arrow at us. He doesn't even need to hit us. The Hellfire will consume the entire trapeze in moments.

But if Agni is gone, the Hellfire will disappear, too. I need something to get rid of Agni, and I need that person to be quick and sudden about it.

I call to Tree, and he appears several yards behind Agni, already prepared to run. He lets out a growl loud enough to shake the Menagerie and then charges at him.

Agni doesn't have time to react. He falls under Tree's weight and is crushed in a medley of screams and the crunching sound of breaking bones.

Hawk grabs me and takes off, cheering for Tree as the flames disappear. I'm too disturbed at the sight of the Menagerie floor, which is a mess of blood and Agni's broken body, to echo her enthusiasm. But I murmur my appreciation for Tree's efforts and return him safely to his Trunk.

We soar out of the tent and over Gomorrah. There's a battle raging not far outside the Menagerie, to the tune of screams and swords clashing. Even from upside-down and far away, it's easy to see that Gomorrah has the advantage because of its jynx-workers. Shadow-workers clutch the shadows of the officials and toss them dozens of yards away, and all of our weapons carry some kind of strengthening charm.

I don't think Hawk is thinking about where she's flying because she's taking us north, beyond the burning Skull Gate. "We need to find Villiam," I tell her. The cold wind up here slaps against my skin.

"You still haven't told me what the hell is even going on." Her face is pale, and obviously all of this has shaken her as much as it has me. I told Nicoleta and Unu and Du about Agni, but I didn't tell her. I simply brought her out when I needed her, right in the middle of danger, which wasn't fair. Yet she acted fast. She saved my life. And, by doing so, saved all our lives.

I'm suddenly reminded of how very young she is.

"I know. I'm sorry."

"I just need to be in a tree somewhere. Three dead mice in my hands. And then I'll be good."

But we don't fly to a forest. We turn around and fly back to our tent, beside Villiam's. Once we land on the ground, we rush around the path's corner toward our home. The guards who usually protect us are gone—probably dealing with the battle at Skull Gate.

"I'm not a jynx-worker," someone says nearby. "I'm not. I swear."

"I can see your shadow twisting."

Hawk and I creep closer, careful to keep ourselves hidden from sight. It's Jiafu, cornered by an official. They stand in a clearing surrounded by caravans and tents with their doors sealed and shut, including Villiam's.

"Who is that?" Hawk whispers. She has no idea who Jiafu is, or that I work with him. I shush her so the official doesn't spot us.

"Everything's lit by bloody torches. Of course my shadow is moving," Jiafu says. Though even as he denies his jynx-work, his shadow twists into a spiral on the grass, as if trying to give away its master.

"If your shadow comes near me, I'll put this sword through your gut," the official says.

I'm frozen. I don't know what I could do at this point. Any illusion I could create to scare the official away would probably only make him retaliate.

Jiafu takes a step closer to a tent, farther away from the nearest torch. His shadow dims and doesn't twist so much. But it still flickers. He puts up his hands. "I'm just trying to get back to my home," he says. "I know the proprietor. He personally—"

The official stabs his sword through Jiafu's neck.

I bite my tongue to keep from screaming and cover Hawk's eyes with my hand. When he pulls out the sword, spurts of blood follow. Jiafu collapses on the ground, and even from far away, I can see that he dies within moments. The official wipes off his sword on Jiafu's shirt.

Nausea races through me. I should've done something. I shouldn't have been frozen. But I didn't expect this to happen. Jiafu always squirms his way out of trouble.

"He just killed him," Hawk whimpers.

"We need to get inside."

I am almost too shaken to maintain even the simple moth illusion. I don't bother to conceal the sound of our footsteps as we run.

I collapse on our living room floor and bury my face in a pillow. My clothes reek of smoke and sweat, and my heart pounds erratically. I feel like my chest could burst, and I breathe in the comforting, familiar scent of the kettle corn kernels that litter our floor.

I open Luca's Trunk. Maybe he'll wake now.

He appears lying down, his head resting on my lap, unconscious. "Luca. Luca," I plead, but it doesn't do any good. I also open Nicoleta's Trunk, because I need someone to talk to who can keep a level head through all of this. Hawk has already left to find food in the next room. I hear the wooden bowls clunk together as she rummages around for dead mice.

Nicoleta doesn't stumble when coming out. She's gotten used to coming and going between my head and the real world. "What happened?" she asks. "You smell like a cigar shop."

"Agni showed up and attacked me. Tree trampled him, and Hawk flew us to safety."

"You're saying Agni's dead? And that he was behind all of this?"

"Yes."

"That doesn't make sense. There's a mind-worker involved; I'm certain of it."

"I don't know. Maybe Agni was a mind-worker, too? I just

need to breathe. Can I just breathe for a moment?" I'm crying, nearly hyperventilating, shaken to my core. I squeeze Luca's limp hand for comfort.

Nicoleta does what Nicoleta always does—pace. "Maybe we *should* leave Gomorrah," she says.

"Where would we go? We're as far up in the Up-Mountains as you can get—"

"Anywhere is better than here. There's another killer here, Sorina. There's someone else. I can feel it."

This isn't what I meant by "just breathe." I feel as though I need months to gasp for air, if not years. To sleep and not worry about any of this, and to get the sound of Agni's bones crunching out of my head.

"I need to talk to Villiam," I say.

"Then go check if he's next door. Hawk and I will stay with Luca."

I thank her and hurry outside to Villiam's caravan. As I knock on the door, I realize just how much I need to hear his voice. I need him to hug me. To tell me it will be okay. I need my father to sort this out.

There are voices inside.

"There are people dying in Gomorrah over this nonsense," Villiam says. "Your officials are terrorizing them for no reason."

"The officials are under direct orders from the new lord Exander to ensure you leave. If you want them to stop, take your Festival away from here and back to where you came from."

"We had permission to come here a month ago. From the lord."

"It's been revoked, now that the previous lord is dead. May he rest in peace."

"Why?"

"It doesn't matter why."

I knock harder. This time, someone throws open the door.

It's a Leonitian city official, dressed all in white. He stares at me and my strange mask.

"Go home, girl," he says.

"Sorina?" Villiam's eyebrows furrow. "What are you doing here?"

"I need you. *Please.*"

Villiam turns to the officials. "We'll be leaving Leonita soon. And I suggest you remove your officials from our Festival. We didn't come here looking for violence—we're fleeing the war behind us. But if you continue to attack, know that you are against an entire city, one far more ancient than yours and one full of magic."

His expression is intimidating, almost threatening, even despite his crutches. Before I knocked, it sounded as though the officials had the upper hand, but Villiam turned the course of the conversation in an instant. Would I ever be able to do that, as a proprietor? I doubted it.

"Ovren champions those who serve Him," one of the officials says, but he pulls the other by the shoulder and they leave.

"What has happened, Sorina?" he says, once the door closes behind them. "You look frazzled."

"We were attacked," I say, burying my face in his chest. "It was Agni. Agni killed Gill and Blister and Venera. Luca is innocent."

He stiffens. "No, that's not possible. I've known Agni for years—"

"It was Agni. He came after us with Hellfire."

Villiam closes his eyes and takes a deep, staggered breath. "He's been…shaken since his son was taken. I thought the work was good for him. But…our informants were certain. Where is Agni? I want to speak with him immediately."

"Agni is dead," I say quietly, feeling almost guilty when I see the stricken expression on my father's face.

Villiam covers his mouth with his hand and takes a deep breath. "And Luca?"

"He's in my tent. So are the others. They'll tell you what happened."

We hurry back to my tent, where Nicoleta has managed to awaken Luca. As soon as we enter, I have the urge to release all the illusions, to sit among what remains of my family and let Villiam clear our problems away. It's over. It's over at last.

Luca watches us approach with wide eyes.

"Sorina. No," he says weakly.

"What happened?" Villiam asks. "Is everyone all right?"

"No," Luca says again, a panicked expression on his face. "It's him, Sorina. He's the mind-worker. He's been a jynx-worker all along."

CHAPTER TWENTY-FOUR

My heart leaps into my throat. No, that's impossible. What is Luca talking about? He's obviously mistaken, and I turn to Villiam, ready to apologize, to make excuses for Luca's confusion.

Villiam takes a few steps closer to Luca, hobbling on his crutches. Nicoleta lunges in between them, as if protecting him, as if she believes him.

Before I can think about what's happening, I hastily hoist Luca's and Nicoleta's Strings into their Trunks. Luca is disoriented, and neither of them know Villiam like I do. I'm tired of the accusations. Tired of jumping to conclusions. Villiam doesn't have any jynx-work. And he'd never hurt anyone in our family.

Nevertheless, my pulse quickens, and I'm hyperaware of the silence in the tent.

"You put them away?" Villiam says.

"Yes. What were they talking about?" I ask.

"I have no idea," he says. "They looked traumatized, which isn't surprising after what Agni did. We've both known Agni for years—this is a shock for everyone. To think that he'd be driven to this point... And I can't blame anyone more than myself..."

Why would Luca think Villiam is a jynx-worker or that he had anything to do with this? I take a few steps away from him, hating myself as I do so. It's only Villiam. My father. The man who's watched over me for years. I don't need to protect myself from him.

Luca must've made a mistake. Did he hear Agni talking about Villiam? Or is he only jumping to conclusions, since Agni is Villiam's assistant?

"Can I make you some tea, my dear?" Villiam asks. When I shake my head, he takes a seat on the floor and motions for me to join him. I do, leaning my head against his shoulder, my thoughts twisted.

"Do you want to talk about what happened?"

"I..." My mouth runs dry as I picture the fire. The cruelty in Agni's voice. The horror of finding Luca unconscious in the cage, of realizing he's my illusion. It's been too much. I can't possibly begin to process it all.

"I want to help you, but you need to talk to me," he says. "Tell me what happened."

I hesitate. I can't help it—I'm tense. Why do I always trust Luca's judgment more than my own? I can think for myself, but it seems as if I always listen to everyone else before I trust my own instincts. When I ran to Villiam, the first thing he did was make sure we were all safe. Why would he do that if he was involved?

But I need to ask questions, even if they're difficult. Gill, Blister and Venera died because I opted for easy answers to difficult questions, and it's time I assume responsibility. Even though Villiam is innocent, I need to ask...

Then, suddenly, my train of thought stumbles. I just made Luca disappear, yet Villiam hasn't asked how that was possible.

I lift my head off his shoulder. "Aren't you surprised that Luca is an illusion?" I ask. "I just made him disappear, after all."

He clears his throat. "I figured you would tell me when you're ready. I didn't want to push you…"

But his words don't ring true. Villiam has helped me create all of my illusions, so if I'd made another one without telling him, he would be shocked—hurt, even. I share all of my illusion plans with him, every step of the processes.

I stand up and put several feet between us. "Luca said you're a mind-worker. Is that true?" My breath quickens, and all the anxiety of the past month seems to hit me one hundredfold. I'm stupid, stupid, stupid.

I search Villiam's eyes as my question lingers in the air. It felt silly to even ask it. Of course he'll tell me he's not a jynx-worker. He'll laugh. The idea is…preposterous.

"I don't like lying to you, Sorina," he says, avoiding my face. His words make my knees almost give out. "I'm a mind-worker with a talent for peering into people's memories and meddling with them as I wish."

My heart leaps into my throat. That isn't true. It can't be true.

"It's been safer to keep it hidden. Do you think the Up-Mountain officials would want to interact with Gomorrah if they knew the proprietor could twist their very minds? Hiding it has brought prosperity to the Festival. I've brought us to more and farther places than any proprietor before me."

"You're the reason I forgot about Luca," I say. "It was you. Have you been killing the illusions, too? Has it been you all along?"

The resigned expression on his face is all the answer I need. I stumble back in horror.

"How could you do this to me? To our family?" I cry out.

He looks at me sadly, pityingly, as if I'm still the naïve child he rescued all those years ago. "This has never been about you. I have only done what was needed to protect Gomorrah. I must take my responsibilities as proprietor more seriously than my role as your father, which you ought to understand. Even you have risked your life for Gomorrah, bravely, selflessly." He sighs and holds his face in his hands. I should run from him, run far away, but I'm rooted to the spot. I have to hear him out. I have to understand.

And then I'll run. I'll leave Gomorrah and never look back. We can start over in the Down-Mountains. We'll find some place to be a family again. To be safe again.

I squirm away from him.

"Your illusions are the imaginary friends of a child," he says, his voice suddenly cold and condescending. "They've never been *real*. I never hurt them myself, not that it matters to you, I'm sure." He stands and approaches me, but I back away. I don't know what he means to do—hug me? Plead forgiveness? But I don't want him anywhere near me. He doesn't sound like my father.

A spark of madness twinkles in his eyes. "But the others we've killed together...the princess, the duke, the prince...they were *very* real. Together, you and I are creating the war that will save the Down-Mountains and millions of people. The Alliance shall fall."

"I never helped you kill anyone," I whisper.

He laughs, and the sound chills me to the bone. "You've never been aware, but you've been instrumental to our cause. The crown jewel of the entire plan is in your head this very moment. The new, young lord of Leonita, Exander, leader of the Alliance. Without his power over the city, Leonita will fall, and the entire region will follow. When the Up-Mountains are no longer united, our people can strike."

"Luca," I say. "Luca is linked to Exander."

"Yes. The boy you made to be a lover. Your illusions never do turn out as planned, do they? From the rumors I've heard...he's hardly much of a lover at all." He laughs again, as if this is all a joke to him, the way we'd laugh if Blister tried to pronounce a curse word or Unu lost five straight rounds of lucky coins. As if he's teasing me, not insulting me and destroying everything I've always believed to be true.

So that was the reason I created Luca? To be my lover?

He was made to love me. That's the explanation. Only someone forced to could actually love a freak like me.

I'm trying desperately not to cry as my heart breaks. "You knew about Luca from the beginning?" I ask.

"I suggested the idea," Villiam says. "And it was our secret—you were too embarrassed to tell the other illusions. I had every intention of giving you a happily-ever-after—I never wanted to use Luca. Our suspicions about the prince as the leader were very slim then. But by the time you finished the process, the lord of Leonita had developed the snaking sickness, and Leonita is too important to gamble with. I didn't want to risk you learning the truth. So I used your mind to give Luca a past and then wiped your memory of him entirely. He was born a stranger to you. He would have remained a stranger had you not met. By the time I discovered it, I couldn't undo it—you'd already told Nicoleta, whose mind I cannot mold. So I watched and I waited for the opportunity to take him."

If a worker looks into your mind, then pieces will be left behind. So Kahina said. If Villiam has been playing with my mind for years, then that explains why pieces of my memory have disappeared. With Jiafu... With Agatha...

This revelation makes it difficult for me to breathe, and I can't hold myself together anymore. I break. I sob.

Villiam reaches into his pocket and takes out a sapphire ring. "Do you recognize this?"

It's the ring Jiafu stole from Count Pomp-di-pomp on the night of Gill's murder. "How do you have that?"

"As you know, the thieves of Gomorrah work for me. I've known you've been working with Jiafu for quite a while. I assigned him his projects, though, admittedly, a few you likely don't remember." He points to Blister's top on the table. "Charm-dolls need something to connect them to the original person. An item close to them. You don't remember, but you helped steal Nicoleta's hairpin. Venera's lipstick. Luca's pocket watch. Then Jiafu gave them to me, and I gave them to you. Your illusions wouldn't even exist without my help."

That's why Luca's pocket watch was engraved with Exander's name. It did belong to him, once.

A new determination takes hold of me. "I won't let you hurt Luca," I say.

"If you're going to become Gomorrah's proprietor one day, you need to make the tough decisions." He reaches forward to touch me, but I back away again. His face falls. "If we finish what we started, we can free the Down-Mountains from the greed of this region."

"There are other ways," I say. "I'm not letting you touch him. I won't let you touch any of them." I wish my voice sounded firmer, more confident, but it quivers instead.

"Ways the Up-Mountains could see coming. We don't have the money or the organization to fight a proper war. But because of you, we might not need to."

He's trying to guilt me into this. As if I would ever agree to let him hurt any more of my family. To let him hurt *anyone*, period.

"I'm leaving Gomorrah," I say, sniffling. "You can't hurt us. And you can't hurt him. Only a fire-worker can kill Luca, and Agni is dead."

"There are plenty of fire-workers in Gomorrah. And there is more than one way to destroy Leonita's lord through Luca tonight."

"How?"

He shakes his head. "Let me take care of it, Sorina. You've barely known him a month. Look the other way, and let me save Gomorrah. Let me do my job. We can work this out together—"

"No!"

I lunge for the exit, already planning my escape from Gomorrah in my mind. Hawk can fly me for a while, and my illusion-work can keep us from the notice of Up-Mountainers. But, on foot, how long will it take us to reach the Down-Mountains? Probably months.

Villiam grabs my arm but, in doing so, nearly falls over. "I have to do this, Sorina."

"Let go of me." I try to wrench my arm away, but his grip is too strong. Even wounded, he is hardly weak. I'm crying so hard that my chest aches.

"I don't want to hurt you. I love you, Sorina." He shakes his head. "I wish I'd known how close you were to learning the truth. I could've spared you from this pain. I should've kept Luca close to me instead of where you might find him on your own. He's too clever. Without him, you would've never figured this out."

"*I* was the one who realized I have two kinds of jynx-work," I say indignantly. "*I* was the one who thought of Agni. Who realized the illusions were linked to the politicians. I'm cleverer than you think I am. Just not enough to realize that you're a monster. I *trusted*—"

His face twists into a scowl. "I'm hardly a monster."

"You've been manipulating me. Killing people."

"You know of the evils of the Up-Mountains as I do. You know what happened to my uncle. To Agni's son. About your own past. I am *not* a monster."

What happened to Agni's son and Villiam's uncle were trage-dies, and I know the evil that lurks in the Up-Mountains. I want to help the Down-Mountains and the people of Gomorrah—but not like this. Maybe that means I won't make a good proprietor. I don't care anymore. Not about pleasing my father, whom I've tried to please my entire life. Not about a legacy built on lies and murder.

"Sorina, you never would've been able to create your illusions without me. Look at Tree. He's barely sentient. He's dangerous and violent. That was the extent of your powers before. I was the one who helped your powers grow. Without me, you wouldn't have had any of them. I've been training you for *this* since I found you."

"How can I believe anything you say?" I ask. "You could've altered all of my memories. Did you actually save me from slavers, or is that just a story you made up to guilt me into working with you?"

He ignores the question and gestures behind him, to the commotion happening outside the tent. "After the Up-Mountains fall and the Down-Mountains are free, you can always recreate your friends. They're only imaginary, after all. They're not real."

I squeeze my hands into fists. How can he say that? He attended both Blister's and Venera's funerals. He sent them presents on their birthdays. Asked me how they were doing with school. Watched their performances.

But it was all for show. All so that he could kill them in the end.

Nausea falls over me, and I cup a hand over my stomach. I should've seen the truth. I should've seen this side of my father. All those years, I thought he wouldn't share the responsibility of Gomorrah's proprietorship with me because I was too young, too stupid. But really, he didn't want me close to the truth. Had I simply stepped outside the Freak Show tent, ventured more than a few times to the Downhill, I could have learned the truth on my own.

This is my fault.

"You've been plotting to kill them from the beginning," I say. "I've just been a tool for you. Not a daughter, not your heir. Just a tool you could use to start a war."

"No. Never," he says, almost like he means it.

But I don't believe him. Not anymore.

"Let me *go*."

"Don't leave. We're so close." He squeezes me tighter until my arm hurts. "It would've been easier to make you forget them altogether, to save you the pain."

"Then why didn't you?"

"Because, as I've found out, I cannot use mind-work on your illusions, just as Kahina cannot see them in her fortune-work. It ends up messy, imprecise."

Then it's over. Nicoleta knows the truth. He won't be able to make her forget.

Unless he kills her.

He reaches toward me and unties my mask. It drifts to the floor.

"The pain of losing a loved one… Wouldn't you rather forget? I could do that…simply wipe them all from your mind, the way I first did when you created Luca. You could start over. Start fresh—"

"I'm not going to forget them," I hiss. I try to squirm out of his grip. "I don't want to."

"Why waste the opportunity for relief? I would've been grateful for such relief after my mother died or when my uncle was killed where he stood by a religious zealot. If only I could ease my own mind the way I can ease yours."

Villiam leans down to my forehead, as if to kiss me, and I instantly cover it with my hands.

"I don't want to force you, my dear," he says, through gritted teeth. He grabs my other arm, as well, and yanks both away. In the process, he drops his crutches and, wincing, puts pressure on his broken leg. He presses his thumb against my brow bone.

When he touches my skin, a pain stabs through my head, as if Villiam has clawed his way into my brain. I shake. I should run. I should get out of here. But my legs won't move, as if the pain is rooting me to where I stand. He lets go of me, now that I can no longer flee. I raise one shaking hand to cover my forehead where he touched me, where the pain still lingers.

"Exander is evil," he says. "You know what he thinks of us? That we're scum. He'd burn all of Gomorrah and our people's homes in a heartbeat. With him alive, the deaths of your other illusions will be meaningless. The Alliance will survive. Yet you'd let him live."

"I'd let *Luca* live," I say.

"Luca isn't a real person. He's a figment of your imagination, one you and I brought to life."

"I won't let you hurt him," I say again.

I press past the pain in my mind to search for some kind of illusion, anything, even the moth. Something I can use to escape. But it's hard to concentrate beyond the pain, beyond the shrieking outside, beyond the smell of Villiam's cologne. It's hard to delve deep enough in my mind to escape the reality in front of me.

He lifts my chin up, forcing me to look at him. "I can make you forget this whole conversation. I can make you forget anything. You only need to move your hands."

Agatha told me that there is magic in a kiss. That must be what Villiam needs to dig into my mind properly—a kiss, on my forehead. I'd always thought it was meant for comfort. For love.

He rips my hands away from my forehead and kisses me. The pain in my head increases tenfold, and I scream as he splits my mind in two. I see flashes of my memories, as if I'm caught in a dream. I see the night of Gill's death and my argument with him about working with Jiafu. I see Jiafu's blood spill to the ground when the official stabbed him in the throat. I see Luca's head rolling at my feet. I see the apothecary where Luca told me he suspected Hellfire could kill him. I see the charms he kept in his vest, the charms crushed on the ground outside the Menagerie.

The pain squirms around my thoughts like a worm. It reaches my row of Trunks, then it slithers to the farthest one: Luca's. It yanks the Trunk open.

Luca appears beside me. He groans as he fights to move, but, like me, Villiam has him frozen. He presses his thumb to Luca's forehead. "It does not take precision to break someone," Villiam murmurs.

"Get. Out. Of. My. Mind," he snarls at Villiam, his dark eyes almost black with rage.

"It won't last long."

Another scream. Luca falls to his knees.

"Don't touch him," I beg. "Please. *Please.*"

"This wouldn't hurt so much if you had only listened to me, Sorina. If you hadn't gone looking for answers yourself and lied to me. You never would've met him to begin with. Nicoleta tried to warn you. So did Venera. If you hadn't met him…this mess would never have happened."

Villiam leans down and kisses Luca's forehead.

Luca screams.

The pain in my mind lessens. Slightly. With Villiam focusing so much energy on Luca, I now have more room to breathe. I don't dare move an inch to clue Villiam in to this but instead frantically search through my mind for some kind of an illusion. I settle on hornets.

We hear the buzzing first.

Then they appear, one by one, as if sprouting from the earth. They circle the air around me and Villiam, so loud they drown out the noise of everything but Luca's screams.

"I can see through your tricks, Sorina," Villiam says. "You can't actually hurt me."

Still, I order the fake hornets to attack Villiam. Whether or not he *knows* they aren't real won't stop him from feeling the pain of their stings.

Villiam grunts, but his concentration must not waver, as Luca doesn't stop screaming. However, the pain in my own head lessens. Sweat rolls down the side of my face, and I lift my hand to wipe it away.

My mind eases open to me like a sigh, and I search around

it as if I'm crawling and reaching for things in the dark. I find a Trunk—I'm in too much pain to identify whose it is. Hopefully it's Tree, who could stampede over Villiam just like he did to Agni. This time, I'll be ready for the sound of bones crunching. I'll be ready to watch my justice carried out.

But if it isn't Tree, who is seven feet tall and capable of protecting himself, then whichever illusion it really is could be in danger. How could Unu and Du save Luca? By slapping Villiam across the face?

But it's the only shot I have.

I open the Trunk, and the Strings slip out like a rope dropping off a cliff. They run and run and run until a silhouette appears beside me in the darkness, one with sharp hair curling on his head.

Crown.

His face hardens as he examines the scene before him, of Luca screaming, of me sweating and trembling on the ground. I curse. It could've been anyone other than Crown. Crown has been weak after Blister's death, and this...this could kill him.

Crown, however, doesn't hesitate. Not for a moment.

He takes off the glove on his right hand and drops it to the ground, exposing the razor-sharp fingernails beneath.

And he stabs his arm straight through Villiam's heart.

Villiam, Crown and I each let out a cry—Villiam's of agony, Crown's of anguish and mine of horror. Luca collapses, gasping for breath. The hold on me breaks, and I immediately rush to Luca's side. I place his head in my lap.

"Are you all right?" I ask. "Please, please be all right."

He squeezes his eyes shut, and he doesn't speak for almost a minute. Just when I am certain he is gone, he manages, "I'm fine. Just a migraine."

"Thank goodness," I say, over and over. I kiss his cheek. "I'm sorry. I'm so, so sorry."

He takes a deep breath, but his expression remains rigid. "I know."

Crown pulls his arm out from Villiam's chest, and my father falls face-first into the grass. His usually clean shirt is stained a deep scarlet. Even knowing everything he's done, all the hurt he's caused me, I still cry out. Another member of my family is dead.

"You killed my little boy." Tears spill from Crown's eyes. He grabs his glove off the ground and covers his blood-soaked hand. "Evil, evil man."

Handsome;
a performer;
witty;
no back hair;
bedroom brown eyes;
charming;
INDESTRUCTIBLE?
HELLFIRE.

LOOKS UP-MOUNTAINER; BELIEVES
HE IS FROM THE CITY-STATE OF RASKE.

LIVES ALONE IN DOWNHILL; PERFORMS
A SHOW WHERE PEOPLE PAY TO KILL
HIM. APPEARS INDESTRUCTIBLE.

CONCEITED, RUDE, CONDESCENDING.
CALLS HIMSELF A GOSSIP-WORKER.

KEEPS COMPANY WITH PRETTYWORKERS
BUT LACKS SEXUAL INTEREST.

CHAPTER TWENTY-FIVE

I help Luca to his feet, but he's so weak that he needs to lean on me for support. Not that I have much to give him. I'm so shaky from crying that I can barely stand myself. Like mine, his hair is stringy with sweat, and his whole body feels hot to the touch. "Are you sure you're all right?" I ask him.

He winces. "I'm fine."

"What do we do with him?" I ask, nodding toward Villiam's body, which I refuse to look at. Several hours ago, he was my father. Now he's a killer. It's going to take me more than a few minutes to be able to process that. For now, I can only feel as though I've lost someone else I loved. Someone who betrayed me.

How much of my love was genuine and not the result of his manipulation?

How much was his?

"Move him to his caravan," Crown snarls. "Then leave him for someone else to find."

I startle at Crown's tone. He so rarely says anything hurtful; his words are almost always full of kindness and encouragement. The harsh look on his face, the blood on his arm—this is a Crown I don't recognize.

The Crown after Blister's death.

"We'll walk back to Kahina's caravan," I say. "She's probably worried sick." And I have no desire to stay here, with my father dead on our floor.

"You can summon Nicoleta," Crown says, "if you don't want to move him yourself."

I examine my father's body. "No. I should do it." I can't keep allowing Nicoleta to deal with all of my problems for me. And he was my father, not hers.

While Luca rests against the table, Crown and I pick William up. I grab him under the arms, and Crown grabs his feet. I cringe. I have no desire to touch him or to be within five hundred feet of him. But we can't leave him here. So I cast my moth illusion, and we carry him arduously to his caravan. We lay him on the floor by his bookcase.

Afterward, I dunk my hands in the water basin in our tent to wash away the smell of his cologne. I wipe the snot and sweat from my face, and Crown comfortingly rubs my back.

"It's okay," he says.

"I can't believe it," I say. "I can't believe he did this to me. To us."

Crown, Luca and I walk down the path to Kahina's caravan, and I continue to cloak us in the illusion of moths. This is a strictly residential neighborhood, made up primarily of schools, homes and orphan tents. I picture Zhihao, Jiafu's younger brother, and how he will cope with the news of Jiafu's death.

Those who aren't fighting by Skull Gate are packing and hiding in their caravans, as if prepared to leave at any moment. Several caravans are missing from their usual spots—perhaps they've already left. The usual smells of kettle corn and bonfires are gone. Everything smells of the smoke still smoldering over Skull Gate.

I bang on Kahina's door until my fist hurts. She opens it and pulls me into a hug. "Sweetbug, sweetbug," she says. "I was so worried. What's happened to you?" She eyes the blood on Crown's arm.

Kahina helps us inside the caravan, and I immediately collapse on her cushions. The other Trunks in my mind fly open, unable to be contained a second longer, and suddenly Kahina's caravan is quite full with her, me, Luca, Crown, Nicoleta, Hawk, Tree and Unu and Du…as well as Kahina's many potted plants.

"What happened?" Nicoleta asks. "Crown, your arm, are you hurt?"

"No, no, I'm fine," he says softly.

All eyes turn to me to tell the story. I take a deep breath, slide my hand into Luca's for support and begin.

I have to stop several times to cry, or to hear the way my words hang in the air—to hear the truth in them. Villiam, my father, killed the illusions, and he's been planning to since the moment that I created them. The entire time I'd been paranoid about the killer watching us, I'd been right. He *had* been watching us. For much longer than I imagined.

And the worst part is to remember him at Blister's and Venera's funerals, helping us dig the graves. And how he comforted me after every single death. I was so naïve. And he…he'd been so cruel tonight. I'd never heard such harsh words escape him. I trusted him. I considered him my family. And that's how he thought of me all this time. Not as a daughter but merely a tool.

But, still, I'm not sure about that. I don't think I ever will be.

"All that matters is that we're safe now," I say.

"You killed him?" Unu asks Crown. "You killed the proprietor?"

"What was it like?" Du asks.

Nicoleta hushes them as Crown pales. "It's rude to bring up things like that."

"That man got what he deserved," Crown says. "That's all I have to say about it."

And yet, I grieve for him. I grieve for the man I always thought of as my father.

"And, Luca," Kahina says, "are you sure you're all right?"

"I'm fine," he says. "A bit nauseous. Agni used charms to make me pass out. And my head hurts, of course, but that will pass."

"Is there anything I can get for you?" she asks.

"Do you have any gin?"

She clicks her tongue. "Afraid not."

"But there's something that still doesn't make sense to me," Nicoleta says. "If each of us are tied to some...person, why not simply kill us anywhere? Why bring us all the way north, into the middle of a war? Villiam could've carried out his plans in the Down-Mountains, anywhere."

"Because Sorina is a charm-worker, obviously," Luca says. We wait for him to continue, but he doesn't, as if that explanation is sufficient.

"I'm still not sure I understand you," Nicoleta says with a hint of annoyance.

"Charms only work in close proximity. I had protective charms, but they only worked if I wore them. If one of you— us—are killed, it doesn't mean anything unless we're close enough to the person to whom we're tied."

You. Us. I'm reminded once more that Luca is one of the illusions, another person I made up. Which means that everything he remembers about his life before Gomorrah is a lie. He never had a life before Gomorrah.

I squeeze his hand. He doesn't squeeze back.

"So are we going to leave now?" Hawk asks. "Gomorrah will go back south?"

"Who's going to be proprietor now?" Unu asks.

"Luca could do it," Du says. "Luca's a genius, aren't you, Luca?"

I am almost hurt that Du didn't say anything about me. *I* was Villiam's protégée. I've been training to become the proprietor for a long time, but no one had expected it to happen so soon.

But I cannot imagine myself succeeding Villiam. Not after everything he's done. I don't want anything to do with him or the Gomorrah family.

I wouldn't make a good proprietor, anyway.

The corner of Luca's lips twitch into a smile. "As if Gomorrah would want an Up-Mountainer to be their proprietor."

"Then what about Nicoleta?" Hawk says. She tugs on Nicoleta's sleeve. Though Nicoleta also resembles Luca's people, she is hardly the only one in Gomorrah to do so, and she is from the Festival. People know her. People respect her. "You could be the proprietor. You'd keep everything very...organized."

She laughs. "I could hardly—"

"I think that's a great idea," I say. "I think that's perfect."

Nicoleta watches me with apprehension, and I can almost see the questions floating around in her mind. Would Gomorrah take to a proprietor who isn't a real person? But then a determined glint shines in her eyes, and she smiles.

I sit at Villiam's table, holding an insect vial that Villiam must've intended to give me. It's an oyster spider—not technically an insect but interesting nonetheless. Its eggs look like pearls, and it buries them in the sand near areas of salt water. I'm alone inside the caravan, debating about whether to keep the exotic gift from such a hateful man.

Outside, Gomorrah is burying Villiam's body. Rumor has it that an Up-Mountain official murdered him.

They want war.

I shouldn't feel guilty for missing my father's funeral after what he did, yet there's a part of me that does. But I can't bear to go. I've attended three funerals in the past five weeks because of him. I will not attend his. I won't stand there as Gomorrah buries him like a hero.

People will talk about the proprietor's daughter not showing up. Let them. Nicoleta will become proprietor and soon, they'll forget about me. They never wanted a freak as a proprietor anyway.

Worse than that is the guilty feeling that everything that has happened is my fault. Even if Villiam orchestrated all of this, I was willingly ignorant. Had I only asked questions, had I only taken a moment to think, none of this might have happened.

Someone knocks on the door.

I open it, and it's Luca, dressed in a fresh set of clothes without any stains of blood or dirt. He peers up at me through the rain. His blond hair is soaked and dripping down his neck. "May I come in?"

I nod, holding my breath and bracing myself for the conversation that will inevitably follow. Our relationship, which had already begun with complications, has now developed into something impossible. I created him, whether or not I remember it. All of his memories—everything he is—came from Villiam, the man who intended to murder him.

And I almost let it happen. I'm shocked he can even look at me.

He climbs into the caravan and stands at Villiam's desk. He removes his hat and soaked coat and looks up at the ceiling. "The warrior constellation," he says.

"I forgot you knew about stars," I say.

"My father and I used to examine them from the clock tower..." He taps his cane on the toe of his shoe. "But I suppose that never truly happened. The City of Raske and the clock tower are very real places. I'm simply not a part of them."

My heart aches when I look at his face. At his dark eyes. At the way he bites his lip. This is the boy I've come to love, the only person I suspect in the world who could ever also love me.

Because I made him up.

But he feels so real. The smell of his sandalwood soap. The groans of the caravan shifting from his weight as he paces around the room. The burning in my chest. All of it is so real that I could burst from the pain of it all.

"I'm very sorry about Villiam," he says, still standing. He doesn't touch me the way he usually does. Five feet span between us. "I'm sorry about all of this."

He was the one who almost died.

"I'm sorry, too," I say bitterly. "I don't know if I can ever say it enough. I didn't trust you—"

"It doesn't matter," he says, but, by his tone, it does.

"How are you feeling?"

"Better. My headache is gone. Doesn't seem like any lasting harm was done, though I can't seem to stop my right hand from trembling." He lifts it off his cane to show me the tremor. "But I didn't come to you for small talk. Gomorrah is leaving Leonita."

"I know that," I say. "Everyone is packing up now."

"Despite the fact that you and I disagree with Villiam's motives, the Alliance is real. With the other Up-Mountain city-states in turmoil, Exander will act. What are you going to do about it?" He leans on his walking stick. "Nicoleta isn't proprietor yet."

"I'm not going to kill you."

"I was hardly suggesting that," he says.

In truth, I'd rather abandon the proprietorship entirely. The Festival isn't my responsibility, and I want nothing to do with the Gomorrah family.

"What would you have me do?"

"You can do nothing. You can take Gomorrah away from here and let history play out. But that isn't the purpose of Gomorrah," he says. "You should give Exander something to remember. Something that will make him think twice about taking on the Down-Mountains, when the Ninth Trade War does begin."

He wants me to create an illusion.

"I don't want to be part of a war."

"It's inevitable. Just as it is inevitable that Gomorrah will be caught in the middle of it. That's the nature of these things." He stares out the open window. "What will you do to protect the Festival?"

It isn't fair for him to ask this of me. I've already gone to extraordinary lengths to protect my family and, by extension, this Festival. I am not the proprietor. I'm merely his daughter. This isn't my city.

My crusade is over.

"Why do you want me to do this?" I ask. "What is it to you?"

He grimaces. "You're right. I'm an Up-Mountainer. Why would I possibly care about world events? Why would I not dwell, even a little, on the fact that I only exist because Exander exists? I have been fashioned in the image of prejudice and terror. Everything I remember about my life was invented by your father. Why would I possibly care that you are sitting in your dead father's chair, mourning him and the future he promised you?"

I wince. "Do you hate me now?"

"No. No, I don't hate you. Even in the Menagerie, trapped and feeling very much betrayed, I did not hate you." He sighs, and I'm too overcome by guilt to speak. "But I know you. You aren't going to do nothing. While Gomorrah remains in Leonita, you're the proprietor. So…what are you going to do?"

He holds out his hand.

His eyes are questioning, but he already knows my answer.

I take it.

The walk to the outside of Gomorrah takes over forty minutes, from Villiam's caravan to the obelisks at the edge of the Downhill. The Festival moves behind us, a roar of wheels turning and wood creaking. Neither of us speak.

I am not certain who I am doing this for. For my family? To help finish Villiam's goals feels like a terrible insult to their memory. But Luca is right: the Alliance is a real danger. They always have been.

Am I doing this for myself? I was once a slave, according to Villiam's stories. Even if he lied about so many other things, I don't really think he lied about that. But I was so young. I cannot even imagine my life then. The evils of the Up-Mountains' empires have harmed thousands, and I feel almost guilty for not remembering my past. It's my story, yet it doesn't feel like mine to tell. Maybe Villiam stole that from me. Maybe the Up-Mountains did.

I shouldn't merely do this for Luca, simply because he wishes more of me. Everyone thinks I am a warrior, but I don't believe there's any fight left in me.

We stop in the field, its grass trampled and brown from accommodating Gomorrah. It looks as if we've left a wasteland behind us. Even in the sky, we have stained the clouds black.

"Leonita's officials even reached the Downhill," Luca says. "Look. One of the obelisks is broken."

The one to our left is missing its point. They are no longer twins.

"What are you going to do?" he asks.

"I usually make my illusions up on the spot."

"But this isn't the Freak Show."

"Isn't it?"

"You sound like you don't care."

"What makes you think that?" I ask. Really, I don't have enough in me to feel anything at all.

"Your voice is flat. You're..." His face darkens as he searches for a word. *Broken* would be the best choice. He touches my mask. Matte, black, plain. "Where are the feathers? The sequins?"

"My father just died."

"And the rest of your family is safe."

"Are they?" I ask. "Safe from Villiam and Agni, I suppose. Agni probably forced Dalimil to lie about the spy. But Gomorrah is currently fleeing from a possible war. A Ninth Trade War, everyone is saying. This battle might be over, but there are more to come. Gomorrah has asked my family to defend it before; who is to say they won't do it again?"

"You are. Right now." His voice rises, and the wind carries it. We are alone in this field—the iron gates of Leonita ahead of us, the fraternal obelisks of Gomorrah behind us. "The Wandering City will always wander into trouble. You must convince Exander not to follow us there." He points his walking stick toward the castle jutting out over the Leonitian skyline. "He should be in his castle."

"I don't think I can single him out from such a distance," I say.

"Then show the whole city your illusion."

I wither. That must be thousands of people. I don't normally perform illusions for such a large crowd. I perform in small details: in the scurries of insects, in the glittering of stars.

"I don't know if I can do this."

He rests his hand on my shoulder. I'm so startled, I nearly flinch away at his touch. "I'm connected to Exander, aren't I? Use me to find him."

I hesitate.

"Sorina. You can do this."

I'm not a warrior.

"You're Gomorrah's proprietor."

I don't desire any battles.

"Make him remember."

But maybe…I can stop them before they begin.

I lift my arms toward the Leonitian skyline, all iron and angles on its hilltop. I picture Gomorrah's smoke—the thickness of it in the air, in every mouthful we breathe. The towers of the castle twist into the spires of the Menagerie. The gates bend as if, bit by bit, someone is twisting them into a new shape: a skull. Its mouth gaping into a scream.

With everything I have, I push the illusion from my mind until I feel it seeping into reality. The dark clouds descend over the city as if falling from the heavens, cloaking its buildings, and its angles and contrasts disappear into shadow. The castle twists like a top spinning until the Menagerie tent spreads open wide and covers it completely, semitransparent.

I imagine Exander stepping to his window to look outside at the city below him, only to find Gomorrah. The churches of Ovren have vanished into the smoke. His people disappear entirely. I don't grace him with the smells of licorice cherries and kettle corn—I bring the rot, the manure, the tobacco smoke.

There's an obvious disturbance in Leonita. The gate falls shut. Horns blare out in the distance.

Luca squeezes my shoulder, and I focus on his touch. I don't know anything about charm-work—Villiam stole that knowledge from me. But I sense a presence in the city that reminds me of Luca in a way I cannot describe. A presence in the tower.

I'm so far, so incredibly far, but I grasp hold of that presence and use it to propel me closer. Whether or not my vision is real, I picture him at his window. With the smoke surrounding the city, he cannot see Gomorrah retreating in the distance. He might not understand. I'll have to show him who is responsible.

I allow the scene to continue for another thirty seconds before the next illusion comes to me. Beside that window on the tallest tower, I picture myself: maskless, in my performance robes. I hover in the smoke several feet from him, my hands stretched out menacingly like they are now. The image of me burns and flickers like the faint glow of fire within the city below.

I beckon to him, as if urging him to jump. I know he won't.

But I inch toward him. The wind stirs, and I turn around for a moment to admire what Leonita has become. When I meet his gaze again, my skin cracks. White grains of salt fall from my hands, my cheeks, my lips. The lord of Leonita watches as my remains are scattered across his city.

All at once, the illusion vanishes. The castle returns, the gate, the dark stone, the angles. All the lord sees is the smoke of Gomorrah in the distance. But even as we leave, he still catches the faint smell of burning in the air. Our ghost remains.

I drop my arms and lean against Luca to steady myself, entirely exhausted. That was all I have.

"Marvelous," he whispers.

He picks me up to carry me back to Gomorrah.

"I can walk," I say.

He ignores me. "I think I felt his fear, when you focused on him. I trembled in my soul."

"I have that effect on people." This earns me a hint of a smile, and I allow myself to relax. Maybe he doesn't hate me, after all. He can carry me if he likes. He isn't that strong—he will only tire himself out—but I don't mind the feeling of my cheek against his chest, and I'm tired. I won't argue.

"I'm sorry," he says. "I didn't mean to be harsh earlier."

"I deserved it."

"No, you didn't. I wish I'd seen through Villiam earlier. It was all there, right in front of me."

"It wasn't all in front of you," I say. "The puzzle pieces, they were *my* puzzle pieces. The mystery was my mystery. The problems were—"

"All of those were mine, as well. We've both avoided asking the tough questions."

We enter the edge of the Downhill. For a moment, we pass through a flicker of heat. It is only a moment, so quick it feels as though I imagine it, but it burns like Hellfire. I think back to the proprietor who supposedly stored the souls of Gomorrah in our gates so that we would forever burn, how the memory of heat still lingers at the edges of the city. The Festival's proprietors have always had a fondness for theatrics.

"My memories have always been fuzzy," Luca says. I don't know if he even noticed the heat. "I assumed it was the change of scenery, from a place like that to a place like this. Turns out I have eighteen years' worth of memories and only a year of them are real."

"I'm sorry—"

"For what? Creating me?" he asks, his face painfully emotionless. "I'd rather you not apologize for that. I like being alive, you know." He closes his eyes. "It's just—my father, my mother, I still remember them. I remember losing them. I remember running away. And now that I know none of it was real, I can't help but revisit it all again, in my memories. I can barely picture his face anymore..."

"Luca..."

"I'm not done," he says. "I've rehearsed my little speech several times. At least let me perform it." His voice cracks. Luca's voice never cracks. "I considered leaving, going to Raske, visiting the place I never grew up in. But I'm not going to do that. I can't leave Gomorrah. I can't leave you."

"I'll be fine," I say, though the thought of him leaving makes my heart ache. "I understand if you need to go...find yourself..."

"I can't leave because I love you, Sorina," he says. His expression becomes pleading, one of such vulnerability that I'm taken aback. "I love you, even if doing so is mad. And why travel to a place I've never been when I can find myself with you?"

I let out the breath I've been holding. I don't know what to say. I want to squirm out of his arms so I can avoid looking at him and the embarrassment on his face. His cheeks flush, and I am certain my chest will burst.

"But you're an illusion," I say. "I created you."

"That doesn't mean I'm not real."

I wince, remembering Villiam's harsh words about my illusions. "What I mean is, you don't have to love me. Even if I created Hawk to be my sister and Crown to be my grandfather, you don't *need* to be connected to me."

"It's not a *need*," he snaps. "It's a want. But if you don't want me—"

"It's not that at all! When Villiam accused you, I was distraught over Venera's death. I let him confuse me, and I'll forever hate that he so easily turned me against you." I bite my lip, uncertain if I should go on, if I want to bring up the misery of those days, but Luca nods at me to continue.

I owe it to him to apologize properly. "I was distraught and devastated. I still struggled to wrap my head around the accusations because…I love you, and it was impossible to see beyond it. When I thought you were gone…it was terrible." My voice has reduced to a whisper, and Luca's expression has softened. "So it's not that I don't love you. I'm just scared because the only people in my life are figments of my own imagination."

He sets me down. We have reached his caravan. It would feel better to stand, to pace, but Luca sits on the edge and leans against the door. He motions for me to join him. I sit close to him, my legs dangling several inches from the grass.

"I am not a toy," he says. "And neither is the rest of your family. Your illusions, whatever you imagined them to be, don't turn out the way you plan because you cannot control us. I've made my own decisions, and you're one of them. Don't diminish me to something less than a person. If I want to try to be with you, it's because I *choose* you."

His face is inches from mine, and I stare into his dark eyes. My heart, broken and exhausted from weeks of tragedy and betrayal, manages to flutter. He wants to be with me.

"I'm sorry. I didn't—"

"It doesn't matter. I just need to know if…" He squeezes my hand, his eyes peering through me as if I'm not even wearing a mask. I brace myself for what he is about to ask. I'm prepared to give him anything, if only he will forgive me, if only he will keep loving me. "If you will let me apply for the vacant position in your show."

I bark out a laugh. "What?"

"If Nicoleta is going to take over the duties as proprietor, you'll need a new manager." His eyes glint mischievously. "Were you expecting me to say something else?" He wraps an arm around my waist, pulling me closer to him.

"The pay won't be much," I say.

"I'll take a pay cut if it means not being slayed for sport." He smiles, dimples and all, as he presses his forehead against mine.

I'm breathless.

"Unu and Du bicker incessantly."

"I'm sure I can tolerate that." His breath warms my cheeks.

"Crown's food... It's really terrible." My voice grows quieter with each word.

"I don't doubt it."

Luca runs his hand through my hair, making me tingle all the way down my back.

I kiss him, and he kisses me back in a way that makes me dizzy. Not dizzy from his lips, or the taste of him, or the smell of his soap, but dizzy in my thoughts. I'm kissing Luca, the boy who loves me, who sees me as more than a freak. The boy who'd call himself a freak, too.

"Just say yes," he whispers.

"Yes."

CHAPTER TWENTY-SIX

I peek behind the curtain at the audience from a southern town in the Up-Mountains, a quiet place used to the comings and goings of Gomorrah but no less delighted with our visits every few years. They wear simple clothes and, due to the harsh mountain winter, coats buttoned all the way up from their knees to their necks. They chatter about the last time they visited Gomorrah and other acts they've seen earlier tonight, like the fire-juggler who wears all black or the swan dragon at the Menagerie.

I search the front row for Nicoleta and then spot her at the end. She wears her light brown hair down and wavy, and she laughs and whispers into the ear of her date, a gorgeous girl of mixed background, a charming smile and delicate, feminine features. Whatever joke Nicoleta told must have been crude, as several visitors around them turn to glare, which only makes the pair laugh harder. It's been a long time since I've seen Nicoleta grin like that.

The patrons have no reason to expect a young woman in such casual clothing to be the Festival's proprietor.

On the opposite side of the backstage stands Hawk with her fiddle and Unu and Du with their drums. Beside them, dressed in scarlet satin robes, is Luca. He nods at me, my cue to raise the curtain.

The music plays. The curtain rises. And Luca struts onto the stage, his cloak swinging behind him. The silver piercing he usually wears in his nose has been replaced by a deep amethyst for the show. "Welcome to the Gomorrah Festival's famous Freak Show," he says in his practiced performance voice, meant to project across the tent. "I'm Luca, the show's manager, and I'd advise anyone of faint constitution, or those who've recently filled their stomachs with treats, to leave now. The show is filled with horrors, and there's no need to add to them by overturning your food in the second row."

He pauses to let the music fill the tent. Hawk, in addition to playing her fiddle, sings an eerie aria. The audience members watch the stage with apprehension and curiosity, exactly the way Luca wants them.

"And now, without further ado, let the show…begin!"

Thump. Thump.

"I'd like to introduce you to a friend of mine," Luca says. He sits on the edge of the stage and casually crosses his legs, as if completely unconcerned by the near-earthquake thundering behind him. He smiles the dimpled smile that I've pined over agonizingly for the past six months. "He comes from the Forest of Ruins. A rare half man, half tree."

Tree emerges on the stage, and most of the audience leans back in their seats. Tree glances at me for a moment, and I smile at him as if to say, *Go on, you're doing magnificently.* He waves at the audience without me needing to control him. He even grins.

"Wonderful, isn't he?" Luca says. "You'll notice that, even in winter, his leaves are still a vibrant green. Could I have a volunteer to come onstage, then?"

No one raises their hands. No one ever does.

371

Luca jumps off the stage. "Oh, don't be ridiculous. You, there." He points at a frumpy woman with his walking stick. "You look like you could do with some flowers."

She shakes her head vehemently.

"Nonsense." He takes her hand. "I simply won't allow it. My friend Tree will be upset, as he would very much like to present you with a flower." He hoists her up and leads her onstage. She trembles from the attention and more so the closer she walks toward Tree. Luca points his walking stick up toward Tree's head, at his impressive mess of branches and leaves. "There, see, there are flowers. Would you like to pick one?"

The audience cheers. Encouraged by their enthusiasm, the woman nods. She reaches up and plucks off a pink blossom from one of Tree's branches.

Adding more participation to the show was Luca's doing. It's been one of his better ideas. His other idea involved having his old assistant pretend to run up to the stage to kill him, only for him to miraculously come back to life, but that had our audience screaming and running out of the tent. Now Luca remains alive throughout the entire performance.

"Thank you, Tree," Luca says. "And now, I'd like to introduce my next friend, who I assure you is gentler than he looks. Crown, would you come out and greet our cheerful audience?"

While Tree joins me backstage, Crown walks out, leaning against his cane. He carries two heavy wooden boards with his other hand.

"You were great," I whisper to Tree, who smiles. I sit on the ground at his feet, looking up at the shade of his leaves and recalling a time when he could pick me up and swing me around. When it was only me and Tree. "You're still my bud, you know."

He picks off a flower and hands it to me. I slip it behind my ear.

"Now, I'm looking for two volunteers this time," Luca says. He chooses two small boys sitting near the back, who look more than pleased to have been chosen. "Each of you, take a board. This one is thicker, you see. Knock on them. Hit them. They're quite solid, aren't they?"

"What's he gonna do with them?" the one boy says.

"Crown, tell them, what are you going to do with them?"

In his feeble, elderly voice, Crown says, "I'm going to punch straight through them." I love that line.

The first boy, with the thinner board, holds it out for Crown. Crown takes off his glove, revealing his long fingernails, and slices clean and straight through the board. The boy gapes and shows the hole to the audience.

Crown moves on to the second, heavier board and does the same. The audience claps.

"That's wicked," the first boy says, and Crown winks at him.

"My next friend goes by the name of Hawk because...well, you'll see why." Luca peers backstage. "Hmm, we seem to have misplaced her. Where—"

Hawk screeches from outside the tent and then flies in through the visitors' entrance behind the audience, swooping onto the stage. The audience shrieks and then chuckles nervously and straightens their hats once they see her, a young girl no more than fourteen.

"Hawk is a very talented fiddle player," Luca says, "but her greatest virtue is her singing voice. So we're going to have her sing for you."

While Hawk sets up her act, I slide into the dressing room, where Kahina sits, as she does during all our shows now that her snaking sickness has finally cleared. She brings baskets of treats.

I pop a licorice cherry into my mouth. "He's improving."

"He's been delightful," she says. "And did you see Nicoleta's date? I ran into them outside. A really sweet girl, she seems like."

Hawk clears her throat and begins her song. It's a sad one, the same she sang at Blister's funeral, which serves as a memorial during our show for Blister, Gill and Venera. Her lyrics speak of friends who have gone for the night but will return in the morning, and every time, I need to fight back my urge to cry. Until I see Luca onstage, with Hawk, Tree, Crown and Unu and Du watching from backstage, and I'm reminded of the family that I still have here with me. It's what Kahina has often told me to do.

I return to my spot behind the curtain just as Hawk makes her exit. Luca sits again in the center of the stage, dangling his legs off the edge. "How am I doing as the manager?" he asks. "I'm rather new. The previous manager is on to bigger and brighter things."

The audience claps for him, and Nicoleta laughs from the front row.

"I used to work in this other show. People paid to try to kill me. You can imagine why I was eager for a new position."

This only gets a few laughs, one being from Luca. He's the only one who finds his morbid jokes amusing.

"My next friends come in a pair. *They* actually believe they're funnier than I am," he says, straightening his cloak. "But I'll let you decide for yourselves." He stands up in an almost-jump. "Unu, Du, I think the audience could use some lightening up."

Unu and Du step onto the stage to begin their new comedy routine, which has proven much more popular than their previous dancing one. They tell their jokes in a rhythm to match their drumbeats.

Luca steps off the stage for a few moments and stands beside me. "How am I doing?" he asks. He grabs a cup of water and chugs it.

"You're marvelous," I say and kiss his cheek. "You really are quite the performer."

"I still think we could have a dancing routine. Once, you know, you obviously practice up a bit—"

"Hey, I'm a fantastic dancer," I say, elbowing him in the ribs.

"You're terrible. But it's all right," he says. Behind us, the audience laughs at one of Unu's jokes. Most of their punchlines involve insulting each other. Shockingly, their routine was not difficult for them to come up with.

"I thought, after this, we could go watch the fireworks," he says. "All of us. You, me, the whole lot."

"First you join our show, and now you're planning family outings," I tease.

"But it will have to be fast. The Leather Viper wants to have tea again. He claims he has a juicy secret about the ex-lover of the Cougar that I'd love to hear—"

"Tell Ed I'd love to go, but I promised Nicoleta I'd meet her new girlfriend." Over the past few months, Luca has been steadily introducing me to more and more people in Gomorrah, particularly in the Downhill. Gomorrah is my home, and I should know more people in it. It's nice to wave at the man who provides my family with produce or to stop for a conversation with the palm-reader across the path.

"I heard she's a charm-worker with a successful shop in the Downhill—"

"She doesn't look like she'd be from the Downhill."

"We all know Nicoleta prefers a bit of the wild side when it comes to her romantic interests."

The audience claps as Unu and Du's act ends. The second they are offstage, they resume their bickering. Their latest argument is about a lucky coin they recently commissioned—the Illusionist. The attack stats are rather pitiful, but the defense leaves little to be desired. And, as the only one of its kind in existence, it's a collector's piece. They forgot to ask for a second, so they keep debating about who it belongs to.

Luca quickly breaks apart from me and returns to the stage. "And now, for the final act, I'd like to introduce you to the Girl Who Sees Without Eyes."

I make my grand entrance, wearing my floor-length black cloak, red sequined mask and brilliantly violet lipstick.

"How do we know she doesn't have eyes if we can't see under

the mask?" a woman in the front row asks haughtily. "She should take it off."

"Honestly, you should at least take her to dinner first," Luca scoffs.

I hold my breath. This isn't the first time the audience has asked, and I've done it before. But I will freely admit that it still scares me.

I untie the ribbon in the back, let the mask slip off and shove it in my pocket.

The audience gasps, and then the room goes quiet. My back sweats a little. I remind myself that my face isn't a deformity. It's magic. *I* am magic.

"Where would we like to go today?" Luca asks the audience. "A rainforest? To the stars?"

Before he can make another suggestion, I put a hand on his shoulder to stop him. "No, I have something special planned. Tonight, I'm going to take all of you on a tour though Gomorrah." The planning part is a lie. I never plan out my routines. But I *did* have the idea ten minutes ago, which, to my mind, counts as preparing.

The audience quiets, waiting for my act to begin.

The room around us changes to the field just outside Skull Gate. It's nighttime, and the black glittering eyes of the skull twinkle in the starlight. Its mouth gapes open wide, and we enter in a rush through the dark tunnel, soaring past the ticket booth and into Gomorrah. Vivid colors of pink, purple, red and black greet us all around, from the flags that wave above the tents to the costumes of the performers around us—jugglers, beast-tamers, shadow-workers. The night sky is invisible, cloaked by the cloud of smoke that always covers Gomorrah like a mist. But it's a mist that smells of licorice and cigars, spiced cider and rum. We speed and spiral around the Uphill, past the Menagerie tent, where the roars of a dragon thunder over the festivities, past the caravans of jewelers and fortune-workers, past the fence of spikes and bones separating the Uphill from the Downhill.

In my mental sweep of Gomorrah, I pass the tents and caravans of people I now know. The owner of the Menagerie. Kahina. The Leather Viper. Yelema. Zhihao. But to the visitors, they are merely nameless silhouettes in the ever-present smoke. Before I met Luca, that's what they were to me. I felt like an outsider in Gomorrah, never a participant.

I could show the audience this part of Gomorrah, but I know they're not here to learn about the secret lives of orphans and businessmen, prettywomen and charm-workers. They're not here to learn about what happens backstage. My Gomorrah is a home. Their Gomorrah is a show.

The Festival comes alive in a rush of opium smoke, the blinking lights of dancers, the smell of pastries that stick to your fingers, the thundering of the fireworks. We spin around Gomorrah as if on a carousel, going faster and faster until even I am dizzy, and the world has become a kaleidoscope of purple, pink, red and black.

But soon the colors fade, because dawn is drawing closer, and the light of the sun peeks through the smoke shrouding Gomorrah. The fortune-workers pack away their spirit boards. The fire-workers change out of their glittering costumes. Gomorrah children run home with leftover sweets in their hands, waving to their neighbors and any remaining visitors. The Festival quiets as morning arrives, settling into bed, still windswept with the feeling of desire and anticipation for the next night, when Skull Gate will open once more.

★ ★ ★ ★ ★

ACKNOWLEDGMENTS

Many months have been spent enjoying the wicked delights of the Gomorrah Festival, and I have dozens of people to thank for agreeing to travel with me and Sorina's family through all of this hard work, panic and excitement.

Thank you to all of my lovely critique partners and readers, whose thoughtful guidance and encouragement made Sorina's story possible. To Jena Debois, who patiently read my first drafts to ensure that I finished this book like I promised myself I would. To Sylvia Park, who provided me my total "Aha!" moment right when I needed it. To Sarah Hudson, who pushed and challenged and demanded more from my writing, like no one else. More thanks to Kristy Shen, Deeba Zargarpur, Hafsah Faizal, Christine Lynn Herman, Darci Cole, Hanley Brady, Roshani Chokshi, Kat Cho and the writer cult for all of your support throughout this journey.

So much appreciation goes out to Brianne Johnson, my agent, who understood my exact vision for this freak show murder mystery and for my career. It has been a pleasure to work with you.

Thank you to my editor, Lauren Smulski, who remembered

me from my book about murderous card games, and whose infectious enthusiasm reminded me why I love writing in the first place. Sorina and her family's story has improved dramatically in your hands, and I cannot wait for our next editorial adventure on that card game book.

To the entire team at Harlequin TEEN for their support for *Daughter*, thank you for taking a chance on me and working tirelessly to bring the Gomorrah Festival into the hands of readers. You all deserve many bags of licorice cherries.

To my creative writing and English teachers over the years, thank you for supporting all my projects—and for not making fun of me for taking my writing so seriously while I was so young! My experience in your classes has touched every sentence of this book.

To Zoe, who was subjected to living with me and my panic sessions when I realized my childhood dream was coming true. To Ben, who patiently listened to me squeal a billion times (and counting) about said dream.

To my siblings, who cannot decide if my writing is weird or cool. (Answer: it's weird.) To my parents, who instilled in me my love for reading, and who have put up with my compulsive storytelling since I was very small. Thank you for not worrying about my sanity when I told you about Sorina's lack of eyes, or what covered Crown instead of skin. I'm still uncertain where these ideas came from, but if anyone asks, I inherited my imagination from you.